A KILLING IN MOSCOW

A KILLING IN MOSCOW

Clive Egleton

St. Martin's Press
New York

Library of Congress Cataloging-in-Publication Data

Egleton, Clive.
A killing in Moscow / Clive Egleton.
p.   cm.
ISBN 0-312-10487-1
1. Intelligence service—Great Britain—Fiction.   2. British—
Russia—Moscow—Fiction.   3. Moscow (Russia)—Fiction.
I. Title.
PR6055.G55K55   1994
823'.914—dc20   93-44059   CIP

First published in Great Britain by Hodder & Stoughton Ltd.

First U.S. Edition: August 1994
10 9 8 7 6 5 4 3 2 1

For the women in my life –
Joan, Janet and Harriet

Chapter 1

The dark-haired girl who had followed Joyner into the hard currency bar on the mezzanine floor was wearing a single-breasted black pinstripe jacket and matching skirt with a mini hemline that showed off her legs to considerable advantage. The executive briefcase she was carrying sent one message; the heavy make-up, four-inch heels, and plunging neckline of her silk blouse semaphored a conflicting one. A momentary doubt that he could be picking up the wrong signal was dispelled for Joyner when she brought her drink over to his table and asked if he minded her joining him.

"Be my guest," he said.

"You are American, yes?"

"No, English."

"Oh."

The smile was still there on her lips and Joyner thought she didn't sound too disappointed. But that was understandable because she wasn't exactly spoilt for choice when the only other patrons of the hard currency bar were a couple of Africans with their wives.

"You are a tourist perhaps?"

"Businessman."

"What line?"

"Commodities," he told her, maintaining the clipped exchange.

"Me also. I have a seat on the Russian Commodities and Raw Materials Exchange."

Joyner gazed at her with new-found interest. When the Exchange had been set up in the old Central Post Office back in 1990, a seat had cost sixty thousand roubles; nowadays, they were changing hands at four point four million. Even though the

1

rouble had plummeted from parity to a hundred and seventy to the pound, that was still an impressive amount of money, more than she was likely to see in her lifetime. No, he had been right the first time around, she was a *valutnaya*, a two-hundred-dollar-a-trick hooker. He had seen her like before in hotels all over Moscow. They had to grease the palm of the security guard to ply their trade in the lobby, but sometimes they came across someone they couldn't bribe and ended up getting themselves arrested. They rarely appeared in court though; most hotels had a police cage in the basement where the hookers were detained for three or four hours and then released.

"Did you do any business today?" she asked.

"I clinched a couple of deals, bulk orders for clothing and electrical goods in US dollars."

"You are pleased?"

Joyner smiled. Even as she asked the question, her eyes were wandering around the room, hoping no doubt to find an unattached Japanese tourist or businessman. They were the only people who were mugs enough to pay her two hundred dollars for a perfunctory roll in the hay that would be about as exciting as drinking yesterday's flat beer.

"Let's say I'm not dissatisfied."

It was the understatement of the year. He was talking about a five hundred per cent profit on bankrupt UK stock bought for knock-down prices at auctions held by Official Receivers up and down the country.

"I also had a good day."

"Yeah?" Joyner raised a quizzical eyebrow. "I don't recall seeing you at the Commodities Exchange."

"I don't remember seeing you there either, Mr . . .?"

"Joyner, Colin Joyner," he told her, and wondered what had made him so indiscreet.

"And I am Nina Golodkinova," she said, and reached across the table to shake hands with him. "Can I get you another drink, Mr Joyner?"

"Oh no, allow me." He raised his free arm and snapped his fingers to summon one of the bartenders. "What'll you have?" he asked. "Vodka? Brandy? Rum? Whisky? Gin?"

"I'd like some Scotch." Her English was a little quaint but she knew what she wanted.

"Water, soda, ginger ale, lemonade?"

"On the rocks," Nina said, as if to prove how sophisticated she was.

"Make it two of the same," Joyner told the bartender.

"In England where you live, Mr Joyner?"

It took him a few moments to realise she wanted to know whereabouts he lived in England. His Russian was marginally better than her English and switching to it, he told Nina he had a large house on the outskirts of Liphook some fifty miles south-west of London. He told her a lot else besides; how he had got started in the export/import business, his likes and dislikes and what he did for relaxation. Joyner did not, however, tell her about his wife and stepdaughter; they were more than a taboo subject, they simply did not exist when he was away from home and chatting up a girl.

And this Russian one was worth chatting up. Nina Golodkinova was a hooker all right, no two ways about that, but she had a touch of class, and her more obvious physical attributes were not to be sneezed at either. She was perched at an angle on the edge of her armchair, knees pressed together and pointing to the left, a deliberately awkward posture that gave him a tantalising glimpse of a stocking top and suspender. Shapely legs in dark nylons a shade lighter than black – Joyner could feel himself beginning to erect.

"I spent two years studying medicine at Moscow University," Nina informed him. "Then I came to my senses and realised I couldn't afford to become a doctor like my father."

Joyner didn't say anything; if Nina Golodkinova had been a medical student, he thought, then he was a brain surgeon and winner of the Nobel Prize. But like most lies, it contained a grain of truth. The Russian economy might be out of control and heading for the rocks with hyperinflation but a hospital intern's salary was still pegged to five hundred roubles a month, which equated to three pounds or four dollars eighty at the present rate of exchange. A cab driver could earn twice that amount on a single nineteen-mile journey from the centre of Moscow to Sheremetyevo 2 International Airport, always provided his fare was a foreigner with hard currency.

"You are very thoughtful, Mr Joyner. Perhaps you are wondering if I have any regrets?"

"No, I was waiting for you to suggest it was about time we went on up to my room."

A faint smile curled her lip. "I don't think you can afford me," Nina told him insolently.

"Thirty pounds should cover it."

"Is that what you call a joke in your country?"

"The laugh'll be on you if you turn the offer down," Joyner said.

"I think not."

"Oh well, maybe you want to spend the next three hours locked up in a cage down in the basement because that's what will happen to you if I walk out of this bar on my own. I'll go and see the hotel security officer and tell him you tried to proposition me. That's all it will take."

"You wouldn't dare."

"Try me."

He got to his feet and walked out into the mezzanine, confident that Nina Golodkinova would follow him. The click-clack of high heels on the parquet floor in the bar told him he was not mistaken. By the time Joyner reached the lifts, the Russian girl was at his shoulder, matching him stride for stride. The only company they had on the way up to the eleventh floor was a bespectacled Sikh and a middle-aged German couple.

The key lady was seated behind her desk in the corridor. She was a thin woman in her late thirties or early forties, who wore her greying hair in a bun and looked perpetually sour. Joyner produced his hotel pass, waited patiently while she found his room key in the drawer, then gave her a dollar bill, which most Russians preferred to a pound coin even though it was worth considerably less. The money didn't bring a smile to the key lady's face but it did ensure she was prepared to turn a blind eye in Nina Golodkinova's direction.

Joyner unlocked the door, reached for the switch inside the hall and put on the light. He stepped to one side so that Nina could pass through into the room before he closed the door and attached the security chain.

"Don't want the maid disturbing us," he said with a lewd grin.

The bathroom, bidet and toilet were on the left side of the hall; the double room beyond was furnished with twin beds, two easy chairs, an oval-shaped occasional table, a standard lamp, a colour

4

television with remote control and an all-in-one unit consisting of a chest of drawers, dressing table and hanging cupboard. The large picture window at the far end of the room looked out on to a concrete jungle of low-cost apartment blocks behind the Mira Prospekt Hotel that stretched as far as the eye could see. Joyner switched on the standard lamp and drew the curtains to blot out the ugly view, then took out his wallet and gave Nina thirty pounds.

"I hope you are going to earn this," he said.

"I don't think you will be disappointed, Mr Joyner."

She took off the black pinstripe jacket and laid it carefully on the bed nearer the bathroom. Reaching behind her, Nina unzipped the skirt and allowed it to fall slowly around her ankles. Every other Russian hooker Joyner had been with had performed like a robot but this one shed her clothes with a certain amount of style. With mounting excitement, he watched her step out of the skirt and remove the white silk blouse and cravat.

"You like?" she asked and smoothed the brief nylon slip against her body.

"Very nice."

Nina moved towards him, smiling. "Very nice? Is that all you can say, Mr Joyner?"

"Colin," he said hoarsely as her right hand unzipped his fly and reached for him.

"Colin," she repeated and tickled his scrotum until he was close to ejaculating. "I think I am making you too excited, yes?"

"You could say that."

She pushed him down onto the bed, then backed away, smiling. "Try to calm down while I get myself ready."

Nina turned away, picked up her executive briefcase and disappeared into the bathroom. Never one to waste time, Joyner kicked off his shoes, stripped to the buff and dumped his clothes on the spare bed. But eager though he was to crawl into the sack with the Russian girl, he didn't believe in taking unnecessary risks. Retrieving his wallet, he took out a condom and rolled it over his erect penis.

As he lay there on the bed waiting for Nina, he heard her flush the bidet. Above the noise of the rushing water, he did not hear her remove the security chain on the door before she came to him. Apart from high heels, dark nylons and a black suspender

5

belt, all she was wearing was a ready-made bow tie.

Valeria Sorokina was forty-three years old and looked more. Married at nineteen, she had divorced her alcoholic first husband eighteen months later and had had little better luck with the second who had ended up under a train on the Metro. He had left her to bring up three small children under the age of ten, which Valeria couldn't have done without the help of her widowed mother who had looked after them while she went out to work. Although the two eldest were now married and off her hands, inflation meant that she now had to hold down two jobs in order to survive. From five until eight each weekday morning, she was employed as an office cleaner at the Russian Foreign Ministry on Arbat Street and Smolensky Boulevard. Her other place of work was the Mira Prospekt where she was one of three key ladies who looked after the hotel guests on the eleventh floor. Currently, she was working the four to midnight shift.

Valeria Sorokina was an embittered woman. Thanks to Gorbachev and Yeltsin, prices had gone through the roof, food was practically unobtainable except on the black market and her life's savings had been wiped out. The one good thing about being a key lady these days was the hard currency tips foreigners occasionally gave her. Tonight she had earned the equivalent of a week's salary with the dollar bill she had received from the Englishman in Room 1141. Not that she felt grateful; truth was the largess only made her despise him. But she reserved her real hatred for the *valutnaya* who was with him, who could earn a fortune in one night.

There had always been prostitutes in Moscow, but Glasnost, Perestroika and all that rubbish had brought the lice out of the woodwork in their thousands. She had seen them in the Mira Prospekt, no-good sluts mincing about in high heels and skin-tight dresses that didn't leave much to the imagination. The police ought to lock them up and throw away the key, but, of course, everybody was on the take and nothing was ever done about them.

"Valeria Sorokina?" A KGB shield in a plastic wallet appeared under her nose and she looked up to find three tough-looking men in civilian clothes grouped in a half-moon around her desk. "You are Valeria Sorokina?" repeated the officer who had produced his badge for her inspection.

"Yes." She cleared her throat nervously. "Who are you?"

"We need your pass key."

"What for?"

"That's none of your business, mother."

"I am not your mother," Valeria said angrily.

"Why not tell her, Mikhail?" the tallest officer suggested.

"This is police business, she doesn't need to know."

"Maybe so, but where's the harm in telling her if it saves us a lot of hassle?"

Mikhail hesitated, then shrugged his shoulders. "Joyner," he said, "the Englishman in 1141. You see a girl with him when he picked up his room key a few minutes ago?"

Valeria sensed trouble and tried to look blank but was unable to fool the KGB man.

"Listen, it's okay," Mikhail continued. "I mean, we know how things are, the foreigner gave you a greenback to look the other way and you thought the girl was a *valutnaya*. Right? Hell, we're not blaming you, a person has got to eat. But this Nina Golodkinova isn't a hooker; she sells heroin a hundred per cent uncut straight from the poppy fields of Tadjikistan. Even as we are talking, a deal is being struck in Room 1141; that's why we have got to have your pass key. Okay?"

"I'll have to ask the hotel security officer."

"Are you mad?" Mikhail demanded. "How do you suppose she was able to walk in here with a briefcase full of dope? She greased his palm, that's how." He unbuttoned his leather jacket so that she could see the Makarov automatic in his shoulder holster. "Now, let's have that damned key."

Valeria opened the centre drawer and took out the master. "I shall have to come with you," she said.

"What?"

"I'm not supposed to let this pass key out of my sight."

"Now I know you're crazy. There's every chance that Golodkinova is carrying a gun, but maybe you don't mind getting your head shot off."

"It's all right," the tall one said. "Valeria Sorokina can come with us, I'll see she doesn't come to any harm."

Mikhail thought it over, then nodded. "Just be sure you do, Nikolai," he said. "I don't want her getting in the way."

★ ★ ★

Joyner gritted his teeth and tried to hold back, but it wasn't easy because Nina Golodkinova was on top riding him to a climax. What made it even more difficult was the way she kept talking the whole time, the language she used, Russian and English, to describe how good it felt to have him inside her. Every other hooker he had screwed in Moscow had been totally passive, totally limp, but this girl acted as if she really had the hots for him. He grunted, shoved and writhed to his own litany of four-letter words. Approaching the high peak of coitus, he did not hear the door open, nor was he aware there were intruders in the room until Nina suddenly withdrew and he found himself looking into the barrel of an automatic pistol.

"Who are you? What do you want?" he gasped, first in English, then Russian, his voice a frightened whisper.

"I'm Mikhail," the gunman told him quietly. "And this is my friend Igor," he added, pointing to the muscular blond on the left side of the bed. "You owe us two million dollars."

"Me? Owe you two million?".

"Your name is Mr Joyner?"

"Yes."

"Then there is no mistake."

"You've obviously got the wrong Joyner. I've never done any business with you people."

"Don't listen to him." Nina Golodkinova retrieved her skirt and jacket from the spare bed and moved towards the bathroom. "He was at the Commodities and Raw Materials Exchange this afternoon. He told me so himself."

"Stop worrying about it," Mikhail told her. "You'll get your money."

Joyner caught a knowing wink from the Russian and wasn't sure what to make of it. He looked towards the hall in time to see Nina Golodkinova disappear into the bathroom. Igor, the muscular tow-headed intruder was only a few paces behind her, his right arm trailing by his side, the oversized pistol in his hand pointing downwards at the floor. It did not remain that way for long. As Nina ordered him to back off and went to close the door in his face, he suddenly raised the automatic and squeezed the trigger. Joyner saw the pistol buck in his hand before he heard the muffled report and the solid thump of a bullet striking home. Nina grunted and went down hard, cracking what sounded like

8

her head on the tiled floor. Igor remained outside in the hall looking into the bathroom, then apparently concerned to make absolutely sure she was dead, he took deliberate aim and calmly put another round into her.

It didn't make sense, that was the really terrifying thing about the murder. Nina Golodkinova had picked him up and gone to his room just so that she could slip the security chain off the door and let them in, and then Igor had shown his appreciation by pumping her full of holes. If they could do that to Nina, what hope was there for him? But maybe it wasn't for real. Maybe it was a mock killing, a piece of theatre to put the fear of God up him. Joyner considered the possibility and latched on to it.

He kept his eyes on the ceiling, unwilling to look in the direction of the hall in case he saw something which would prove beyond all reasonable doubt that the Russian girl really was dead. Think positively, Joyner told himself, think positively. He had already tried telling Mikhail that he had got the wrong man, now the only thing he could do was buy himself some time by convincing both gunmen he had what they wanted. He tried to unstick his tongue and swallow but his mouth was bone dry and he couldn't find any saliva.

"Listen," he croaked, "I'm sure we can work something out. You think I owe you two million dollars – "

"We know you do," Mikhail said, interrupting him.

"You're right. I made a mistake but I can rectify that if you'll let me. I can make you rich beyond your dreams."

"Money is no longer important," Mikhail said tersely. "Thing is, we are here to make an example of you."

"A what?" Joyner said hoarsely, unwilling to believe he had heard the Russian correctly.

"You want to turn over onto your stomach and make it easy on yourself?"

"Please . . ." Joyner tried to hold back the tears welling in his eyes. "Please," he choked, "please, I've got a wife and daughter."

"Listen, I'm easy. You can lie there and watch me squeeze the trigger or you can bury your face in the pillow. You've got five seconds to make up your mind and I'm counting. One . . ."

"Please . . ."

"Two."

Joyner rolled over and closed his eyes tight. Unable to control his bladder, he urinated into the condom and was bitterly ashamed of himself. "I'm sorry," he sobbed.

It was the last thing he said. With clinical precision, Mikhail shot him in the back of the head and then retrieved the ejected cartridge case; detaching the silencer, he slipped the Makarov automatic into his shoulder holster.

"You ready to leave?" he asked Igor.

"Yes."

"Picked up all your empties?"

"What do you think I was doing while you were chatting with the Englishman?"

Mikhail went to the door, opened it a fraction and got a thumbs up from Nikolai out in the corridor. Signalling Igor to go ahead, he hung the "Do Not Disturb" sign on the outside, then closed the door behind him and set off towards the bank of lifts in the connecting passageway opposite the key lady's desk. There was no sign of Valeria Sorokina, but that was no surprise. Nikolai would have disposed of her; the only mystery was where he had hidden the body. Mikhail had to wait until they had left the Mira Prospekt and were walking towards the Metro station before he learned the answer.

Chapter 2

It was only the second time Ashton had visited Moscow. On the previous occasion he had been on a package tour and had flown economy class, though British Airways liked to describe it as World Traveller, which was something of a public relations exercise. Today he was masquerading as a Queen's Messenger carrying a diplomatic pouch, a subterfuge which had enabled him to sample the Rolls-Royce treatment accorded to pop stars and the like who regularly went first class. Last August the tour operator had bussed the group to their hotel; seven months later, the embassy had sent a chauffeur-driven limousine to pick him up. Apart from enjoying the VIP status, precious little else had changed. Sheremetyevo 2 International Airport was still the same chaotic place, his suitcase still ended up on the wrong carousel and getting through Customs and Immigration still took for ever.

The driver of the Rover saloon which the embassy had sent for him was one of the locally employed Russians who formed the bulk of the administrative staff. His name was Feliks, he was forty-three years old, a good fourteen pounds overweight for his sixty-seven inches and was rapidly losing his jet-black hair. His command of English was better than good and he took advantage of every opportunity to practise it on the unsuspecting. It also quickly became evident that he was extremely nosy. Before Gorbachev, Perestroika and Glasnost, Ashton would have assumed that Feliks was attempting to gather information for the KGB; now the Russian was simply trying to discover what he planned to do while in Moscow in the hope of earning a little extra on the side.

"I'm not going to be here long enough to take in the Bolshoi or the State Circus," Ashton told him. "All being well, I shall be on the British Airways flight tomorrow afternoon."

"There's always this evening," Feliks said hopefully.

"I'm dining with the Head of Chancery," he lied.

"Perhaps you will have time to do some shopping before you go?"

"It's possible."

"I can give you the address of an artists' co-operative where you can get some very nice jewellery for your wife, Mr Ashton."

"I'm not married."

"Your fiancée or girlfriend?"

Ashton wondered how Jill Sheridan would describe herself – ex-fiancée, colleague, platonic cohabitant or joint mortgager of a flat in Surbiton? Probably, the latter. They had been engaged once but Jill was regarded as a high-flier by the Secret Intelligence Service and she had broken it off in October '89, wanting to achieve her full potential. Jill's father was an executive with the Qatar General Petroleum Corporation and she had spent much of her childhood and early adolescence in the Persian Gulf. Arabic had been her second tongue; Persian was an additional qualification she had acquired at the School of Oriental and African Studies. To the Head of the Middle East Department at Century House she had seemed the ideal choice to run the Intelligence set-up in the United Arab Emirates.

Unfortunately, in that part of the world a woman was definitely a second-class citizen. In order to function at all, it had therefore been necessary to disguise her true status and on the Bahrain Embassy staff list she was officially the personal assistant to the Second Secretary Consul. It had not been a happy arrangement but she had stuck it out for twenty-one months before requesting a transfer. Now Jill was back in London running the Persian Gulf Desk at Century House and living in their jointly owned flat.

"Do you know what that sculpture is on your right?" Feliks asked.

Ashton turned to look at the rows of angle iron pickets cast in bronze and arranged like dragon's teeth to form an antitank obstacle.

"I haven't the faintest idea," he said, even though it wasn't too hard to guess what event the sculpture commemorated.

"It marks the limit of the Fascist advance on Moscow in 1941," the Russian told him proudly.

The M10 motorway became the Leningrad Chaussee and then

the Leningrad Prospekt before changing its name altogether as they approached the Garden Ring Road. Throughout the nineteen-mile drive into town, Feliks kept up a running commentary, pointing out various places of interest. All Ashton had to do was respond with a grunt now and again, which left him free to think about other things, like what the future might hold for Jill and himself.

The Persian Gulf Desk had been a sideways move, not a demotion. Jill was still a rising star and would go a long way, but she would not be the first woman to become Director General of the Secret Intelligence Service. The Arabs had seen to that.

There had been a time when he too had been going places. If he had distanced himself from a certain GRU officer and had refrained from kicking over a number of stones which the Foreign and Commonwealth Office would have preferred him to ignore, the Russian Desk would probably have been his by now. Although he had won through in the end, there were those who thought he had become slightly contaminated by the KGB in the process. So he had been removed from Century House and transferred to Security and Technical Services at Benbow House over in Southwark where he did not have constant access to Top Secret and codeword material.

"We're almost there," Feliks announced.

The British Embassy was on the Maurice Thorez Embankment south of the River Moscow. Despite considerable pressure and all kinds of inducements, the Foreign and Commonwealth Office had steadfastly refused to move from the large, elegant Tsarist villa to a purpose-built embassy in a less attractive part of the capital. Cynics maintained that their resistance to change had a lot to do with the fact that in its present location, the embassy enjoyed the best vista in all Moscow. From their offices, the diplomats had an unrivalled view of the Great Kremlin Palace, the golden onion domes of the Cathedral of the Annunciation and the Ivan the Great Bell Tower. On Ashton's first visit to the city seven months ago, he had been photographed outside the gates with the other tourists in the group; this time, he swept through them in a chauffeur-driven limousine.

The general dogsbody of the SIS cell was waiting for him inside the entrance. Although they had never met before, he greeted Ashton like an old friend, then whisked him up to Head of

Station's office on the top floor where the view across the river was even better.

Ashton hadn't met Hugo Calthorpe before either, nor had he seen a photograph of him when he'd been on the Russian Desk. He had, however, formed a mental picture of the man from reading his despatches. His phraseology and choice of vocabulary had suggested a small, rather pernickety individual; in the flesh, Calthorpe was a touch over five eight, hovered on ten stone and cultivated a moustache that was more luxuriant than his head of light brown hair. He was, in fact, three and a half inches shorter and thirty pounds lighter than Ashton, and at forty-five he also happened to be a dozen years older.

"The Ambassador sent for me shortly before you arrived," Calthorpe said after the obligatory niceties.

Ashton thought he knew what was coming. No one liked a security inspection; there was an ingrained feeling that London had sent one of their snoopers to prove that standard operating procedures were not always being observed correctly. There was another irritant, and his name was Hicks. When he arrived to sweep the office for bugs, no one else was allowed to be present. Depending on what was found, the spring-cleaning could take an hour or half a day, a fact of life which everyone accepted with good grace. Unfortunately, Hicks had an uncanny knack of rubbing people up the wrong way, and he had arrived a week ahead of Ashton.

"Has Mr Hicks been putting a few noses out of joint?" he asked.

Calthorpe looked surprised. "Not that I know of. This has to do with a Mr Colin Joyner who was found murdered in his hotel room at the Mira Prospekt. The Chief of Police, Major General Gurov, has asked for our assistance and the Ambassador would like to show willing."

"What exactly does he have in mind?"

Calthorpe didn't find it an easy question to answer. Gurov wanted to demonstrate just how open police methods had become since Yeltsin had come to power and according to the Ambassador, who had consulted the Foreign and Commonwealth Office, London was in favour of co-operating with the Russian authorities.

"The Director General has indicated that he is quite happy for you to meet the chief investigating officer," Calthorpe said finally.

"With a view to doing what?"

"Assessing how best we can help them. It shouldn't take you more than a couple of days at the most."

"I hope you're right," Ashton said. "I didn't come equipped for a long stay."

"The Chief Investigator is Major Oleg Lysenko; Feliks will take you to his office."

"Thanks. Does this Lysenko speak English?"

"Not a word." Calthorpe smiled. "Still, that's not a problem for you, is it?"

"So long as he doesn't speak a dialect."

Ashton had read German and Russian at Nottingham University and had graduated with a good upper second. A member of the University Officers' Training Corps, he had joined 23 Special Air Service Regiment in the Territorial Army when he had been taken on by British Aerospace as a technical author and translator. A nine-month tour of duty with the regular army's Special Patrol Unit in Northern Ireland and a further spell of active service in the Falklands had got him into the SIS via the back door.

"What about the next of kin?"

"The family was notified earlier this morning. Mrs Joyner should arrive later today to identify her husband's body."

Twenty-three years in the Service had made the Head of Station, Moscow, extremely reluctant to disclose more than he had to. By dint of patient questioning, Ashton learned that the dead man came from Liphook and had been in the export/import business. Significantly, he had never sought advice from the First Secretary, Commerce at the embassy.

"Is there anything else I can tell you?" Calthorpe asked.

"When is Lysenko expecting me?"

Calthorpe glanced at his wristwatch. "About ten minutes ago," he said laconically.

Before the break up of the Soviet Union, the Second Chief Directorate of the KGB had been responsible for internal security. In simple terms, this meant it had controlled the everyday life of the indigenous population and monitored the activities of

15

all foreigners living within the borders of the USSR. Of the various departments which came under the Directorate, the Twelfth was charged with investigating such economic crimes as graft, corruption, currency speculation and black-market activities. The collapse of the old order had seen the emergence of the *Mafiozniki* and a collosal growth in drugs, prostitution and protection rackets with a murder rate equal to that of the United States. To combat this threat, Major Oleg Lysenko was one of the top-flight officers who had been drafted into the Criminal Investigation Division which had grown out of the former Twelfth Department.

Lysenko's office overlooked the Lubyanka Prison behind the rococo-style All Russian Insurance Company building on Dzerzhinsky Square. The larger-than-life-size statue of the KGB's founder might have been removed from its plinth in the centre of the roundabout fronting the building but nothing could change the menacing atmosphere, not even Lysenko, who was twenty-nine years old and good-looking, had a ready smile, and was like the nice boy next door every mother wanted her daughter to marry.

"It's a privilege to meet you," he said and pumped Ashton's hand with considerable enthusiasm.

"The feeling's mutual," he told the Russian, and even managed to sound as if he meant it.

"You speak our language well."

"Thank you. I don't know how I can help you but the embassy said you were in charge of the investigation . . ."

"You wish to see the body?" Lysenko asked eagerly.

Ashton shook his head. "I don't think that would be particularly helpful. I've never met Mr Joyner and I'm not a doctor so I wouldn't be able to say how long he's been dead."

"The body was discovered late yesterday afternoon approximately twenty-four hours after death had occurred." Lysenko opened the centre drawer of his desk, took out a batch of photographs and passed a selection to Ashton. "These were taken at the scene of the crime."

Joyner was stark naked. He was lying on his stomach, his face buried in the pillow, which was soaked with blood. A close-up showed that a pistol had been held close enough to the deceased's head to singe the hair around the neat entry wound. Photographs

16

taken later in the morgue concentrated on the exit wound above the right eye where a large piece of the forehead was missing.

"The killer used a 9mm Makarov," Lysenko said in a matter-of-fact voice. "We were able to identify the weapon from the bullet we found buried in the mattress under his body. It had retained the greater part of its ballistic profile after passing through the victim's head and pillow into the mattress. Regrettably, the same can not be said for the rounds discharged from the second murder weapon."

Another selection of colour photographs was pushed across to Ashton's side of the desk. The young woman on the bathroom floor was in a similar state of undress but unlike Joyner, she had been shot twice, once between the eyes and then again in the chest, though not necessarily in that order. It looked as if she had been standing just inside the doorway when the killer had shot her and the impact had slammed her into the bidet before she finished up on the floor, chin resting on her chest.

"Her name was Nina Golodkinova," Lysenko announced in the same neutral tone. "She was the only child of Sergei and Raisa Golodkinov and was twenty-four years old. Both parents are doctors and Nina herself studied medicine for two years at Moscow University before electing to do Economics. She came from a privileged background and was thoroughly spoiled. A taste for the good things in life, which Golodkinov could no longer afford once prices began to soar, led her into prostitution."

"Any idea why they were killed?"

"Well, robbery wasn't the motive; Golodkinova still had a hundred and sixty dollars and thirty pounds in her purse. The killers would have taken the hard currency if it had been."

Killers – the plural again. Ashton rearranged the photographs so that he could look at both sets simultaneously. Lysenko had already referred to a second murder weapon, and with some justification, because it seemed unlikely that one man could have shot both Colin Joyner and Nina Golodkinova without either victim crying out for help.

"Did anyone see the killers enter Joyner's hotel room?" he asked.

"We believe there was a witness."

Ashton found himself looking at a third set of photographs.

"God Almighty," he exploded, "what have you got here – a massacre?"

"The third victim is Valeria Sorokina; she was a key lady at the Mira Prospekt. Her body was found in the linen room on the eleventh floor."

She had been strangled and dumped in one of the laundry baskets, her legs dangling over the edge. Her absence had first been noticed at eight o'clock the night before when one of the hotel guests had complained that he was unable to obtain his room key because no one was on duty at the desk.

"Since her pass key wasn't missing, the undermanager assumed she had simply gone home without telling anyone. Although Valeria Sorokina had never done anything of the sort before, it was not an unknown occurrence with other members of the staff. Knowing this, he merely found someone to replace her and didn't bother to organise a search. Her body was discovered the following morning by one of the maids."

"What about the other two victims?"

"They remained undiscovered until late yesterday afternoon. The killers had hung a 'Do Not Disturb' sign on the door."

Although the linen cupboard where Valeria Sorokina had been dumped was no distance from Joyner's room, the police had taken the "Do Not Disturb" sign literally. The way Lysenko told it, the bodies of Joyner and Golodkinova could have remained undetected for a lot longer than twenty-four hours had the relief key lady not observed that the guest in Room 1141 was obviously sleeping the clock round.

Ashton returned the photographs to Lysenko. "Have any of the hotel guests on the eleventh floor complained that their rooms had been burgled?" he asked.

"No."

"So they were after Joyner, and Valeria Sorokina was murdered because they needed her pass key to get into 1141." Ashton ruled out the possibility that the killers had targeted Golodkinova because they could have got to her any time, any place, anywhere.

"That's the way I see it," Lysenko said. "Though what he had done to offend them is far from clear. Your embassy wasn't able to tell me very much about him."

"I don't think they were holding out on you; from what I

gather, he never went near them. Maybe Mrs Joyner can shed a little light on his business activities in Russia." Ashton paused, then said, "Don't take this the wrong way, but there's no point in causing the widow unnecessary pain. In fact, it could be counter-productive, so perhaps you could avoid mentioning Nina Golod-kinova when you question her?"

"I was hoping you would do that."

"Me?"

"We don't want a diplomatic incident on our hands as well as a triple murder investigation. That's why Major General Gurov appealed to the British Embassy for assistance."

Ashton could see what was going to happen. Some urbane first secretary would give the widow tea and sympathy while he was left to do the dirty work. He hoped Mrs Joyner didn't have reason to suspect that her late husband was in the habit of sleeping around when he was away from home, otherwise things could get very sticky.

"Most hotel rooms have a security chain on the inside of the door," Ashton said, changing the subject. "Is the Mira Prospekt any different?"

"No."

"Well, it doesn't seem to me that Joyner was the sort of man who would take a hooker up to his room and forget to put the chain on the door. Matter of fact, I wouldn't mind betting that Nina Golodkinova was hired to set him up and make sure they didn't have any problem getting into the room."

"She certainly stalked him." Lysenko went over to the filing cabinet in the corner of the room farthest away from the window, opened the top drawer of three and returned with a typewritten statement, which he gave to Ashton. "This is what Georgi Zakharov, the bartender at the Mira Prospekt, told us."

The statement ran to half a page. After giving his name, address, identity card number, date and place of birth, the first thing Zakharov wanted to make clear was that not for one moment had he suspected that Nina Golodkinova was a prosti-tute. She had arrived shortly after Joyner, had taken a seat at the bar, ordered a whisky and paid for it with US dollars. She had told Zakharov that as a commodity broker, she insisted her commissions were paid either in US dollars or pounds sterling. During the course of their brief conversation, she had glanced around the room and had immediately recognised Joyner who was sitting at a table by himself. Questioned by the investigating officer, Zakharov was adamant that she had referred to the Englishman by name and had claimed they were business acquaintances. Observing the Englishman's reaction when she joined him at his table, Zakharov had formed the opinion that they appeared to know one another rather well.

"Did anyone see Nina Golodkinova in the lobby before she went up to the bar on the mezzanine floor?"

Lysenko nodded. "One of the girls on the reception desk claims she noticed her looking at the goods displayed in the window of the souvenir shop, then sometime later, she was seen by the Beriozka shop at the other end of the foyer where foreigners can buy duty-free gifts. I think it's safe to assume she arrived at the Mira Prospekt some ten to fifteen minutes before Mr Joyner did."

"And he went straight up to the bar?"

"Yes. Apparently, he usually had a drink before going to his room."

"Golodkinova was waiting for him."

"I don't think there's any doubt about that," Lysenko said.

"So what was the militiaman doing?" Ashton demanded. "I mean, isn't it his job to prevent unauthorised persons entering the hotel? Isn't that why every guest is issued with a hotel pass?"

"The answer is yes to both questions." Lysenko retrieved the statement and put it back in the filing cabinet. "That's why I had the hotel security staff brought in for questioning."

Ashton guessed where they were being held when the Russian walked him down the corridor to the lift serving the rear entrance. In the past, it was said that if Muscovites preferred not to know about the All Russian Insurance Company building, the Lubyanka immediately in rear of it was their worst nightmare. Until Stalin died, it had been the death factory, the slaughterhouse where thousands upon thousands of so-called enemies of the State had been executed in the basement cells. Even in the early sixties, a prisoner could be terminated with a bullet through the neck. There was, Ashton thought, no more intimidating place on earth to bring a man for interrogation.

The interview rooms were on the floor above the cells. When they entered the Lubyanka from the inner courtyard, Lysenko turned left and made straight for a room three doors along from the entrance on the opposite side of the corridor. The interrogator was a militia sergeant with fists the size of hams, a short muscular neck, which disappeared between ox-like shoulders, and a lumpy face that looked as if it had been used as a punchbag in the none-too-distant past. There was an equally intimidating NCO standing guard behind the detainee but his presence was entirely superfluous.

The small, immature twenty-year-old militiaman under interrogation was clearly terrified of the sergeant and couldn't stop trembling. He had, it transpired, been dragged out of bed in the middle of the night, thrown into a prison van and whisked off to the Lubyanka. Somewhere along the way, he had collected a black eye and a split lip.

Lysenko picked up the statement the sergeant had taken down and read it quickly, then turned to Ashton. "This man was on duty at the Mira Prospekt when Nina Golodkinova arrived. After he asked to see her hotel pass, she made a great show of going through her handbag before pretending to have mislaid it. When he tried to eject Golodkinova from the hotel, she became extremely agitated and demanded to see Yuri Ivanovich Babkin."

"Who's he?" Ashton asked dutifully. From the moment he had arrived at the KGB headquarters in Dzerzhinsky Square, it seemed to him that he had been participating in a charade that was being staged entirely for his benefit.

"Babkin is chief of security at the Mira Prospekt Hotel," Lysenko informed him. "He took the militiaman here to one side and said Golodkinova was to be left alone because she was involved in a highly secret KGB operation and he had better keep his mouth shut or he would find himself in serious trouble."

"I see. So what happens now?"

"We are going to confront Yuri Ivanovich Babkin with this man and see what he has to say for himself."

Lysenko rounded on the burly sergeant and ordered him to fetch the prisoner on the double, then made small talk with Ashton while the two NCOs collected Babkin from the cells in the basement. They were back five minutes later, highly excited, grim-faced and without the prime suspect. What they had to say caused a stampede.

21

The cell in which Yuri Babkin was confined measured some eight feet by six. The only items of furniture were a bedboard and galvanised latrine bucket, while the only natural light came from a window that was out of reach for even the tallest of men. The warders had confiscated the tie Babkin had been wearing at the time of his arrest and they had also removed the laces from his shoes. They had, however, neglected to do anything about his leather belt. For reasons only Babkin could have answered, he had threaded the belt through the bars of the inspection grille in the door and had then knotted the ends around his throat to slowly strangle himself.

Chapter 3

The inspection grille was less than five feet off the ground. To hang himself, Babkin would have needed to adopt a sitting position with his legs out straight in front of him rather than bent at the knees. That way he achieved the necessary weight suspension ratio to cause death by strangulation. There were a number of signs that suggested it had been a slow and painful exit for him, the black face, the ruptured blood vessels in the bulging eyes and the protruding tongue. The scuff marks on the floor by his heels indicated that at some stage he had apparently changed his mind about committing suicide but had lacked the strength to get up in order to relieve the pressure on his throat.

"He left it too late," Ashton said, thinking out loud.

"What do you mean, he left it too late?" Lysenko said sharply.

"Look at the marks on the floor. It appears that at the last minute Babkin tried to stand up but the effort proved too much for him and he blacked out."

"This was a very bad place, Mr Ashton, especially when Stalin was alive. Hundreds of men and women must have been confined in this cell. Look at the messages they scratched on the walls, their names, the dates they were arrested, where they came from, their loved ones." Lysenko pointed to one directly below the window. " 'Valeri Aleksevich Fatayev from Maloyaroslavets, October the seventeenth 1929. You are always in my thoughts Irka Danilova.' Come here, see for yourself."

"I don't have to," Ashton told him. "There are plenty of other inscriptions nearer."

"Do you know why these cells have never been cleaned up and redecorated?" Lysenko demanded, then proceeded to answer his own question. "Because those who controlled the Lubyanka wanted a prisoner to know how many others had been and gone

23

before him. They wanted him to read those messages of despair so that it would undermine his resolve and persuade him to give them the voluntary confession they needed. It's called psychological pressure, my friend."

"What are you trying to say?"

"I'm saying those scuff marks may have been there for years because they certainly don't look fresh to me, and if by chance Babkin did make them, we can't be sure they weren't simply caused by the death throes of the nervous system. One shoe has been kicked off and he's only just got his toes in the other." Lysenko crouched beside the body. "There is a leather strap around your throat, Mr Ashton, which is choking you to death. What's the first thing you instinctively do?"

"I'm pretty sure I would claw at the thing that's strangling me – wouldn't you?" Ashton hunkered down beside the KGB officer. Babkin's face was a hue of purple and black but there were no lacerations on the flesh. Although the deceased's fingernails had been cut fairly recently, they were still long enough to inflict some damage to the neck and cheeks. "I think you've got a point, Major," he said.

"I'm glad we agree on something." Lysenko straightened up. "What's keeping that cretin of a photographer; we can't dispose of the body until he's taken his blasted pictures." He rounded on the militia sergeant. "Get after him, Oroblinsky, kick his arse and get the little prick down here on the double."

Ashton continued to examine the dead man's hands, his eyes drawn to a faint weal on the inside of both wrists – a thin band no more than half an inch wide and less noticeable amongst the dark hairs on the back of the hands. It was not the sort of chafing you would get from a rope but something more rigid. Handcuffs? The police would have manacled Babkin when they arrested him.

"When was this man taken into custody?" he asked.

"He was picked up at approximately 0100 hours this morning," Lysenko told him.

"Was he under restraint?"

"Only until he was admitted."

Ashton bent a little closer to the dead man and examined his mouth. "What about the cells on either side? Are they both occupied?"

"They were earlier on . . ."

"And the warders – how often do they look in on a prisoner?"

"At irregular intervals – there is no set pattern." Lysenko clucked his tongue. "Would you mind telling me what you're getting at?" he asked.

"I'm just curious, Major."

"Is that why you are peering into his mouth?"

Ashton got to his feet. "I'm no doctor, but whoever performs the autopsy might care to pay particular attention to the wrists. Those marks look recent to me."

"They would, it's only seventeen hours ago that he was arrested."

"There is also a piece of lint wedged between two of the left upper incisors."

"What are you implying?" The faintly amused smile had disappeared and Lysenko's tone was now icy.

"I think there's a possibility that Babkin did not commit suicide. His wrists could have been manacled behind his back rendering him virtually defenceless and it looks as though he was gagged with a wad of lint. You can see he wasn't a big man – I doubt if he weighed more than a hundred and forty pounds – and he wouldn't have proved all that much of a handful for a couple of guards to slip a noose around his neck and hold him down while he choked to death. He probably fought them all the way, and that would account for the scuff marks on the floor."

"You've overlooked something," Oroblinsky growled.

Ashton glanced over his shoulder, wondered how long the militia sergeant had been standing there behind him. "Like what?" he asked.

"The door opens inwards, we had to put our shoulders to it to force our way into the cell. Babkin was literally a dead weight and it was just as if somebody had jammed a wedge under the door. That's how his shoes made those scuff marks, it's how one of them came off his foot."

Lysenko snapped his fingers. "And another thing," he said. "If Babkin had been manacled and really had been fighting for his life, surely there would have been blood on his wrists as he struggled to free himself?"

"It was only a thought," Ashton said.

"I'm afraid this place stirs up the imagination, but you were right to voice your doubts. I can't understand why the prison staff didn't remove his belt either. That's a piece of gross negligence we shall have to look into, won't we, Sergeant?"

"I'll personally attend to it, Major." Oroblinsky jerked a thumb in the photographer's direction. "Can he get started now?"

"Certainly, we'll get out of your way. Would you like to come with me, Mr Ashton?"

It wasn't an invitation he was predisposed to decline. A more liberal régime might be in power but the Lubyanka hadn't changed. It was still an evil place and no one in his right mind would want to spend a minute longer within its walls than was strictly necessary. Compared with the prison, the headquarters of the KGB's Second Chief Directorate was almost a cosy and hospitable establishment.

"What happens now?" Ashton asked when they were back in Lysenko's office.

"Katya Babkina will have to be informed that her husband is dead and it's possible she may be able to help us with our enquiries."

"Well, I don't see how I can help you there. I'll let you know if Mrs Joyner has any useful information."

"You are leaving?"

"That's the general idea," Ashton said.

"How do I get in touch with you should the necessity arise?"

"Ring the embassy, they'll know where to find me."

Lysenko smiled. It made him appear almost boyish. "No doubt you are anxious to get on with the annual security check."

"That sort of thing is not within my remit, I've only just been taken on as a Queen's Messenger."

"Nonsense. You're SIS."

Ashton laughed. "Whoever told you that must have been hitting the vodka."

"I think not. Let me tell you what our First Chief Directorate used to do in the bad old days. Every year they purchased a copy of the British Foreign Office Diplomatic List from Her Majesty's Stationery Office. Every year every KGB Resident throughout the world obtained a copy of the staff list relating to the British Embassy they were responsible for monitoring. These individual staff lists were fed into one of the First Chief Directorate's computers at Yasenevo and compared with the full Diplomatic

List. This was done year after year, which is how they know you have never served in an embassy. You are almost thirty-four, Mr Ashton, and you have ten years service; you are not senior enough to be a policy maker in Whitehall."

"Your informant has put two and two together and managed to come up with the wrong answer. It was precisely because I was never given a foreign posting that I resigned from the Diplomatic and became a Queen's Messenger. At least I now get to see more of the world, if only briefly."

The explanation would not stand up in the long term, but Lysenko had caught him on the hop and it was the best he could do in the circumstances. The way the KGB were supposed to have identified him as an SIS officer was a load of crap. He had come to the notice of the First Chief Directorate, the foreign Intelligence branch, in the wake of the attempted coup aimed at replacing Gorbachev in August '91, and London should never have involved him in the Joyner case where he was bound to be noticed again.

"Well, I suppose it wouldn't be the first time those geniuses over at Yasenevo got it wrong," Lysenko said genially.

That the Russian didn't believe it became very evident before they parted company when he asked to be remembered to Hugo Calthorpe. It was, Ashton thought, a neat way of letting him know that the KGB also knew who was running the show in Moscow.

There was no sign of Feliks in Dzerzhinsky Square. Like most Muscovites, he was still leery of the KGB and preferred to give them a wide berth. After quartering the immediate vicinity, Ashton eventually found he had parked the car in the rear of the Children's Department Store a quarter of a mile away and was fast asleep behind the wheel.

It was well after six by the time they returned to the embassy. Given the relatively late hour, Ashton had expected to find that everyone had gone home with the exception of the duty officer and the wireless operator on night watch, but the downstairs noticeboard showed that Calthorpe was still in his office, as was the Head of Chancery and the Third Secretary, Commerce. With Hicks waiting for him by the gate to the secure area, it wasn't hard to guess why they were working overtime.

"Who have you offended now?" Ashton asked wearily.

"That's right, blame me," Hicks said in an aggrieved tone. "I find a bug in that little prick of a commercial attaché's office and it's all my fault."

"Are we talking about Mr Vaughan?"

"Who else would fly off the handle when I told him he could expect to kiss goodbye to his locally employed secretary."

"Is that what you told him in so many words?"

"I don't believe in beating about the bush. 'Course he got all uptight because he thought I was hinting that he was having it away with that dishy bit of goods who's always bringing him cups of coffee." Hicks jerked a thumb towards Calthorpe's office at the end of the corridor. "Vaughan's in there now with the Head of Chancery making a formal complaint about me."

"Have you been told to wait?"

"No, I just want to make sure they hear my side of the story."

"Well, I've heard it," Ashton told him, "so now you can run along and leave everything to me."

"But – "

"No buts. At the moment, you are like a red rag to a bull and you should get out of this particular field while you still have a head start. Now, just give me the device you found and make yourself scarce."

Hicks gave every sign that he was about to protest before he had second thoughts and nodded judiciously to himself. "I'll see you tomorrow then," he said, and dropped a miniaturised transmitter into Ashton's outstretched palm.

The junior Commercial Attaché emerged from Calthorpe's office some five minutes after the electronics technician had departed. Michael Vaughan was in his early twenties and was one of those bouncy little men who walk with a spring in their step as if to compensate for a lack of inches. He also looked enormously pleased with himself and it wasn't difficult to understand why he and Hicks would have fallen out.

Head of Chancery appeared a few moments later and gave Ashton an enigmatic smile as they passed each other in the corridor. It didn't tell him anything, neither did Calthorpe when he walked into his office, but the SIS chief in Moscow didn't have to speak; the long-suffering expression on his face said it all.

"Don't tell me," Ashton said. "Hicks has been ruffling a few feathers again."

"That's something of an understatement."

"I was warned before leaving London that tact was not one of his strong suits and of course I'll have a word with him. But the fact is a bug was found in Vaughan's office and it's no good him getting heated with Hicks because chances are his Russian secretary planted the damned thing. These days, the opposition is more interested in obtaining sensitive commercial information than they are in acquiring military intelligence. Vaughan should have known that and it was up to him to take appropriate security measures."

"Quite so." Calthorpe cleared his desk, stacked the in-, pending and out-trays one on top of the other and locked them away in his safe, then spun the combination dial. "Will you be seeing Elena Andrianova tomorrow?" he asked.

"Who?"

"Michael Vaughan's secretary."

"Ah yes. I'll want to have a talk with her first thing, before word gets around that she has been rumbled."

"I thought you would. How did you get on with Major Lysenko?"

"He seemed friendly enough," Ashton told him, then said, "Were you aware that whoever murdered Joyner killed two other people in order to get at him?"

Calthorpe stared at him, seemingly unable to take it in. "What . . . simultaneously?" he asked incredulously.

"More or less." Ashton paused. "Could be there's been a fourth murder," he added, then told the Head of Station why he didn't think Yuri Babkin had committed suicide. "Lysenko hasn't come up with a motive for Joyner's murder; he's hoping the widow may be able to shed a little light on the mystery. I said I would have a word with her."

"Good." Calthorpe took one last look at his desk before gently steering Ashton towards the door. "Better leave it until tomorrow; she doesn't arrive until late this evening."

"Fair enough. Any idea where I'm staying tonight?"

"With Richard Quennell, the senior First Secretary. After all, you are supposed to be a Queen's Messenger and we've got to keep the opposition guessing, haven't we?"

"I'm afraid I was compromised several months ago."

"Never mind," Calthorpe said cheerfully. "Your suitcase has been delivered to Richard's house and the duty officer knows where you are staying. Now all we have to do is find you a pool car. Wouldn't do for the two of us to be seen together."

"Lysenko asked to be remembered to you," Ashton said. "He seems to know you are the Head of Station."

"Does he really?" Calthorpe said, apparently amused. "Well, I suppose that means no more foreign postings for me, except as a decoy."

They went on downstairs and out into the cold night air. Spring was only three days away but winter was still making its presence felt and the gentle rain, which had started shortly after Ashton had left Dzerzhinsky Square, had now turned to sleet.

Frances and Mandy Joyner arrived on the Aeroflot flight departing Heathrow at 13.25 hours, which touched down at Sheremetyevo 2 a few minutes late at 20.05.

According to his passport, the deceased was thirty-eight. The Second Secretary for Consular Affairs who met the Joyners at the airport was surprised to find that the widow was accompanied by a grown-up daughter who was only a dozen or so years younger than her stepfather. Instead of the dazed and grief-stricken woman he had expected, Frances Joyner was dry-eyed and unemotional almost to the point of seeming callous. There were other shocks in store; offered the choice of staying with the Head of Chancery and his wife or a suite at the Ukraina, she had opted for the hotel. Without so much as a thank you for the hospitality she had declined, Frances Joyner and her daughter had proceeded to bombard him with a shopping list of questions on the way to the Ukraina. Amongst them were a number that only Ashton could answer. Since the widow wanted to get everything settled as soon as possible so that she could fly home the following day, the consular officer was only too happy to summon Ashton to the hotel even though it was gone nine thirty.

"Mother and daughter are in Room 1098," he informed Ashton when he met him in the lobby. "And a right pair they are too – hard as nails."

"Anything else I should know?"

"The widow is knocking on forty-seven, has dyed blonde hair

30

and has been married before. She isn't exactly grieving over the loss of hubby number two. The daughter's first name is Mandy and she's twenty-four and a brunette, and like her mother, doesn't appear to be mourning."

"Perhaps that will make my task easier then," Ashton said and went on up to the tenth floor.

Frances Joyner didn't look her age. Her figure was good, there were no crow's-feet under her eyes and no signs of either a double chin or a recent face-lift. She was wearing a Jaeger pleated skirt and a beige-coloured, hip-length blazer over a white sweater. Except for the high-heeled boots and the expensive leather slacks, the daughter appeared to have purchased her wardrobe at a jumble sale.

"I understand you know the officer in charge of the murder investigation?" Frances Joyner said as soon as Ashton had introduced himself and expressed his condolences.

"I've met Major Lysenko," he said cautiously.

"The Foreign Office got the local police to break the news of Colin's death before they rang me at home. They needn't have bothered because there was precious little they could tell me other than that my husband had been murdered in his hotel room."

"He was shot," Ashton said quietly. "If it's any comfort, death would have been instantaneous."

"Do the police have any idea why he was killed?"

He thought Frances Joyner could have been talking about some casual acquaintance for all the emotion she showed.

"Robbery wasn't the motive," he told her. "Your husband's wallet containing well over a hundred pounds was still in his suit."

"Did the murderer kill the wrong man by mistake, Mr Ashton?"

"Major Lysenko doesn't think so."

"And what's your opinion?"

"There are no witnesses but there is strong circumstantial evidence that more than one man was involved. They murdered the concierge on the eleventh floor to get her pass key."

"What time of day did this happen?"

Ice cool and detached. Ashton wondered why he should be surprised by her cold-blooded attitude. He had only to look at her eyes to know that Frances Joyner had not shed too many tears over her husband.

"Around eight pm," he said, then qualified his answer. "At least, that was when the hotel undermanager learned that the key lady was missing. He assumed she had gone home without telling anyone. It sometimes happens."

"So when did he discover that she had been murdered?"

"The following morning when one of the maids found her corpse in the linen room."

Ashton took note of the thoughtful frown and guessed what was coming before she asked why no one had looked in on her husband until late in the afternoon. He could shrug his shoulders and pretend he didn't know or else he could lead Frances Joyner to believe that the hotel staff frequently didn't get around to making up the beds in some rooms until very late in the day. He could try, but she was too sharp to believe it and the truth was bound to come out in the long run.

"The killers put a 'Do Not Disturb' sign on the door."

"I doubt if they did." She laughed harshly. "Ten to one it was Colin, ten to one he took a woman up to his room." She searched through her handbag, found a packet of cigarettes and lit one. "No need to look so shocked, Mr Ashton, I know what my husband used to get up to when he was off the leash. Frankly, I can't think why I put up with it. I should have given him his marching orders long ago."

"Oh come on, Mother, not that hoary old chestnut again." Mandy tossed her head. "You were besotted with that rampant stallion from the day you first met him when Daddy was still alive. The truth is, you were frightened of losing him; that's why you always turned a blind eye to his infidelities."

The outburst didn't seem to bother Frances Joyner. She didn't flush with anger, didn't snap at her daughter, merely removed the cigarette from her lips and inspected the lipstick on the filter tip, half smiling to herself.

"How soon will the authorities release Colin's body after I have officially identified him?" she asked.

"They will have to carry out a post mortem . . ."

"To establish the cause of death when they already know he was shot? How very droll."

"It's a formality . . ."

"Really. Well, they can stick to their red tape but I'm not staying a minute longer in Moscow than I have to. I'm leaving tomorrow with or without the body. I'll fill in all the necessary forms, give the embassy a cheque or my gold card number and you people can do the rest. And don't say you can't because that's what we pay our taxes – "

"The police are looking for a motive," Ashton said, interrupting her. "They are wondering if he made any enemies as a result of his business activities?"

"How would I know what he got up to in Russia, apart from screwing every little tart who was happy to drop her pants for a consideration?"

"Would he have made any bad enemies in England?"

"Yes, me," Mandy snapped, then added, "among a good many others."

"You mustn't pay too much attention to my daughter, Mr Ashton. She is still getting over a very unhappy love affair and is feeling bitter."

The saccharin-sweet smile and regretful tone only served to sharpen the underlying malice. It was also calculated to anger her daughter.

"Well, at least I didn't have to buy my sexual favours," Mandy retorted. "Why don't you tell Mr Ashton how Colin got started and who he turned to every time one of his business ventures failed or was in financial difficulties?"

"I'm not the only wife to have bailed her husband out."

Frances Joyner got up and crossed the room to stub out her cigarette in the ashtray on the bedside table. Then, instead of returning to the easy chair she had just vacated, she continued to walk up and down while she spoke of the timber yard she had inherited from her father. It had been worth a cool three-quarters of a million after the Inland Revenue had presented their demand for capital transfer tax. Large sums of it had been dissipated by Colin Joyner on one failed enterprise after another.

"First it was a casino, then he went into the haulage business, dabbled in the property market and ended up dealing in commodities and futures. I don't see how he could have made any serious enemies along the way when he was God's own gift to any conman peddling a get-rich-quick deal. Of course, I'm not saying there couldn't have been an angry husband in the wings who had a score to settle."

"Do you have anyone in mind?" Ashton asked her.

"Oh no. I never bothered to find out who he was cuckolding. It simply didn't interest me."

It didn't interest Ashton either, nor could he see why it should concern the SIS. Nevertheless, he thanked Frances Joyner for being so helpful, then said goodnight to mother and daughter while fervently hoping this would be the last he ever saw of them. When it came to escorting the bereaved to the mortuary, there was not the slightest doubt in his mind that the consular officer was the obvious man for the job.

First thing tomorrow he would phone Lysenko and tell him that the family were unable to suggest a motive, then he would tackle Vaughan's Russian secretary and see what she had to say for herself. With a bit of luck, the Joyner affair would only have extended his sojourn in Moscow by a mere twenty-four hours. It was a small consolation to hang on to as he left the hotel and walked out into the sleet.

Chapter 4

According to her record of employment card, Elena Andrianova had become one of the British Embassy's locally engaged administrative staff in 1984, some nine months after graduating from the Lenin Institute of Foreign Languages. The intervening time had been spent on a secretarial course where she had learned shorthand and typing. When tested at her job interview, Elena Andrianova had reached a standard only marginally below that required of an entrant to the UK civil service. With East-West relations then in a highly volatile state, it was accepted that she had also received some training in espionage techniques and would undoubtedly be controlled by a KGB case officer. By employing her in the Commercial Attaché's office, it was considered that the risk to security would be negligible. Elena Andrianova was, in fact, no different from any other member of the locally engaged staff, all of whom were under the thumb of the KGB.

Elena Andrianova was thirty-one. She lived with her elderly parents in the Babuskin District of Moscow, had a six-year-old daughter and was in the process of divorcing her husband, who had left her for another woman. All the UK members of the staff thought she was a bright, attractive, intelligent and outgoing young woman. Furthermore, no one could remember seeing Elena without a smile on her face and she was said to get on well with the other locally engaged personnel. Normally, the Russian supervisor would have been present when she was being interviewed, but this wasn't the annual staff assessment season and Ashton had made sure that no one else knew about the tête-à-tête. The fact that he had decided to conduct the interrogation in the office normally occupied by Michael Vaughan, the Third Secretary, Commerce, also allayed her suspicions. The really nasty surprise Ashton literally kept in his hand until she was seated opposite him.

"You want to tell me what this is?" he demanded, and pushed the miniature wire transmitter across the desk.

"I can't . . . I don't know . . ." Her voice was breathless and barely audible.

"Well, let me explain how it works. This thin strand of wire is a highly sensitive directional mike; the transmitter and power source is the metal tab at the other end. One surface of the tab is magnetised so that it can be anchored to some piece of metal furniture." He swivelled round in the chair and pointed behind him. "See that filing cabinet in the corner? Notice how there is a wafer-thin gap between the bottom of it and the floor? You anchored this bug to the underside where it couldn't be seen."

"No." Elena shook her head. "No, that isn't true."

"The transmitter has a maximum range of a thousand metres, as I'm sure you know," Ashton continued remorselessly. "Any kind of shielding, like a wall, would of course weaken the signal and reduce the operating distance. But that limitation didn't matter because you work in the outer office and the communicating door is always kept ajar. Now, the only question is, are you going to remove the earpiece or am I?"

"I don't know what you are talking about."

Ashton hit the desk with his palm, making a noise like a pistol shot that caused Elena to flinch and rear back in the chair. "Don't give me that shit," he shouted and repeated it in Russian in an even louder voice.

It wasn't in his nature to bully and browbeat a woman, reducing her to tears, but it was something that had to be done in this instance because Elena Andrianova wouldn't admit to anything unless she feared him more than the KGB.

"Did you hear what I said?" he snarled and hit the desk a second time.

Elena nodded dumbly, tears welling in her eyes. She reached up, removed something from her right ear and placed it on the desk. Although the receiver was no bigger than a pinhead, the device was embedded in a cone-shaped holder to prevent it disappearing into her inner ear where an operation would be necessary to remove the obstruction.

"Thank you." Ashton picked up the transmitter. "Now, the

36

first thing I want to know is how long this bug has been in place?"

She wasn't going to tell him, he knew that even as he posed the question. The KGB might have been emasculated but it still had the power to instil fear.

"Let's see what we have here," he continued in a soothing tone. "Your mother, Ludmilla, has a heart condition and has been a semi-invalid for the past four years, which means she is unable to obtain gainful employment. Your father, Konstantin Kirillovich, is one year away from retirement and his state pension won't keep the family in food for more than one week in four. You are the real breadwinner because your salary is paid in hard currency. How long that continues is entirely up to you. Given your present uncooperative attitude, I would say you are facing instant dismissal."

"You have already made up your mind to dismiss me," Elena said quietly and with a great deal of dignity.

"I would be lying to you if I said you could continue to work in the embassy, but there are other jobs."

Elena looked up hopefully. "Where?" she asked.

"With the British Council."

Literary evenings with visiting authors, lectures on the British way of life, exhibitions, musical concerts, a reading room and a library containing all the latest novels published in England. The place was a hotbed of culture and Elena would have absolutely no access to sensitive material, commercial or otherwise. It should be possible to secure a post for Elena even if her salary had to come out of the SIS vote.

"Will the British Council have me?" she asked.

"You have my word on it."

"I don't know . . ."

It was, he realised, another way of saying that she would like to believe him but had her doubts. "I'm afraid you have to trust me," he said.

She thought about it, her eyebrows close together in a worried frown. Her hands were still shaking even though they were clasped and resting on her lap.

"I put it there last October," she whispered, suddenly coming to a decision.

"Now we are getting somewhere. Answer a couple more questions like that and you'll be off the hook. Okay?"

"*Da*," Elena said, lapsing into her native tongue before correcting herself. "I mean yes."

"So tell me, who ordered you to bug this office?"

"I can't – "

"Can't or won't?" Ashton said severely.

"I can't tell you because I don't know . . ." She had found a handkerchief from somewhere in her jacket and was busy knotting it. As a means of physical therapy to steady her nerves, it wasn't exactly a howling success. "I never met him," Elena blurted out, "he was just a voice on the telephone."

The man had phoned her parents' flat one evening in early October after she had returned from work and had asked to speak to her. The caller, who had identified himself only as Mikhail, had rapidly made it very clear that he knew a great deal about her.

"He knew I worked for Mr Vaughan at the embassy and where my daughter, Vera, went to school. He said that if I didn't obey his instructions, she would suffer. I said I would report him to the police."

Two days later, Mikhail had picked up Vera from school and had taken her out to Gorky Park before abandoning the six-year-old outside the Sviblovo Metro station almost a mile from the street where she lived. The message behind the abduction could not have been clearer. Next time, he wouldn't be gentle with Vera. In the circumstances, it was hardly surprising that Elena had chosen to put her daughter first.

"Are you sure you never met this Mikhail face to face?" Ashton asked her.

"I've already told you – he's never been more than a voice on the telephone."

"So how did he get the transmitter to you?"

"I was told where to find it."

"In other words, you collected the device from a drop?" The suggestion met with a blank look of incomprehension. "A hiding place," Ashton explained in Russian.

"Yes, a hiding place in the grounds of the Exhibition of Economic Achievements. It was near the Pavilion of Technology. You wish to see the exact location?"

"That won't be necessary. What sort of information did Mikhail ask you to obtain?"

38

"He wanted details of any inquiries the embassy received from British companies – forecasts and assessments of the Russian economy by UK analysts. Also of interest were gold and silver bullion prices on the London market, plus future quotas for oil and gas."

"Yeah? How did you smuggle this information out of the embassy?"

"I committed the facts to memory and wrote them up at home," Elena told him.

"Then sometime later you left the notes at a drop where Mikhail subsequently collected them?"

"To begin with . . ."

Somehow Ashton managed to disguise his irritation. Extracting information from Elena was like pulling teeth.

"Would you like to explain that?" he asked with a tight smile.

The arrangement, she told him, had been changed after the second delivery. On Mikhail's instructions, she had gone to McDonald's in Pushkin Square one evening to meet the girl who was to act as a go-between in the future.

"She was younger than me," Elena continued, "and a lot taller. A very striking girl – by that I mean good-looking – black hair and the bluest eyes I've ever seen. I'd never met her before but she recognised me and introduced herself."

Ashton thought Mikhail had probably photographed Elena when she had collected the transmitter and had subsequently given the go-between a copy. "Did she have a name?"

"Nina Golodkinova."

It wasn't only the name which brought Ashton up with a jolt; the description fitted the hooker who had been killed with Colin Joyner. The connection suggested that the motive for the triple murder at the Mira Prospekt Hotel could be buried somewhere in the files of the Commercial Attaché's office.

"I don't get it," he said aloud.

"What?" Elena sounded genuinely puzzled.

"It doesn't matter. When did you last see Nina?"

"Monday lunchtime. She gave me twenty-five American dollars as a reward for the information I had obtained for Mikhail."

Monday lunchtime. The day of the triple murder at the Mira Prospekt. Either Elena Andrianova wasn't aware that her contact had been shot or else she was remarkably cool. Ashton made a note to check how much the general public had been told about the case on TV or read in the newspapers.

"When do you expect to see Nina Golodkinova again?" he asked casually.

"On Tuesday next. We meet every eighth day."

"Not any more you won't."

"Good. I never wanted to get involved. You may not believe this, Mr Ashton, but I'm glad you found out."

"Glad or not," Ashton said grimly, "the fact is, Nina Golodkinova is dead. Someone put a 9mm bullet into her pretty little head, then gave her another in the chest to make absolutely sure."

Elena Andrianova flinched as if he had struck her. She had a sallow complexion but what little colour there was in her face rapidly drained away. "When did this happen?" she asked in a hoarse whisper.

"Sometime on Monday evening."

"There was nothing about it in my newspaper." She raised her head and stared at him wide-eyed. "I don't think it was reported on television either."

"We can always go down to the mortuary if you want to see the body."

"No, no." She shook her head. "I couldn't bear the smell. I'd be sick." She played with her handkerchief, using it like a flannel to wash her hands. "What am I going to do?"

Ashton didn't have to tell her that she was at risk; the note of desperation in her voice showed that Elena had already worked that out for herself.

"We have to find this Mikhail before he gets to you, and there's only one way the militia can trace him. That's why I want you to go back to your office and write down everything you told him."

He did not explain how this would help Oleg Lysenko to apprehend the killers and he was glad she didn't think to ask him because he hadn't the faintest idea. The sole point of the exercise was to ascertain the kind of economic data Mikhail had been keen to obtain.

Some days were better than others. As far as Oleg Lysenko was concerned, this one had got off to a bad start with a phone call from Ashton and the news that Mrs Joyner had apparently been unable to shed any light on her late husband's business activities in Russia. On top of that, Ballistics hadn't come up with anything new and the report from the pathologist who had performed the autopsy on Nina Golodkinova hadn't told him anything he hadn't already deduced for himself. And just to round everything off, the English widow and her spiteful-looking daughter had been less than helpful when they had finally turned up at the mortuary accompanied by an official from the British Embassy. Mrs Joyner had done no more than formally identify her late husband's body. When he had asked her if she could think of a possible motive, she had coolly informed him that she hadn't the faintest idea why anyone should have wanted to kill Colin. All Frances Joyner had wanted was to get the formalities over and done with in the shortest possible time so that she could catch the first available flight back to London.

No motive, no eyewitnesses and precious little in the way of forensic evidence; Lysenko just hoped that Katya Babkina whose late husband had been chief of security at the Mira Prospekt could give him the lead he so desperately wanted. She was a thin, rather plain woman in her mid-thirties who had done a lot of crying since learning that Yuri Ivanovich had gone and strangled himself with his own leather belt. She had, in fact, been living on her nerves from the moment Sergeant Oroblinsky had picked up her husband and carted him off to the Lubyanka. To learn that he had then committed suicide within twenty-four hours of being arrested had been enough to tip her right over the edge.

As a result, Katya Babkina had spent last night under sedation in the nearby Sklifososki Institute with a woman police officer in constant attendance at her bedside. This was therefore the first opportunity Lysenko had had to question her and the interrogation was proving more difficult than he had expected. The political climate might have changed for the better but few citizens were ready to trust the KGB yet and most people were still frightened of the organisation for state security. Katya Babkina was one such citizen and was only giving him a straight yes or no to every question he asked because she was scared of incriminating herself.

"You've got nothing to worry about," he told her for the umpteenth time. "You haven't committed a crime and I'm not about to lay one on you. Okay?"

"Yes."

The one word answer again. Lysenko gritted his teeth but still managed to keep a smile on his face. "Yuri Ivanovich was a good man," he continued. "Ten years in the militia after army service, and four commendations. You can understand why the management of the Mira Prospekt were happy to have him as their chief of security. He was said to be incorruptible, but the fact is he wouldn't allow one of the militiamen on hotel duty to eject Nina Golodkinova, a known prostitute, from the lobby. He told him she was involved in a KGB undercover operation. Now, contrary to what most people think, I don't believe Yuri Ivanovich took a bribe."

"You don't?"

Two words this time and Lysenko thought he detected a note of relief in her voice. "No, I have a feeling your husband was duped by someone he knew and trusted but who ultimately betrayed him. I'm not saying this man was a close friend." Lysenko opened the top right-hand drawer of the desk, took out a sheet of typing paper and held it out to Katya Babkina. "In fact, I'm pretty sure his name isn't on this list we compiled. Maybe you would like to run your eye over it?"

It was meant to be taken either as a suggestion or an invitation but Katya reacted as if he had given her an order. In her anxiety to appear co-operative, she snatched the list from his grasp and held it up in front of her face.

"Are you short-sighted?" he asked.

"I left my reading glasses at home," she said and returned the list.

"Are they all there?"

"What?"

"The names of your husband's friends," Lysenko said. "You see, we had to get them from your brother-in-law, Leonid Ivanovich, and while he obviously did his best, we can't be sure that nobody got overlooked. Which is why I wanted you to see these names."

"They are all there Comrade Major. No one's missing."

Although the assurance came too quickly to have any validity, he didn't believe Katya was trying to protect anyone. Nor was she being deliberately obstructive. The way she had addressed him by the now defunct title of Comrade Major was revealing because it was indicative of the very real fear the KGB still inspired in her. She undoubtedly remembered how it had been in the old days when you could end up doing a ten-year stretch in a gulag for having the wrong attitude. No matter what the politicians said, Katya wasn't convinced that times had changed all that much and was simply telling him what she thought he wanted to hear. Somehow he had to persuade her that she could trust him.

"We checked your husband's deposit account with the Kincevo branch of the Nowotny Savings Bank," Lysenko told her. "Their records show that Yuri Ivanovich increased his savings to fifty roubles a month three years ago and had four thousand two hundred in his account as of the first of March this year. It's a modest enough sum and as there are no luxury items in your two-room apartment which he might have bought for cash on the black market, we know he wasn't on the take. Perhaps you can now see why I believe he was duped."

"Yuri would never have knowingly done anything wrong," she murmured.

"Quite so. It's very clear to me he thought he was dealing with the KGB." Lysenko clucked his tongue. "Did Yuri ever talk to you about his job?" he asked thoughtfully.

"He used to tell me about the hotel guests . . . the people he met . . . things like that." Katya Babkina opened the cheap plastic handbag she had been nursing on her lap. "Do you mind if I smoke, Comrade Major?" she asked hesitantly.

Lysenko took out a packet of Marlboro. "Please," he said, "have one of mine. They're American and very good."

"Thank you." She leaned forward, took one from the pack and accepted a light from the Zippo he'd acquired from a street trader on Arbat Street. "Thank you," she repeated as she drew the smoke into her lungs. "Yuri Ivanovich was always saying what a small world it was . . ."

"Because he often bumped into some acquaintance he hadn't seen for years?" Lysenko suggested.

"Yes."

"When was the last time this happened?"

"About two weeks ago." Katya removed a flake of tobacco from her bottom lip and inspected it closely. "He walked right up to him in the hotel."

"Who are we talking about?"

43

"Mikhail," Katya said quietly. "Mikhail Yerokhin."

It was a breakthrough, but he needed more than just a name, and that was the tricky part because Katya Babkina was on the edge of hysteria and it wouldn't take much to make her throw a wobbly. The tears welled in her eyes and her throat started working overtime whenever she spoke of Yuri Ivanovich.

"Can I get you a coffee or something stronger?" he asked solicitously, only for Katya to raise her head and stare at him uncomprehendingly. "I can offer you some Armenian brandy."

"No thank you."

"Can we talk a little about this Mikhail Yerokhin?" Lysenko asked, feeling his way.

"Isn't that why I am here?"

Lysenko noted the bitter tone and trod even more carefully. "Suppose you tell me what you know about him," he said gently.

"He came from the same part of the country as Yuri – "

"Just a minute, are you saying he isn't a Muscovite?"

"Yes, he came from Novogorsk, a small village seventy-five kilometres west of Minsk."

A Belorussian and a country boy. Lysenko could guess the outcome even before she told him that, when conscripts, the two men had served in the same motor rifle regiment and had joined the militia when they were demobbed because neither one had wanted to return to the land. Their sights had been set on Moscow, but outsiders needed special permission to live in the capital and that was rarely given. Joining the militia was the only way a country boy could jump that particular hurdle.

"Do you know when your husband joined the militia?" Lysenko asked.

"It was before I met him. I don't know the exact date but it was sometime in August 1976."

"And Mikhail Yerokhin enlisted with him?"

"So Yuri said."

With a date, he could put a face to the name. The Soviet Union might have broken up but the militia archives were still intact and it was a simple enough matter to pull Mikhail Yerokhin's Record of Service card. And in the top right-hand corner there would be a head and shoulders photograph of the subject.

"Why did you kill my husband, Major?"

The unexpected question took his breath away, much as if

someone had punched him in the stomach. Katya Babkina had to be crazy to accuse him of such a crime. Had to be? She *was* crazy, sitting there with the cigarette end burning her fingers and not feeling the pain. He leaned across the desk, grabbed hold of her right hand and shook it until she dropped the glowing ember onto his desk.

"Listen to me," he said passionately. "No one murdered Yuri Ivanovich, he committed suicide."

Lysenko wanted to believe it but he couldn't help remembering that Ashton, the English Intelligence officer, had not been convinced.

Chapter 5

The sky was the colour of slate and although the day was still young, there was little prospect of the sun breaking through the overcast. The temperature had fallen below zero during the night and it was still only a few degrees above freezing now when it was almost eleven o'clock. Milder weather the previous week had led to a steady thaw but enough impacted snow remained in the parks, under the hedgerows and in the back streets of the city to remind Muscovites of the long hard winter. But as far as Ashton was concerned, this was not a day to feel depressed; despite the business with Major Lysenko and Elena Andrianova, he had completed the security check on time and was booked on the British Airways flight to Heathrow departing at 17.30 hours.

One of the first things Ashton had learned in his new appointment was that it was customary to discuss the results of the inspection with the SIS Chief and Head of Chancery before leaving. In this instance, the wash-up conference took place in Calthorpe's office with Richard Quennell, the senior First Secretary and Ashton's host for the past two days, deputising for the Head of Chancery who was an overnight victim of flu. Most security checks revealed the odd minor irregularity in the accounting procedures for classified material, but this was unique in that it had uncovered a hostile Intelligence agent in the person of Elena Andrianova.

No one liked the revelation, the diplomats least of all because it made them look bad. The abrasive and cordially disliked Hicks might have discovered the bug, but it had been Ashton who had pointed a finger at one of the locally engaged personnel, and he got the distinct impression they couldn't forgive him for that. It was also apparent that Richard Quennell was more concerned to learn what he was going to put in his report to London than assessing what damage, if any, had been inflicted by Elena Andrianova.

"Let's be clear about one thing," Ashton said quietly. "I'm not seeking to make a reputation for myself at the expense of someone else's." He picked up a photocopy of the statement Elena Andrianova had made. "She claims this is the total amount of information Mikhail received from her in the five months she has been spying on Vaughan. What I want to know is, does the Commercial Attaché believe she is holding something back, or does he accept this is a truthful account?"

"On balance, he doesn't think she is lying," Quennell said, choosing his words carefully. "But as I have already intimated, he can't give you a categorical assurance until every letter, every document and every cable received by his department during the past five months has been checked against this statement. Then he might be in a position to ascertain how much material she apparently overlooked."

Ashton acknowledged that the Commercial Attaché and his staff had every reason to be cagey. Their hundred per cent check wouldn't prove anything one way or the other. They only had Elena's word that she had planted the device in October '91 and to be really safe, they would need to go all the way back to the previous February when Hicks had last swept the embassy. This would be a time-consuming process and it would leave them none the wiser.

"Elena was getting twenty-five dollars a time for this stuff." Ashton put the statement on one side. "Question is, was she being overpaid?"

"Depends on whether this Mikhail regarded the money as an on-going retainer. The unauthorised disclosure of this information won't harm our commercial interests; conceivably it could have been of some value to the recipient." Quennell smiled. "If it was, he will lose his source this evening when Elena Andrianova leaves our employ."

"I've promised her a job with the British Council."

"I don't think we can agree to that, Peter."

By "we" Quennell meant the Foreign and Commonwealth Office. The British Council existed to promote a wider understanding of Great Britain and the English language abroad and to develop closer cultural relations with other countries. Although a wholly independent organisation, it was funded in part by the FCO.

"Is that going to be your recommendation to London?" Ashton inquired.

"The Ambassador's. I'm only a first secretary."

But not for ever, Ashton thought. Richard Quennell had left Cambridge with a double first and his star had been in the ascendant ever since. He was just forty, had married well, and was widely regarded as a future permanent under secretary. His advice would probably carry more weight with the Ambassador than that tendered by the Head of Chancery.

"What are your objections?"

"The British Council has only just been established in Russia; I don't see why they should be landed with someone we know isn't trustworthy."

"Elena Andrianova saved us a lot of trouble," Ashton said. "If she hadn't confessed, we would still be trying to work out who had planted the bug and when."

"I'm opposed on principle to making deals," Quennell told him pompously.

"She was coerced – "

"We've only her word for that. The fact is, there are still a large number of dedicated Communists in this country who don't like what has been happening and are prepared to do anything they can to reverse the situation. Now I'm not saying Elena Andrianova is a dedicated Communist, but I don't think we should take any chances. We shouldn't give her the opportunity to sabotage the work of the British Council."

Ashton knew it wasn't any use looking to the SIS Chief to support him. Hugo Calthorpe still had a year to do in Moscow and had no desire to find himself isolated in a minority of one. Once back in London, he would have to persuade Century House to back him against the FCO; fortunately, Victor Hazelwood was still the Assistant Director in charge of the much depleted Eastern Bloc Department and Ashton reckoned his former boss owed him at least one favour.

"About Nina Golodkinova?" Calthorpe said before he was asked to take sides. "What have you told Major Lysenko about her involvement?"

"Nothing," said Ashton. "I haven't seen him or been in touch since Hicks found the transmitter. What Lysenko doesn't know won't hurt him and his continued ignorance will spare us a lot of embarrassment."

"And Elena Andrianova?"

"I don't think she's likely to go to the KGB, but – "

"I agree," Quennell interrupted before Ashton could qualify his remark.

The telephone curtailed any further discussion. With a muttered excuse, Calthorpe lifted the receiver, conducted a brief monosyllabic conversation, then cupped a hand over the mouthpiece.

"It's the Chief Archivist," he said, looking at Ashton. "Says he has Major Lysenko on the line asking for you." He looked to Quennell. "Do you think Peter should take it?" he asked and received an affirmative nod.

"Tell him I'm not here," Ashton said.

Calthorpe took no notice, hooked the phone into the amplifier on his desk and told the Archivist to put Lysenko through, then angled the voice box towards Ashton. The KGB man barely gave him time to say hello. Unable to contain his excitement, Lysenko bubbled over, telling him at machine-gun speed that there had been a breakthrough in the Joyner case. He wasn't prepared to give any details over the phone but he wanted to see Ashton and would brief him as soon as he arrived at Dzerzhinsky Square. This was the last place Ashton wanted to go but it was impossible to refuse when Calthorpe and Quennell could hear every word Lysenko was saying over the amplifier and he was receiving notes from both men informing him that the Ambassador would be extremely displeased if he turned the Russian down.

"Okay," Ashton told him, "I'll be with you in half an hour." He hung up, determined that no matter what anyone had to say about it, he was going to be on the British Airways flight to Heathrow. "I'll need transport," he said.

"I'll get you a car from the pool," Quennell told him.

It was almost inevitable, Ashton thought gloomily, that he would end up with the lugubrious Feliks as his driver.

If anything, Lysenko's office looked even more cheerless than it had when Ashton had first seen it. Except for the metal filing cabinet, the furniture was heavy Germanic circa 1900, the walls

50

were a depressing lavatorial green, the carpet a grubby beige and the ceiling was too high to ascertain precisely what shade of cream it was meant to be. Lysenko, however, had gone out of his way to compensate for the décor and greeted him with coffee and Armenian brandy. Although it resembled linseed oil and tasted much the same, at least the thought was there.

"We have something to celebrate," Lysenko announced with a broad grin that made him appear positively adolescent. "A major breakthrough."

"So you said on the phone."

"Well, believe me, Katya Babkina was most helpful," Lysenko bubbled. "She remembered the name of the man who had served in the army and later the militia with her husband. He's Mikhail Yerokhin. The two men hadn't seen each other for eight years when Mikhail Yerokhin walked into the Mira Prospekt one day last week. This is his photograph."

Ashton found himself looking at three mugshots of the same man showing the left side of his face, the right profile and full frontal where the subject was holding a board across his chest showing his militia serial number. Mikhail Yerokhin had a narrow, heart-shaped face with high, prominent cheekbones and a cleft chin. The eyes looked Asiatic.

"After leaving the militia in 1986, he became a licensed taxi driver for the Moscow municipal authority. In this capacity, he came to the notice of the police on several occasions."

"For doing what?" Ashton asked.

"Pimping. He supplied Western businessmen with high-class hookers for a consideration. Of course, there was never enough proof for the police to arrest him."

"Maybe he was paying them a consideration too?"

"It's possible," Lysenko admitted.

"You think he recruited Nina Golodkinova to set up Joyner?"

"That's the way I see it, Mr Ashton."

"Then he posed as a KGB officer to persuade Yuri Babkin to allow her into the Mira Prospekt?"

"Exactly."

"Have we any idea how many evenings Nina Golodkinova was working the hotel?"

"Is it important that we should know this?"

"I'm not sure," Ashton said. "But it is a fact that Joyner had

51

already spent four nights in Moscow before he was killed. Why did the killers wait that long? Did they have to photograph him first so that she would recognise him?"

"Will it help us to apprehend the men who killed your fellow countryman if we could answer that question?" Lysenko countered.

"No, I doubt if it would."

"Then it will have to wait until we have Mikhail Yerokhin in custody. This, by the way, is a photograph of his close friend, Igor Ponomarenko."

"Another militiaman?"

"Certainly not."

"An old army buddy?"

"Wrong again," Lysenko said triumphantly. "He was a nurse in a psychiatric hospital."

Igor Ponomarenko was blond, muscular and in his mid-twenties, or at least he probably was when the photo was taken. Judging by the head and shoulders, Ashton estimated he was roughly six feet tall and could weigh as much as two hundred pounds.

"He has two convictions for disorderly behaviour," Lysenko continued, "the first in '82 when he was fined one hundred roubles, the second in '87 when the court sentenced him to twenty-eight days in a correction centre."

"What constitutes disorderly behaviour?"

"Drunkenness, Mr Ashton. He should have been arraigned for inflicting grievous bodily harm, but his father was an important man in the Communist Party in those days so the charge was watered down on both occasions. Igor was into drugs back then; he stole them from the mental hospital – tranquillisers, uppers, downers – and sold them to students at Moscow University. Anyone who was slow to pay up for goods received could reckon on having a few bones broken. Rumour has it that he soon had the resident physician and chief psychiatrist of the hospital on his payroll, supplying him with drugs and cooking the poisons register so that the discrepancies were concealed." Lysenko paused long enough to take out a packet of American cigarettes and light one before continuing. "It's probably true. Under Brezhnev, doctors and nurses were among the worst paid in the whole Soviet Union. Selling the odd grain of morphine kept them off the breadline."

"What are you doing about Mikhail Yerokhin?"

"We're looking for him in all his usual haunts, same goes for Igor Ponomarenko." Lysenko blew a smoke ring towards the ceiling. "Of course, if Igor has done a bunk from Moscow, we could be in trouble."

The statement hung in the air awaiting the obvious question. For some time Ashton ignored the invitation but eventually bowed to the inevitable. He had a plane to catch and was prepared to humour the Russian rather than miss the flight.

"How come?" he asked, and knew straight off he wasn't about to get a snappy explanation.

"Igor's father used to be a political commissar with the Baltic Fleet; his mother is an Estonian and he was born in Tallinn. If he is lying low in one of the Baltic Republics, we'll never get him out. We've no extradition treaty with Latvia, Estonia or Lithuania and there is nothing they would like better than to give us the old two-fingers-up-yours routine. Things were different when there was a Soviet Union."

Lysenko sounded almost wistful, and perhaps with reason. Things had been much easier for the police when Brezhnev and Andropov had been around and the KGB had been a power in the land. Every citizen had had to carry an ID card that constrained an individual to a particular location. Keeping track of people had been a doddle in those halcyon days because an internal passport was needed to move from one geographical area to another with the result that the police in your new home town knew you were coming even before you left your former haunt. Ten years back, the Balts would have crapped in their collective pants at the very idea of defying Moscow.

"So what are you going to do when all else fails?"

"Hope for the best," Lysenko told him with a shrug.

Ashton was about to wish him the best of luck, but he didn't need it. Not all messengers are the bearers of bad tidings and the one who came knocking at Lysenko's door was positively jubilant, and with some justification. Sergeant Oroblinsky had put the word out on Mikhail Yerokhin and one of his snitches had called in to report that the wanted man had been observed entering the municipal public baths on Slobodin Road in the

Nagatino District no more than half an hour ago. Although Lysenko didn't actually punch the air with a clenched fist, there was no doubting his genuine and intense excitement. It showed in his voice and in the string of unnecessary orders he continued to deliver even after Sergeant Oroblinsky made it clear that he had already alerted the nearest militia precinct house.

"You'll be coming with us, Mr Ashton?"

Uttered in a different manner, it could have been either a question or possibly an invitation. Delivered at the same speed and in the same tone he had addressed his subordinates, it sounded very much like an order.

"What for? You don't need me to hold your hand, Major."

In Lysenko's experience, not too many people refused to fall in with his wishes and he was momentarily taken aback. There had hardly ever been an occasion in the past when it had been necessary for him to inveigle another person into doing something they didn't want to do and he had yet to acquire a persuasive tongue. But he did his best, stressing how much importance Major General Gurov, the Chief of Police, and His Excellency the British Ambassador attached to closer co-operation between their two countries.

"I'll give you two hours," Ashton said, cutting him short. "If you haven't found Mikhail Yerokhin by then, I'm leaving, no matter what. Clear?"

"No one could ask for more," Lysenko said, confident in the knowledge that his wishes weren't about to be flouted after all.

This time Ashton didn't have to go looking for Feliks. The Russian was parked outside the front entrance under the watchful eye of a sentry armed with a Kalashnikov AK47. His pensive face brightened as Ashton got into the car, then became gloomy when he told him to make a right turn into Dzerzhinsky Street and tag on to the police Ladas as they emerged from the inner courtyard between the All Russia Insurance Building and the Lubyanka.

Slobodin Road in the Nagatino District wasn't mentioned in Baedeker's or any other guidebook for that matter. It was a long grey street in a particularly mean-looking part of the city that had first begun to disfigure the landscape in the immediate post-war years when Stalin had decided to transform Moscow. Nowhere on Slobodin resembled the wedding-cake architecture of Moscow

University, the Foreign Ministry or the Ukraina Hotel; indeed, the only building of any note among the drab tenements was the private bath house. Before Perestroika and Glasnost, its facilities had been open to the general public. In keeping with the spirit of the enterprise culture, it had been taken over by the local *Mafiozniki* who had turned it into an exclusive social club. Even so, it was easily one of the grimmest places Ashton had seen in a very long time.

"Looks as if somebody reckons there is going to be a war," Feliks observed sourly.

Ashton was inclined to agree with him. Militiamen from the local precinct house were there in force and armed to the teeth with tear gas projectors, stun grenades, riot control shotguns and AK47 assault rifles. Two roadblocks had been established using police vans, the first a hundred yards short of the bath house, the other roughly the same distance beyond it. Since they already had the place surrounded and marksmen were covering the front of the bath house from the rooftops of the tenements across the road, it was difficult to see what purpose they served. Ashton supposed the roadblocks could have been set up to keep rubber-necking spectators at bay, but none of the residents seemed the least bit curious. That was the eerie thing about the whole business.

"You'd better wait here," Ashton said as he opened the door on his side.

"Don't worry, I intend to," Feliks told him. "I wouldn't go near those cowboys for all the gold in Russia."

Ashton got out of the Rover and walked past the Ladas they had followed to the first roadblock where Lysenko and Sergeant Oroblinsky and four plainclothes detectives appeared to be in conference with the police lieutenant in charge of the militiamen. Oroblinsky was wearing combat boots, a black all-in-one jump-suit and a baseball cap. He had also equipped himself with an armoured protective vest, which included a high-velocity panel and detachable groin shield. Unlike the other members of his squad, who were armed with Makarov automatic pistols, he was carrying a 7.62mm Kalashnikov with the double strut metal butt stock in the folded position.

The conference broke up before Ashton got within earshot. The militia lieutenant edged his way across the road, then doubled forward to join an NCO who was observing the bath house from the entrance to a block of flats. Sergeant Oroblinsky and his squad crossed the pavement on the right-hand side of the road, then advanced towards the bath house in single file, hugging the buildings in order to present the minimum target to any gunman who might be lurking inside. Approximately twenty yards short of the objective, they made a sharp right turn into one of the narrow alleyways that separated each block of flats from its neighbours.

"What's going on?" he asked Lysenko.

"It's very simple, Mr Ashton. My men will go in the back while the militia create a diversion out front. That's how we achieve surprise."

It seemed unlikely after all the commotion that had preceded their deployment. The klaxon on Lysenko's vehicle hadn't stopped warbling from the moment he had emerged from the inner courtyard fronting the Lubyanka until he had reached Slobodin Road. The militia had got there first and while he might be doing them an injustice, Ashton was prepared to bet they hadn't exactly pussyfooted their way into the neighbourhood. To find that Mikhail Yerokhin and his friends were still inside the bath house would therefore be a genuine surprise.

"When are you going in, Major?"

Lysenko ignored the question. His attention was concentrated on the second hand of his wristwatch to the exclusion of all else. Presently, he raised the dry-cell, fixed-channel radio to his mouth, counted down from ten to zero, then said, "Go, go, go."

A four-man team led by a corporal doubled past them and reached the bath house without incident. The NCO in charge and the second in command of the squad were armed with Kalashnikov AK47 assault rifles; the remaining two militiamen had a riot-control shotgun and tear gas projector between them. Moving as a team, they positioned themselves either side of the front door, their backs to the outside wall. What followed was pure farce, at least to begin with.

The corporal used the folding butt of his Kalashnikov to hammer on the door. It was opened some moments later by a stout, elderly woman with iron-grey hair who poked her head out into the street and nearly had a heart attack when she spotted the armed policemen in the doorway of a block of flats on the opposite side of the road. She got as far as uttering a high-pitched squawk of alarm before the corporal bundled her aside and stormed into the bath house with the rest of the squad hard on his heels. A back-up team appeared from a tenement a little way down the street and scampered across the road to join the first entry squad.

"I'm going in now, Mr Ashton." Lysenko slipped the walkie-talkie into a pocket of his anorak, took out a Makarov automatic and jacked a round into the breech. "You don't have to come unless you want to," he added.

"I'd like to see you try and stop me," Ashton said, trying to sound as if he meant it.

Two teams going in the front door, a third entering from the rear; there was no better recipe for a "blue on blue" firefight. Ashton had seen it happen in the Falklands campaign and there was a strong possibility of a repeat performance on Slobodin Road. But he hadn't liked the condescending tone Lysenko had used when offering him a let-out, and consequently had no scruples about using the Russian as a human shield.

The bath house was still relatively quiet when they went inside. The old woman who had opened the door to the militiamen was now sitting on a ladderback chair just inside the entrance, fanning herself with a hand. A second, much younger woman in a distinctly off-white linen smock was gaping at them from behind the counter towards the back of the hall. She was supporting a bath towel on the palms of both hands and holding it out to them like a peace offering.

The war started as they were working their way towards the sauna at the rear of the building. It opened with a deafening explosion from a stun grenade that brought down large chunks of plaster from the ceiling above their heads and was immediately followed by sustained bursts of automatic fire. Ricochets screamed off the walls, gouged lethal splinters from the wooden lockers in one of the changing rooms to their right, and blew away the jaw of a young militiaman some twenty feet in front of them at the far end of the corridor. With the instinct for survival endemic amongst infantrymen the world over, Ashton hit the deck while Lysenko was still thinking about it.

The firefight died slowly, punctuated with spastic eruptions as if the weapons had a mind of their own and were reluctant to call it a day. But finally the wounded and the dying were able to make themselves heard and a kind of peace returned. Like an avenging angel, Sergeant Oroblinsky appeared through the smoke screen of brick dust and plaster with a huge grin on his face.

"We got the bastards, Comrade Major," he shouted. "Got them bang to rights."

The wanted men were lying in the slaughterhouse that was the changing room directly across the corridor from the sauna. There were at least two innocent victims among the dead and dying, but that sort of thing was always happening to people who were unfortunate enough to be in the wrong place at the wrong time. Mikhail Yerokhin was sitting on the floor, his back resting against an overturned bench, which left him free to use both hands in an effort to prevent his entrails from sliding out of his stomach. Igor Ponomarenko was face down in a pool of blood, stark naked except for a pair of socks. He had tattoos on both forearms, the shield and dagger motif of the KGB on the left, a winged dragon on the right.

"Well, that would seem to be it," Lysenko said in a satisfied tone of voice.

"If you say so."

"What is that supposed to mean, Mr Ashton?"

"Whatever you choose to make of it, Major. For my money, it's just a little too neat and if I were you, I'd keep a sharp eye on that sergeant of yours."

"I resent the implication – "

"Quite frankly, I don't give a shit what you resent," Ashton told him. "I'm going home and that's an end of it."

He turned about and walked out of the bath house into the street, glad to breathe air that didn't stink of cordite.

The departure time of the BA flight to Heathrow was delayed by approximately forty minutes at Sheremetyevo 2 International Airport due to some problem with the local in-flight caterers. Although the pilot did his best to claw back the lost minutes, they had encountered strong headwinds all the way home and had then got caught up in an emergency landing at Heathrow and had found themselves stacked up with eighteen other planes all waiting to get in.

Had everything gone to plan, Ashton would have been home in

time for dinner, but even though Moscow was three hours ahead of British Summer Time, it had been going on eight o'clock by the time they had touched down. An hour and three-quarters later, having collected his car from Airways Cranford Parking, he let himself into the flat on Victoria Avenue.

Jill Sheridan wasn't at home, but he had known she was out when he'd parked the Vauxhall Cavalier in the yard behind the apartment house and found that her XR3 was missing. She had, however, left a welcome home note on the worktop in the kitchen, which, amongst other things, invited him to eat up the cold ham in the refrigerator. Since he had eaten on the plane, Ashton fixed himself a whisky and soda, then went out into the hall to call Victor Hazelwood.

The house known as Willow Dene which Hazelwood owned in Willow Walk near Hampstead Heath was described as a maisonette. One of three identical properties, it was part of a much larger Edwardian residence that had been built in 1900 from Mendip stone. Outwardly, little appeared to have changed since the turn of the century with the exception of the Virginia creeper, which had gradually increased its stranglehold on the mortar. Internally, it was a different story. Over the years, various builders and interior decorators had created the kind of showplace usually found between the covers of *Ideal Home*.

Hazelwood had bought the property in 1970 before house prices went totally crazy and two people didn't have to go out to work in order to pay off the mortgage. Unlike his neighbours, he had been content to leave things pretty much the way they were when he and Alice had first moved into Willow Dene. In fact, the installation of telephones in the study, kitchen and master bedroom to supplement the one in the hall was the only change he had made. His apparent deafness to all four could mean one of two things: either the Hazelwoods were out or Alice was giving one of her famous dinner parties. Ashton suspected it was the latter, a supposition confirmed by the mellifluous voice on the line when Hazelwood finally got around to answering the phone.

"It's me – Peter," Ashton told him. "I think I've probably called at a bad moment. If you are entertaining, I can always phone back later . . ."

"Don't hang up," Hazelwood said briskly. "I'm glad you rang, gives me a chance to have a cheroot. How was Moscow?"

"That's why I wanted to talk to you."

"I sense trouble . . ."

"As a matter of fact, something did come up, but I don't think you need lose any sleep over it."

"That's a relief," Hazelwood said cheerfully.

"On the other hand, I do need a favour."

"You've only to ask, Peter."

"Thanks. Unfortunately, it's not something we can discuss over the phone."

"I see . . ."

Ashton thought the momentary pause was significant and he could picture Victor standing there in his study, a Burma cheroot burning away between his fingers, a vexed frown creasing his forehead while he tried to come up with an excuse to avoid meeting him face to face. What he eventually settled for was long-winded, centred around a very full diary and lacked conviction even before he suggested Ashton should ring his PA to arrange a date.

"You owe me, Victor . . ."

"You think I am not aware of that?"

"I was beginning to think you had a convenient memory."

"Oh come on, Peter, you should know me better than that."

"So why don't we meet in your office first thing tomorrow morning?"

"On a Saturday?"

"Monday morning then."

"Okay, it's a date."

"Thanks."

"Just make sure you are there by seven fifty," Hazelwood growled, then hung up before he had a chance to reply.

Ashton put the phone down, made for the spare bedroom and unpacked his suitcase. The stuff he had worn in Moscow went straight into the Bendix to await the next wash day; then he stripped off, crawled into bed and fell into a restless sleep. Amongst other nightmares, he dreamed there was a man crawling around the kitchen bleeding like a stuck pig because half his face had been shot away.

Chapter 6

Ashton removed the five-pound note from the small plastic folder containing his season ticket and British Rail identity card and slipped it into his jacket pocket. The train had just clattered through Vauxhall and would be pulling into Waterloo in another three or four minutes and it was therefore extremely unlikely that an inspector would catch him for the excess fare at this late stage of the journey. He wondered why he had bothered to travel first class when Jill Sheridan had been sheltering behind the *Financial Times* from the moment they had boarded the train at Surbiton. Maybe it would have been different if she hadn't picked a compartment where the only available seats had been diagonally opposite each other, and he then wondered if perhaps her choice had not been entirely haphazard.

Jill had made herself pretty scarce over the weekend. She had arrived home in the early hours of Saturday morning only to take off again before lunch to stay the night at some hotel on the Thames between Windsor and Marlow. Of late, she had been seeing rather a lot of someone called Henry; not that the name mattered to Ashton. As far as he was concerned, Jill could date any Tom, Dick or Harry; their relationship was over and he was relieved to discover that he no longer cared. All he wanted to do now was come to some permanent arrangement about the flat and find a place of his own.

The train passed under the first of five signal gantries outside Waterloo, caught up with the tail end of the Solent Express from Portsmouth Harbour, then abruptly diverged to pull into one of the suburban line platforms. Like most other commuters in the compartment, Jill folded her newspaper away, lifted the executive briefcase down from the rack above her head and moved out into the corridor. A large percentage of the doors on the old-fashioned rolling stock comprising the eight-car unit were already open before the train came to a halt. Within seconds, the great surge towards the exit began.

Jill was a good ten yards ahead of him by the time he alighted. Hemmed in on all sides, Ashton held his season ticket aloft for the benefit of the bemused collector as the crowd bore him through the gates. The worker ants spilled out into the concourse and became individuals once more, hiving off in all directions while somehow managing to avoid colliding with one another. Sidestepping and weaving his way past every obstruction, he finally caught up with Jill at the York Road exit.

"What kept you, Peter?" she asked with an amused smile.

"Jet lag, I guess; I just didn't feel like fighting my way through the crowd." He hesitated, uncertain how to broach the subject, then said, "Are you going anywhere tonight?"

"I'm not sure. Why do you want to know?"

"I think we should have a serious talk."

"There's no turning back the clock, Peter," she said. "I hoped you had understood that I simply don't see myself as Mrs Ashton any more."

Ashton had been reluctant to accept that for a long time after she had broken off the engagement. Now he considered it a lucky break. In the matter of their joint ownership of the flat, Jill had shown him a side of her character he'd never suspected. In Bahrain she had wanted him to sell it and had threatened to cancel her standing order to the building society if he didn't accept the first serious offer, even if it meant they wouldn't get their money back on the property. She had changed her mind as soon as she'd heard that her request for a transfer back to London had been granted. Ambitious, selfish, inconsiderate of others and motivated by self-interest; in choosing to compete in a man's world, Ashton supposed it was only to be expected that Jill would acquire some of the less attractive traits of the male.

"Actually, I was thinking about the flat."

"Oh, I wouldn't worry about that, Peter; there'll be another reduction of the mortgage rate of interest any day now."

"I'd like one of us to move out."

"Feel free. I like it where I am."

It sounded as though Jill had something up her sleeve which

could affect him. "Who's Henry?" he asked, hoping to bounce her into disclosing what it was.

"Someone I met in the Persian Gulf."

There was no doubt Jill had chosen the right vocation for herself. No one he knew was better at safeguarding information; she hoarded it like a squirrel stockpiling nuts for the winter.

"I think I spoke to Henry one night last July when I phoned you in Bahrain."

"It's possible," Jill said without elaborating.

Realising it was futile to probe further, Ashton lapsed into silence as they walked on down Westminster Bridge Road to the twenty-storey concrete, steel and plate-glass structure that was Century House. The security guard on duty in the lobby greeted Jill by name and offered profuse apologies for asking to see her identity card. There were two reasons why Ashton wasn't accorded the same grovelling treatment; he wasn't an attractive female and his ID card was only good for the less sensitive establishments such as Benbow House. It was rather like the difference between a gold card and a simple Access, he thought wryly. Directed to the reception desk, Ashton completed a visitor's pass, then waited to be escorted up to Hazelwood's office on the top floor.

Victor Hazelwood was a big man in more than one sense of the word. Few people of his seniority were prepared to admit to mistakes and errors of judgement as and when they occurred, but he did so with scant regard as to how it could affect his career. Anyone who was fortunate enough to work for Hazelwood knew they could rely on his support in foul and fair weather.

"I presume you want to talk to me about Elena Andrianova?" he said, waving Ashton to a chair.

"You've heard from Moscow then?"

"Two cables arrived over the weekend, one from Hugo Calthorpe, the other, from the Ambassador to the Secretary of State, was copied to us." Hazelwood opened the ornately carved wooden box on his desk, which he had bought on a trip to India, and helped himself to a Burma cheroot. "They are both opposed to finding her a job with the British Council."

"That doesn't come as a surprise."

"So convince me why we should."

"She put her hand up, Victor, and saved us months of work.

Vaughan's office is outside the secure area and is open to all the locally employed staff. But for Elena Andrianova, we would be faced with a protracted and possibly inconclusive investigation."

Hazelwood struck a match and lit the cheroot. "You'll have to do better than that, Peter," he said between puffs.

"If it's a question of money, I can find her salary from my contingency fund."

"You must have a generous budget."

"I'm talking about one thousand pounds a year – it won't exactly break the bank, Victor."

"Perhaps not . . ."

"Convert it into roubles and Elena will think she is being paid a fortune."

"I don't doubt it, but before he goes in to bat, our Director General will want to know why we are being so kind to her."

"What did Hugo Calthorpe have to say about the Joyner case?"

"Quite a lot." Hazelwood opened a buff-coloured file cover, picked up the top enclosure and passed it to Ashton. "See for yourself."

The signal from Moscow ran to five pages and gave a very comprehensive account of the murder and subsequent investigation by Major Oleg Lysenko. However, although Calthorpe drew attention to Nina Golodkinova's involvement with both Joyner and Elena Andrianova, he expressed no opinion and had no comments to make on a number of puzzling aspects of the investigation either.

"Well? Has Hugo left anything out?"

"Not a thing," said Ashton. "On the other hand, he just states the facts and leaves it at that."

"Whereas you have a number of reservations?"

"Joyner was the victim of a professional hit, yet it seems he was a nobody. If he had been a hot-shot entrepreneur, I might have understood it, but I get the impression that the biggest and smartest deal he ever made was marrying Frances Joyner. None of the commercial attachés had ever heard of him before he ended up on a slab in the morgue."

"So what do you read into that?"

"I think he may have been killed as a warning to someone else."

"Bit far-fetched, isn't it?"

Ashton had been around long enough to know Hazelwood's scepticism wasn't meant to be taken literally. It simply meant he was open to persuasion and wanted him to develop the argument.

"Everybody who had anything to do with Joyner's murder has been put in the ground. First it was Nina Golodkinova, who made sure the killers could get into his room, then they got to Babkin, the chief of security at the Mira Prospekt, who'd been led to believe she was involved in some undercover operation. Finally, the two hit men got the chop in a police shoot-out. It's too damned neat, Victor. No arrest, no arraignment, no trial, no awkward questions from defence counsel; there was never any chance that Mikhail Yerokhin and Igor Ponomarenko were going to be taken alive."

"So who signed their death warrants? Major Lysenko?"

"Maybe." Ashton pushed the cable across the desk, index finger on the final paragraph. "But, if you read that again, the man to watch has to be Sergeant Oroblinsky. I'm not saying he organised the whole thing but he's certainly the executioner."

Hazelwood ignored the suggestion. "This Mikhail who suborned Elena Andrianova," he said thoughtfully, "could his other name have been Yerokhin?"

"I think it's highly likely."

Although Mikhail was a common name in Russia, for it to be someone else with the same first name was rather too much of a coincidence. Furthermore, if the KGB had provided him with the requisite documents to pass himself off as an officer from the state security organisation, they had also put him on to Elena Andrianova. Amongst other records maintained by the Second Chief Directorate were the names and home addresses of all Russian nationals employed by the various foreign embassies in Moscow.

"You still haven't given me one good reason why we should find a niche for Elena with the British Council."

"I don't see how else we are going to save her life," Ashton said bluntly. "If word gets out that she was sacked, the people who had Joyner killed may think we are on to something and take remedial action. It might be a different story if they are led to believe she had been transferred out on promotion."

There was no need for him to point out that Elena could hardly go to the police and ask for protection when they were deeply implicated. Victor was in possession of all the facts and was quite capable of drawing the appropriate conclusion.

"You're right," Hazelwood told him, "she has to go to the British Council. The Foreign Office will object, but I think I can persuade the DG to do some arm twisting. They won't be quite so intractable once they are told we shall hold them responsible should anything happen to her."

"Thanks, Victor. The thing is, we don't have too much time. As far as the rest of the locally employed staff are concerned, Elena has a week's holiday coming to her and she is taking it now before moving to her new post."

"Leave it with me." Hazelwood paused long enough to flick the ash from his cheroot into the wastepaper bin, then said, "See what you can dig up on the late Mr Joyner."

"I'd already planned to do that."

"Good. Could be a job for that new assistant you're getting from MI5."

"Yes, I'll put Williamson on to it as soon as we've said hello."

"Wrong name. Someone fell sick and MI5 have been playing musical chairs while you were in Moscow. Williamson has gone to the Foreign Office Security Department. You've got Egan."

"Egan?" Ashton frowned. "Can't say I've heard of him."

"Wrong sex," Hazelwood said with a grin. "It's a her, first name's Harriet."

Harriet Egan was half an inch under six feet, a fact of life which she tried to disguise by wearing low-heeled shoes, hunching her shoulders and walking with a slight stoop. She tipped the scales at ten stone five and there was no way she could shed any weight without looking like a poster for War on Want. She had large hands with long tapering fingers and was very self-conscious about the size of her feet, which was strange because she would have looked rather overbalanced with anything less than a seven and a half. Although she had a good figure, it was the perfect symmetry of her face that claimed everyone's attention and remained firmly imprinted in their minds afterwards. Harriet was, in fact, quite beautiful though she herself was unaware of it.

Born in Lincoln, Harriet Egan was twenty-eight years old and had joined the civil service straight from university after obtaining a good upper second in Geography at Birmingham. As a graduate entrant, she had expressed a wish to join the Home Office where she had been talent spotted by the Security Service while still on probation. The original attraction of the Home Office was that it dealt with those internal affairs in England and Wales which had not been assigned to other departments. Amongst other things, its responsibilities ranged from the grant of licences for burials, cremations, exhumations and firearms to the general policy on laws relating to shops, gaming, lotteries and charitable collections. It had, however, rapidly become clear to Harriet that she was unlikely to be concerned with the administration of justice and criminal law without the appropriate legal qualifications. The talent spotter from MI5 had little difficulty therefore in persuading her that she would find greater job satisfaction with the Security Service.

After her induction course at the training school, she had been attached to the Armed Forces Desk in Bolton Street for the next eighteen months before moving to K2, the section that dealt with subversives. Opportunities to serve outside the UK were few and far between and Harriet had been delighted when she had been selected for a job with the British Services Security Organisation in Germany, even though the establishment was soon to be disbanded. Her posting had been changed at virtually the last moment and instead of going to Berlin, she had left Gower Street for Benbow House, south of the river in Southwark.

More than a little disappointed by the switch, Harriet Egan had reported to Benbow House on Friday and had spent the whole day with the Assistant Director in charge of Administration. A rather pompous man in his middle fifties, he had walked her around the building so that she could meet all and sundry. She had been photographed, issued with a security pass, invited to read standing operational procedures, and had then been taken to Century House to meet the Director General. As far as the SIS vetting and security branch was concerned, Ashton was the one person Harriet had not met. She did not, however, wait to be formally introduced; having asked the clerks to let her know when he arrived, she tapped on the door of his office and walked straight in.

"Hello," she said, "I'm Harriet Egan. I understand we shall be working together."

"And I'm Peter Ashton." He smiled. "If you haven't already guessed."

He got up and walked round the desk to shake hands. Ashton was, she estimated, exactly her height, but he carried himself well and Harriet found herself looking up at him. Instinctively, she straightened up and braced her shoulders.

"I'm sorry I wasn't here when you arrived on Friday."

"It was a private arrangement," she told him, "made on the spur of the moment. Officially, I was supposed to report this morning."

"Well, why don't you take a chair and tell me all about yourself?" He shook his head ruefully. "Forget I said that, it sounds terribly pompous. Fact is, I haven't seen your CV yet."

"I joined MI5 six years ago," Harriet told him. "I did eighteen months on the Armed Forces Desk, then moved to K2 where I screened people from other government departments who needed a positive vetting clearance to do their job."

She wanted Ashton to know that he was not being saddled with a novice. Far from it, she had probably forgotten more about vetting procedures than he had learned in the six months he'd held his present appointment. Even more galling was the job description for her particular post, which was set out under the heading of "Staff Assistant to Head of Security, Vetting, and Technical Services". It was the assistant bit that rankled with her.

"What else did you do with K2?"

"Liaison with Special Branch . . ."

"Well, they're your foot soldiers, aren't they? I mean, MI5 have no powers of arrest, so you have to use the police."

"I was also the link between the Royal Ulster Constabulary and the Met's Anti-Terrorist Squad," she said, trying not to sound irritated.

"That's a bit of an unnecessary duplication, isn't it? Why can't the two law enforcement agencies talk to each other direct instead of going via a third party?"

Harriet wondered if Ashton was deliberately trying to needle her and vowed she wouldn't give him the satisfaction of knowing how close he was to succeeding. Her smile when she spoke was a little on the tight side but she managed to crinkle her eyes to show she was amused.

"I also did a lot of ferreting for the Cabinet Office when Margaret Thatcher was PM."

"Ferreting?"

"Civil servants are the guardians of the status quo; understandably, there were occasions when the government wanted to seek an independent view from someone who was not part of the Establishment. Sometimes, the person or persons whose advice they sought had not been cleared for access to the sort of classified material they needed to see before venturing an opinion. It was my job to ferret out all I could about them in order to decide whether or not they were a security risk."

"Colin Joyner, date of birth the twenty-ninth of August 1953." Ashton scribbled the details on a slip of paper and passed it across the desk. "Would you like to see what you can dig up on him?"

"Is this some kind of test?" she asked, keeping her voice light.

"Colin Joyner was in Moscow on business. He was murdered in his hotel bedroom a week ago. Wasn't it in the newspapers?"

"I don't remember seeing anything. It certainly wasn't reported in any of the TV newscasts, but then we're in the middle of a general election and what happens elsewhere in the world hardly rates a mention." Harriet frowned at the slip of paper in her hand. "Am I allowed to know why the SIS is interested in this man?"

"A number of people around him came to a sticky end, there is no apparent motive for his murder and the Russians would like us to believe their investigation is a hundred per cent kosher. I think there is enough there to make us curious."

"I suppose so. Do we have a place of birth for him?"

"Afraid not. You could try the consular department of the Foreign and Commonwealth Office. They will have had a spate of signals from Moscow concerning the repatriation of the remains."

"Thanks for the tip."

It was what she had planned to do anyway but telling him she was hoping to save time and effort if they already had the information would only have made her sound petulant. Returning to her office along the corridor, Harriet looked up the consular department in the FCO's internal telephone directory and rang the deputy head who could not have been more helpful.

Joyner, he informed her, had been born in Wealdstone, Middlesex. She also learned that on the widow's instructions the embassy in Moscow had arranged for the body to be conveyed to Beresford and Son, Funeral Directors in Kimberley Road, Harrow. This last piece of gratuitous information was only of passing interest; what mattered was that she now had the place of birth as well as the date and was able to start the ball rolling with the National Identification Bureau, previously known as the Criminal Records Office.

Like other government departments, the SIS had its own special delivery service, which operated at three-hourly intervals between Century House and the administrative branch in Southwark commencing at 08.30 hours. The photocopy of the latest communication from Moscow arrived at Benbow House with the 11.30 am delivery and was on Ashton's desk fifteen minutes later. It was accompanied by a compliment slip on which Hazelwood had written, "Thought you would be interested to see this."

The latest from Moscow was a resumé of a ballistic report the embassy had received from the Criminal Investigation Division of the KGB's Second Chief Directorate. The two 9mm Makarov automatics which had been recovered from one of the changing rooms at the public baths in Slobodin Road after the shoot-out, had been examined by Ballistics. After test firing both weapons, they had been able to match one of the handguns to the bullet that had killed Colin Joyner. From the latent palm and fingerprints found on the butt, the police now had conclusive proof that the murder had been committed by the late Mikhail Yerokhin. The final sentence was pure Calthorpe. It said, "From our point of view, I would suggest the case is now closed."

Ashton initialled the photocopy and tossed it into his out-tray. Head of Station, Moscow, was right, the case was closed. No one would ever know for sure who had shot Nina Golodkinova because the bullets had shattered on the tiled floor of the bathroom after passing through her head and chest, but it was a safe bet that Igor Ponomarenko, the other gunman killed in the shoot-out, had done it.

So who had killed the key lady, opened the linen room and dumped her body in a laundry basket? Mikhail? Igor? Or had there been a third man, someone who had kept watch in the corridor and signalled the other two when it was safe to leave the bedroom after they had shot Joyner and Golodkinova? But what the hell did it matter if there had been a third man? Major Oleg Lysenko was unlikely to break his back looking for him. Ashton told himself to forget it and reached for the next file awaiting his attention in the in-tray.

Chapter 7

Although there was a cafeteria in the basement of Benbow House, few of those who worked in the SIS building used it. People either went out for a pub lunch at The Bunch of Grapes, The Wheatsheaf or The Hero of Inkerman or else they brought something in from the nearest delicatessen. Ashton was about to unwrap the cheese and onion roll he'd bought from the sandwich bar in Duke Street Hill when Harriet Egan appeared in the doorway of his office. One look at the polystyrene cup of coffee he had obtained from the vending machine on the first floor was however enough to stop her crossing the threshold.

"Come on in," Ashton told her as she started to back off. "You're not interrupting anything."

"Well, if you're sure . . ." Harriet slipped into the room and promptly sat down on the one and only spare chair, then crossed one leg over the other to rest a notebook on her thigh. "The late Mr Joyner didn't have a criminal record," she said without preamble, "not even a spent conviction. He wasn't a member of the Communist Party, had never been involved with Militant or the Socialist Workers Party. There is no record of his subscribing to the *Morning Star* or any other left-wing journal. The same applies to the National Front, the British National Party and other neo-Fascist organisations. Consequently, he never came to the notice of MI5. In short, Colin Joyner was Mr Clean."

"That's impossible," Ashton said. "What happened in Moscow was not a chance encounter between an innocent tourist and some junkie armed with a pistol. Joyner was targeted by professional killers."

"I didn't say I believed he was whiter than white, Mr Ashton."

"Peter," he said, correcting her.

"Peter," she repeated dutifully, then said, "The next logical

73

step is to look into his business affairs, and the best place to start is with the Registry of Business Names here in London. Then I'll have some idea what to look for when I approach the Companies Office in Cardiff. After that, we could endeavour to find out whether the Inland Revenue had their beady eyes on him and it would be worth checking with HM Customs and Excise to see if they have had any problems with his VAT returns. It's also possible that the Department of Social Security might be able to shed some light on his activities. All we need is an excuse to involve the Fraud Squad and that will give us access to his bank accounts."

"Can you really do all that, Harriet?"

"Let me ask you a question, Mr Ashton. How official is this investigation?"

A minute ago she had called him Peter, now they were back to Mr Ashton and Miss Egan. It was, he suspected, her way of warning him that she wouldn't hesitate to go over his head if he gave her a less than satisfactory answer.

"I don't have to ask anyone's permission to start the ball rolling," he told her.

"That isn't what I meant," Harriet said with just a trace of steel in her voice. "Everybody is entitled to approach the registration office and ask for information about a specific company. You can also legitimately obtain a copy of the latest balance sheet for a small fee, but involving the Inland Revenue, Customs and Excise and the Social Security people – well, that's a different story altogether. What I suggested is highly illegal and will involve a number of friends and acquaintances doing me favours which could lead to their dismissal if word got out. Now, what I want to know is can we rely on your Director General to support us should somebody blow the whistle?"

Ashton knew there was no way the DG was going to do that when he hadn't even been briefed. Furthermore, he would certainly veto the idea if it were put to him. The last thing he wanted was to see the SIS being pilloried in the quality newspapers for infringement of civil liberties.

"I think we had better stick to what is legal for the time being," he said cautiously.

"And will this take priority over anything else that happens to come across my desk?"

74

"Absolutely."

"Good." Harriet stood up. "Now I can ignore the in-tray with a clear conscience."

"One final point," Ashton said, calling her back. "Since Joyner lived in Liphook, you might try the local Chamber of Commerce to see what they know of him."

"Liphook?" She frowned. "That's funny, I was under the impression his home was somewhere in the Harrow area."

"What makes you think that?"

"Because the consular department of the Foreign Office told me that, on Mrs Joyner's instructions, the embassy in Moscow had arranged for his body to be consigned to Beresford and Son, Funeral Directors in Harrow."

Frances Joyner had made no secret of how much she had despised her husband when Ashton had met her in Moscow. Maybe she wanted nothing more to do with him now he was dead but there had to be some kind of family connection with the area for the body to be sent to Beresford and Son.

"Is there anything else I need to know?" Harriet asked.

"I don't think so."

"Then I'll leave you to enjoy your lunch in peace," she said.

Ashton opened the paper bag on his desk, took out the cheese and onion roll and ate it slowly. Although he was curious to know more about the funeral arrangements, the security inspection report on the Moscow embassy had priority. Completing the various boxes on the standardised proforma was child's play; it was the general remarks and recommendations at the end of the question and answer section which made him pause for thought. If you looked hard enough, it was always possible to find fault with something and therefore no embassy was immune from criticism. A so-called meticulous eye for detail was said to be a sure-fire way of establishing a reputation with the Assistant Director in charge of Administration, or so his predecessor had led him to believe. But making a name for himself at someone else's expense wasn't his style and never would be. What had to be said needed to be put across in terms which would not offend people. Consequently, he had to rewrite completely the notes which Hicks had produced for inclusion in the report.

The task completed, Ashton walked the draft round to the clerks' office for typing, and returned with the north-west

London telephone directory. He looked up the number for Beresford and Son, only to have second thoughts as he reached for the telephone. As far as the SIS were concerned, how the family intended to dispose of the body was really none of their business; their involvement with the Joyners had begun and ended in Moscow. But although Ashton couldn't refute the argument, curiosity rapidly triumphed over logic; lifting the receiver, he obtained an outside line, then punched out 081 followed by the area code and subscriber's number.

After explaining who he was and what he wanted to the girl on the switchboard, he found himself repeating everything to Beresford's secretary before she consented to put him through to "Mr Simon". Ashton supposed it was only par for the course that he too should want to know how he could be of assistance.

"I'm inquiring about the funeral arrangements for the late Mr Colin Joyner," he told him.

"I see." There was a noise on the line that sounded like a truck grinding along in low gear as Beresford cleared his throat. "Are you a member of the family?" he asked.

"I'm with the Foreign Office."

"Ah." It was evident from his tone that Simon Beresford was deeply suspicious and believed he was dealing with a hoaxer.

Although reluctant to disclose the unlisted number for Benbow House, Ashton realised he would get nothing from the funeral director until his doubts were allayed. "Be sure to ask for Extension 212," he said before putting the phone down.

Two minutes later, he picked it up again to profuse apologies from Beresford. It subsequently took almost as long to assure him he had every right to satisfy himself that his caller was genuine.

"You wanted to know about the funeral, Mr Ashton?"

"Yes, the embassy in Moscow has asked me to represent them at the service."

"Well, it's on Thursday, nine forty-five at the Breakespear Crematorium in Ruislip." Beresford found it necessary to clear his throat again. "I was told it would be strictly a family affair," he added.

"Well, naturally we shall respect their wishes, but I presume there will be no objections to our sending a wreath?"

"That's just it. Mr Neville said the family didn't want any flowers but if people wished, donations should be sent to the Red

Cross. There will be a notice to this effect in tomorrow's *Daily Telegraph*."

"Who is Mr Neville?" Ashton asked.

"I was told he is a legal executive, though I must say I find that hard to believe." Beresford gave a nervous laugh before going into his throat-clearing routine. "Looked more like a boxer than a lawyer, if you know what I mean."

Ashton didn't, but was soon to find out. Neville, he learned, had the barrel chest as well as the broad shoulders and narrow waistline of a prizefighter.

"Somebody had definitely used his face as a punchbag, Mr Ashton."

"What – recently?"

"Oh no, judging by the scar tissue above the right eye, it must have been some time ago."

"But he's the man I should contact about the estate?"

"If those people in Moscow are hoping to be paid for the work they did on the late Mr Joyner, they're likely to be disappointed if Mr Neville has anything to do with it."

The phone call to Beresford and Son had been in the nature of a fishing expedition. Now that it looked as if he'd got a bite, the trick was to land the catch. "Nothing gets past him?" Ashton suggested tentatively.

"George Neville wasn't born yesterday. First thing he did was photograph the body from all angles to prove what a slipshod job the Russians had made of touching it up. After that he chose the cheapest coffin in our brochure."

"In that case I don't imagine he'll give us a lot of hassle. Mrs Joyner is due a rebate on the traveller's cheques she gave the embassy to cover the cost of sending the body home by air freight."

"That should please the widow."

"Not immediately," said Ashton. "The money has to go into the estate, so I need to know the name and address of the solicitors Neville works for."

"Hold on a moment." There was a faint clatter as Beresford put the phone down before opening and closing one of the drawers in his desk. "Yes, here it is," he said presently. "I've been instructed to send our account to Harold Raeburn and Associates, 625/626 Finchley Road."

"Thanks."

"My pleasure," Beresford said and replaced the phone.

Frances Joyner had identified the body in Moscow and would have seen that a large piece of the forehead above the right eye had been destroyed by the 9mm bullet when it had exited. Faced with such a wound, not even the embalmers who had preserved Lenin like a waxwork dummy could have made the corpse look more than halfway presentable. Naïve was not a word Ashton would have applied to Frances Joyner but if she really was thinking of suing the Russian government for compensation, he wondered why she hadn't gone to a firm of solicitors with a big case reputation.

Harold Raeburn and Associates: Ashton looked at the address he'd scribbled on his notepad and decided it might be an idea to leave the office a little earlier than usual and look them up before going on home.

The Assistant Director in charge of Administration was responsible for courses, clerical support, internal audit, claims, expenses, departmental budgets, control of expenditure and Boards of Inquiry. He was also the secretary of the promotion board. His empire included the financial branch, the motor transport and general stores section, and Ashton's Security, Vetting and Technical Services division. To run such a diverse and compartmentalised department required a sense of humour, something which the present incumbent sadly lacked.

Roy Kelso, the current head of Administration, was a pain; there was no other word to describe him. He was fifty-one, tired, disappointed, embittered and small-minded, qualities which were not calculated to endear him to his subordinates. Ashton had learned from experience that the best way to get on with Kelso was to avoid him as much as possible. It was, however, difficult to ignore a request to spare him five minutes, especially when it was delivered in writing by his PA.

"Do take a seat, Peter," he said affably when Ashton presented himself at his office on the top floor. "How was the trip to Moscow?"

It was a loaded question. Ashton knew that as a matter of courtesy he should have reported to Kelso before he did anything else. That he had stopped off at Century House to see

Hazelwood on the way to the office was no excuse. Neither was his new assistant; he should have told Harriet Egan he would see her later and the security inspection report could have waited too.

"It was pretty eventful," he said cautiously.

"So I gather."

Uttered in any other tone of voice, it would have been a reproof, but the smile was still there on Kelso's face and he didn't appear to resent the fact that he had had the news second hand. If the coffee-pot, best china cups and saucers and the plate of chocolate biscuits were anything to go by, it seemed he intended to treat him like a prodigal son.

"Black or white, Peter?"

"White, please – no sugar."

"I wish I didn't have a sweet tooth." Kelso poured the coffee, added a dash of milk to both cups and passed one to Ashton. "Chocolate biscuit?"

"No, thank you."

"I shouldn't either," he said and promptly took one. "I've been hearing good things about you."

The kindly housemaster giving the head of house a friendly pat on the shoulder and telling him well done. It was enough to make Ashton squirm.

"Well, I can't take all the credit," he said. "After all, it was Hicks who found the bug."

"And ruffled a few feathers afterwards by all accounts."

"He's inclined to be a bit acerbic on occasions."

"You'll have to be more firm with him, Peter."

Although he was still smiling, still affable, Ashton could recognise a dig when he heard one. What made it especially irritating was the knowledge that while Hicks invariably treated the Assistant Director with contempt, Kelso had never once had the courage to reprimand him for his impertinence.

"I think we are talking at cross purposes, Peter. Actually, I wasn't alluding to your interrogation of that Russian employee – what's her name now?"

"Elena Andrianova."

"Yes, Elena Andrianova. I don't imagine she was in a position to do us much damage but it's as well you persuaded her to make a voluntary statement. I don't suppose it will be difficult to recruit a suitable replacement, given the present economic situation in Russia."

"Quite." Ashton wondered if he should tell him that he had asked Hazelwood to get Elena a job with the British Council. As a result of her activities, she had been kicked out of the British Embassy. What use the Eastern Bloc Department subsequently made of her talents was really none of Kelso's business. It would, however, become his concern if the money for her salary had to be found from one of the votes he controlled. The trouble was, Kelso might be tempted to put a spoke in the wheel if he was told about the proposal.

"I was in fact referring to the extremely good rapport you established with Major Oleg Lysenko. You earned yourself a good chit there."

The change of topic resolved Ashton's dilemma. "Were you consulted before I was thrown into the arms of the KGB?" he asked, thankful for the unexpected reprieve.

"The DG was keen for you to liaise with them and I agreed you were an ideal choice."

"It effectively blew my cover as a Queen's Messenger."

"You made yourself a known face months ago, Peter." Kelso removed his glasses and polished them with a handkerchief. "It happened when you got a little too close to a certain KGB officer in Germany. The DG felt we should use this fact to our advantage."

In his devious way, the DG was making a point. By pushing him into the limelight, the 'Old Man' was effectively telling the KGB that he was expendable and it would be a waste of their time, money and effort if they had it in mind to cultivate him. Now you know the score, Ashton thought, and couldn't help feeling rather deflated.

"While you are here, you might as well have this." Kelso replaced his spectacles, dipped into his pending tray and handed him a memo from Century House. "A team from the US Defense Intelligence Agency is arriving on Wednesday to exchange information with their opposite numbers. As our Deputy DG will be attending the conference the following morning, you'd better look into the security arrangements."

"But the conference is being held in the Ministry of Defence."

"So?"

"So the MoD has its own security organisation," Ashton said.

"Then check with them and offer to help. We'd all look pretty stupid if the IRA managed to smuggle a bomb into the conference room."

"Right." Ashton gulped down the remains of his coffee and stood up. "Will that be all?" he asked.

"I think so." Kelso waited until he had almost reached the door before he said, "Next time you go away, Peter, I would appreciate it if you would make a point of seeing me on your return."

Even though Ashton knew the Assistant Director was due an apology, the words stuck in his throat and nearly choked him.

Returning to his office, he rang MoD Security to enquire about the arrangements for the conference on Thursday, then asked if he could be of any assistance. As he had surmised, the offer was received with some amazement and politely declined. On that note, he cleared his desk, locked everything away and left the office to call on Harold Raeburn and Associates.

The offices of Harold Raeburn and Associates were about a hundred yards from the Metropolitan and Jubilee Line station at Finchley Road. The People's Law Centre, as a placard inside the window informed Ashton, was in the middle of a typical high street block of shops that had appeared all over outer London between the two world wars. The firm was staffed by lawyers drawn from the Asian, West Indian and Chinese ethnic minorities amongst the community as well as the indigenous population. Since they donated their services free of charge, the number of associates varied from week to week, if not day to day. Unable to find George Neville on her list of volunteer solicitors and legal executives, the Chinese receptionist quickly referred Ashton to a Mr Patel who was equally quick to whisk him upstairs to Harold Raeburn, the head of the People's Law Centre.

Raeburn's office overlooked the street and was big enough to have been the lounge-diner in the days when the rooms above the shop had been a self-contained flat. It was more impressive than the man behind the desk, who was small, untidy and in his late forties or early fifties. He was wearing a sports jacket with leather patches on the elbows over a Fair Isle pullover and a pair of grey slacks that had a food stain on the right thigh.

81

"Ashby?" he repeated vaguely after Patel had left them alone together.

"It's Ashton actually."

"From the Foreign Office?"

"Yes. The Consular Administrative Department."

"Can't say I've heard of it." Raeburn waved a hand in the general direction of a shabby ladderback chair. "Do take a seat," he said, then added, "and tell me what the problem is," before sinking back in his chair.

"My business is really with a Mr George Neville. I understood he was a legal executive at this law centre."

"News to me."

Raeburn wasn't giving anything away; years of tangling with authority on behalf of the underdog had obviously turned him against anyone he regarded as part of the Establishment. Despite appearances to the contrary, he was probably as keen as a cut-throat razor and at least as dangerous. Ashton found himself wishing he had asked Harriet Egan what her colleagues in MI5 knew about the People's Law Centre before he'd set off to Finchley Road.

"It's what I was told by Simon Beresford of Beresford and Son, Funeral Directors of Harrow. You may have heard of them? If you haven't, you soon will because, on Mr Neville's instructions, they will be sending their account to you."

"Yes."

"What does that mean?" Ashton asked.

"It means I am aware that their bill will be sent to me. I don't know if Mr Neville is a legal executive but we have been retained by him acting on behalf of Mrs Frances Joyner."

"Do you have an address for him?"

"I do," Raeburn said calmly, "but it would not be ethical to disclose it without knowing why you wish to see Mr Neville."

Ashton had anticipated the question from the moment Patel had introduced him to the head of the People's Law Centre and was ready with an answer. He told him about his conversation with Simon Beresford and why he believed the family were thinking of suing the Russian authorities.

"If that is their intention," he said, "you can probably understand why we should be concerned."

"Yes indeed."

Polite but unhelpful, that was Raeburn, and his slightly condescending manner was beginning to irritate Ashton although he
kept a smile on his mouth.

"We are not trying to obstruct Mrs Joyner," he said. "It's a
free country and she can do what she likes with her money. But I
think someone ought to advise her that she won't get a penny out
of the Russian government."

"We haven't been asked to initiate legal proceedings."

Ashton thought it likely that he wouldn't know how to begin if
he had been so instructed, and that meant Neville was handling it,
which was a little ambitious of him because, by his own account,
he was only a legal executive, not a fully fledged solicitor and was
therefore still learning the ropes.

"Liphook's not the far side of the world," Ashton said, trying a
different approach. "I could go down there myself and seek out
Mrs Joyner, but I don't believe the lady would listen to me, much
less take my advice. I'm a Foreign Office man and chances are
she would simply convince herself that our only concern was to
make sure she didn't rock the boat."

"You're probably right."

"Someone in her own corner has to tell Frances Joyner the
score."

"Quite."

"And that's where Mr Neville comes in."

"Yes, I'd say it was his responsibility."

"So how do I get in touch with him?"

The question went begging with 'Stonewall' Raeburn making a
virtue out of being uncooperative. Ashton's smile had long since
left his lips and it was getting harder and harder not to show his
irritation.

"Why the reluctance to tell me?" he demanded. "If you have
any doubts about my version of the family's intention, you can do
one of two things. Either telephone the widow and ask her direct
or else you can ring Beresford at the funeral parlour. He'll tell
you why Neville photographed the body."

Raeburn glanced at his wristwatch. "Too late for that, he will
have gone home by now."

"You could look him up in the directory to see if his private
number is listed."

"I don't want to waste any further time on Mr Neville. We have only been retained to settle the estate; since he has not chosen to brief us on the matter with the Russian government, disclosing his business address can hardly be a breach of confidence.''

It had taken a long time to get there and Raeburn's sudden about-face owed more to a fit of pique than to the concoction of half-truths which Ashton had been feeding him. But that was unimportant; what counted was the slip of paper the solicitor pushed across the desk. On it was written: "Mr George Neville, UK Representative Trans Globe Services Incorporated, Arlington House, 36/38 Arlington Gardens, London SW1W 5BS – Telephone 071-976 2000.''

"He's not a legal executive then," Ashton observed.

"I never said he was. Mrs Joyner told me that he had been in business with her husband and was a friend of the family.''

Ashton wondered why she had chosen the People's Law Centre to obtain a grant of probate but knew better than to ask. It would not take much to arouse Raeburn's suspicion and he didn't want the lawyer telephoning the Foreign Office to check up on him. A heartfelt vote of thanks drew a vapid smile, the mandatory apology for taking up so much of his valuable time was rewarded with a limp handshake.

On the way back to the Underground, Ashton used one of the pay phones in Finchley Road to call the offices of Trans Globe Services Incorporated. The number rang out half a dozen times before the answering machine cut in. A gruff voice announced that Mr Neville was not in the office at the present moment but would get back to him as soon as possible if, after the tone, he would like to leave a message together with his name and telephone number. It was the last thing Ashton planned to do.

84

Chapter 8

Ashton showed his season ticket to the collector on the gate and passed through onto the concourse. The day before, he had travelled up to town with Jill Sheridan, this morning he was on his own. The serious talk he had wanted had started on a slightly unusual note and had never looked back; Jill had arrived home from the office yesterday evening with Henry in tow and a solitaire diamond the size of a grape on the third finger of her left hand. One glance at the engagement ring and he'd known that the future ownership of the flat was as good as settled. In the event, the discussion had been even briefer than he'd anticipated because Henry had announced that he proposed to buy him out and take over his share of the mortgage. All he had to do now was find somewhere to rent while he looked round for a place he liked and could afford.

Ashton rode the escalator down to the Underground, fed a pound coin into the vending machine, then followed the directional signs for the Northern Line. Alighting at the Embankment, he caught the first westbound train and got out at Victoria. From a pay phone opposite the bus depot he rang Trans Globe Services and got the answering machine again. Most businessmen were at their desks long before nine; it seemed that George Neville was one of the exceptions.

Just how Arlington Gardens had got its name was not apparent at first sight. The only greenery in sight was a narrow grass strip on the central reservation of the dual carriageway; there were no trees, no flowerbeds, no shrubs, and Ashton could only assume that either at some time in the distant past a garden had existed in that part of Victoria or else it was a case of poetic licence. Arlington House itself was an unpretentious seven-storey purpose-built office block which, according to the information board in the entrance hall, was occupied by fifteen assorted companies. Trans Globe Services shared the top floor with a firm of chartered accountants and Lifeguard Insurance Brokers. Ashton also noted that the only tenants on the fourth floor were Jerome, Jerome and Bowker, Solicitors and Commissioners for Oaths. With an obviously thriving practice on the doorstep, he wondered why Neville had found it necessary to go to the People's Law Centre in Finchley.

He walked over to the lift, joined the tail end of a queue of office workers and just managed to squeeze into the car without fouling the door. The crush eased significantly at the fourth floor; by the time the lift reached the sixth, the only other occupant was a petite brunette in a brown leather skirt, matching bomber jacket and a stone-coloured sweater.

"Nice morning," the girl remarked nervously and immediately distanced herself from him.

Ashton smiled, hoping to put her at ease. "Let's hope it stays that way," he said.

Two-thirds of the office space on the top floor was rented by the chartered accountants, Lifeguard Insurance Brokers had leased roughly a quarter and the remaining five per cent or so was occupied by Trans Globe Services. In bald terms, this meant the UK representative of the corporation had to make do with a couple of rooms. Ashton tried the nearest door, walked into an office that was little more than a box room and found himself face to face with the same petite brunette who had shared the lift with him.

"It's all right," he said hastily, "I'm not following you. I was looking for Mr Neville."

"He's not here," she told him.

"So I gathered. What time does he normally get in?"

"Nine o'clock or thereabouts, but you won't see him today, he's in Switzerland."

She couldn't tell him when Neville would be back. The cryptic message he had left on the answering machine had merely instructed her to look after the shop while he attended to some urgent business in Geneva. What Ashton wanted was an excuse to spin things out so that he could get the feel of the place and, with luck, learn something about Neville, the man who looked like a boxer, who had told Beresford he was a legal executive and had passed himself off to Raeburn as a friend of the family.

"Perhaps you can help me," he said. "I understand Mr Neville is in charge of the funeral arrangements?"

"What funeral arrangements?"

"For his late partner, Mr Colin Joyner."

"I didn't know he had one." She frowned. "Of course, this is only the third week I've been working here. I'm a temp, you see."

"Who are you filling in for?"

"No one. The previous secretary was also a temp, came from the Brewer Street Bureau like me. Libby was here for two months before she moved on but I think I'll pack it in at the end of next week."

Once the ice had been broken and she had been inveigled into talking about herself, the rest was easy. Her name was Debbie Roxburgh and there were lots of reasons why she liked being a temp. You never had time to get bored with a job because you were always meeting new faces and learning new routines; you could also go away on holiday when you felt like it, unlike a regular job where you had to put your name down on the office roster months in advance.

"As a temp, you are self-employed," Debbie told him. "That means your National Insurance contributions are much smaller."

"Any other advantages?"

"Well, they do say a change is as good as a rest."

"So what's different about this job compared with others you've had?"

"Trans Globe works like a dating agency. For instance, if some hospital in a Third World country wanted to buy a kidney dialysis machine at a rock-bottom price, they would come to us and we'd put them in touch with a health authority who had one to sell. It isn't always money that changes hands; sometimes we barter stuff like crude oil for meat and dairy products – that sort of thing. Happens quite often when we are dealing with the Russians or one of the former republics of the Soviet Union. Of course, we have to find a buyer from somewhere for the crude before we can receive our commission."

"Who handles that side of the business when Mr Neville is away from the office?"

"I do," Debbie said, "provided the latest commodity prices are on the computer."

There was a visual display unit on her desk, part of a stand-alone system that was linked to another screen in the adjoining office where the input was initiated by Neville. Much of his information came from a second terminal on line with the data bank in Geneva which only he could access.

"I can't enter the system because I don't know the password." Debbie opened her handbag, took out a pack of American cigarettes and offered one to Ashton. "You smoke?" she asked.

"No, thanks," he said. "I gave it up some years back."

"Wish I could do the same."

Ashton reckoned he would be a rich man if he had a pound every time he'd heard that. No one addicted to cigarettes ever meant it and he had only to observe the pleasure she got from inhaling to know that Debbie Roxburgh was no exception.

"Of course, it wouldn't do me any good even if I did know how to enter the system," she continued. "I saw a print-out on his desk once and it was all in some kind of code."

It was not unknown for large international corporations to use a commercial code in order to hoodwink their competitors. Whether Trans Globe Services belonged in the same league as the multinational giants was open to question. Ashton didn't think they were, if the amount of office space needed to run the UK operation was anything to go by.

"Still, I expect you've got plenty to do even without access to the main frame," he said, fishing for more information.

"Some days are busier than others."

"Well, suppose I had some office equipment for sale. What would the Russians give me for a hundred Rank Xerox machines?"

"Are you in that line of business?" she asked.

"No, I'm Foreign Office, but it's something our commercial attachés in Moscow should be telling the Department of Trade and Industry."

"A hundred Rank Xerox machines. Well, okay, let's see what we are likely to be offered for them." Debbie left her cigarette to burn in the ashtray while she keyed the details into the desktop computer. A few moments later, the barter details appeared on the screen. "We could get twenty-five tractors from the Kirov factory dealing through Moscow's Commodities and Raw Materials Exchange. Alternatively, there's an office supplier in Kazakhstan who'd be prepared to give you a ton of dried apricots for every machine."

"It's mind boggling." Ashton shook his head in feigned wonder. "Do you think I could have a copy to show the Department of Trade and Industry?"

"I don't see why not," she said and keyed in the printer, then picked up her cigarette. "Fascinating, isn't it?"

"The job or the machine?"

"Both."

"Then why do you want to leave at the end of next week?"

"Because it gets lonely and there's nobody I can have a good chinwag with. You may find this hard to believe but you are the first person I've met since I started here."

"Really?" Ashton made a point of looking at his wristwatch. "Looks like you're going to be on your own again, I'm afraid."

"You're leaving?"

"Got to, I'm late as it is."

"Next thing you know, they'll be docking your pay, huh?" She ripped the print-out from the machine and gave it to him. "Is there a message I can give Mr Neville when he returns?" she asked.

"Yes. Tell him to get in touch with the consular department if he or Mrs Joyner is thinking of suing the Russian government." Ashton backed away towards the door. "The number is 071-233 3000," he added and managed to leave before Debbie Roxburgh had the chance to ask him for his name.

Measured in a straight line, Victoria and Southwark were only five miles apart. The number 70 bus which dropped him off outside the door of Benbow House made it seem like twenty. Roadworks, a burst water main and an accident in Stanford Street helped to create the mother and father of all traffic jams. Ashton doubted if Neville had encountered anything like the same amount of hassle on the way to Geneva.

Ashton barely had time to open up the safe before the files began to arrive.

"Looks worse than it is," the chief clerk told him after he had deposited a round dozen in the in-tray. "This lot is mostly for information only. The Mid East Directorate is borrowing a couple of people from the army and they've asked you to run your eye over their security dossiers. They want to know what you think of them."

"Okay." Ashton glanced at the intimidating number of files and tried to summon up a little enthusiasm. "Have there been any phone calls for me?" he asked as the chief clerk was leaving.

"If there were, they didn't come through to me."

No word on Elena Andrianova then, but perhaps that was expecting too much too soon. Hazelwood would need to wait for the right moment to tackle the DG.

Ashton plucked the file marked 'Conferences – General' from the stack awaiting his attention and found the top enclosure was a brief letter from the MoD advising addressees of amendments to the list of officers from the US Defense Intelligence Agency who would be attending the seminar on Thursday. On it he wrote, "Chief Clerk – we don't have the original letter this amendment refers to – please chase", then signed it and tossed the file into the out-tray. The others followed in rapid succession until he uncovered the first security dossier.

"I guess this isn't the ideal moment to ask for five minutes of your time," Harriet Egan said.

She was standing in the doorway clutching a thin, brown-coloured folder in her right hand. Yesterday Harriet had worn the bottom half of a pants suit with a roll-neck sweater; today, it was a dark navy-blue suit over a white blouse and low-heeled shoes. The style was modest and deeply conservative. As if hoping to make herself appear neat but unglamorous, she had also tied her dark shoulder-length hair back and dispensed with any kind of make-up. However, if that was the intention, she was singularly unsuccessful and still came across as an attractive and stylish young woman.

"Come on in and sit down," Ashton told her. "There's nothing here that can't wait."

"Yes, well, I thought you would like to know that the Registry of Business Names and the Companies Office in Cardiff both came up trumps." Harriet placed the brown folder on his desk and sat down. "Ten different companies in almost as many years – you have to say this for the late Mr Joyner, he was a busy little entrepreneur."

Ashton opened the folder and read the neatly typed memo. If variety was the spice of life, Joyner had done his best to sample it to the full. Car hire, leisure activities, gaming, real estate, restaurateur, furnishing, office supplies, wholesaler for durable goods, road haulage and secondhand dealer; he had tried his hand at all of them and failed at every one.

"He never filed for bankruptcy," Harriet said, pre-empting his next question. "In every case, he simply ceased trading and placed the company in suspended animation after paying off his creditors. At the time of his death, he was still in business as a secondhand dealer in electrical goods."

"Do we have a copy of the latest balance sheet for that company?"

"No, but I can get you one, Peter, though I doubt it will differ much from the others his accountants filed. It started with the usual share capital of one hundred pounds."

"What did the local Chamber of Commerce have to say about him?"

"Nothing," said Harriet, "there isn't one. It's likely he was a member of the local Rotary in Liphook but I decided it was too risky to sound them out."

"You did a good job, Harriet, and I'm very grateful." Ashton was conscious of sounding pompous and wondered why she always seemed to have that effect on him.

"Thanks. The list of his directorships is on the reverse side."

Ashton turned the page over. He recalled what Frances Joyner had told him in Moscow about her late husband, how he was supposed to have dissipated most of her inherited fortune on one hare-brained enterprise after another. He had got the impression that she had had to sell the timber yard to settle his debts but the business was apparently still in her hands. So were others she had failed to mention – the building firm, the plumbing and central heating business. Colin Joyner may not have been the managing director but she had kept him on the board of all three companies.

"I don't see Trans Globe Services Incorporated on the list," he said.

"Who are they?"

"I don't know, that's what I would like you to find out. Head Office of the UK subsidiary is in Arlington House, Arlington Gardens, Victoria."

"Does this task also have priority over everything else?" Harriet asked.

"Yes."

"There's nothing like an unequivocal answer," she said and started to get up, only to sit down again when she realised he hadn't finished.

"The UK rep of Trans Globe is a man called George Neville. I can't tell you where he was born or when but I want to know him better than his own mother does."

"May I ask why we are so interested in him?"

"He led Beresford, the funeral director, to believe he was a legal executive but he told the solicitor who is applying for grant of probate a different story. Said he was a close friend of the family and claimed Joyner had been a business associate. But his secretary had never heard of him and wasn't aware he had a partner."

"Of course I'm only an outsider, Mr Ashton, but I can't see why any of this should concern the SIS."

He noted the 'Mr' and the hint of steel in her voice wasn't lost on him either. He guessed the next thing she would ask was whether the DG would be prepared to support them in this instance and wasn't disappointed.

"The answer is the same as before," he told her. "In fact, I'll go further; he'll run for cover if anything goes wrong."

"I see."

"Neville's present secretary is a girl called Debbie Roxburgh. She came from the Brewer Street Bureau like her predecessor. Check with them to see if this is a regular pattern with him – "

"I'm not happy about this, Mr Ashton," she said, interrupting him.

"Look, if you're worried we'll open a branch memorandum file on George Neville and I'll give you written instructions. Then you can send me a memo expressing your disquiet and everything will be on record, which means you will be fireproof."

Harriet got to her feet. "That won't be necessary," she said coldly. "I'm quite capable of looking after myself."

Ashton watched her put the upright chair back in place before walking out on him. "So where are you off to now?" he asked.

"To get your bloody information," she told him angrily from the doorway.

Listening to her footsteps as she stalked off, he regretted what he had asked of Harriet. He had this feeling that Neville was in some way connected with what had happened in Moscow, but it wasn't her fault that he had failed to get this across. He had asked her to go out on a limb for him and he had no right to trash her with all that rubbish about opening a branch memorandum simply because she thought he was in the wrong. Ashton got to his feet and started towards the door, intending to go after her, but the phone began to ring and he turned back.

"My office – now," Kelso told him and put the phone down before he had a chance to say a word.

There were times when Ashton felt it would have been better all round had he tendered his resignation instead of moving to Benbow House to head the Vetting, Security and Technical Services Division. The new appointment was practically the kiss of death anyway and, unless the Fates were extraordinarily kind to him, he would be lucky to make Assistant Director in charge of Administration before he was pensioned off. Furthermore, had he decided to call it a day, he would have been spared the aggro of serving under Roy Kelso.

"Elena Andrianova," Kelso snapped, the moment Ashton walked into his office. "What's all this nonsense about getting her a job with the British Council? I hadn't the faintest idea what the DG was on about when he phoned me."

The Assistant Director was suffering from a bad case of injured pride; he had also been made to look a fool, which was worse because it could have been avoided.

"I'm sorry," Ashton said. "That was my fault. I should have briefed you after I had been to see Victor Hazelwood."

"So why didn't you, Peter? You had plenty of opportunity to do so yesterday afternoon. You sat there in that very same chair telling me what had happened in Moscow and you never said a word about it."

"Yes, that was wrong of me."

"It certainly was. At the very least, I should have been consulted before you offered to pay her damned salary. You may be the account holder but I'm responsible for the internal audit."

"Well, the truth is, I didn't think we would have to find the money. Hell, I only offered the thousand pounds if the question of Elena Andrianova's salary became a sticking point with the Foreign Office."

"You obviously misjudged the situation," Kelso observed tartly. "Though how you could contemplate such an expenditure without first discussing it with me is beyond my comprehension."

"We are talking about a thousand pounds from a vote which is consistently underspent. We are talking about a woman whose life expectancy could take a sudden nose dive if she isn't taken on by the British Council before the week's out."

"Nevertheless, it would have been politic to seek my support before going to Hazelwood. He was under the impression that my agreement was a formality."

Kelso was right, he should have gone to him first. It would have taken a little longer to get things started but how much difference would a few hours have made?

"I'm sorry," Ashton said again. "I'll make sure it doesn't happen again."

"I don't imagine it will. The DG asked me for my opinion and I told him it was a nonstarter."

"You did what?"

"We are not in the business of rewarding people who spy on us," Kelso continued blandly. "Think of the precedent it would create if we found alternative employment for Elena Andrianova. Every Russian in the Moscow embassy would think she had been on to a good thing and would be tempted to follow her example."

There was a lot more of the same as Kelso warmed to his theme and the longer he went on, the more obvious it became to Ashton that he was relishing the opportunity to lecture him. He could understand now why Hicks, along with many others, detested the man and he longed to tell the Assistant Director exactly what he thought of him, but that was a luxury he couldn't afford. Elena Andrianova's whole future rested with him and he had to sit there and take it if he was to stand any chance of persuading Kelso to change his mind.

There was, however, a time and a place to begin the conversion and it definitely wasn't here and now. He counted up to ten and went on counting until Kelso finally ran out of steam, then somehow managed to eat humble pie and thank him for his sound advice. Still keeping his temper in check, he strode past the ancient lift and used the staircase to reach his office two floors below. His outwardly calm exterior vanished the moment he unlocked the door and stepped inside. He walked over to the desk, stood there looking down at the in- and pending trays, which were still far from empty, then sent them flying into the wall where they shattered on impact.

"Fuck you," he exploded.

Immediately ashamed of his childish outburst, Ashton surveyed the damage, then stooped down, retrieved the files and stacked them in two equal piles on his desk. Both wooden trays were beyond repair and went straight into the wastebin. He buzzed the chief clerk, explained that he had accidentally dropped a couple of his filing trays and asked if they could be replaced.

The phone rang shortly after the archivist had produced two wire baskets with a knowing smile. After the fracas with Kelso, he had a premonition it was Hazelwood and knew it was going to be bad news.

"I couldn't swing it," Hazelwood told him bluntly. "You want to switch to secure speech so that we can talk more freely?"

"Sure." Ashton depressed the button on the cradle and checked to make sure the green light was showing on the scrambler positioned on the floor by the desk. "Whenever you're ready," he said, raising his voice slightly to compensate for the reduced power.

"The DG was dead against the idea," Hazelwood continued. "Moscow had already made their views clear to the Foreign Office and he virtually threw in the towel after talking to your Assistant Director."

"In other words, he doesn't give a damn what happens to Elena Andrianova?"

"He's convinced she won't come to any harm, that it's pure conjecture on your part."

"And that's it?"

"Not quite," Hazelwood told him. "For what it's worth, I've asked Head of Station, Moscow to look out for her."

"Thanks, Victor."

"I wish I had been able to do more," Hazelwood said and hung up.

Ashton put the phone down. Hugo Calthorpe was all right but it was difficult to see what protection he could afford Elena.

Moreover, as the only breadwinner in the family whose salary had been paid in hard currency, she had lost her job and was unlikely to find another with anything like the same remuneration in roubles. She had put her trust in him and he had let her down, albeit not entirely his fault, but that was the bottom line.

There was approximately eight hundred and fifty pounds in his current account with Lloyds Bank and he had a further two thousand on deposit but he would have to give fourteen days' notice before he could get his hands on the latter. He picked up the phone again, rang his bank manager in Surbiton and asked for a temporary overdraft facility of one thousand pounds. He also asked for a one-time drawing arrangement for the same amount with the Regent Street branch in case he needed to get hold of a large sum in a hurry. The money would go some way to solving Elena's financial problems in the short term if he could just find some way of getting the cash to her.

Elena Andrianova, Rusanova Prospekt 1258, Babuskin District 095-91.16. Her home address and phone number had been on the record of employment card maintained by the embassy and he had noted the details in his diary for the report he had submitted later. He would ring her and explain what he had in mind. But not from the office where the call would eventually be traced back to him.

Chapter 9

The British Museum was at one end of Gower Street, University College at the other. Between these two well-known landmarks in the heart of Bloomsbury, there were a number of anonymous buildings, none more so than the one occupied by the 'Kremlin Watchers' and 'Russophil Observers' of MI5, officially known as K1 and K2 Sections respectively. It was the task of K1 to ferret out the KGB and GRU officers who, contrary to popular belief in the UK, continued to operate as before within the cover provided by the diplomatic service representing the Commonwealth of Independent States, the associated consular offices and the permanent trade delegation.

Before the break up of the Soviet Union, K2 had been responsible for keeping an eye on all known extreme left-wing activists and the identification of potential subversives in sensitive areas of government and industry whose political convictions might lead them to offer their services to the USSR. Much of their work was therefore of special interest to K1. Consequently, in the four years that Harriet Egan had been at Gower Street, she had got to know all of the 'Kremlin Watchers' very well, especially Clifford Peachey whom she regarded as a good friend.

Clifford Peachey had started as an interrogator and had earned himself a reputation in this field second only to that of Jim Skardon who, in the 1950s, had broken a whole string of Communist agents including Klaus Fuchs, the atom spy. Like Skardon, he was renowned for his tenacity and refusal to abandon the chase once he had scented his prey. To Harriet, his sharp, terrier-like features were a mirror image of this characteristic. He had grey-flecked dark hair cut short back and sides, and a neat toothbrush moustache which was not at all flattering. A shy manner with strangers had led a number of adversaries to dismiss him as a nondescript little man, an error of judgement they subsequently had had good reason to regret. If, as some of his colleagues maintained, he deliberately cultivated a sphinx-like attitude, they might have revised their opinion had they witnessed his obvious pleasure at seeing Harriet again.

"Well, this is a pleasant surprise," he said. "I thought you had been seconded to that rival firm south of the river?"

"You're right – unfortunately."

The smile left his face. "As bad as that?" he said quietly. Then added, "You want to talk about it?"

"I need your advice, Clifford."

"Well, you'd better close the door, draw up a chair and tell me what the problem is."

"My problem begins and ends with the Head of Security, Vetting and Technical Services at Benbow House. He wants all the information he can get legally and illegally on a man called George Neville, and expects me to do his dirty work for him." Harriet frowned. "On reflection, 'expects' is the wrong word; it would be more accurate to say that he has ordered me to use my contacts in the Inland Revenue, the DSS and the Fraud Squad to fill in any of the blank spaces."

"What's the name of this SIS officer?"

"Peter Ashton. Have you heard of him?"

Peachey nodded. "I met Ashton a little over six months ago when he was on the Russian Desk. An Intelligence Corps officer called Whittle had been murdered in Dresden and the Foreign Office didn't want anyone blaming the Russians for it because officially the Cold War is over. Century House despatched Ashton to Germany to make sure the army and the local *Polizei* attributed the crime either to the IRA or some Iraqi hit squad hellbent on avenging the humiliation of the Gulf War. Unfortunately for the Foreign Office, the SIS had picked the wrong man for the job and he started turning over a number of stones London would have preferred him to ignore."

"That sounds like the Peter Ashton I know," Harriet said with feeling.

"Well, he may not be everybody's cup of tea but he gets results."

"What are you telling me, Clifford? That Peter Ashton's a good bet and I should do as he asks?"

"He's not a good bet as far as you are concerned. He got very close to a senior Russian Intelligence officer and there was a time when his superiors believed he had been turned by the KGB. They asked for our help, told us when it was safe to go into his flat, and we bugged the place. We also found his latest statement from Access which showed he had spent approximately seven hundred pounds with the Getaway Travel Agency. It didn't take our people long to find out that he had been to Leningrad and Moscow on a two-city break without seeking permission."

There was no need for Harriet to ask how he knew all this. If the SIS had believed their man had been turned, they would have alerted the 'Kremlin Watchers' of K1 to look out for any contacts between Ashton and the KGB Resident at the Russian Embassy.

"Of course, all this happened before Ashton wiped the floor with the Russians," Peachey continued. "When he did, the bugs were removed and all surveillance measures were terminated. But if he has been transferred to Security, Vetting and Technical Services, it can only mean they still don't entirely trust him."

Harriet was on the point of challenging the assertion when she thought better of it. In the short time she had been seconded to Benbow House, she had already discovered that the Security, Vetting and Technical Services Division was not in receipt of any Top Secret material. It was therefore an ideal slot to put Ashton in.

"So what I am advising is this," Peachey said, winding up. "If you are unhappy about the assignment you've been given, go over his head and explain the situation to the Assistant Director in charge of Administration. This is one instance where you can't be accused of telling tales out of school."

She thought about Roy Kelso and repressed a shudder. "I can't do that, Clifford."

"I admire your loyalty, Harriet, but I think it's a mistake."

"There's more to it than that."

Harriet told him what she knew about George Neville, the lies he had told the director of the funeral parlour and the head of Raeburn and Associates, the People's Law Centre, and how little she had been able to discover about Trans Globe Services

Incorporated and why, since talking to Clifford, she was beginning to think Ashton could be on to something after all.

"So what are you saying, Harriet?"

She smiled wryly. "I guess it means I am going to put my neck on the chopping block," she said. "I was given a job to do. I may not like it but I can't spend the next two years avoiding Peter."

"It's Peter, is it?" Peachey observed and raised an eyebrow.

"Don't go all coy on me, Clifford. I'm not interested in him in that way and I doubt he is aware of my existence."

Peachey found that hard to believe. Harriet had only to walk into a room to become the centre of attention; she had that effect on both men and women without even trying.

"What have you dug up on this George Neville so far?" he asked, changing the subject.

"Precious little. I still don't know his date and place of birth or where he is living now. The one thing I have found out is that in the two and a half years Neville has been the UK rep, he's never had a regular secretary. All of them have been temps supplied by the Brewer Street Bureau." Harriet glanced at her wristwatch. "Time I was leaving," she said. "I'm going to be an hour late into the office as it is."

"Can you give me the names of any of these temporary secretaries?"

"I've got a fairly comprehensive list of former employees."

"All right, let's have the address of Trans Globe; it'll save me looking it up in Yellow Pages."

"What are you up to, Clifford?"

"I'm going to put Neville under the microscope for you."

"Why?"

"Why? Because I like you, because I've been in the Security Service a lot longer and have many more contacts, because I know where all the skeletons are buried and because no one can risk sacking me. Now may I please have that address?"

"It's Arlington House, 36/38 Arlington Gardens," Harriet told him with a grateful smile.

The pay phone was near the junction of Southwark Street and Blackfriars Road, a little over five minutes' walk from Benbow House. Although Ashton wasn't in the habit of leaving the office in the middle of the morning, he did so today for one very good and pressing reason. Yesterday evening he had left the flat he shared with Jill Sheridan to phone Moscow. He had rung Elena Andrianova's apartment in Babuskin four times before and after dining at the Beijing Restaurant in the town centre. On three occasions he had got an unobtainable signal and while he had managed to get through at the fourth attempt, the call had gone unanswered. He had tried again this morning on the way to the station and had been equally unsuccessful. He was hoping for better luck this time round.

The pay phone was unoccupied. Stacking a pile of coins on top of the box, Ashton fed three pounds into the meter, then lifted the receiver and punched out the international dialling code and Elena's number. There was a fairly lengthy pause before he heard the digits begin to click like the tumblers of a combination safe lock falling into place. Moments later, the number began to ring out. When no one answered it readily, he instinctively glanced at his wristwatch for an explanation; Moscow was three hours ahead of London, which meant it was two o'clock over there. He wondered if anyone was at home, then recalled that Elena's mother had a heart condition and was therefore a semi-invalid.

There was a faint click and for no apparent reason, the meter started running. Ashton held on, watching the money tick away. With just twenty-five pence left on the clock, someone picked up the phone and a harsh, guttural voice said, "Who's there?"

"I'm a friend of Elena Andrianova," Ashton said in Russian while feeding coin after coin into the box to keep the line open. "May I speak to her, please?"

"Not here."

"Who am I talking to?"

There was a prolonged silence as if the Russian needed time to consider the propriety of the question. "This is her father, Konstantin Kirillovich Andrianov," he said eventually. "Who are you?"

No matter how many times he asked, Ashton was not going to identify himself when there was no telling who might be listening to their conversation. If the KGB had put a phone tap on the Andrianovs, they would know by his accent that he was a foreigner, they might even be able to guess who he was, but he didn't propose to make life easy for them by confirming their supposition.

"I've already told you," he said. "It's important I talk to Elena."

"She's not here."

Ashton closed his eyes briefly. Konstantin Kirillovich was like an old, cracked 78, repeating the same phrase over and over.

"Do you know when she will be back?" he asked.

"No one will tell me."

"What do you mean – no one will tell you?"

It was a stupid question. Anyone with an ounce of common sense should have picked up the inference and drawn the appropriate conclusion, but the meter was counting down at an alarming rate and his only concern was to keep the Russian talking while he primed the pump.

"She has been . . ."

A car with a hole in the silencer went past the open kiosk, the deep-throated snarl from the exhaust making it impossible for him to hear the rest. Ashton waited until the noise had subsided to a low rumble as the vehicle approached Blackfriars Bridge before asking Konstantin Kirillovich to repeat it.

"I said she has been hurt and is in hospital," the old man said querulously and put the phone down.

Ashton replaced the receiver, gathered up his remaining change and slowly retraced his steps to Benbow House. He told himself that because Elena Andrianova was in hospital, it did not necessarily follow that her injuries had been inflicted deliberately. She could have tripped over some obstruction and broken her leg, ankle or arm. She could have cut herself accidentally or been knocked down by a car. If he put his mind to it, there were dozens of possibilities and none of them sinister. But it was hard to shake off the feeling that Konstantin Kirillovich Andrianov had sounded frightened and that his daughter had been the victim of an unprovoked assault.

He picked up a cup of coffee from the vending machine on the first floor of Benbow House and took it up to his office. Elena Andrianova was in serious trouble; the more Ashton thought about it, the more he was convinced this was the case. Unfortunately, he could hardly go to Victor Hazelwood and urge him to order Head of Station, Moscow to check it out without revealing that he had been in touch with the family. And when you got right down to the nitty-gritty, what sort of response could you reasonably expect from Hugo Calthorpe? According to Major Oleg Lysenko, the KGB had already identified him as Head of Station, so he had little to lose by going to see the family himself. But then again, if he did go to their apartment on Rusanova Prospekt, the nark who undoubtedly followed Calthorpe everywhere he went would report the fact to his master in the Second Chief Directorate, which wouldn't do the Andrianovs a whole lot of good.

Hugo could hardly send one of his minions to see Konstantin Kirillovich without blowing their cover. On the other hand, there was no reason why one of the commercial attachés shouldn't call on him. Vaughan was the ideal choice. His face was probably known to the KGB and, since Elena had been his secretary, it was only natural that he should want to find out how she was. It wasn't beyond the wit of man to devise an explanation for his surprise visit to Rusanova Prospekt, but would HM Ambassador okay it? On balance, Ashton thought it highly unlikely he would allow one of his diplomats to be used by the SIS, especially if Richard Quennell, the First Secretary, was given an opportunity to put a word in.

Ashton finished his coffee and tossed the empty polystyrene cup into the wastepaper bin. He would have to go himself. Apart from there being no alternative, he held himself responsible for what might have happened to Elena Andrianova. A quick in-and-out trip over the weekend when he wouldn't be missed; that was the way to do it. The next question was – how? No point using a tour operator; it would take them three weeks to obtain the necessary visa from the Russian Embassy and any bargain break they offered was likely to involve a minimum of three nights. He would go as an individual, make his own flight arrangements and rely on folding money to get him into a suitable hotel after he had arrived in Moscow. The requisite visa and other documents were relatively easy to arrange; not for nothing was he the Head of Security, Vetting and Technical Services.

For the first time since being attached to Benbow House, Harriet felt that she had been asked to do something that was not at odds with the job description of her appointment. The two security dossiers which had found their way onto her desk had been accompanied by a brief memo from Ashton informing her that the Middle East Department wanted the warrant officer and lieutenant colonel for observation duties on the Turkey-Iraq border, and did she think they were suitable?

The warrant officer had spent sixteen years in the Royal Signals and had a totally clear positive vetting clearance. The lieutenant colonel had served even longer in the infantry and had also been cleared for constant access to Top Secret, but had been made a referred posting category 'B' for NATO appointments and Europe generally. The referral had been imposed because he had married an Australian of Polish descent who had relatives living in Warsaw and Zakopane. At the height of the Cold War, the possibility that indirect pressure could be brought to bear on the colonel would have to be considered before his selection for a NATO appointment was confirmed. Although Turkey was a member of the Treaty Organisation, the political situation in Poland had changed out of all recognition, and he wasn't being considered for a staff appointment at a military headquarters.

Harriet uncapped her fountain pen and was in the process of writing a brief note to this effect when Ashton appeared in the doorway of her office.

"You've just saved me a job," she told him and pointed to the security dossiers. "There's nothing wrong with those two."

"That's what I thought." Ashton pursed his lips. "Actually, I came to see you on another matter."

"Are you referring to Mr George Neville by any chance?"

"Well, yes . . ."

"I'm still working on him," Harriet said tersely before he could finish. "It'll be at least another day or two before I have anything."

"I was thinking about Joyner's funeral at the Breakespear Crematorium in Ruislip. It takes place at nine forty-five tomorrow and since Neville has made all the arrangements, I imagine he will be among the mourners. It might be an idea to get a photograph of him."

"You'd like me to go?"

Ashton shook his head. "No, as it happens, I've arranged for Hicks to pick me up from the Underground station. He lives out that way." He paused, as if wondering how to phrase the next request, then said, "I'd like you to cover for me and take any calls while I'm away from the office. Before I leave tonight, I'll switch my extension through so that your phone will ring automatically."

"Fine, that will save me the trouble of informing the exchange supervisor."

"There is one other thing," he said, trying to sound casual. "A team from the US Defense Intelligence Agency will be visiting the MoD tomorrow. Roy Kelso is running around like a cat on hot bricks because the Old Man is attending the conference. Told me to check on the security arrangements and offer our services which the MoD politely declined."

"I see," Harriet said, but didn't.

"The conference is being held in the Main Building," Ashton went on. "The officer responsible for the security arrangements is Major Timothy on extension 0028. I thought perhaps you could make your number with him so that you are in a position to field any questions from Kelso when he starts flapping tomorrow morning."

"Of course I will."

"Thanks a lot, that's a great help." He glanced at his wristwatch. "I'd better be moving along," he said. "Got a lot of things to do in this lunch hour."

Ashton didn't enlarge on the statement. He didn't leave either and she had a feeling he was waiting for her to say something which would give him an excuse to tell her. "Is there anything that I can do?" she asked dutifully.

"Not unless you know of a furnished flat I can rent."

"I'm one of those fortunate people who live in Dolphin Square," Harriet told him. "I don't think there's anything going in our neighbourhood."

"Just my luck."

He gave her the friendliest and warmest smile she had received from him thus far, then started to leave, only to stick his head round the door again to tell her that he might well be taking an extended lunch hour. After he had gone, she asked herself what it had all been in aid of and was at a loss to think of an answer.

From Yellow Pages he had learned that Finnair was in Clifford Street. The map on page 140 of the London Streetfinder showed that it was only a short walk from the British Airways office in Regent Street, which itself was practically opposite the branch of Lloyds where his own bank manager had arranged a one-time drawing facility for up to a thousand pounds. Ashton thought he couldn't have planned things better if he'd tried; he hoped it was a good omen because everything depended on the availability of seats on the right airlines at the right times.

From Benbow House, he walked across Blackfriars Bridge, caught a train to the Embankment, then changed on to the Bakerloo Line. Alighting at Piccadilly Circus, he rang the British Airways office from a pay phone in the concourse and enquired about flights to Helsinki. He then called Finnair to obtain much the same information and discover how much he would need to draw from his account. Once he knew this, he left the Underground station, walked up Regent Street to Lloyds Bank and cashed a cheque for six hundred pounds.

There was no way he could use his Access card with Finnair, nor could he write them a cheque. Although no such restriction applied to BA, they wouldn't let him have the plane ticket until payment had been cleared by the bank, which could take up to four days. He crossed the road, turned into Burlington Street and made his way to the offices of Finnair.

"My name is Messenger," he told the blonde girl behind the counter. "I phoned your office about ten minutes ago to enquire about flights to Moscow from Helsinki."

"Yes, you spoke to me. Do you wish to confirm your reservation, Mr Messenger?"

"Please," he said.

The girl looked down at her millboard. "You asked for an economy seat on Flight AY702 departing Saturday at 09.25 hours arriving Moscow 12.05 local time, returning same day leaving Moscow 22.50 arriving Helsinki 23.40 hours. Yes?"

"That's correct." He would have ten hours in Moscow, which was more than enough for what he had in mind. The flight times also meant that he wouldn't have to grease someone's palm to get him a hotel room. Even better, the KGB wouldn't begin to check the visas collected at the airport with their computer record until after he had boarded the flight to Helsinki.

"You wish to pay by credit card or cheque?"

"Cash," Ashton told her and took out his wallet.

106

"The return fare is one hundred and eighty pounds."

"Yes, so you said on the phone."

He peeled off nine twenties, waited for her to write out his plane ticket, then went on to the British Airways office in Regent Street. This time, he used his real name and booked himself on to Flight BA798 departing Friday evening at 17.55, returning Sunday on Flight 797 leaving Helsinki at 16.45 hours. By using his real name, he was able to pay for the ticket with his Access card.

Chapter 10

Ashton left the Piccadilly Line train at Alperton and walked out of the station to find Hicks waiting for him in a Ford Sierra. He didn't have to ask the electronics expert if he had remembered to bring a camera with him; it was there on the back seat, an expensive-looking job with a huge telephoto lens and a tripod.

"Haven't you got something a little more discreet?" Ashton enquired hopefully.

"Got a Canon Sure Shot in the glove compartment. Of course, if I'm to get the kind of high-grade picture you want of Neville, I'll need to be pretty close to him."

"Don't worry, you'll have plenty of time to choose a good vantage point."

"You think so?" Hicks said doubtfully.

"It's only just after eight thirty; we'll arrive at the crematorium long before the family does."

"I wouldn't bet on it – wait till you see the traffic. We'll be okay once we're on the A40 heading out of town but that could take for ever the way things are this morning."

Hicks was right, it was the rush hour and the traffic was double banked heading into London. It was stop and go from Alperton station, up Ealing Road, across the Grand Union Canal into Hanger Lane. With the traffic barely moving and the inevitable roadworks, it took them forty minutes to cover the three-quarters of a mile to the North Circular. Turning right at the lights, Hicks edged his way into the outside lane as they went over the underpass and then made another right into the slip road leading to the A40. With everything now heading in the opposite direction, they virtually had a clear run out through Perivale, Greenford and Northolt. Ignoring the speed limit, Hicks put his foot down and held it there until he turned off on to the minor road leading to Ruislip and followed the signs to Breakespear Crematorium. With a little over ten minutes in hand before the funeral service was due to begin, they swept in through the gates. As they went on up the approach road, Ashton saw that Frances Joyner and her daughter had beaten them to it.

"Go to the far side of the car park," he said brusquely. "Find a slot behind the hedgerow where the widow can't see us."

"I told you we would be lucky to get here before they did," Hicks reminded him sourly.

"Then you'll just have to hold off until I've managed to distract them."

Ashton got out of the car and walked back. Although there were two chapels, there was never a slack moment; as one service ended, so another began. The mourners varied from a mere handful to a large congregation depending on how many relatives and friends the deceased had. In this instance, the number of people who had come to pay their last respects to Colin Joyner could be counted on the fingers of one hand.

The immediate family consisted of Frances Joyner looking very chic in a tailored dark coat and Mandy, whom Ashton suspected was in the same clothes he had seen her wearing in Moscow. There were two other people standing nearby, a man in his forties dressed in a bulky anorak and a thin, sour-faced woman of pensionable age who was leaning heavily on a stout walking stick.

"Why, Mr Ashton, this is a surprise." Frances Joyner greeted him with a brittle smile. "What are you doing here?"

"Representing the Foreign Office," he told her.

"Well, isn't that thoughtful of them," she said with more than a trace of irony, then waved a hand in the direction of the older woman. "You haven't met my mother-in-law, Mrs Winnie Joyner, have you?"

"No, I haven't had that pleasure." Ashton smiled, shook hands with the late Colin Joyner's mother and was told she was pleased to meet him.

"And I'm Winnie's next-door neighbour in Headstone Road," the man in the anorak said, introducing himself. "We came in my car," he added as he pumped Ashton's hand enthusiastically.

"You live near here?"

"Harrow – roughly seven miles away."

A red top-of-the-range BMW 720 cut across the parking area

and nipped into a space a few yards behind the Joyners. The man who got out and walked towards them was about five feet nine and had the broad shoulders, barrel chest and narrow waistline of a prizefighter, just as Simon Beresford, the funeral director, had described him. As he drew near, Ashton could see the scar tissue above the right eye and knew he was George Neville even before Frances Joyner introduced him as Colin's business associate.

"From the Foreign Office, huh?" Neville said and stared at him with cold, unblinking grey eyes.

"We met Mr Ashton in Moscow, George. He was in touch with the police and told us how the investigation was proceeding."

Neville made no comment. Instead, he glanced over his shoulder at the hearse, which had drawn up outside the chapel while they were talking, then made some excuse about needing to have a word with the pallbearers before the service began. In the event, he didn't get the chance. As he set off towards the hearse, a clergyman emerged from the chapel and began to shepherd the mourners inside.

Ashton tagged on to the end of the small procession and was ushered into a pew directly behind the family. Ignoring the verger, Neville chose to sit across the aisle from him and immediately took refuge in the Order of Service, holding the card up at an oblique angle as if to shield his face. Although he stood up, sat down and bowed his head in prayer in time with the other members of the tiny congregation, Ashton knew he was surreptitiously watching him.

The address was mercifully brief with the parson telling them what a fine man Colin Joyner had been and how it would not be only the immediate family who would miss him. They moved on to the final hymn and then suddenly the casket disappeared through the curtains and they were filing out of the chapel past two economy-size wreaths, the priest pressing flesh and murmuring words of sympathy.

"You were a close friend?" he asked.

"You could say that," Ashton told him in an equally low voice.

"Time is a great healer."

"So I hear," he said and moved on towards the car park.

Hicks was waiting for him in the Ford Sierra. The solemnity of the occasion seemed to have escaped him; he had the window down on his side, was smoking a cigarette and listening to Radio

111

One with a faraway expression on his face.

"I hope you remembered to get a photograph of Neville," Ashton said when he got into the car.

"The blond guy with the BMW?"

"That's him."

"Used a whole reel," Hicks said.

"Good. You can drop me off at Ruislip station, then go on home and get the film developed. I want the pictures on Miss Egan's desk this afternoon."

"You don't want to see them first?"

Ashton shook his head. "I'm going to be busy checking the stores. It's a job that's likely to take up most of the afternoon."

The various items of equipment held by Technical Services were classified under two broad headings – hardware and software, neither of which had anything to do with information technology. Communications, surveillance aids and small arms came under hardware and were stored in separate lock-ups in the basement of Benbow House. Software included blank passports, visa application forms, protected currency and identity papers of every description. At the height of the Cold War, it had been the proud boast of the SIS that they possessed the necessary documents to insert an agent into any member state of the Warsaw Pact. Although the big thaw meant that much of the software material was now only of academic interest, it still had to be accounted for.

When Kelso had been appointed Assistant Director in charge of Administration, he had amended standing orders for the duty officer of the day to include a spot check of three items of controlled stores chosen at random. As Head of Security and Technical Services, Ashton was required to submit a return on the thirtieth day of every month certifying that, unless otherwise stated, all items shown on ledger charge were physically present and accounted for. In theory, it was not a particularly onerous task; in practice, it was not easy to set aside a complete day for what amounted to a hundred per cent stocktaking exercise.

His predecessor, a cheerful, work-shy extrovert who had taken early retirement, had signed every certificate blind and had rarely been seen in the basement strongrooms. Ashton didn't have that cavalier attitude and preferred to submit a certificate showing the dates on which the check had been conducted. In the five months he had been head of the division, his subordinates had become accustomed to him carrying out a random inspection without prior warning. No one was therefore surprised when, after an early lunch, he went down to the basement to check the communications equipment on charge to the division. Within a few minutes he was joined by his deputy, Frank Warren, who had learned on the grapevine that he was on the prowl.

Warren was forty-nine and had six years to do before he was eligible for minimum pension. He had been an administrator all his working life and should have been able to run rings around someone who was fifteen years his junior, but he lacked self-confidence. Even when the stores were a hundred per cent correct, Frank Warren acted as though he expected to be hauled over the coals for not doing something or other by the book.

"What are you checking today, Peter?" he asked, then laughed nervously. "Not the damned authentication tables, I hope?"

The authentication tables were a pain to account for. They were used whenever an operator suspected that a bogus station had joined the net and basically consisted of a challenge and countersign which were automatically changed every hour on the hour. Each station was issued with three months' supply, which had to be accounted for while they were on the shelf and a destruction certificate rendered when they became time expired. The primary users were the armed forces but because they were equipped with the same type of radio, the SIS was obliged to conform with NATO procedures.

"I thought we would have a look at Brahms," Ashton told him.

"Thank God for that," Warren said with feeling.

Ashton didn't have the heart to tell him that he was thinking of checking the fill guns as well. Brahms was the codename for an encrypted radio telephone which was built into an innocent-looking executive briefcase. It came complete with a three-pin plug and could be set up and operated from any hotel bedroom with a power point.

The fill gun was a much more complicated gadget. Resembling the type of laser weapon favoured by the crew of the Starship *Enterprise*, it was loaded with electronic ciphers from the master grid and was then used to transfer these key variables to an infinite number of compatible radio sets. A hostile station trying to intercept transmissions on a crypto-protected net merely

113

picked up a cacophony of electronic sounds. Although this discordant symphony could be recorded on tape, it was claimed by the Royal Signals Research Establishment that it would take every computer the Russians possessed a full week to unscramble the original message. If the code setting was changed every seven days, one squirt from the fill gun gave a radio three weeks' supply of crypto. Should control decide to change the setting on a daily basis, then the set was crypto-guarded for seventy-two hours.

They checked the Brahms by the serial numbers stamped inside the lid of the briefcase, then went through the same procedure for the fill guns, except that here, the registration number was etched into the equivalent of the butt. There were, of course, no discrepancies, a fact that appeared to surprise Warren.

"That's a relief," he said. "There would be a hell of a fuss if we lost one of those bits of kit."

"Let's go up to your office," Ashton said casually. "While we're at it, I'd like to have a look at the documents we are holding."

"Documents?"

"Passports, visa application forms and so on."

"Oh right." Warren nodded emphatically. "Matter of fact, I've been meaning to raise the question of the old ten-year passports with you ever since we received the new European Community issue. I was wondering if we shouldn't destroy the old blanks, or at least some of them."

Ashton turned away so that the older man wouldn't see the smile he was unable to contain. The whole purpose of the charade in the basement had been to put Warren on edge and make it that much easier for Ashton to palm one of the blanks. How he was going to return the passport in pristine condition after he had used it was something he had yet to work out. Now a large slice of luck coupled with a chance remark had delivered the solution.

"Refresh my memory," he said. "How many have we got of the old type?"

"Thirty," Warren said promptly.

"Okay, we'll keep half a dozen and bin the rest."

"That's what I was about to recommend."

"Well, you know the old saying, Frank – great minds think alike."

The documents were kept inside the security cupboard located in Warren's office. In accordance with standing orders, the combination was known only to him and Roy Kelso, who had placed his record of the setting in a sealed envelope which, in turn, was kept under lock and key. Warren, however, was easily distracted by small talk and it did not occur to him that Ashton was watching his every move as he went through the sequence. Four complete turns in a clockwise direction starting from zero before stopping at thirty-one, followed by three anticlockwise revolutions to number twelve. Even as he turned the dial in a clockwise direction again, Ashton knew the last number in the sequence would be forty-two. In seeking to memorise the combination, Warren had broken every rule in the book by setting the lock to his birthday, the thirty-first of December 1942.

Ashton turned away. The rest of the procedure was standard and there was no need for him to watch his deputy. Two complete revolutions in an anticlockwise direction to zero, then forward until the tumblers clicked. Knowing this, he did not move up to Warren's shoulder until he heard him yank the locking bar and open the cupboard.

"Might as well start with the old passports," he said. "You want to switch on the waste destructor, Frank?"

"Shouldn't we check them off first?" Warren asked doubtfully.

"Why make unnecessary work for ourselves? All we need do is record the numbers of the six we retain."

"You're right."

Ashton placed half a dozen on one side, waited until Warren's back was turned as he went over to the destructor, then slipped a blank passport into his jacket pocket before carrying the remainder over to the machine.

"Okay, Frank, grab some of these and let's get on with it."

Ashton ripped the pages from the stiff cover and fed both halves of the document into the destructor. The blades whirred, emitting a high-pitched scream as they sliced the pages into thin strips no thicker than a strand of cotton. The hard cover produced a different noise, a cross between a bass singer hitting the bottom-most note and a hollow groan that sounded like someone in pain. There was also a noticeable loss of power as if the machine was in danger of grinding to a halt. To hoodwink his deputy, Ashton started to rip the stiff covers in half before feeding them into the machine between wads of dismembered

115

pages. A barrage of unrelated questions also helped to distract the older man; the intrusive summons from the telephone, coming when it did, ensured he lost count of the number of passports they had destroyed.

"It's for you," Warren said, raising his voice to make himself heard above the racket.

"Thanks." Ashton switched off the destructor and took the phone from him.

"I'm afraid I didn't catch the name, Peter, but your friend sounds as if he hails from the other side of the Pond."

There was no need for Tony Zale to identify himself. Ashton recognised his voice the moment he said "Hi", even though he hadn't heard from the American in six months. Back in October '91, they had spent a hectic week flying around the old East Zone of Germany in a Hind helicopter of the Russian Air Force to satisfy themselves that no unpleasant surprises were left in place after the Red Army withdrew. He was about to ask Tony Zale what he was doing in London when it dawned on him that the American was probably among the names on the original list he'd asked the Chief Clerk to obtain.

"You're over here to attend this get-together the MoD is holding. Right?"

"Got it in one. I was hoping we could get together over a drink."

"Nothing I'd like better," Ashton told him. "How about this evening?"

"That's what I was about to suggest. I'm staying at Brown's Hotel in Dover Street. Why don't we meet in the bar around six?"

"I'll be there," Ashton said and put the phone down.

It was going to be easier than he had dared to hope. As soon as he completed the check, he would let the clerks and security guards know that he would be returning to Benbow House during the evening to finish off some work. Then, while no one else was around, he would open the security cupboard in Warren's office and fix himself up with a Russian visa, identity papers and residential permit. Everything he needed was to hand – application forms, official stamps and a trace which would enable him to forge the signature of the consular official in charge of the visa section.

Tony Zale was slim, had short blond hair and was a compact five feet ten. After graduating from Cornell in 1985, he had joined the Defense Intelligence Agency and was now thirty years old, though most strangers observing his youthful appearance found that hard to believe. In 1991 his tour of duty in Berlin had been cut short at the instigation of the *Kriminalpolizei* and with the connivance of the State Department who regarded him as a troublemaker. Recalled to Washington, he had been put out to pasture in Computer Records, his career apparently finished. But now it seemed he was back in the fast lane once more.

When Ashton walked into Brown's Hotel, he found him sitting at a corner table looking the part of the well-dressed man about town in a dark grey suit, button-down shirt and knitted tie. If the frankly appraising glances Zale was drawing from two young women at a nearby table were anything to go by, it was evident the American wouldn't have lacked company had he been unable to meet him for drinks.

"Hi there, Peter." Zale half rose to greet him with a broad smile. "You're looking great," he added and sank back in the chair.

"You too," Ashton told him.

"So what'll you have to drink?"

"A whisky with a lot of soda."

"You've got it."

Zale didn't have to snap his fingers to get attention. The waiter simply appeared at his elbow, took their order and returned in double-quick time with a selection of canapés to go with the drinks, which he placed on two absorbent coasters.

"I'm impressed," Ashton said. "How long have you been here?"

"The boss and I checked in yesterday afternoon. Brown's is practically his second home."

"No wonder they look after you." Ashton raised his glass. "*Skol*," he said.

"Cheers." Zale gave an appreciative sigh. "You can't beat Chivas Regal for Scotch on the rocks."

Ashton had a feeling that the American was about to dispense with small talk and was proved right in the next breath.

"I hear you are no longer with the Russian Desk, Peter?"

117

"You heard correctly. I'm Head of the Security and Technical Services Division these days which is another way of saying I'm in charge of vetting and office cleaners. It's small potatoes."

"That's tough."

Ashton shrugged. "These things happen."

Zale looked about the room, apparently to satisfy himself that no one could overhear what he was going to say. "Our little trip around the old East Zone didn't do me any harm."

"So I guessed. What are you doing now, or is it Top Secret?"

"I'm what you people call a SANSI," he told him, "Senior Analyst Special Intelligence. The photo interpreters tell me what they figure they've seen, then I look at the pretty pics and try to come up with some profound observation."

"What are you looking at, or can't you tell me?"

"I don't see why you shouldn't know. This is the year of the freight train; we've been keeping track of them as they roll out of the Ukraine into Romania. Trouble is, we are apt to lose them the closer they get to Bucharest."

"How come?"

"We start out with one freight train of eighty boxcars and end up with four trains with twenty or some other combination. What we would like to know is how many are crossing yet another border into Yugoslavia."

"The US of A is not about to get involved in that nasty civil war, is it?"

"Well, Bush may be up for re-election this November but the Agency isn't anxious to be found wanting should the Executive ask for an assessment."

"And you came over here to compare notes with the MoD?"

"Yeah. We were hoping your Military Intelligence people might know something we didn't."

"And did they?"

"No. Matter of fact, they didn't seem too interested in the Jugs. Guess they are waiting to see who forms the next government."

Ashton doubted if domestic politics had anything to do with their inertia. Even at the height of the Cold War, the army had never had the resources to do more than keep an occasional eye on the country. There were few Serbo-Croat speakers in the ranks and no one was going to waste time, money and manpower

118

training linguists from scratch when Yugoslavia belonged to the group of nonaligned nations and the USSR was the chief protagonist. Maybe 13 Signal Regiment in Germany was eavesdropping on the national army but it was the local Serbian irregulars who were doing the killing and they weren't operating a sophisticated command net. That probably meant 13 Signals wasn't picking up much in the way of communications intelligence.

"What are the odds on John Major still being the Prime Minister on April tenth?"

"Not good. All the opinion polls have Labour in front. But it won't make any difference who gets in; the way we're disarming, I can't see any government committing our ground forces to Yugoslavia."

A diminishing and already overstretched army, which was going to be critically short of infantry by the time the cuts were completed, was not the only reason for staying out of it. Ejecting the Iraqis from Kuwait might have been a quick surgical operation with limited casualties but military intervention in Yugoslavia could well prove a long, hard and bloody business. In the Second World War, Tito's partisans operating in the mountains had pinned down almost forty divisions of varying Axis strengths. What had been done before could be repeated almost fifty years later, especially as there was no reason to believe the Serbian militia would be a pushover.

"I can't believe that you of all people are happy to sit back and do nothing about the situation." Zale reached for his glass and finished the whisky. "Thousands of civilians, men, women and children, are being systematically killed out there and you aren't interested to know who is keeping the Serbian irregulars supplied with artillery ammunition? Well, one thing I can tell you, they sure as hell aren't getting it from the National Army, at least not directly . . ."

There was no holding the American once he began to develop his theme. The ammunition was coming in from the Ukraine, possibly even as far afield as Russia itself and was being routed through Romania. The boxcars containing the artillery natures were tacked on to regular freight trains and were then detached once they were safely across the border. Sometimes the consignment was offloaded onto trucks for onward movement to the final destination; other times, the boxcars were hitched to yet another freight train. Rumour had it that a number of them had subsequently passed through Sofia before reaching Belgrade.

Sensing he was coming to the end of his diatribe, Ashton signalled the barman to bring them the same again and indicated that he wanted the bill.

"Are you saying Yeltsin is supplying the war materials?" Ashton asked when the American finally paused for breath.

"He wants hard currency to kick-start a terminally sick economy. Right? So what else has he got to sell but a huge arsenal of conventional weapons?"

"I think you're wrong about Yeltsin; he's going to be on the side of the angels while he's looking to the European Community, the United States and Japan for aid. Besides, if he did go down that road, the Iranians would be his number one customer. They need to re-equip their army and, unlike the Serbians, they've got the money to pay for it."

"The Russians are supplying them," Zale continued doggedly as if repeating an article of faith.

"Can you prove it?"

He couldn't, that was the trouble. After collating all the statistical data they had been able to gather over a time frame of eight months, the American Embassy in Belgrade had come to the conclusion that, if anything, there had been a downturn in economic activity since Croatia had broken away from the federation. The ordnance factories were working normal shifts and in the view of the Military Attaché, the Serbian irregulars would have exhausted current war reserve stocks of the National Army within three months. The expended munitions had to be replenished somehow and the Defense Intelligence Agency was quite sure they knew where it was coming from. Unfortunately, the pattern of rail traffic did not support Zale's contention; there were now fewer freight trains entering Romania than at any time since the fragmentation of the Warsaw Pact.

"It's the way these boxcars are shunted around once they're across the border that makes me suspicious."

"Have you got any people who would be willing to do a little train spotting for you when they're in Romania?"

"It's not a country that attracts too many of our businessmen."

"I was thinking of relief workers, adoption societies and the like." Ashton frowned. "Maybe we could do something."

"We'd surely appreciate any help you can give us."

As part of the so-called peace dividend, the establishment of the Eastern Bloc Department was being cut by forty per cent and Hazelwood was desperately looking round for ways and means of staving it off. Zale's problem could be his salvation, but Ashton had simply been thinking aloud and Victor might not be in favour of the idea.

"I'm not guaranteeing anything will come of it," Ashton said, "but I'll see what I can do. When are you returning to Washington?"

"Monday. Tomorrow we fly out to Moscow, departing Heathrow at 08.55 hours."

"What for?"

"Goodwill visit," Zale told him. "They're going to pull the wool over our eyes, we're going to do the same to theirs. Should be a nice vacation; the Russians are putting us up at the Hotel Metropole in Marx Prospekt. All expenses paid."

"Ring me from the airport if you have time."

"You're not expecting to get a decision by then, are you?"

"No chance, but I can let you know Hazelwood's reaction after I've spoken to him tonight." Ashton caught the waiter's eye, pointed to the five-pound note he'd left under an ashtray and stood up. "I'm afraid I've got to be going."

"Must you?"

"Can't keep a lady waiting."

Ashton left Brown's Hotel, walked up to Piccadilly and caught a train to Victoria from Green Park, then changed on to the District Line and got out at Blackfriars. By the time he crossed the river to Benbow House, it was gone seven thirty, was pitch dark and drizzling with rain. Except for the duty officer, duty clerk and three security guards, the building was deserted.

Ashton checked in with the gateman, took the lift up to his office and rang Hazelwood at home. There was no secure speech facility at Willow Dene but he got round the problem with veiled speech and said just enough for Hazelwood to catch on. By the time he had finished, he was in a position to tell Zale in all honesty that the Eastern Bloc Department was interested in the idea. It was also a more productive way of filling in time than re-reading files he had already dealt with.

Satisfied that it was now safe to make his move, Ashton locked the door of his office behind him and made his way along the corridor to Warren's. Every door open, every window closed, the lights burning in every room; the measures that were intended to make the building more secure and easier to check during silent hours put him on tenterhooks. He went through the combination swiftly – 31-12-42 – opened the security cupboard and helped himself to visas, internal passport, residential permit, laminating kit, adhesive, signature trace and official stamps. Just when every second counted, his fingers were all thumbs and he had the devil's own job attaching colour photographs to the flimsy visa applications. For the blank passport he'd stolen that afternoon, he used a head and shoulders picture, showing him in shirtsleeves without a tie, which he had tried to age by rubbing the sheen off the snapshot. Whatever else they might be, the Russian immigration officials were no fools and they would smell a rat if they saw the same photograph on both sets of documents.

The various tasks took Ashton longer than he had allowed for. He was still waiting for the laminated strips to adhere over his photograph on page three and the date stamp and the place the passport was issued on page four when he heard footsteps in the corridor. Pulse racing, he put the laminating kit, adhesive, signature trace and official stamps back inside the security cupboard and quietly turned the locking bar. There was no time to spin the combination dial; grabbing the passport, visas and other documents he'd left on Warren's desk, Ashton moved swiftly and silently across the room to position himself back to the wall on the right side of the door, which opened inwards.

The hanging card on the round locking handle was reversed, the red side facing the corridor with the magic word "CLOSED" stencilled on it in block capitals. Ashton hoped it would satisfy the guard because if he took it into his head to enter the office and try the cupboard, the bloody thing would open and he could scarcely fail to see him behind the door when he turned about after securing the combination.

The footsteps drew nearer and nearer, then stopped outside Warren's office. Ashton closed his eyes and prayed as he had never prayed before: Jesu, Jesu, Jesu, don't come in for God's sake. Beads of sweat broke out on his forehead, trickled into his eyes and made them smart. The seconds multiplied, each one seeming like a full minute; then, just when it seemed there was only one way the impasse could end, the watchman suddenly walked off.

Ashton waited until he was sure the guard had left the floor to check out the rest of the building before he secured the combination dial and showed himself in the corridor. He had covered almost half the distance to his own office when Harriet Egan emerged from a room on his right. Somehow he managed to stretch his mouth in a smile and even put some warmth behind it.

"What are you doing here at this time of night, Harriet?" he asked in what he hoped was a normal tone of voice.

"I'm the duty officer," she told him.

"Really? That's a bit hard considering it's your first week with us."

"The actual DO was taken sick this morning while you were out. I'm standing in for him."

"I see." From the quizzical expression on her face, he thought Harriet was waiting for him to explain what he was doing in Benbow House, but he wasn't about to fall into that particular trap. When in a tight corner, it was always better to wrong-foot any would-be interrogator rather than resorting to some defensive explanation. "Did Hicks deliver those photographs of Neville?" he asked her.

"Yes. What do you expect me to do with them?"

Unwittingly, she had given him the perfect opening. "I expect you to use your initiative," he said abruptly. "Show them to your friends in Scotland Yard, see if anyone recognises him. Neville might not be his real name; could be he's got a criminal record and has changed it."

Ashton dug out the key to his office, turned his back on Harriet to unlock the door and then walked into the room, leaving her high and dry. She probably thought he was the rudest man she had ever met, but that couldn't be helped. He did not know her well enough to take her into his confidence and he was feeling too vulnerable to make small talk. He did not think she had been lurking in ambush but he didn't want to do or say anything which might arouse her suspicions.

Chapter 11

Sheremetyevo Airport didn't look any better from the air than it did from the ground. All Ashton could see of the surrounding countryside from his window seat was flat open grassland and a chequerboard of woods – some birch, some fir. There was a sinking feeling in the pit of his stomach which had nothing to do with their rate of descent, but it was too late now for second thoughts. He should have had those before he had boarded British Airways Flight BA798 to Helsinki on Friday evening.

He could have aborted in Finland itself, hired a car and spent the weekend looking at the forests and lakes until it was time to catch the flight home. But he hadn't, and no doubt a psychologist would have a fun time analysing his behaviour. Although he felt responsible for Elena Andrianova, her plight was only part of the rationale for going to Moscow. Yesterday morning he had again discussed the possibility of assisting the Defense Intelligence Agency with Hazelwood and had been told by Victor that, while he was in favour of monitoring the number of freight trains reaching Belgrade from Russia, they were up against the Foreign Office and they were interested only in negotiating a ceasefire between the opposing forces. Intelligence gathering was definitely out. One of the mandarins had even told Hazelwood privately that he thought recognising Croatia as an independent state had been a grave error.

It was being said around Whitehall that with the Foreign Office and the Treasury running the affairs of state between them, the country had no need of enemies. Ashton was inclined to agree with that sentiment and thought that in the last four years, no Treasury forecast had been worth the paper it was written on, and the Foreign Office enjoyed a reputation second to none for getting it wrong. Anger, frustration and contempt had much to do with his decision to go on. It had also been tempered by the not unreasonable belief that should he run foul of the Russian Intelligence Service, he was unlikely to be put on trial in the present climate. He would, of course, be kicked out of the SIS with no preserved pension rights or terminal grant but as he had been tempted to resign the Service before taking up his present appointment, that would hardly be the end of the world.

The McDonnell Douglas MD80 of Finnair touched down and went into reverse pitch. Constantly losing speed, the plane swept past maintenance hangars, freight sheds, airport buildings, parked aircraft and fire tenders, then slowed almost to a jogging pace before taxiing back to the terminal building. At 12.05 hours, exactly on schedule, Flight AY702 from Helsinki nestled alongside its appointed gate and the engines were stilled. Airline passengers were the same the world over. As always, everyone started moving at once; as always, the line ground to a halt until the crush sorted itself out. Ashton shuffled forward towards the exit and got a warm smile from the blonde stewardess at the door of the aircraft as he left the plane to follow the directional signs to the arrivals hall.

By travelling light with just one piece of hand baggage, he didn't have to wait for the plane to be unloaded. A lugubrious official took the customs declaration form he'd completed during the flight, which showed he had three hundred pounds on him plus an Omega wristwatch. But it was the passport in the name of Peter Messenger which was of most interest to the Russian, who spent what seemed an age examining every page before retaining one copy of the forged visa and stamping the other two.

Ashton moved out into the concourse. He had cleared the first hurdle and the alarm bells were unlikely to start ringing in Dzerzhinsky Square before the hotel registration slips were collected on Sunday morning. By the time the KGB discovered that there was no record of a Mr Peter Messenger staying anywhere in Moscow, he would be back in Helsinki. Dismissing the thought as dangerously complacent, he walked out of the terminal and was immediately surrounded by at least half a dozen taxi drivers, most of whom weren't licensed.

For a ten-pound note, any of the drivers would have taken him to the Kremlin and back again, but all Ashton wanted was a one-way ride to the Belgrade Hotel opposite the Foreign

Ministry. Narrowly avoiding a riot, he chose a small, cheerful-looking man in his early forties and climbed into the back of a Moskvich saloon that had definitely seen better days. Before leaving the cab rank outside the terminal building, the driver was obliged to hand over forty roubles to the despatcher and a militiaman relieved him of another sixty, a sort of road tax for using the Kliminki highway into town.

Ashton paid off the cab outside the Belgrade Hotel, waited until the driver had pulled away from the kerb and the Moskvich was swallowed up in the traffic on Smolensky Boulevard, then used the underpass to cross the road. He skirted the Foreign Ministry, turned into the pedestrianised Arbat Street and ambled past the market stalls. The choice of merchandise was somewhat limited and restricted to *matryoshka* dolls, lacquered jewellery boxes, old Red Army regalia, balalaikas, pop records and cassettes. Arbat Street was also a favourite stamping ground for the unofficial money changers who were only too eager to buy dollars and pounds above the official exchange rate. Ashton did not have to go looking for them; his overnight bag identified him as a tourist and he was approached by two different currency dealers within the first hundred yards. The statute which made it an offence to change foreign currency on the black market was still in force and the KGB frequently resorted to the old entrapment routine. Only when satisfied that he was dealing with a genuine speculator did Ashton trade in twenty pounds for two thousand five hundred and sixty roubles.

The transaction completed, he walked on towards the Metro station at the top of Arbat Street. On the way there, he stopped to buy a fur hat from a stall purely in order to change a note into more manageable denominations and obtain a handful of kopeks for the train fare. Sviblovo was the nearest Metro station to where the Andrianovs lived in the Babuskin District; travelling across the town centre, he changed on to Line 1 at Kirovskaya.

The Second Plan for the development of Moscow was adopted in 1951. Apart from altering the skyline with seven examples of the grandiose 'wedding cake' architecture favoured by Stalin, the plan also called for the widening of inner city boulevards to eight lanes, which could only be achieved by the demolition of existing streets. In this connection, Rusanova Prospekt was among several housing projects that had been needed to accommodate those who had lost their homes as a result of the Second Plan, as well as providing additional living space for a rapidly growing population.

The apartment houses on Rusanova Prospekt were dull, cement-coloured, eight-storey barrack blocks wherein each floor was subdivided into sixty units of varying sizes. Elena Andrianova's parents lived in 1258; as Ashton discovered for himself, this meant they occupied a three-room apartment on the fifth floor of the third block on the left-hand side of the road. The building was served by only two lifts; fortunately, both were in working order.

Although the family was lucky enough to have a private telephone, Ashton had decided not to ring the flat. The old man had told him that his daughter had been hurt and was in hospital. He hadn't said how she came to be there, but if her injuries had been deliberately inflicted, there was a chance that the KGB was involved somewhere along the line. If they were, the Andrianovs' phone was probably tapped.

Ashton tried the doorbell and heard a low buzzing noise somewhere inside the apartment. Getting no response, he pressed the button again, confident that even if the old man was out, his wife would be at home, given that she had a heart condition and was practically housebound. Footsteps inside the flat proved his assumption; moments later, the door opened a fraction and a lined face appeared in the gap.

"Konstantin Kirillovich?" he asked and received an unintelligible grunt.

"I am a friend of Elena Andrianova, the Englishman you spoke to the other day." Ashton reached inside his jacket, took out his passport and waved it in front of the old man. "May I come in?"

"Your Russian is very good," Konstantin Kirillovich said and continued to keep him standing on the doorstep.

It was obvious that something more than the front cover of a British passport was required to gain admittance. Ashton put it away and produced a ten-pound note from his wallet instead. "This is for you," he said. "I have others for Elena."

He did not have to point out how much ten pounds would fetch on the black market. From the calculating expression in his eyes, it was patently obvious that Konstantin Kirillovich had already worked that out for himself. But if the Russian was a poor man, he was also a proud one and he was torn between taking the money or slamming the door in his face. Angry with himself for what he was doing to the old man, Ashton tried to restore his injured pride.

"I have offended you," he said contritely, "and that's the last thing I wanted to do."

"What is it with you people? Why do you think money can buy everything?" There was no anger in his voice, only an infinite weariness.

"I'm sorry." Ashton spread his hands. "What more can I say? Except that I'm concerned for Elena and have come all the way from England to find out how she is."

"You'd better come in," Konstantin Kirillovich said reluctantly and stepped aside.

There was no hallway, the door opened into the living room, which also doubled as a kitchen diner. It had less floor space than a single integral garage back home in England and was crowded with cheap furniture, some items of which he assumed Elena had brought with her when she had moved in with her parents.

Ludmilla Andrianova was sitting in a wing chair staring blankly at the fourteen-inch black and white television in the near corner of the room. The embassy was under the impression that Elena's mother had angina but their information was clearly out of date. At some time in the not-too-distant past, Ludmilla Andrianova had had a severe stroke which had paralysed the whole of her left side. Her mouth was now a diagonal slit and she drooled continuously from the lower corner, the saliva running down her chin to fall on an old cardigan.

"She can't talk since the stroke," Konstantin Kirillovich told him when he went to greet her.

"When did it happen?"

"Last September."

And the following month, Elena had started her short-lived career as a spy, eavesdropping on Vaughan, the Third Secretary, Commerce, for a paltry twenty-five dollars a month. Ashton glanced at the little girl who was playing with a rag doll as she sat on the floor by the wing chair. Elena had told him that she had planted the transmitter because she was frightened of what 'Mikhail' would do to her daughter, but that was only part of the story. In the end, she had done it for the money. Someone had to look after her mother and collect Vera from school while she and her father were at work, and they would expect to be paid for their trouble.

"How do you manage?" he asked.

"It isn't easy."

It was, Ashton thought, a sublime understatement. Ludmilla Andrianova wasn't housebound, she was a vegetable, unable to do the simplest things for herself. Vaughan should have noticed that Elena wasn't her usual self and should have made it his business to find out what was troubling her. But it seemed he had either been too blind to notice anything or else he hadn't cared. The more Ashton considered the shabby way Elena had been treated by the Foreign Office, the angrier he became. If ever he needed an excuse to justify his actions, the totally avoidable plight of the Andrianovs provided one.

"Of course my daughter has been a big help," Konstantin Kirillovich began, then fell silent.

"What did happen to Elena?"

"Some thugs attacked her on Lomonovski Prospekt shortly after she had left the Metro station."

At first, Konstantin Kirillovich hadn't known what his daughter had been doing in that part of town. He had understood her to say that she was going to see an old school friend. It was only after she had been admitted to hospital that he'd learned that her friend was a lecturer at Moscow University up in the Lenin Hills. The attack had occurred a few minutes before seven o'clock in the evening when it had been getting dark. Two men had grabbed Elena off the street and bundled her into a van. One man had pinioned both arms while the other punched her in the stomach and face after she had screamed for help, but that was all she could recall. She had been unable to describe her assailants, not even the one who had beaten her up.

Some students from the university had found her lying unconscious in the grass midway between the Luzhnikovski Bridge and Holy Trinity Church. She had four cracked ribs, a dislocated elbow, fractured pelvis and a broken nose. Both eyes had also been closed and a gash above the left eye had needed eight stitches. When the ambulance arrived, it had taken her to Piragow Hospital off Lenin Prospekt where she was still detained.

"Do the police know why your daughter was attacked?"

"Elena told them she had been robbed. They took her purse containing fifty roubles."

At the official rate of exchange, fifty roubles was worth twenty-five and a half pence or fractionally more than the cost of a first-class postage stamp. But Ashton supposed robbery could have been the motive; these days, people were being murdered for a few pounds – in hard currency, of course.

"When did this happen?" he asked.

"Tuesday night."

The day she would have met her contact at lunchtime in McDonald's had Nina Golodkinova still been alive.

"Did anyone telephone Elena on Tuesday?" he inquired.

"How would I know? I wasn't at home, I was on shift at the Vladykino power station."

Konstantin Kirillovich was a member of the emergency repair team responsible for the power lines in the north-east sector of Moscow; Ashton recalled that the embassy had made a note to that effect on Elena's personal file.

"First thing I knew about it was when I got home." Konstantin Kirillovich took out a crumpled packet of cigarettes and lit one. The acrid smoke went straight down into his lungs and made him cough and splutter so that it was some moments before he was able to catch his breath and continue. Even then, his voice sounded wheezy. "I let myself into the apartment and there she was all dressed up and ready to leave. When I asked where she was off to, Elena said she'd arranged to meet an old school friend she hadn't seen in years. Claimed she told me about it a week ago."

Elena was a grown woman in the process of divorcing her husband by whom she'd had a daughter who was now six years old. Even allowing for the claustrophobic nature of family life in Russia, Ashton couldn't believe she would have let her father know that far in advance.

"I didn't mean to lose my temper with Elena. She was on a week's holiday between jobs and she had every right to go out after meeting Vera from school and seeing to her mother. It was just that Ludmilla has to be waited on hand and foot and I'd had a lousy day at work . . ."

Elena had lied to her father. She hadn't left the apartment to keep a long-standing date with an old school friend. There was no university lecturer either; Elena had responded to a phone call she had received that afternoon. There was, however, only one person who could confirm the supposition.

"How do I find this hospital?"

"You are going to see Elena?"

"Yes. Do you mind?"

"No, I'd be happy for you to go. It is very difficult for me to leave Ludmilla Andrianova. I have to ask one of the neighbours to sit with her."

"So how do I get there?"

Konstantin Kirillovich told him that the nearest Metro station was Oktyabrskaya on the Circle Line. As soon as he came out onto the street, he was to keep the Warsaw Hotel on his right and head south-west on Lenin Prospekt. The hospital was the fourth turning on the right, approximately one and a half kilometres from the station.

"I know what you are going to say," Ashton told him. "I can't miss it. Right?"

"No, I was thinking perhaps it's not such a good idea after all."

"Why not?"

"You may speak our language very well but you do not look like a Russian; your clothes are too good. I would not like to see you in trouble with the authorities."

"Don't worry, I plan to change into something a little more informal." Ashton picked up his overnight bag. "Do you mind if I use the bedroom?" he asked.

"Please." Konstantin Kirillovich pointed to the appropriate door.

It was one of the smallest double rooms Ashton could remember seeing. One large bed and two single divans had been pushed hard up against three of the four walls to form a hollow square. There was a hanging cupboard to one side of the door and a dilapidated chest of drawers on the other. There was just enough floor space for two people to stand upright.

Ashton closed the door, shed his raincoat, then placed the overnight bag on the double bed and unzipped it. He took out a pair of black trousers that looked suitably worn and would go with the pale grey ski jacket which had been all the fashion when he had bought it in 1983. Last was a pair of down-at-heel shoes he should have thrown out long ago but somehow never had.

He changed swiftly, packed his suit away in the zipper bag, then hid his wallet, plane tickets, forged visa and the two British passports under the chest of drawers. Checking his appearance in the speckled mirror on the back of the door, he decided the tie didn't look right and removed it before returning to the living room.

"How do I look now?" he asked Konstantin Kirillovich.

"Better. You should pass inspection, Mr Englishman."

"Good. Is it all right if I leave my bag here?"

"But of course."

"I'll see you later then."

Ashton let himself out of the flat. He had two ten-pound notes and a little over two thousand four hundred roubles on him. He also had a Russian internal passport and a resident's permit in the name of Peter Pavlovich Zaitsev.

There were eighty beds in Elena's ward, all of which were occupied. Judging by the noisy babble of conversation which greeted him when he walked in, Ashton estimated there were roughly three times as many visitors. If the hospital had been in England, he would have arrived with flowers and a bunch of grapes. In Russia, they did things differently. Here, family and friends brought food to supplement the meagre and unappetising hospital fare. Knowing this, Ashton had stopped off on the way and bought two loaves of bread, some liver sausage, butter and a selection of cheeses which he carried in a string bag he'd purchased from another street trader.

Elena was one of the few patients in the ward who didn't have a friend or relative sitting at her bedside. She was lying flat on her back with a fracture board under the mattress and a steel cage over her legs to keep the weight of the bedclothes off them. She was not aware of his presence until he whispered her name, then she turned her head in his direction and peered at him through her one good eye. A second later, her jaw dropped in astonishment.

"Yes, it's me, Peter Pavlovich Zaitsev," he said in Russian before she could ask him what he was doing in Moscow. "Konstantin Kirillovich sends his love. He would have come himself but of course he cannot leave your mother and Vera.

Anyway, he asked me to deliver these cheeses, bread and liver sausage."

"Thank you, Peter Pavlovich."

He was glad to see that Elena had her wits about her even though she had been severely beaten. She looked terrible; her left eye was still closed and the gash above it, which had been stitched up, now resembled a zip fastener. The other eye wasn't in much better shape with a purple and yellow bruise on the cheekbone the size of a golf ball. But it was her nose which horrified him most of all. It was swollen to more than twice its normal size and badly misshapen. Both nostrils were still partially blocked with congealed blood so that Elena had to breathe through her mouth. No doubt the swelling would go down in time and the bruises disappear but she would never again be "a dishy bit of goods", as Hicks had once described her.

"Is it okay if I sit on the edge of your bed?" he asked.

"Please do."

Apart from the bed, the only other item of furniture was an open locker divided in two by a plywood shelf. "Is this yours?" he asked Elena.

"The top half is," she told him.

"Right, that's where I'll put your goodies." Ashton fiddled around with the string bag and its contents until he was able to fit them into the space without squashing anything. "Could be neater," he observed. "You will probably make a better job of it after I've gone."

"Perhaps."

"So how are you feeling?"

"A little sore, but I'm improving."

"Have they said when you will be discharged from hospital?"

"The doctor told me it would take three weeks for the pelvis to . . ."

Elena broke off in mid-sentence to stare blankly past him, her fingers plucking nervously at the blankets. Ashton followed her gaze, found himself looking at an unsmiling Amazon dressed like a bakery worker in a white smock and headscarf.

"Who are you?" the nurse demanded.

"Peter Pavlovich Zaitsev."

"You are related to the patient?"

"He is my second cousin," Elena said nervously.

"I didn't ask you."

The nurse was all charm. Ashton wondered if she had ever been a guard at a women's camp in the Gulag Archipelago and was missing the old days.

"You heard Elena Andrianova, I'm her second cousin."

"You do not sound like a Muscovite."

"You want to see my resident's permit?" Ashton reached inside the ski jacket and waved the document under her nose. "Well, here it is," he said, then turned his back on her.

Everyone in the immediate vicinity had stopped talking. It seemed no one had spoken to the dragon lady like that before and they were waiting to see what would happen next. The pregnant silence continued for some moments, then the Amazon backed down and stalked away muttering to herself. The spell was broken, the babble of conversation resumed and Elena Andrianova started breathing more normally again.

"You had better go before she makes trouble, Peter Pavlovich."

"I'm in no hurry," Ashton told her.

"You should be."

"I'll leave after you've told me what happened on Tuesday night."

"Two criminals beat me up and stole my purse . . ."

"That's what Konstantin Kirillovich told me. Now I'd like to hear what really happened."

"You already have," Elena said and turned her head away.

"I can understand why you don't want to talk about it. No one wants to relive a horrible experience, so I'll make it easy for you. I believe you had a phone call on Tuesday afternoon from the same man who abducted Vera last October. He wanted to know why you hadn't met Nina's replacement at McDonald's like you were supposed to and you told him you were no longer employed by the British Embassy. He didn't believe it and told you what would happen to Vera if you didn't follow his instructions to the letter."

"No. No, you're wrong."

"No one snatched you off the street, did they? You got into that van of your own free will and you were taken to some abandoned factory or deserted building for questioning."

Elena didn't have to say anything, her fingers worrying the

blankets spoke volumes for her. Maybe he'd got some minor points of detail wrong but, in the main, his reconstruction was correct.

"There was more than one of them and they wanted to know why you had left the embassy and they kept on beating you until they got what they wanted. Then they beat you some more so that you would know what to expect if you didn't keep your mouth shut. Am I right?" Ashton smiled. "You don't have to answer," he added.

The questions they had asked her would be highly revealing but Elena wouldn't tell him what they were until she was satisfied no harm would come to Vera and her parents.

"You are not alone any more," he told her. "I am going to make sure those men can never hurt you again."

"How can you do that?"

"By playing Peter off against Paul."

"I don't understand," she said.

"It's a saying we have." Ashton squeezed her hand. "Don't give it another thought, you just concentrate on getting fit again."

The dragon lady deliberately turned her back on him and pretended to be conferring with one of the hospital porters when he left the ward and walked past her office. Remembering how long he'd had to wait for a lift on the way in, Ashton used the staircase to reach the ground floor.

Lenin Prospekt at four o'clock on a Saturday afternoon was almost as lively as a morgue and twice as depressing. Hands stuffed deep into the pockets of the ski jacket, a chill east wind blowing in his face, Ashton set off at a brisk pace for the Metro. Shortly thereafter, he was aware of an itchy feeling between the shoulder blades. It was a sensation he had last experienced on the streets of Belfast as an undercover agent with the army's Special Patrol Unit, and he instinctively knew someone was following him.

Ashton waited until he reached the entrance to the Metro station before he suddenly looked back. Caught off guard, the tail rapidly changed direction and headed towards the Hotel Warsaw. They were only thirty yards apart and Ashton had no difficulty recognising the hospital porter he had seen in the dragon lady's office.

Chapter 12

Ashton waited until the hospital porter had entered the Hotel Warsaw before he turned about and hurried into the Metro. He fed fifteen kopeks into one of the turnstiles, then ran down the fast-moving escalator and made for the Circle Line rather than the radial that served the outer suburbs. By sticking to the hub, he could use the Metro to shake off the opposition, something that would be more difficult to accomplish once he deserted the interchange system.

There was a train every ninety seconds during the rush hour, but this was still the off-peak period when the average waiting time was up to three minutes. Although this was a better service than London Underground provided at any time of the day or night, it was hard to appreciate that fact when every second counted. He had merely spooked the hospital porter, not thrown him off, and the Russian would be back.

Ashton walked onto the platform, checked the clock at the far end, which ticked off the seconds since the previous train had departed, and saw that he had just missed an eastbound one. Two minutes forty seconds to the next was a lifetime away, especially as a train heading in the opposite direction would do him equally well. He turned into the connecting subway and went on through to the westbound platform only to discover he was hardly any better off.

There were fewer than twenty people waiting for the next train and nowhere to hide. All Ashton could do was stand there and hope the Russian would check the platforms on the radial line first. He stared at the mural on the facing wall which depicted the glorious achievements of the industrial workers of the Soviet Union and wondered idly how much longer it would be before someone got around to altering the décor.

A faint breeze wafted along the platform and got progressively stronger, then a train emerged from the tunnel to his left, drew into the station and slowed to a halt. The doors opened with a pneumatic hiss; as he moved to board the nearest car, Ashton caught sight of the hospital porter loitering near the bottom end of the platform.

He had three options. He could wait until the doors were about to close before boarding the train in the hope of leaving the Russian stranded, or he could do the same thing in reverse and wave goodbye from the platform as the train disappeared into the tunnel with the tail still on board. On the principle of better the devil you know, Ashton decided on the third alternative and made no attempt to shake him off. There was another consideration; if the hospital porter had a back-up, it was possible he could use him to spot the second man.

Someone had arranged for Elena Andrianova to be kept under surveillance while she was in hospital; someone wanted to know if she had any visitors other than her family. But who? A *Mafiozniki* crime syndicate or some clique within the KGB? Ashton frowned; he would know the answer to that question soon enough if ever they caught up with him. Elena had collected four cracked ribs, a fractured pelvis, a dislocated elbow and a broken nose. He was unlikely to get off quite so lightly and would be lucky not to end up in some dark alleyway with a 9mm bullet in his head.

The train pulled into Park Kultury. The elderly woman in the shabby coat who had been sitting opposite him got out, a young couple with two little girls under ten got in. If there were two men on his tail, they would try to box him in. One in front, one tucked behind; that was the standard procedure in this situation. Or so the detective sergeant from Special Branch who had given a lecture on surveillance techniques had told him and his fellow students on the SIS induction course all those long years ago. They hadn't managed to achieve that desirable state of affairs while he had been waiting for the next westbound, which meant that one of them would have to work his way up the train.

From where he was sitting, Ashton had a clear view of the platform each time they arrived at a station. The trick was to take note of the passengers who were already waiting to board his coach on the premise that anyone who then subsequently went on past it to get on the train farther up was suspect. But nothing untoward happened between Park Kultury and Belorusskaya three stops farther on where Ashton got off.

Whatever else the enterprise culture may have produced, the number of official taxis on the streets of Moscow had not increased. However, there was usually a cab rank outside every rail terminus and the Belorussian station serving Minsk and all points west was no exception. Ashton walked over to the first one in the line and told the driver to take him to the Intourist Hotel at Gorky Street and Marx Prospekt.

As they pulled out of the yard, he looked back in time to see the hospital porter grab the next cab on the rank. A beanpole of a man in jeans and a fur-lined grey anorak that was at least one size too big looked all set to join him, then had second thoughts and made for the Lada saloon behind. The last Ashton saw of him, he was engaged in an altercation with a plump matronly woman who had just beaten him to it and was about to get into the taxi.

Ashton turned about, dug a ten-pound note out of his ski jacket and leaned forward over the front seat. "You want to earn yourself a bonus?" he asked the driver, showing him the Queen's portrait.

"Who do I have to kill?"

"Look into your rear-view mirror and tell me what you see."

"What is this? A quiz game?"

"Humour me."

"You're the boss." The driver looked up briefly, then glanced into the wing mirror. "Sergei Sergevich," he grunted.

"Who's he?"

"The driver of the cab immediately behind us."

"Any sign of a yellow Lada saloon?"

"I'll tell you in a second." The driver drifted out until their vehicle was straddling two lanes. "Yeah, it's behind the Zil truck which is following Sergei Sergevich."

"The money's yours if you can lose both taxis."

"Are you in some kind of trouble?"

"Only with an irate husband and his brother."

"You don't want to go to the Intourist Hotel then?"

"With those two on my back?" Ashton said, feigning amazement.

They were on Gorky Street and approaching the Garden Ring,

139

Moscow's equivalent of the M25 without the nose-to-tail traffic. As the lights up ahead changed to red, the taxi driver nipped into the nearside lane as if intending to turn right into the ring road. Guessing what he had in mind, Ashton waited for the seemingly inevitable crash when he did exactly the opposite.

Determined to make a quick getaway, the driver pressed the accelerator to the floor, let the clutch out and jumped the lights while they were still changing to green. The tyres did not squeal in protest and Ashton wasn't thrown back in his seat; the 1.5-litre engine of the Moskvich needed retuning and the power wasn't there. There should have been a major pile up but somehow the vehicles in the outside lanes managed to avoid them and screeched to a halt, horns blaring.

But it didn't end there. As if hellbent on committing suicide, the taxi driver went straight at the two lines of traffic heading out of town on Gorky Street. There were no hazard-warning lights on the Moskvich but he used the main beams to the same effect, flicking them on and off at machine-gun speed. Engine snarling in second gear, they cut in behind a trolley bus, shot across the front of an oncoming Volvo, then had to swerve out into the middle of the road to avoid ramming into a Zil limousine filtering into the Garden Ring from the right. Accelerating away, the taxi driver changed up into third, overtook a small delivery van and then moved across into the inside lane. Two hundred yards farther on, he turned right into a side road and subsequently kept to the back streets until he was satisfied they weren't being followed. Then he pulled into the kerb and shifted into neutral.

"That Sergei Sergevich," he said, chuckling to himself. "I bet he almost crapped in his pants back there."

"He wasn't the only one," Ashton said and handed over the ten-pound note.

"So where do you want to go now?"

"The nearest pay phone."

"Going to ring the girlfriend at the Intourist Hotel, are we?"

"What do you think?"

"I think I can read some people like a book," the taxi driver said with a leer as he restarted the car.

But not me, Ashton thought. The alleged girlfriend he was going to call was, in fact, Walter Iremonger, one of the few resident press correspondents he hadn't met when he had been on the Russian Desk at Century House. Newspapermen were a valuable source of information and he had made a point of wining and dining them whenever they were on home leave. For this purpose, Hazelwood had arranged for him to join The Athenaeum in Pall Mall whose membership embraced literature, science, public service and the arts. The club was also part of his cover; it was close enough to Carlton House Terrace and Downing Street to lead people to accept the legend that he was a Foreign Office man, pure and simple.

On the assumption that he would eventually meet Iremonger one day, Ashton had compiled a biography of the newspaperman, as he had with all the other British reporters based in Moscow. The purpose of each biography was to help him break the ice when meeting the press correspondent for the first time; the content was therefore brief enough to be committed to memory. It contained the subject's date and place of birth, career to date and awards, if any. It also included the reporter's private address and phone number in Moscow.

The biographical notebook had been Ashton's own idea. Strictly speaking, it should have been destroyed when he was transferred to Security and Technical Services but somehow he had never got around to it. Prudently, he had had the presence of mind to refresh his memory before flying out to Helsinki. Walter Iremonger – Petrowski Avenue 236 – telephone 29 84 61 00. He had total recall.

"This should do you."

Ashton glanced to his left and saw a couple of pay phones on the outside wall of a bank just down the street from Lermontovskaya Metro station.

"Want me to wait for you?"

"No thanks." Ashton gave him the fare, added a tip, then got out of the cab and walked over to the pay phone. He did not look back.

Iremonger turned his back on the twilight view of the Moscow skyline and reluctantly went back to his typewriter. He was stuck for an ending to the piece he hoped the Associated Press would sell to the *Sunday Times* and gazing out of the window wasn't going to furnish him with the necessary inspiration. If he said so himself, it was a good, punchy essay on the demise of

Communism and the resurgence of nationalism. It was going to worry a lot of people back home who looked at life through rose-coloured spectacles because he was quoting the ordinary Muscovite, and what they had to say about democracy would shatter a few cosy myths.

The sudden and ruthless transition from Communism to capitalism had done very little for the average Russian family, except wipe out their savings, debase the currency, create hyperinflation and give them a greater choice of things they couldn't afford to buy. Many of the perks which they had taken for granted under the old régime were now likely to go because the country no longer had the resources to pay for subsidised holidays in the Crimea and a free health cure every four years or whatever.

Iremonger lit a cigarette. It was good all right – clear, concise, objective and fair. He also liked to think it was interesting. But what was he going to put in the concluding paragraph? Something hard-hitting, something which would really make the reader sit up and take notice. He was just beginning to get it together when the telephone rang and broke his train of thought. Vexed by the interruption, he snatched the receiver from the cradle and barked out his home number. There was no response from the caller; all Iremonger could hear was a rushing noise in the background which sounded like traffic moving on a fairly busy road.

"Who's there?" he demanded, then found himself listening to a continuous burr as the mystery caller broke the connection. "Well, fuck you too," he said aloud and put the phone down.

Iremonger stubbed out his cigarette and put his mind to the concluding paragraph again. Russia was a proud and volatile nation; the very same people who'd cheered Yeltsin to the echo last August were now calling him a traitor, the man who had held out a begging bowl to the West and prostituted his country for the equivalent of thirty pieces of silver. There was anger too at the break up of the former Soviet Union and the insults they had had to contend with from the newly emergent tinpot states when everyone knew that, in the Great Patriotic War, nearly all the fighting and certainly most of the dying had been done by the Russians. Hardliners at both ends of the political spectrum were now openly saying that the time was fast approaching when the Russian Empire would have to be reunited by force of arms.

Suddenly, Iremonger knew how to end it. 'There is a dangerous resentment among Russians and it is growing,' he typed. 'At present, it is focused inwards, but the day may come when it is turned in another direction.' He toyed with the notion of adding something about the West discovering just how fragile the new era of peace could be, then decided it was better to let the reader draw the appropriate conclusion.

The article ran to four pages; removing the last sheet of A4 from the carriage, he read the whole piece from beginning to end, pruning the odd sentence here and there. Then he put the essay through the typewriter again and had just reached the final punch line when the phone rang a second time. As before, there was no response when he answered it. For Iremonger, it was a reminder of what things had been like in the old days when the KGB had been fond of harassing correspondents with bogus phone calls, designed to keep them awake all night.

"What's the matter with you bastards," he snarled. "I thought we'd given up playing silly buggers."

Ashton hung up and walked away from the pay phone. He had rung Iremonger to see if he was at home before catching a train from Lermontovskaya, and again just now to make sure he hadn't left his apartment during the time it had taken him to get to Petrowski Avenue. He took out the street map of the town centre which he'd purchased from a bookshop near the Metro and stopped under a streetlight to get his bearings. A five-minute walk, ten at the outside. He folded the map, tucked it into his ski jacket and moved on, hands in pockets, shoulders hunched against the bitter cold. The temperature was already several degrees below freezing and still falling. There was ice in the Moscow River and the leaden sky before dusk had suggested there could be a snowfall during the night. He walked on at a brisker pace, then broke into a jog to warm himself up. He checked off the numbers as he trotted past each apartment block – 232, 234, 236. There was nothing to distinguish one building from another. All had been built around the turn of the century, town houses in solid, neo-German style for rich merchants, minor aristocracy and government officials. After the Bolshevik Revolution, they had been converted into flats. The electronic door lock and call button system looked in mint condition and was obviously a more recent addition. Ashton pressed the appropriate button for Iremonger's apartment and got a tinny reply through the squawk box in Russian.

"Mr Walter Iremonger?" he asked in English.

"Yes. Who's that?"

"Michael Vaughan from the embassy. Do you think you could spare me five minutes? It is rather important."

"You'd better come up."

There was a buzzing noise, then the lock clicked back. Ashton pushed the door open, stepped inside the hall and took the spiral staircase up to the reporter's flat on the third floor.

Iremonger had evidently been waiting for him. As he reached out to press the button, the newspaperman opened the door just far enough to inspect his visitor. The way his eyes narrowed told Ashton he didn't like what he saw.

"You're not Michael Vaughan," he growled.

"No, I'm the man who rang you twice within the last half-hour." Ashton put a foot into the jamb; there was no sign of a security chain on the door and if need be, he was prepared to force his way into the apartment.

"Take your foot out of the way before I damage it," Iremonger snarled.

"All I'm asking for is five minutes of your time."

"You can piss off."

"Believe me, you won't regret it."

"Didn't you hear what I said?"

"Look, why don't you calm down and let me explain . . ."

Iremonger thumped the door into his foot, then opened it a little wider to have another go at him. As he did so, Ashton hit the panel with his right shoulder with sufficient force to send him reeling back into the hall. Before Iremonger could recover, he stepped inside the apartment and heeled the door shut behind him.

"Take it easy," he said quietly, "I'm not going to hurt you."

"You're asking for it."

Iremonger wasn't short of courage but that was the only thing he had going for him. He was ponderous, unfit and signalled his intentions so well in advance that Ashton had no difficulty in blocking the haymaker with his forearm, as he did all the other flailing punches.

"This is ridiculous," he said. "Keep this up and you'll have a heart attack."

"Sod you." Iremonger tried one more swing, then dropped both hands to his sides, his arms feeling like lead weights. "Sod you," he gasped.

"Come and sit down and rest awhile." Ashton took him by the elbow. "Where's the living room?" he asked.

"First door on the left."

The room was half as big again as the entire flat occupied by Elena Andrianova and her parents. In the days before Glasnost, no Russian would have been allowed to rent the apartment; even now Iremonger's flat and others like it were reserved for foreigners, a measure designed to keep them isolated from the indigenous population.

Most of the furniture belonged to a bygone age. The chintzy three-piece suite with lace antimacassars, old-fashioned standard lamp, and nest of tables would not have looked out of place on a stage set depicting a drawing room in the thirties. Neither would the bookcase-cum-bureau in the alcove to the right of the window. The portable typewriter and oval table, which had been pressed into use as a desk, struck a wrong note.

"I should throw you out," Iremonger said plaintively.

"Don't let's have any more of that nonsense," Ashton told him. "You're forty-four years old, you smoke too much and you never walk when you can ride."

"What?"

"You were born in Lancaster on the eighteenth of December 1947. In 1971 you married Paula Willis and were divorced eight years later. You have two daughters, Christine and Emma, aged seventeen and fifteen whom you haven't seen since 1986."

Iremonger stared at him, mouth agape. "How do you know so much about me?"

"I've been following your career."

"You've been doing what?"

"And I'm about to give you the story of the year."

"Me?" Iremonger threw back his head and faked a derisive laugh. "What have I done to deserve this honour?"

They had never met and he'd happened to be at home. Too many other newspapermen knew Ashton by sight and might be tempted to break a confidence. It was his own colleagues, more than the KGB, that he had to look out for. But it wasn't politic to let Iremonger know that.

"You're a good journalist and I respect your integrity."

"By God, you really mean that, don't you?"

"Yes." The best lies were always the shortest.

"All right, let's hear what you've got."

"Remember the Joyner case?"

"Of course I do, it's less than a fortnight since he was murdered. A small-time businessman who was dealing in drugs on the side and overreached himself. Got shot to death in his hotel bedroom with a hooker. There's no mileage in that story; it never ran when it broke and it won't run now."

"There's another strand to it, goes all the way to the British Embassy."

"Oh come on, you must think I was born yesterday."

"Michael Vaughan has got a new secretary . . ."

"You call that news?"

"His previous Girl Friday was Elena Andrianova; she was fired just over a week ago for passing information to Nina Golodkinova."

There were no further interruptions. Iremonger was still sceptical, but he was interested and prepared to listen. Without mentioning any names, Ashton told him about the security check and the discovery of a bug under the filing cabinet in Vaughan's office. He also told him how much Elena was paid, where and when she met Nina Golodkinova as well as how often.

"I don't suppose it's any use me asking who you are?" Iremonger said.

"None whatever," Ashton assured him.

"How do I know this isn't a hoax?"

"Because first thing tomorrow you ring the duty officer at the embassy and ask if there is an Elena Andrianova on the staff."

"And if he denies all knowledge of the lady?"

"You tell him that's funny because you have just come from her bedside at the Piragow Hospital and she is wondering why no one from the embassy has been to see her."

"What is she doing there? Is she sick or something?"

"You could put it like that," Ashton said drily. "Fact is, a couple of thugs beat the crap out of her when they learned she had lost her job. They wanted to know what she had told the

British, then gave her another kicking as a foretaste of what to expect if she opened her mouth."

"That's some story." Iremonger gazed at him speculatively. "You mind telling me what you expect to get out of it?"

"Nothing. Elena Andrianova is in danger and I want the embassy to ensure that she comes to no harm. Right now, she is persona non grata with the Foreign Office, but their attitude will change once they realise you are on to the story."

"She's at the Piragow Hospital?"

"Yes, it's just off the Lenin Prospekt."

Iremonger walked over to the bookcase-cum-bureau, lowered the drop leaf and rummaged through the pigeon holes. "Should have a street map somewhere," he muttered.

"I've got one."

"Good. Let's go; I want to see this patient for myself."

"I don't know what the visiting hours are but it's past six o'clock."

"So what? With the right kind of money you can unlock any door these days."

Ashton hesitated, wondered how much worse it would make Elena's situation if he happened to run into the dragon lady again. On the other hand, if he refused to tag along, he would lose all credibility, and that wouldn't do her any good either.

"Are you coming or not?"

Iremonger's belligerent tone settled the quandary. He would accompany the newspaperman to the hospital and then tell him why he wasn't going anywhere near Elena's ward.

"Of course I am," he said.

They left the apartment, walked down the spiral staircase and out into the cold night air. Iremonger owned one of the last Volkswagen 'Beetles' to come off the production line. It was, he claimed, the only car which was a hundred per cent reliable in the depths of winter. As if to prove it, the engine fired the first time he cranked it. Unfortunately, the heater wasn't quite as reliable.

Chapter 13

The hospital had been built when few ordinary Muscovites owned a car. After looking in vain for somewhere to park the VW, Iremonger settled for the approach road to the casualty department and put the nearside wheels up on the kerb to leave plenty of room for an ambulance to get past.

"Okay, Mr Anonymous," he said, "time we saw the patient."

"I'm not coming with you," Ashton told him.

"Say that again."

"Elena Andrianova is being watched . . ."

"You really are something . . ."

"I was here this afternoon. When I left, I had two shadows, one of whom I had seen talking to the staff nurse in charge of the ward. He was then dressed like a hospital porter. It took me some time to lose him."

"I don't believe any of this," Iremonger said angrily.

"Listen to me. Elena is in a ward on the fourth floor . . ."

"I'm tired of this hoax, buster. Its subtlety has been lost on me but I assume you must have got a kick out of it. Anyway, I'm calling it off here and now and I'd like you to get out of my car. Or shall I call a militiaman?"

Ashton took out a wad of folding money, peeled off five hundred roubles and parted with the remaining ten-pound note. "Here, use this to buy your way into the hospital. Don't bother calling for a lift because it will take for ever."

"You must be deaf. Either that, or you don't understand plain English."

It took a lot to make Ashton fly off the handle but when he did, it was quite awesome. "Will you shut up a minute," he said in a voice full of suppressed fury.

Iremonger looked as though he was about to say something and then thought better of it.

149

"All right, let's start again," Ashton said in a quieter tone. "Like I said, Elena is on the fourth floor. Her ward is to the left of the staircase and she is halfway down it on the right-hand side. You won't have any difficulty recognising her because she is the only patient with a hoop over both legs. Her face is also pretty banged up; she's got a broken nose, and the stitches above the left eye look like a zip fastener. Naturally, her name is on the chart at the foot of the bed, but the printing is on the small side and I don't want you bending down to peer at it if your eyesight isn't good enough. One thing you don't do is talk to her."

"If I'm not going to interview the woman, what the hell am I doing here?"

"You're here to ascertain that Elena Andrianova exists. By the time you leave, you will also know that she was the victim of a particularly brutal assault."

"You know something? I've just tumbled to what your game is. While I'm in the hospital, you are going to steal my Volks and flog it on the black market. Right?"

"Oh for Christ's sake . . ."

"Okay, okay." Iremonger raised both hands in a gesture of surrender. "I was only joking."

"I should hope so," Ashton said angrily.

Iremonger removed the key from the ignition, got out of the car, then went round the back and raised the bonnet. A few minutes later he returned and tapped on the side window to show Ashton the rotor arm. "I don't believe in taking chances," he said before moving off into the darkness.

Although the heater on the VW wasn't a hundred per cent, it functioned well enough to make the interior tolerably warm while the vehicle was mobile. Within minutes of switching off the engine, it went to the other extreme and the car became exceptionally cold. Ashton zipped the ski jacket up to the neck, then blew on his hands before stuffing them into the pockets. Apart from stamping them, there wasn't much he could do about his feet, which soon began to feel like two blocks of ice. To cap it all, it began to snow.

Time dragged, with the cold making each minute seem more like five. The snowflakes swirled in the wind, stuck to the windscreen and windows to draw a veil over the outside world. He did not see Iremonger return and only became aware of his presence when he raised the bonnet to put the rotor arm back in the distributor. He slammed the bonnet down with unnecessary force and did the same with the door when he got into the Volkswagen.

"I can see you're in a bad temper," Ashton said. "I'd like to know why."

"I'm surprised you should ask."

"Well, I have, so let's hear it."

"There is no Elena Andrianova. What's more, there is no patient in that particular ward with the kind of injuries you described."

"They must have moved her."

"You never give up, do you?" Iremonger tossed three crumpled fifty-rouble notes into Ashton's lap. "Your change," he snapped. "The rest went on bribes. Now get out of my car and find yourself a taxi."

"No, I can't do that. We're going back to your place because I am going to convince you Elena Andrianova is a real person even if it kills me."

"Like hell. You're not putting a foot inside my apartment again."

"Please, I'm asking you as nicely as I know how to let me have one more try."

Iremonger sighed. "I know I'm going to regret this," he said and cranked the engine until it caught and fired on all cylinders.

He drove out through the hospital gates, went on up to Lenin Prospekt and turned left. He didn't say another word, just kept his eyes fixed on the road while he whistled tunelessly to himself. It stopped snowing before they reached the Garden Ring but it needed Ashton to point this out before it occurred to him to stop the windshield wipers.

The heater threw another temperamental wobbler. This time it turned the interior into a hothouse and there was no lowering the temperature no matter what Iremonger did with the controls. In the end, Ashton wound the window partway down to allow the cold air in, then closed it again as soon as the atmosphere inside got too chilly. By the time they reached the apartment house on Petrowski Avenue, he had developed the manual ventilation system to a fine art.

Iremonger parked the VW on the verge between the road and

151

the pavement and, still maintaining his vow of silence, led the way inside. He didn't break it until he had fixed himself a whisky and soda.

"You want one?" he asked.

"I wouldn't mind," Ashton said.

"Help yourself then."

"Thanks, I will. Have you got a Moscow telephone directory?"

"On the bureau."

"Look up the number for Andrianov, K. K. and tell me what it is."

"Don't you know?"

"Of course I do, I just want you to see that there is a listing for Andrianov."

Iremonger gave another of his theatrical sighs, left the whisky and soda on the floor by his chair, then walked over to the bureau and riffled through the directory. "All right," he said presently, "there is such a listing. The number's 095-91.16."

"So now tell me the name of the English language officer in charge of the British Council."

"Ullswater. Roger Ullswater."

"Right. Now I'd like you to phone Andrianov and pass yourself off as Ullswater."

"Oh my God . . ."

"Elena will have told her parents that she has got a job with the British Council starting on Monday. You tell her father, Konstantin Kirillovich, that you were expecting to see Elena yesterday afternoon and can't understand why she didn't keep the appointment. Then you listen to what he has to say and take it from there. Think you can do that?"

"Does Andrianov speak English?"

"Not a word."

"My Russian isn't all that good."

"That's okay," Ashton told him cheerfully, "Ullswater doesn't speak it too well either."

Iremonger lifted the receiver and dialled the number slowly, pausing briefly between each digit in case the automatic exchange failed to identify the sequence correctly and connected him with the wrong number. When Konstantin Kirillovich answered the phone, Iremonger followed the guidelines Ashton had given him and was thoroughly convincing. Without any prompting, he expressed a hope that Elena would make a speedy recovery and asked Konstantin Kirillovich to assure his daughter that her job would still be waiting for her.

"All right, I'm convinced," Iremonger said after he had put the phone down. "I was wrong, you're not a hoaxer, and Elena Andrianova is a real person." He pursed his lips. "What do you think the hospital authorities have done with her? Transferred her to another ward?"

If they had, Ashton thought it would only have been a temporary measure until they could sort out a more permanent arrangement. Putting himself in their shoes, he would take steps to ensure that there was no record to show that she had ever been admitted to the Piragow Hospital and would keep her under wraps in a KGB-controlled psychiatric clinic. Pure conjecture, however, wouldn't get them anywhere.

"First thing we have to do is find Elena," he told Iremonger.

"We? Meaning you and I?"

"No, I had someone else in mind, someone I'd rather you didn't know about." He smiled at the journalist. "It's not that I don't trust you, that goes without saying. But I think it would be better if you didn't hear our conversation, and I am bloody hungry."

"Are you suggesting I should cook dinner for you?"

"A sandwich would be most welcome."

"You're not short on cheek, I'll say that for you, and I ought to kick you out. Must be the journalist in me that makes me want to see it through, I guess." He moved towards the kitchen. "Give me a shout when you've finished."

Ashton waited until he had left the room, then rang the KGB's Second Chief Directorate in Dzerzhinsky Square and asked for Major Oleg Lysenko of the Criminal Investigation Division. Although the Russian investigator was unlikely to be in his office on a Saturday evening, he was banking on someone in his team knowing how to reach him. He just hoped it wouldn't be Sergeant Oroblinsky who picked up the phone and was relieved when a young woman with a very pleasant voice took the call. However, like KGB officers of old, she gave nothing away, not even her name. She also tried her best to convince him that Major Lysenko hadn't left word where he could be reached.

"Tell the major that the Joyner case isn't closed," Ashton said, interrupting her. "Tell him the Englishman says so."

"The Englishman? I don't understand."

"Major Lysenko will. I'm going to call again in fifteen minutes and you'd better have a phone number where I can reach him."

"That's impossible."

"Because if you fail me, the British Embassy will be in touch with Major General Gurov, the Chief of Police, to complain about your lack of co-operation."

Ashton heard a bleat of alarm as he hung up and knew the young KGB officer would do everything she could to get hold of Lysenko. He walked into the kitchen where Iremonger was busy making coffee and a pile of corned beef sandwiches.

"Courtesy of the Beriozka shop," he said, pointing to a tin of ground coffee. "Same with the corned beef."

The Beriozkas were hard currency shops for foreigners only, which stocked durable goods and foodstuffs that were not available elsewhere.

"Help yourself to a sandwich."

"Thanks."

"Did you get through to your friend?"

"I'll know when I call back in fifteen minutes," Ashton told him between mouthfuls.

"I see you're still holding the cards close to your chest."

"I have to. And you wouldn't thank me if I gave you all the facts. If the British Embassy ever discovered who had put you on to Elena Andrianova, they would move heaven and earth to get you expelled from Moscow, and the Russians would be happy to oblige."

"So how do I use the information you've given me?"

It was an easy enough question for Ashton to answer. Iremonger was to imply he had initially got his information from one of the locally employed members of the embassy staff and had then been to see Elena's father.

"The embassy will want to know the name of your source on the staff but naturally you will refuse to betray a confidence. And the more pressure they try to apply, the better your story. Right?"

"I'm way ahead of you."

"Start the ball rolling with a phone call to the embassy early tomorrow."

"You already told me that." Iremonger grinned. "Should make their Sunday."

"Oh, I think I can safely guarantee that." Ashton wolfed down another corned beef sandwich, then wiped the crumbs from his lips. "Do you mind hanging on in the kitchen while I call my friend?"

"Do I have much choice?"

"Not a lot."

Ashton returned to the living room, picked up the phone and rang the Criminal Investigation Division again. The same young woman took the call and gave him a number where he could reach Oleg Lysenko.

The KGB major started out full of blather, only to end up eating out of his hand. By the time Ashton had finished with him, he had promised to put one of his best officers on to finding Elena Andrianova. He had also agreed to wait for Ashton near the pay phones in the ticket hall of Leningrad station.

A lot of the people milling around the station weren't there either to catch a train or meet one arriving from Leningrad. In addition to the would-be travellers, there were pimps, hookers, bag snatchers, conmen, pickpockets, black marketeers, pushers and pre-pubescent gangs of orphaned children ready to jump anyone they believed would be worth robbing. It was one of those places where, after dark, it was best not to go alone. Ashton did so for one very good reason. The night people were his early-warning system; they could recognise a plainclothes man when they saw one and would melt away if they suspected something was going down.

Ashton walked into the concourse and looked around. He had arrived twenty minutes early at the rendezvous because if Lysenko was going to double-cross him, he would have already deployed his men in and around the station. The signs were that the KGB officer was playing it straight. The street orphans were still around, nine- to-twelve-year-olds with eyes bright and hard as diamonds, their heads shaved, all of them smoking acrid, hand-rolled cigarettes. He spotted four obvious hookers among the riffraff and was accosted by a fifth as he wrote down the numbers of the pay phones in the ticket hall. Satisfied by what he'd seen, Ashton left the station, hired the first taxi in the cab

155

rank and paid the driver a retainer of two hundred roubles to wait for him outside the post office in the adjoining street. Then he found a vantage point near the Metro from where he could keep the main entrance of the terminus under observation.

Lysenko arrived at five minutes to eight in an unmarked Lada, which he parked behind the cab rank. As he disappeared inside the rail terminus, Ashton made his way to the post office where there were a couple of pay phones on the outside wall. After leaving the KGB man to cool his heels for a good five minutes, he then proceeded to go through the list of numbers he had jotted down, dialling them out one by one. Lysenko was waiting in the ticket hall near the pay phones. Although he had not been warned to expect a call, Ashton was confident that with his training and experience, it wouldn't take him long to catch on. His faith in Lysenko wasn't misplaced; the third number in the sequence of four had just started to ring out when the Russian lifted the receiver and asked what the hell was going on.

"There's been a change of venue," Ashton told him. "Take the Lada and wait for me in the car park opposite the Cosmos Hotel on Mira Prospekt."

"Don't waste my time, Mr Ashton."

"I'm not. I just want to make sure you're clean before we shake hands. Now get with it."

Ashton put the phone down, got into the waiting taxi and told the driver to move up to the road junction and keep his eyes open for a dull brown Lada saloon. It worked like a charm. As they approached the T-junction, Lysenko drove past and the cab driver was able to tuck in behind him. If the KGB were going to cover the new rendezvous, Ashton figured the Major would have to keep well inside the speed limit in order to give his men time to move into the area. But instead of dawdling along when he joined the Mira Prospekt, just south of the Metro station, Lysenko actually put his foot down and drew away from them.

"You needn't bother to keep up with him," Ashton told the driver. "I know where he's going."

He paid off the taxi outside the Mira Prospekt Hotel, waited until the driver had pulled away, then walked on towards the Cosmos. The uneven pavement was covered with a light dusting of snow but the wind had dropped and it wasn't as cold as it had been earlier in the evening.

Lysenko was waiting for him in the car park and open-air bus terminal across the broad avenue from the twenty-nine-storey hotel. Ashton approached the car from the rear and opened the nearside front door silently enough to make the Russian jump when he slipped in beside him.

"Where the hell did you spring from?" Lysenko demanded angrily.

"You can always find a blind spot and I knew you wouldn't hear me with the engine running."

"What did you want to creep up on me like that for, Mr Queen's Messenger? I could have shot you."

"I wanted to make sure you weren't talking to anyone on the radio."

"I don't even have one on this car."

"So I discovered. Now, why don't you chauffeur me around while we talk about Elena Andrianova?"

Lysenko shifted into gear, released the handbrake and let the clutch out. Turning left on the Mira Prospekt, he headed north towards the outer ring motorway.

"I hope you are going to pay me for the petrol," he grumbled. "This Lada happens to belong to me."

"First things first. Who have you got looking for Elena Andrianova?"

"One of my best officers."

"Not Sergeant Oroblinsky, I hope?"

"You don't like him much, do you?"

"That's an understatement, the man's a rattlesnake."

"I think you are doing the sergeant an injustice, but you needn't worry, I gave the job to Katya Malinovskaya. You spoke to her earlier this evening."

"She has a pleasant manner. Is she also efficient?"

"Very. Of course, I was unable to tell her precisely why we are anxious to trace this vanishing lady of yours other than that she was involved in the Joyner case."

"Elena Andrianova was a spy," Ashton told him bluntly. "She bugged the office of the Third Secretary, Commerce and passed the information she collected to Nina Golodkinova. She was recruited by a man calling himself Mikhail, but not the Mikhail Yerokhin who was killed in the shoot-out in Slobodin Road. This Mikhail is alive and kicking; on Tuesday evening, two of his

157

henchmen took Elena Andrianova apart and put her in hospital after he'd learned that she had lost her job at our embassy. He wanted to know what she had told us."

"I'm beginning to think you have a vivid imagination."

Ashton could understand why the Russian was reluctant to believe him. The police theory that Joyner had been dealing in drugs and had been killed by the local *Mafiozniki* was no longer tenable. Elena Andrianova's involvement gave the case a whole new dimension on a scale big enough to point a finger of suspicion at one of the Intelligence directorates. There was, however, no need to spell it out for Lysenko; he was quite capable of seeing the implication himself.

"You are not trying to spread dissent, are you, Mr Queen's Messenger?"

"You find Elena and you'll know I'm not doing anything of the kind. But you will have to take care of her whole family and make sure they won't come to any harm. If you don't protect them, she'll just play deaf and dumb."

"Have you got any more words of advice for me?" Lysenko asked in a voice loaded with sarcasm.

"No, but I do have a request. Don't pick anyone to look after the family you wouldn't trust with your own life."

"You are a very suspicious man. I wonder how you can bring yourself to trust me."

It was a question Ashton had asked himself before he had arranged to meet the Russian. He certainly didn't trust some of the men around him, especially Sergeant Oroblinsky. Two things had counted in Lysenko's favour: his superior officer, Major General Gurov, had invited the British Embassy to provide a liaison officer, and while appearances were often deceptive, the young KGB major had struck Ashton as an essentially honest man.

"I wouldn't be sitting in this car if I didn't," he told the Russian.

"Thanks."

"Don't mention it. Now you can take me to Rusanova Prospekt."

"Why?"

"It's where the Andrianovs live."

"But I don't know the way," Lysenko said.

"That's okay, I've got a map. After we've seen them, you can then drop me off at the Belorussian station."

He would get a taxi to Sheremetyevo from the same cab rank he'd used earlier on. With just under two hours in hand before the plane to Helsinki departed at 22.50 it would be a close run thing, but he should make the Finnair flight okay.

"To hear you talk, you'd think I was your bloody chauffeur," Lysenko grumbled.

"Stop complaining," Ashton told him. "I'll see you right."

The Mira Prospekt had become the M9 motorway and they had left the outskirts of Moscow behind them as they headed towards Zagorsk. Fortunately, there was no central reservation and very little traffic on the road, two factors which enabled Lysenko to make an illegal U-turn and double back towards the outer suburbs. Eventually, they drove past a street which Ashton managed to locate on the map and the rest was easy. Rusanova Prospekt looked an even grimmer place in the moonlight than when Ashton had first seen it eight hours earlier.

"Are you armed?" he asked Lysenko.

"Why? Are you expecting trouble?"

"The people who moved Elena obviously know where her parents live. They could be up there waiting, which is why I'd like you to come in with me."

"Shit. I just knew this wasn't going to be my night."

Lysenko got out of the car, slammed the door and waited for Ashton to join him before moving off at a brisk pace towards the apartment house. No one was loitering in the entrance hall and they didn't encounter anyone on the fifth floor when they stepped out of the lift. The family hadn't had any unwelcome visitors while Ashton had been away and things looked pretty much the same. Ludmilla was still staring blankly at the flickering TV screen in the corner, and Vera was still on the floor at her grandmother's feet, though she was now fast asleep.

Lysenko decided he would wait in the car while Ashton changed. Konstantin Kirillovich wanted to know how his daughter was and Ashton was forced to lie in his teeth and tell him she was on the mend. But it didn't end there and he found himself answering a stream of questions until he began to wonder if he would ever get away. But finally the old man relented and allowed him to escape into the bedroom. He changed into his suit, packed the down-at-heel gear into the zipper bag, then recovered his wallet, plane tickets, visa and the two British passports which he had hidden under the chest of drawers before slipping into his raincoat.

Despite Konstantin Kirillovich's protests, he insisted on giving the old man fifty pounds in sterling and told him to buy something for Elena. The Judas money did nothing for his guilty conscience and he thought he would throw up when the Russian embraced him with tears of gratitude. It was almost impossible to escape from his clutches and Elena's father kept pummelling him affectionately as he left the flat and while they waited for one of the lifts to respond to the call button.

The apartment block was on the left side of Rusanova Prospekt going east. They had approached it from the opposite direction which had led Lysenko to park the Lada on the wrong side of the road. The temperature was only just above freezing but it seemed the KGB man was impervious to the cold and had lowered the window. He did not turn his head as Ashton approached the car but continued to look straight ahead. Drawing nearer, Ashton could see there were two small entry wounds in the left temple and realised that only the seat belt was holding the Russian upright.

Chapter 14

Ashton slipped a hand through the window, found Lysenko's jugular with a finger and pressed hard, desperate to find a pulse of life. It was, he knew, a forlorn hope, but it was still a shock to have his worst fears confirmed. Blood was still oozing from the two fatal head wounds and the body was warm to the touch. While he was scarcely qualified to give an expert opinion, Ashton was pretty sure death could only have occurred within the last five minutes or so. The killer had used a small-calibre weapon, possibly a .22 automatic. A pistol of that calibre would have made a sharp crack which, to most people, wouldn't sound like a gunshot. It might even have been fitted with a noise suppressor, but clearly none of the residents had heard a thing because no one else was on the scene.

He was in the wrong place at the wrong time and he needed to get the hell out of it before someone raised the alarm and the place was crawling with militiamen. The Metro station was a mile away and he hadn't the faintest idea where the nearest bus stop was or in which direction. Walk away, don't run, don't even hurry until you reach the end of the road and turn the corner; Ashton followed his own advice and set off towards the Metro at a normal pace. After covering rather less than a hundred yards, he had second thoughts and turned back.

Katya Malinovskaya of the Criminal Investigation Division had been instructed to find Elena. It was probably the last order Lysenko had given; if his body was now found outside the block of apartments where the Andrianovs lived, it could create all kinds of problems for them. It was now 21.05 and he had less than two hours in hand to make the flight but with luck he could still do it.

He put the zipper bag down, looked into the car again, saw the

161

keys were in the ignition and quickly removed them. Before he drove the Lada away, he had to move Lysenko out of the way and that wasn't going to be easy. The Russian was about five feet eight and well-built. At a guess, Ashton thought he probably weighed a hundred and sixty pounds and would be difficult to manhandle in the confined space of the Lada. To haul such an inert mass from behind the wheel, across the floor-mounted gear shift and transmission tunnel into the front passenger's seat was out of the question. There was, in fact, only one solution. Conscious that every second counted, he walked round to the back, unlocked the boot, then returned to the dead man, released the seat belt and dragged him out of the car.

Ashton crouched down, got the body across his shoulders in a fireman's lift and carried it to the boot. With his free hand, he raised the lid then, facing half left, he tipped the Russian into the trunk. The body landed awkwardly, the head and left shoulder propped against the spare wheel, one leg twisted under the other and a foot hanging outside the boot. Ashton had suspected that it was going to be a tight fit but he hadn't bargained for the spare taking up so much space. He heaved and shoved the body into a foetal position, a task made even more urgent by the sound of an oncoming vehicle. He tried to close the boot, discovered after the second attempt that part of the trenchcoat Lysenko was wearing was fouling the lock and hurriedly shoved the offending bit of material out of the way. Slamming the lid down for the third and ultimately successful time, he straightened up and was caught in the headlights of a vehicle.

The car was moving very slowly. For several heart-fluttering moments he thought the driver was going to stop but the ubiquitous Lada went on by. It had to be a drunk; he doubted if anyone who was sober would drive as slowly and carefully when there was nothing else on the road.

Ashton picked up his zipper grip, dumped it on the adjoining seat and got in behind the wheel. The tension had got to him and his hands were shaking; to put the key in the ignition became a feat of manual dexterity requiring total concentration and will-power. He gave the engine a little choke, turned it over and got a slow agonised groan from the starter motor. The cold wasn't the only reason why Lysenko had kept the engine running while he was waiting in the car park opposite the Cosmos Hotel. He could also understand why the Russian had been reluctant to escort him up to the Andrianovs' apartment. The damned battery was on its last legs. He tried again and drew a nerve-racking shriek from the starter motor followed by a loud clunk as it jammed in mesh.

Ashton punched the steering wheel with a clenched fist in sheer frustration, then he lowered the window on his side and got out of the car, his anger spent as suddenly as it had exploded. He faced the door, put one hand on the central pillar, gripped the windshield frame with the other and, watched by a small audience which had appeared from nowhere, began to push the Lada backwards and forwards. Saturday night entertainment on Rusanova Prospekt, he thought, come see a man wrestling with a car, beats a dancing bear any day. He kept the seesaw motion going, felt the car move forward as if the gearlever was in neutral and knew he had rocked the starter motor out of mesh. He got back in, offered up a silent prayer and cranked the engine once more. There was very little response, the panel lights faded and the whole electrical system looked as if it were about to die on him. Then, at what had to be the last moment, the engine caught and he nursed it into life. His whole body wet with perspiration, Ashton shoved the Lada into gear and took off. He had covered the best part of four hundred yards before it dawned on him that he was driving on the wrong side of the road.

He had to abandon the Lada, and soon. He was driving around in a car which didn't belong to him; there was a dead major of the KGB in the boot and a zipper bag on the adjoining seat containing a residential permit and internal passport for Peter Pavlovich Zaitsev. He had two UK passports in his jacket, a British Airways plane ticket for Helsinki to London in the name of Ashton and a Finnair round trip to Moscow for Messenger. Offhand, he couldn't think of a worse situation to be in.

Keeping his left hand on the wheel, he reached across, unzipped the bag on the adjoining seat and plucked the street map from the inside pocket of the ski jacket. With some difficulty, he managed to unfold and drape the map over the bag. The transport system of Moscow resembled a bicycle wheel; the hub was the city centre, the spokes were the Metro lines and bus routes, the rim was the outer ring motorway. He needed to get on to one of the spokes before ditching the Lada in a quiet side street. With this in mind, Ashton made two left turns to put himself on course for Sviblovo Metro station, then made a right on what appeared to be a bus route into town.

Lysenko had been shot by someone he had trusted. The killer had approached the car as bold as brass and the KGB man had lowered the window on his side to speak to him. Towards what was to be the end of their conversation, the gunman must have drawn Lysenko's attention to some imagined incident up the road and had then calmly put two bullets into the left temple when Oleg had looked to his front. From there, it was only a short step to conclude that he had been murdered by one of his own men. This deduction prompted Ashton to glance into the rear-view mirror again, but he had no reason to suspect the truck behind him was following him.

Ashton spotted another Metro station up ahead, cruised on past it and turned off left into a poorly lit side street. There was never a problem about finding somewhere to park in the outer suburbs and he pulled into the kerb midway between two street lights, roughly two hundred yards from the main road to his rear. He stuffed the map into the holdall and zipped it up, then checked to make sure all the other doors were locked before he got out of the car. He hadn't seen or heard the other vehicle, which had coasted in behind him, because the driver had switched off the engine, shifted into neutral and killed the main beams and sidelights. As he turned about to lock the door on his side, a harsh voice that could only belong to Sergeant Oroblinsky told him to hold it right there.

"Drop the bag, put both hands on the roof, move back two paces and spread your legs."

Ashton did as he was told. It was suicidal to argue with an armed man who was out of reach. You had to wait until he was close enough to grab and then you had better make damned sure you caught him off guard. And the best way to do that was by pretending that you were scared stiff.

"You'll find almost a thousand roubles in my wallet," Ashton told him in a nervous voice.

"I'm not after your money, it's you I want."

As he stood there leaning against the car listening to Oroblinsky's footsteps drawing near, he could guess exactly what the militia NCO would put in his report. The sergeant would claim he had been on patrol and had observed a Lada saloon with Moscow registration number 08.93.64.11 which he knew belonged to Major Oleg Lysenko of the Criminal Investigation Division. But, no matter what happened in the next few minutes, it was clear that Finnair Flight AY703 to Helsinki was going to leave without him.

"Take your left hand off the roof and put it behind your back." Oroblinsky jabbed a pistol into his neck. "And do it nice and slow."

"What am I supposed to have done?"

"Malicious damage and grand auto theft. That will do for a start."

The sergeant was on his own. He meant to handcuff both wrists while holding a gun to his head, then he would put him into his vehicle before checking out the Lada. He would find Lysenko's body in the boot and call for help on his two-way radio. Ashton could visualise the whole charade, and he acted the moment he sensed Oroblinsky was about to close the manacle around his left wrist. Groaning, as if in pain, he went down on his right knee, swivelled round and sprang up again, punching his right fist into the sergeant's groin. At the same time, he lashed out with his left hand and knocked Oroblinsky's pistol aside before the Russian could put a bullet into his face. As he straightened up, his head caught the sergeant a tremendous blow under the jaw and dropped the NCO unconscious at his feet.

Ashton shook the open manacle from his left wrist, picked up the zipper bag and ran back towards the main road. He hadn't heard a pistol shot but the deafness in one ear told him that Oroblinsky had got one off. That no one shouted after him suggested that none of the residents in the neighbourhood had heard it either.

When he turned the corner at the top of the street, he forced himself to walk the rest of the way to the Metro station. He was out on the street and there were only two people in all Moscow who might be able to provide him with a bolt hole. One was Tony Zale of the US Defense Intelligence Agency, the other was Walter Iremonger. It took him only a few seconds to decide that the American was his best hope in this particular situation. Feeding fifteen kopeks into the turnstile, he rode the escalator down to the platform.

★ ★ ★

The Metropole Hotel was practically a national monument. Designed by William Walcott and built in 1903, it was now a listed building protected by the State. Located at Number 1 Marx Prospekt, the hotel overlooked the Bolshoi Theatre and was only a few steps away from the Kremlin. It had been completely refurbished by the Finns in 1989 and had then stood empty for almost two years because no one could come up with the necessary hard currency to pay the contractors.

Tony Zale had been given a first category room on the second floor with an uninterrupted view of the Kremlin walls from the Corner Arsenal Tower to the Lenin Mausoleum. Furnished on a lavish scale with two double beds, two armchairs, a coffee table, mini bar, TV, dressing table, chest of drawers, writing desk and a fitted wardrobe that took up the whole of one wall, it was symptomatic of the Rolls-Royce treatment the Russians had accorded the entire team from the Agency. No effort, and certainly no expense had been spared to make them feel welcome from the moment their Aeroflot European Airbus had touched down at 15.15 hours on Friday afternoon. Not for them the excruciating delay at Sheremetyevo Airport. While others waited for their baggage to be unloaded and then went through Customs and Passport Control, they had been taken off the plane first, escorted to the Zil limousine waiting for them in the VIP area and whisked at breakneck speed to GRU headquarters on Znamensky Street.

While their bags were being delivered direct to their hotel rooms, they had sat through a welcoming speech followed by a short presentation on the Intelligence gathering capabilities of the GRU since the demise of the Soviet Union. They had then been driven to the Metropole Hotel and given just over half an hour to unpack and change before attending a champagne reception and buffet supper in St George's Hall, a room some two hundred feet by sixty-five on the upper floor of the Great Kremlin Palace. As if to emphasise the importance the Russians attached to the occasion, their hosts had included Boris Yeltsin, former Soviet Foreign Minister Eduard Shevardnadze and Admiral Vladimir Chernavin, Commander in Chief, Combined Fleets of the Commonwealth of Independent States.

This morning, they had attended another presentation, given this time by Defence Minister Marshal Yevgeny Shaposhnikov, which had been no less impressive either in content or delivery even though it had lasted just a few minutes short of three hours. This afternoon, by way of recompense, the GRU had arranged a guided tour of the State Armoury and Novodevichy Convent situated in a loop of the Moscow River near the Lenin stadium and sports complex.

Tonight they had been taken to the Bolshoi Theatre to see a performance of *Swan Lake*; tomorrow promised to be equally energetic with a farewell banquet in the evening which Zale thought was likely to test his constitution to the limit. He was therefore more than somewhat relieved when the pretty little apprentice ballerina who had been his escort had declined his invitation to have a nightcap in the Shatyor Bar.

Zale saw the girl into a taxi and waved her goodbye, then walked into the Metropole and collected his room key from reception.

"For you," the blonde desk girl said and gave him a bottle of Scotch whisky. "From your friend, Mr Messenger."

Zale was about to tell the receptionist that he didn't know anyone called Messenger when he read the greeting card on the bottle. It said: 'Sorry I couldn't lay my hands on a bottle of Old Fettercairn but hope you will find this acceptable.' The signature was an illegible squiggle, but that was unimportant, it was the message that had told him who it was from. He remembered the night he had first met Peter Ashton at the Holiday Inn near Sky Harbor International Airport in Phoenix, Arizona, and how they had sat in his room drinking Old Fettercairn on ice.

"Did my friend leave a message?" he asked.

"He said he would wait for you in the Night-Time Bar."

Zale thanked her, made his way through the plush lobby and found Ashton sitting alone at a corner table near the bar. He was nursing a whisky and looked dog-tired.

"Hi, Peter," he said, joining him. "Have you been waiting long?"

"Just over two hours."

"Yeah? What have you been drinking?"

"Whisky soda."

"You look as though you could do with another." Zale raised a hand, signalled the waiter to come over and ordered two of the

167

same. "By the way, thanks for the present. I bet you didn't get it at Heathrow?"

"You're right. I bought it here in the Beriozka."

Zale helped himself to a handful of cashews from the dish in front of Ashton. "You didn't tell me you were coming to Moscow when I saw you on Thursday," he said casually.

"It was a spur of the moment thing – completely unofficial."

"Best way to travel," Zale said in a neutral voice.

"I'm in deep shit, Tony."

"I figured you were." Zale fell silent while the waiter placed their drinks on the table, waited until he had moved away, then said, "How can I help?"

"Something you should know first. I tangled with a militia sergeant tonight; could be I croaked him the way he went down and cracked his head on the road."

"Any witnesses?"

"I didn't stay around to find out. This sergeant blew away a major in the Criminal Investigation Division and meant to pin it on me."

Zale managed to keep his face impassive. Life, he thought, was never dull with Ashton around. "Okay, that's the bad news, now tell me the good."

Ashton grinned. "They haven't caught me yet," he said. "And I've got the hearing back in my left ear."

"How did you lose it?"

"The sergeant tried to kill me, the pistol he was holding was close to my ear when he squeezed the trigger."

"Well, like I said, how can I help?"

"I need somewhere to bed down for the night."

"You've got it," Zale told him.

He reasoned he wasn't taking such a big risk. The Metropole was run like any hotel in the West. You checked in and out with the front desk, which meant there were no key ladies on each floor to watch your every move. He was unlikely to meet anyone from the Agency on the way up to his room either; apart from his boss who had been corralled by the Military Attaché from the embassy, the others had gone on to a casino after the ballet.

"Are you sure you don't want to think again?"

"I've already done my thinking. We'll go on up to my room whenever you're ready."

168

"I'm ready now," Ashton said, gulping down the rest of his whisky.

Luck was with them all the way. They had the elevator to themselves and the corridor was deserted when he unlocked the door to his room. Once inside, he signalled Ashton to follow him into the bathroom where he immediately flushed the toilet.

"The room is supposed to be clean, guy from the embassy swept it this morning while Defence Minister Shaposhnikov was lecturing us, but the KGB could have bugged it after he'd left."

"Right."

Zale returned to the bedroom, switched on the TV, then began to rearrange the furniture, moving the coffee table away from the window to position it behind the outside wall, which effectively screened it from Marx Prospekt. He fetched two upright chairs, then produced a small black box from his pocket, placed it in the centre of the coffee table and switched it on.

"Great little gismo," he said. "It'll drive any eavesdropper nuts."

"Won't the KGB know you are deliberately jamming them?"

"Sure they will, but what can they do about it? They won't come busting in here, not when it is supposed to be all sweetness and light between Boris Yeltsin and George Bush."

"I'll believe you." Ashton tossed the raincoat he'd been carrying onto the bed nearest the door and sat down at the coffee table.

"You're travelling kind of light, aren't you, Peter?"

"I've got my shaving tackle in one pocket of the trench coat and a clean shirt in the other, which is likely to be pretty crumpled by now. I had a zipper grip but I ditched that before coming here. Couldn't sit around the hotel with that at my feet, it would have looked too suspicious." Ashton reached inside his jacket, took out two British passports, a Russian internal passport and a residential permit. "Now you know why I couldn't go to the British Embassy," he said with a lopsided smile.

"I think you'd better tell me all about it from the beginning."

"It's a little confusing, Tony."

That proved to be a masterly understatement. He had listened to some confusing stories in his time with the Defense Intelligence Agency but Ashton's was in a class of its own. A small-time businessman set up by a hooker who had ended up getting herself iced along with the intended target and the unfortunate key lady. The hotel security man who was supposed to have strangled himself while under interrogation at the Lubyanka, the convenient execution of the two gunmen who had murdered the businessman. The spy in the British Embassy who had been passing information to the hooker and had now vanished from the hospital where she was recovering from a savage beating. And last, but not least, the dedicated KGB major in charge of the investigation who had apparently been shot to death by his own sergeant.

"The official story is that Joyner short-changed some Russian drug baron and was hit as a warning to other foreigners who might be tempted to follow his example."

"And you don't buy it?" Zale said.

"Why would a drug baron recruit Elena Andrianova to spy on one of our commercial attachés? You think the Stock Exchange is quoting the market value of heroin?"

"Could be they needed her for some other activity."

"And Lysenko? Was he shot by some hophead with a grudge who just happened to come across him? And what about Oroblinsky? You don't seriously believe he spotted the major's Lada while driving around town on patrol, do you?"

"Hey." Zale smiled and raised both hands. "I'm on your side, remember?"

"I'm sorry."

"It's okay. The thing I don't understand is why Oroblinsky allowed you to drive away when he could have taken you outside the apartment house."

"I think he was improvising from minute to minute. My theory is that Lysenko had begun to suspect that he had murdered Babkin, the hotel security officer at the Mira Prospekt and, at the very least, had had foreknowledge that Joyner was going to be killed. When Oroblinsky learned that he was looking for Elena Andrianova, he assumed the worst and panicked."

He'd gone to Rusanova Prospekt, only to find that Lysenko had got there ahead of him. Oroblinsky had parked his car out of sight and had walked back to the block of flats in time to see him get into the Lada. It was impossible to guess what thoughts had gone through his mind when Lysenko had just sat there in the car instead of driving away. Events seemed to suggest he had simply acted on impulse; the KGB investigator was a threat and therefore had to go.

"I don't believe it occurred to him that Lysenko was waiting for someone," Ashton continued. "He may have thought the major was keeping the apartments under observation. At any rate, he must have been walking back to his car when he saw me leave the tenement and go over to the Lada. There were three things Oroblinsky could have done. He could have arrested me on the spot but would then have had to explain what he had been doing in the neighbourhood. Alternatively, he could have tipped off the police anonymously, but I might have left the scene before they responded to the phone call. When it became obvious that I intended to drive off in the Lada, he was presented with a third choice and decided to follow me. You could say I handed him the solution to his problem on a plate. No finger of suspicion would be pointed at him if he arrested me after I had left the scene of the crime. All he had to do was plant the murder weapon on me and he would be the hero of the hour."

"You're right," Zale told him. "You are in deep shit."

"Only if the whole KGB is looking for me."

"Whereabouts did you ditch the Lada?"

"In a side street about two hundred yards from Botanichesky Sad Metro station."

"I think maybe I'll take a run out that way and see what is going on."

"No way." Ashton shook his head. "If the KGB are out there in force, you could find yourself in all kinds of trouble."

"So what are you going to do?"

"Take one step at a time," Ashton said. "Right now, I'm going to get my head down."

"Best thing you can do in the circumstances."

"Yes. What time is it?"

"Eleven forty-three."

"Is that all? I feel like I've been awake all night."

Zale moved the furniture back in place and switched off the TV. By the time he had finished, Ashton had stripped off, crawled into the spare bed and was already breathing deeply.

Chapter 15

The hand that gripped his bare shoulder belonged to a police officer. Somehow the KGB had traced him to the Metropole Hotel, to this particular bedroom, and now they were about to arrest him. Ashton knew this instinctively and reacted accordingly because no one was going to put him away for a murder he hadn't committed. How many officers he was up against didn't matter, that was something he would discover later. Right now, he knew exactly where one of them was and could take the guy even though he did have his back to him. He attacked swiftly, rolling over onto his right side while simultaneously striking upwards with the left hand, the fingers rigid and outstretched aiming for the thorax.

"Jesus H. Christ." Zale reared back and jerked his head just far enough out of the way for the hand jab to catch him a glancing blow on the right side of the face instead of the throat. "Jesus H. Christ," he repeated, "take it easy. You could have killed me."

Ashton looked around the room. Curtains drawn back, dull day outside, no KGB arresting officers, just one very alarmed, very angry American who was bleeding from a graze where the nail of his little finger had evidently ripped the skin.

"I'm sorry," he said, "really sorry. What more can I say?"

"Not a lot." Zale dabbed at his cheek with a handkerchief. "You're dangerous, you know that?"

"I must have been having a nightmare."

"You're not married, are you?"

"Me?" Ashton stared at him, astonished. "No, I'm not."

"Just as well. Take my advice, stay single. You could end up strangling your wife after one of your nightmares."

"Give me five minutes to dress and I'll get out of your hair."

"Hey, this is stupid. What are we getting uptight about? It was an accident. Okay?"

"Thanks," Ashton said and really meant it. "Could we have the TV on?" he asked. "It's coming up for eight o'clock and there may be a newscast on one of the channels."

"Sure."

Zale crossed the room, switched on the set and waited for it to warm up before searching through the channels. *Dallas* was on Channel 1 with an orange-coloured Sue Ellen baring her teeth at JR. Adjusting the colour contrast, he then switched to Channel 2 and got the highlights of yesterday's football match between Moscow Dynamo and Kalinin FC. There was a piano recital on 3, testcards on 4 and 5. He pressed the first button on the remote control and went back to Channel 1 again in time to see the credits roll up. The station logo appeared briefly on the screen and was followed by the news.

The lead story featured the bombardment of Split and Dubrovnik on the Dalmatian coastline by elements of the Yugoslav national navy in violation of the January ceasefire agreement which was supposed to have ended the Croatian war. The rest of the foreign news consisted of a brief report on the American primaries, an even briefer mention of the general election in the UK, and the industrial unrest which was beginning to surface in West Germany. The domestic news was mostly doom and gloom about the state of the economy with the Lysenko murder coming right at the very end in a two-minute slot immediately before the weather forecast. There was a still photograph of the Lada in the side street and one of Lysenko taken with other classmates at some graduation ceremony when he was only a senior lieutenant. Listening to the voice-over, Ashton learned that the body had been found in the early hours of the morning following a tip-off from an anonymous informer. The same source had also provided a description of the man he claimed to have seen running away from the scene of the crime.

"Have you seen all you want?" Zale asked as soon as the weatherman appeared on the screen.

"Yes, you might as well switch it off."

"No prizes for guessing the identity of the mysterious informer. Oroblinsky described the trench coat you were wearing pretty well, but he was rather vague about your physical appearance, wasn't he?"

"I think he was protecting himself," Ashton said. "That side

174

street is poorly lit; if he described me too closely, some people might begin to wonder how the anonymous informer could pick out so much detail in the dark. And if I was identified and arrested because of his accurate description, a smart investigator might suspect the mystery man had seen me somewhere before. Once started on that thought process, it wouldn't be long before Oroblinsky was in the frame as the informer."

There was, however, another explanation which Ashton didn't care to dwell on. If he was up against more than just a few disaffected members of the KGB, it could be the TV report was a ruse to lull him into a false sense of security. Oroblinsky knew him by his real name and the First Chief Directorate, the KGB's foreign Intelligence service, had taken several photographs of him last year when he had been playing footsie with one of their officers stationed in Germany. Distribute enough copies of his likeness and it wouldn't matter what name was in the passport he showed the Immigration officers at the airport.

"Something you should be grateful for," Zale told him. "At least you didn't kill the sergeant."

"You suppose the KGB will take that into consideration if they catch me?"

"What are you going to do, Peter?"

"Get myself on another flight – and it'll have to be Aeroflot. The next Finnair to Helsinki is 22.50 hours tonight and that won't connect with the British Airways flight."

"And Aeroflot will?"

"I hope so."

"There's an Aeroflot desk in the lobby. You want me to ring down and find out?"

"Too risky."

Zale checked the hotel directory next to the phone. "I don't have to go through the switchboard. I can dial them direct."

Ashton weighed the risks, the possibility that Zale would be asked for his room number, the dangers of giving a false one coupled with a bogus identity and the domino effect of arousing the curiosity of the airline staff. The latent threats multiplied in his mind and made him indecisive.

"I'd sooner leave it until later and do it myself," he told Zale.

"Sure. You want something to eat? I can have room service send up a large breakfast which you can share. You could hide in the bathroom while it's being delivered."

There was one lesson Ashton had learned from his brief time in the army. When food was on offer, you ate it, because there was no telling when you would get another opportunity to fill your belly.

"Thanks, Tony," he said. "Let's do that. Just give me a couple of minutes to straighten up the bed."

"You've got all of that and more," Zale told him.

The American was talking from experience. Before the orange juice, cereal, bacon, scrambled eggs, grilled sausage, fresh rolls and coffee arrived, Ashton had time to make up the spare bed, wash, shave and get dressed. He also ripped up the residential permit for Peter Pavlovich Zaitsev and flushed it down the toilet together with the return half of his Finnair plane ticket. He did the same with the internal passport after he had borrowed Zale's nail scissors to cut up the semi-stiff cover.

The doomsday predictions which had temporarily paralysed Ashton proved groundless. No one saw him leave Zale's room and the man on the Aeroflot desk couldn't have been more helpful or less inquisitive. Hard currency got him a seat on Flight SU199 departing at 14.30 hours which, because of the time zone difference, arrived in Helsinki at 15.15. Ninety minutes later he would be on a Boeing 737 to Heathrow.

With three hours to kill before he was due to report to Sheremetyevo, Ashton went shopping. Given any choice, he would have preferred to stay off the streets, but it was impossible for him to remain in Zale's room once the American and the rest of the Defense Intelligence team were collected by their Russian hosts. From a stall in Gorky Street, he bought himself a briefcase and then filled it out with a couple of books for the sake of appearances.

Richard Quennell swept through the gates of the British Embassy on Maurice Thorez Embankment, made a U-turn in the drive and came to a halt opposite the main entrance. He had planned to spend that morning at the amusement funfair in Gorky Park with his wife and two children. Unfortunately, a phone call from the duty officer had put paid to all that, much to the vocal disappointment of both boys. On the whole, he did not greatly care for press correspondents; as of this moment, Mr Walter Iremonger was high on the list of those people he cordially loathed.

The duty officer had shown Iremonger into the visitors' waiting room outside the secure area and had been plying the journalist with coffee while they waited for him to arrive. Both men were in good humour, which was more than Quennell could say for himself though he did his best not to look annoyed.

"Nice to see you again, Mr Iremonger," he said with a forced smile. "I believe the last time we met was at the embassy reception to mark the Queen's Official Birthday?"

"You've got a good memory," Iremonger told him.

"I never forget a face, Walter. Now, what's this fairy tale I've been hearing about Elena Andrianova?"

"It's no fairy tale," Iremonger said cheerfully. "She was sacked for spying on Michael Vaughan, the Third Secretary, Commerce."

Quennell chuckled. "I think someone has been pulling your leg, Walter."

"Are you saying she wasn't given her marching orders?"

"Of course I'm not. If you must know, she was sacked for theft."

"I don't believe it."

"Well, I'm sorry if I've ruined your copy, but it happens to be true."

Quennell fancied he sounded convincing and with some justification. While up at Cambridge he had been a highly talented member of the university's amateur dramatic society and his actor's skill had not deserted him.

"According to my source, she was passing information to Nina Golodkinova, the hooker who was found murdered in the same hotel bedroom as Colin Joyner."

"Really?" Quennell dipped his head, one of his stage tricks which was intended to convey mild astonishment. "Well, if you had told me a month ago that she was on speaking terms with a common prostitute, I would never have believed it. However, she hadn't been caught with her hand in the petty cash then."

"Her father claims she was promised a job with the British Council in return for her co-operation."

"Absolute nonsense."

"Last Tuesday night, Elena Andrianova was beaten up by two thugs who wanted to know what she had disclosed to your security officer under interrogation."

Quennell sighed. "That's complete rubbish. There was no interrogation; she was asked to explain why there was an apparent deficiency in the petty cash and she promptly burst into tears and admitted stealing it."

"The thugs gave her four cracked ribs, a dislocated elbow, fractured pelvis and a broken nose," Iremonger continued remorselessly. "Most of these injuries were inflicted as a warning to her to keep her mouth shut. She was admitted to the Piragow Hospital off Lenin Prospekt and was still there yesterday afternoon. Shortly afterwards, word got around that the police were looking for her and she disappeared."

"Perhaps she was discharged from the hospital?" Quennell suggested.

"I rang the Piragow this morning; they say they have no record of an Elena Andrianova being admitted to the hospital on Tuesday night."

"Did you personally visit her while she was in the Piragow?"

"No, I didn't."

Quennell smiled. For the first time, he began to feel he was in control of the situation. "Well, now, Walter," he said, "isn't it possible that the hospital staff were telling the truth?"

"Did you see the news on Channel 1 this morning?"

"We don't watch television," Quennell told him and was conscious of sounding both smug and patronising simultaneously.

"Major Oleg Lysenko of the KGB's Criminal Investigation Division was murdered last night. You remember him, don't you, Mr Quennell? He was the officer in charge of the Mira Prospekt case. Joyner, Golodkinova, Andrianova and Lysenko." Iremonger raised a hand and ticked them off one at a time with his fingers. "The businessman, the hooker, the spy and the policeman, three dead and one missing. Think what a story that will make."

"What exactly are you trying to say, Mr Iremonger?" The reversion to his surname and the icy tone of voice were intended to intimidate the journalist, but they had no effect.

"I'm saying the embassy ought to show a little concern for one of their own. I'm saying you should lean on the KGB to find Elena Andrianova before she ends up in a ditch somewhere with a bullet in her head." Iremonger stood up. "That is one of the points I shall be making when I cable the story."

"Well, that's your prerogative."

Barely able to contain his fury, Quennell escorted the journalist to the entrance and said goodbye, then went upstairs to his office. Iremonger clearly knew a great deal more about the Andrianova case than he did and had made him look a fool into the bargain, which was particularly galling. It was, of course, up to the embassy security officer to discover the identity of the source but the odds were that it was one of the locally employed staff. However, it was pointless spending further time on mere speculation; the important thing now was to ensure London was fully briefed before Iremonger's allegations appeared in the newspapers. Although quite capable of drafting the cable to the Foreign and Commonwealth Office himself, it was politic to consult his superiors. Lifting the phone, Quennell rang the Head of Chancery.

Sheremetyevo Airport on a Sunday afternoon was no different from any other day of the week. As usual, Terminal 2 was heaving with people; as usual, the KGB officers on Passport Control were doing their level best to add to the general chaos. Every document produced for their scrutiny was examined with suspicion so that it was not uncommon for an official to spend three or four minutes looking at a single sheet of paper. When Ashton arrived shortly after twelve forty, they were having fun and games with a planeload of Vietnamese students.

The KGB hated all students. If there was such a thing as a Race Relations Act, they hadn't heard of it. Although they were openly contemptuous of anyone with a black skin, they really had it in for the Vietnamese. According to KGB folklore, they were all thieves, pimps, prostitutes and currency speculators. The Russian taxpayer paid for their education at the Patrice Lumumba Friendship University and they rewarded their benefactors by smuggling icons, Beluga caviar and hard currency out of the country. Consequently, no Vietnamese got past a Customs official without having every item of baggage tipped out onto the counter.

Ashton checked in with Aeroflot, asked for a seat in the non-smoking section, then tagged on to the shortest queue going through Passport Control. But appearances were deceptive; like all the other lines, it too moved slowly, as if the officials were having a competition amongst themselves to see who could take the longest to process the travellers who had elected to file past their particular booth. A full half-hour after joining the queue, Ashton finally arrived in front of a morose-looking junior lieutenant. The Russian examined his UK passport page by page, compared the photograph on the inside with Ashton and then spent an inordinate amount of time studying the third and last copy of the fake visa before adding it to the pile of others he had already collected. He snapped his fingers, demanded the currency exchange form and accepted without question the fake document which purported to show that Ashton had converted twenty-five pounds into roubles with the cashier at the Hotel Intourist in Gorky Street.

Unable to believe his luck, Ashton went on through to the departure lounge. Gradually, his heartbeat returned to something like normal and the butterflies in his stomach died a natural death. He wasted some time in the duty free shop, but didn't buy anything because that would have been a dead giveaway. He ate an ice cream, drank a cup of coffee, bought a copy of *Newsweek* and read it from cover to cover. At 14.00 hours, Flight SU199 was still waiting to be called forward; by 14.15 it was apparent that they wouldn't make their departure time even though the visual display units in the lounge were still showing precisely the opposite.

The word "Delayed" appeared in Russian against Flight SU199 some five minutes after they should have taken off. There was no word of explanation over the public address system and none of the airport staff knew what was causing the hold-up. In mounting tension, Ashton watched the clock, knowing that the time he had in hand between flights in Helsinki was slowly but inexorably being whittled away. The Japan Airlines flight to Tokyo started boarding at Gate 14; shortly after that, Lufthansa LH2670 to Frankfurt was called forward. Other departures appeared on the visual display unit, Lot Airlines to Warsaw, Aeroflot to Berlin, Air France to Paris, but still the word "Delayed" appeared against Flight SU199. Then, suddenly, Gate 9 flashed up to a ragged cheer from the waiting passengers.

There was another ten-minute delay in the waiting area at Gate 9 and the revised departure time suffered yet another setback when the airline staff decided to allow passengers to board as and when they liked instead of calling them forward in groups by row numbers. At 16.25 hours, the TU-154 backed away from the gate and taxied out to the runway. Ten minutes later, they were airborne two hours and five minutes behind schedule.

He was travelling on a forged passport on a Russian plane in Russian airspace, yet it was his own colleagues back in London who posed the greater threat. It was, he thought, one of life's great ironies.

Aeroflot SU199 was less than halfway to Leningrad when British Airways Flight BA797 departed Helsinki for Heathrow.

Hazelwood backed his car out of the garage, went on up Willow Walk to Hampstead High Street and turned left. Driving in London early on a Sunday evening was almost a pleasure; the roads were practically empty and the only hazard was the possibility of being caught for speeding. It was also a pleasure to escape from the so-called quality Sundays with their pessimistic analyses of the economy and the inept election campaign being waged by the Conservative Party. With only the occasional hold-up when the lights were against him, he made good time through Camden, past Euston station and into Woburn Place. The speedometer needle rarely hovering below forty, he continued onto Southampton Row, managed to catch the lights before they changed at the junction with High Holborn and shot across into Kingsway. He followed the one-way circuit around the Aldwych into the Strand and crossed Waterloo Bridge.

Barely twenty-five minutes after leaving the house, he parked the Rover 800 outside Century House and walked inside the building to find the duty officer waiting for him by the security desk with the cable from Moscow.

"Who else has been told about this bombshell apart from the DG?" he asked, plucking the cable from the duty officer's grasp.

"Mr Kelso. He's on the way in now."

"Right. Tell him I'll be in my office."

Hazelwood walked over to the lifts, pressed the nearest call button and took the first vacant one up to the top floor. The cable from Moscow was punctuated with names that were disturbingly familiar and included one which was likely to haunt them for many a long day. Elena Andrianova was the reason why the DG had called a meeting for six fifteen on a Sunday evening and Hazelwood could understand why the Old Man should want Roy Kelso to be present.

Two against one; although it probably wouldn't come to that, Hazelwood didn't like the odds and decided to redress the balance. Unlocking the centre drawer of his desk, he took out his personal telephone directory and looked up the number of Ashton's flat in Surbiton. Convinced he would find him at home, Hazelwood was mildly surprised when Jill Sheridan answered the phone.

"It's Victor Hazelwood here," he told her. "I'm sorry about this but I was hoping Peter would be there."

"He's gone away for the weekend, left straight from the office on Friday."

"Do you have any idea where he went?" he asked.

"Sorry, Victor," Jill said cheerfully, "and before you ask, I don't know what time he'll be back tonight."

"Never mind, I think I can hear someone who may."

"What?"

"Nothing, I was just talking to myself." He crooked a finger at Kelso, beckoning him to come in from the corridor, then apologised to Jill for troubling her and hung up. "Take a seat, Roy," he said. "Maybe you know where we can get hold of Ashton?"

"Why? Has the DG asked for him to be present?"

"No, but I think he may well do so." Hazelwood picked up the cable from Moscow and gave it to Kelso. "I imagine this is going to be a damage limitation exercise. I don't know anything about this Walter Iremonger, but when Peter was on the Russian Desk he made it his business to meet every Moscow correspondent passing through London. Now even if Peter didn't get the opportunity to make his acquaintance, I'm sure he will be able to tell us which newspaper Iremonger works for."

"So that we can have a word with the proprietor?" Kelso shook his head. "I think that would be counter-productive."

"Is that the DG's opinion or yours?"

"Oh, mine."

"Then I think Ashton should be available in case he is needed. I'm not suggesting we lean on anyone to spike the story, merely tone it down. Most newspaper tycoons support the Conservative

Party and I doubt they will want to embarrass the government when the election campaign is going so badly for them."

"You may have a point. May I use your phone?"

"Please do," Hazelwood said.

Kelso rang the duty officer at Benbow House first, then Frank Warren and finally Harriet Egan. There was a testy exchange when the duty officer was tactless enough to remind him that there was nothing in standing orders which said that Ashton was required to leave a contact address when he went away for the weekend. From Warren he learned that Ashton had asked his deputy to stand in for him but hadn't said where he was going. It seemed he had been more forthcoming with Harriet Egan who understood that a friend had lent him a cottage somewhere in Wales.

"Well, that was illuminating," said Hazelwood drily.

"We don't have to have anyone on call," Kelso told him defensively. "We are not an operational department."

"Quite so."

"I just don't understand why the embassy didn't mention the newspaper Iremonger works for in their cable."

"I'll be sure to make that point to Hugo Calthorpe when I phone him," Hazelwood said mischievously.

One of the first off the plane after it had landed at Helsinki, Ashton made straight for the British Airways desk after he had cleared Customs and Immigration. Finnair AY837, which only ran on Sundays, had already left, and he had to settle for a seat on the BA flight departing at 07.30 hours the following day. With Helsinki two hours ahead of British Summer Time, this meant he would arrive at Heathrow at 08.40 hours. It also meant that he would be up to an hour and a half late into the office, but he didn't think that was anything to get excited about.

Chapter 16

It wasn't exactly a fine day for the end of March; dark, low-lying nimbostratus clouds threatened rain which only a Force five to six wind was holding at bay and the sun was nowhere to be seen. The Thames was a cold grey and a lot of garbage was bobbing against one of the piers supporting Blackfriars Bridge, yet the city had never looked better to Ashton. He had been into the lion's den and come out again without so much as a scratch. And he had covered his tracks; he had destroyed Messenger's passport before boarding the BA flight at Helsinki and the stuff he had bought in Moscow had gone straight into the nearest rubbish bin after leaving Heathrow. Feeling good about it, he walked into Benbow House, collected his identity card from the sergeant in charge of the security office on the ground floor with whom he had left it on Friday evening, and went on up to his office.

He removed his trench coat and hung it on the back of the door, then opened the combination safe and placed the wire filing trays on his desk. When he looked round, Harriet Egan was standing in the doorway.

"Hello, Peter," she said quietly. "How was the weekend in Wales?"

"Very enjoyable."

"That's good. Roy Kelso's been looking for you."

"What it is to be popular," he said drily.

"I think you could be the flavour of the week. He rang me at home yesterday evening wanting to know where you were. He sounded rather flustered."

"I see. Any idea what he was so het up about?"

" 'Fraid not. He didn't confide in me."

"Well, I suppose I'd better go and see him before the phone starts ringing."

Ashton picked up the key to his office and started towards the corridor only to receive a shrill summons from the extension on his desk.

"I didn't hear that, did you?" he said, and locked the door behind him. "About those photographs of Neville," he continued when he caught up with Harriet. "Any joy?"

"The National Identification Bureau rang earlier this morning and confirmed that he doesn't have a criminal record."

"Confirmed? You mean I am supposed to know this already?"

"Yes, I told you on Friday."

"I don't remember."

"I expect your mind was on other things," she said coolly, then added, "like Barmouth."

"What's Barmouth got to do with it?"

"I understood you were going to spend the weekend there at some isolated cottage two or three miles from the seaside resort."

Ashton glanced at her sideways, wondered just what she was up to. Like the best lies, the best cover stories were always simple and imprecise. The more complicated the story, the more chance there was of being caught out. He had merely told Harriet he was off to Wales for the weekend. In fact, he wouldn't have said that much if she hadn't made some comment about the overnight bag he was carrying when he'd happened to bump into her at the wrong moment. He could tell her she was mistaken but that would sound defensive, as if he had something to hide, and she was suspicious enough already.

"Did I say Barmouth?" Ashton shook his head in feigned bewilderment. "I must be getting simple in my old age."

"Not you," she murmured as they parted company outside her office.

The asthmatic lifts were as old as Benbow House itself and belonged in the Science Museum. Sometimes they responded to the call button, sometimes they didn't. When the machinery remained obstinately silent, Ashton took to the staircase and went on up to see Kelso. The wintery smile the Assistant Director gave him when he walked into his office was no more than he had expected.

"I trust you enjoyed your weekend in Wales," Kelso said acidly.

"You wanted to see me?"

"I've been trying to get hold of you ever since six o'clock yesterday evening. Frank Warren didn't know where you were, neither did Miss Egan. The DG was not amused."

"What's happened?"

"I haven't got time to explain." Kelso plucked a folder out of his pending tray and thrust it at him. "Read these cables from Moscow and bring yourself up to date, then we'll talk."

There were four cables in all but Ashton only had to read the opening paragraph of the first to get the whole picture. Iremonger had departed from the script they had agreed and had gone after the embassy, accusing the diplomatic staff of callous indifference towards Elena Andrianova. It had the makings of a story that would run and run and could make her a cause célèbre. It was difficult to be sure how the Foreign Office would react under such sustained bad publicity, but there was a real danger that they would be tempted to keep their heads down and do nothing. The ostrich policy had served them well in similar situations in the past.

"Doesn't look too good, does it?" Ashton observed casually.

"Well, of course it doesn't. You see what the embassy says about Iremonger in their second cable? He's an Associated Press correspondent, which means he sends his copy to the AP bureau in London and they peddle it around."

It was one of the reasons why Ashton had chosen him. As an AP man, there was no way the story could be spiked by some friendly newspaper proprietor willing to do the Establishment a good turn. The other consideration which had influenced Ashton was the fact that, since they had never met, Iremonger wouldn't know who he was dealing with.

"This is all your fault," Kelso continued angrily. "We wouldn't be in this mess if you hadn't promised that woman a job with the British Council. You had no right to do that, no right at all. I can't tell you how many times the Director General has heard that complaint from the embassy."

And if he hadn't promised Elena something, they would still be looking for the spy in the embassy. And if she had gone to the British Council, there was a good chance that, once she felt safe, Elena would have told them precisely what instructions she had received from Nina Golodkinova. But nothing would be gained from pointing this out to Kelso when he couldn't prove it.

"Is that it?" Ashton said coldly. "Or is there something else you want to say to me?"

Kelso reared back, his face turning a delicate shade of pink. He bridled, looked as if he was about to ask Ashton who he thought he was talking to, then collapsed like a pricked balloon and tried instead to pass himself off as the efficient and dynamic department head.

"I want a paper from you analysing the various options open to us in this affair."

"How long have I got?"

"I'd like it on my desk before close of play tonight."

The sporting analogy from the cricketing enthusiast whose greatest claim to fame in *Who's Who* was his membership of the MCC.

"Right. I'll go and knock something out for you."

"Take the cables, you'll need them."

"No, I won't," Ashton told him. "They're not worth the paper they're printed on."

Ashton returned to his office, picked up the phone and rang Hazelwood at Century House. Every assistant director had a personal assistant; the one Victor had inherited from his predecessor saw it as her duty to protect him from unnecessary interruptions. He was therefore either on the phone, in conference or busy.

"Tell him it's about a ministerial enquiry," Ashton said.

Although the SIS was less affected by questions raised by Members of Parliament than any other government department, the possibility of having to answer one was still enough to make people sit up and take notice.

"You're through," she said, and Hazelwood came on the line.

"Let's go to secure," Ashton said and pressed the button on the cradle. "I have a green light," he added, glancing at the box on the floor. "How about you?"

"The same." Hazelwood paused briefly, then said, "I can guess why you are calling."

"Well, you hardly need a crystal ball for that, Victor. And it shouldn't surprise you to hear that Kelso is flying so high he needs oxygen. Naturally, his reaction to the furore is to order me to write a paper on how to avoid a bad press. Hopefully, the Russian Desk is taking a more positive line?"

188

"We are doing what we can."

"You want to tell me precisely what that means, Victor?"

"It means I have cabled Hugo Calthorpe instructing him to inform Moscow's Chief of Police of our concern. Although it will have to be done circuitously, believe me, Major General Gurov will be left in no doubt that we expect him to find Elena Andrianova. Furthermore, she had better be in a reasonable state of health."

"If we don't find a safe haven for the whole family – "

"That's up to the Russians," Hazelwood said, interrupting him.

"She won't tell them anything."

"Maybe so, but there is a limit to what we can do."

"No. No, you're wrong, Victor. The Foreign Office can get the family out of Russia if they want to."

"How?"

"By offering them medical treatment for Ludmilla Andrianova. She has a heart condition."

There was nothing medical science could do for Elena's mother but the Foreign Office wouldn't know that until the embassy's physician had examined her. What he said in his report wouldn't matter. The idea was to stir the embassy up and make it extremely difficult for Her Majesty's plenipotentiaries to wash their hands of the family.

"Let me think about it, Peter."

"By all means. The thing is, Victor, we don't have too much time."

"The police have got to find her first," Hazelwood reminded him and then hung up.

Beneath His Excellency the Ambassador Extraordinary and Plenipotentiary there was, in descending order of importance, one minister and two counsellors who were respectively Head of Chancery and Commerce. Hugo Calthorpe was also shown as a counsellor on the embassy's staff list, but no appointment appeared against his name. As the senior First Secretary, Richard Quennell was therefore some way down the pecking order, though few outsiders who chanced to meet him at an official reception were aware of this. There were times when Hugo Calthorpe felt that Richard Quennell wasn't aware of it either.

The way the younger man had spoken to him on the telephone a short while ago to ask if he could spare him a few minutes had been reminiscent of a summons from the Ambassador himself. Indeed, until he had poked his head round the door, Calthorpe had wondered if he had expected him to run along to his office.

"I've been thinking about Iremonger," he began.

"Who hasn't?" Calthorpe said wearily. "I'm getting tired of hearing his name."

"It was something he said to me concerning his sources. I'm prepared to believe he learned of Elena Andrianova's dismissal from some member of the locally employed staff. It's even conceivable this informer knew she had admitted bugging Vaughan's office, but it was her father, Konstantin Kirillovich, who confirmed it."

"I don't remember hearing that when you briefed us all yesterday morning," Calthorpe said.

"You're right, I didn't say anything of the kind because the significance of what he claimed Andrianov had told him has only just occurred to me. According to Walter Iremonger, her father said Elena had been promised a job with the British Council in return for her co-operation."

Quennell leaned back in his chair, crossed his right leg over the left with the ankle resting on the kneecap, then clasped both hands around the other knee and looked at him expectantly. Calthorpe got the impression that he was expected to make some comment.

"I'm afraid I'm not with you, Richard," he said presently.

"That's my fault," Quennell said in a voice that implied otherwise. "I should have come right out with it. The fact is, I only believe half of what Elena is supposed to have told her father. I just don't think she would have said that she had been promised a job with the British Council if she confessed to being a spy."

"I see what you mean." There was, Calthorpe thought, only one possible explanation. Iremonger had attributed his information to Konstantin Kirillovich in order to protect the identity of the real source.

"Think about it, Hugo. Who was it made such a promise?"

"You're surely not suggesting Ashton is the mysterious source, are you?" Calthorpe asked sharply.

"Let's say I have my suspicions."

"Well, I'd keep them to yourself if I were you, Richard."

"Are you suggesting we close our eyes to the possibility?"

"No, I'm merely concerned how such an allegation could affect your career if it weren't substantiated. Somehow you have got to prove Ashton supplied the information to Iremonger, which won't be easy. On reflection, it's probably impossible."

"Yes, I imagine it would be extremely difficult." Quennell got to his feet. "I'm glad we had this chat, Hugo. I've always valued your advice."

"It's kind of you to say so," Calthorpe told him.

Neither of them meant it. Quennell had never sought his advice before and hadn't done so now. Furthermore, he was one of the most career-conscious men Calthorpe had ever met and he would never do anything which might prejudice his advancement. Why Quennell had therefore seen fit to point an accusing finger in Ashton's direction was past his understanding, but it wasn't something he could safely ignore.

Calthorpe took out a sheet of crested notepaper, uncapped his fountain pen and wrote a brief demi-official letter to Hazelwood, repeating the conversation he had had with Quennell. Although the letter would be despatched to London in the diplomatic bag, he nevertheless double-enveloped it. On the inner envelope he wrote: "Personal for the Assistant Director Eastern Bloc Department", while the outer one was addressed to "The Secretary Box 850".

In Calthorpe's view, forewarned was forearmed. It simply did not occur to him that he had done precisely what Quennell had hoped he would.

The slow measured footsteps Ashton could hear in the corridor did not belong to the duty officer. For one thing, they were too light, for another, the duty officer had completed the security check of the offices on the third floor ten minutes after the last member of the clerical staff had departed at five thirty. He had stayed on after normal working hours because Harriet Egan had asked to have a word with him in private. Now it seemed she was in no great hurry to keep the appointment.

"Is that you out there, Harriet?" he called.

"Yes, it is."

She appeared round the door and walked into his office looking composed, unruffled and very elegant in a plain charcoal-grey two-piece with a cutaway jacket over a deep red silk blouse. It was the same outfit she had been wearing that morning but he'd had other things on his mind then and hadn't paid much attention.

"Take a seat," he said.

"Thanks." She pulled up the one and only spare chair and sat down, right leg forward of the left. He wondered if the posture had anything to do with the fact that the charcoal-grey skirt was shorter than the usual length she favoured and barely covered her knees. He wondered too why Harriet should want to conceal her legs.

"I'm all ears," he said.

"I assume you are still interested in George Neville?"

"You bet I am."

He couldn't think why she should have asked for a private word if they were simply going to talk about the London-based representative of Trans Globe Services Incorporated. He had feared that Harriet was going to inform him that she wanted to terminate her secondment to the SIS and intended to ask Kelso to support her request. It wouldn't have surprised him if she had; they hadn't exactly hit it off, and Harriet had indicated more than once that she wasn't happy about some of the assignments he had given her.

"George Neville comes from my part of the world, more or less. He was born in Grimsby on the eighth of March 1948, the youngest of five children. His father worked on the fish docks, his mother went out cleaning in between her various pregnancies. Neville senior was a heavy drinker and a bully. He would come home drunk on a Friday night and beat up his wife just for the hell of it. One Friday night when George Neville was six years old, he left his favourite pub drunker than usual, staggered out into the road and was killed by a hit-and-run driver. No one in the family mourned his passing."

Ashton picked up a Biro and made a note of Neville's date and place of birth on his millboard. When Harriet had done an in-depth profile of Colin Joyner, she had presented him with a neatly typed report. This time around, it seemed he was expected to make his own notes. Thus far, this had not been a particularly onerous task and there was little chance of him suffering from writer's cramp. The family background, interesting though it was, didn't actually put the spotlight on George Neville. It wasn't really any help to know that one brother had been killed in Korea while the other had died of leukaemia in 1958, or that of the two sisters, one was still living in the same house in Grimsby and the other in Durban, South Africa.

"George Neville left school at the age of fifteen, joined the Royal Signals as a boy soldier, then claimed a free discharge two months later. Subsequently, he was employed as a shop assistant, petrol pump attendant, deck hand and a labourer on a building site before emigrating to Australia. In 1969 he joined the Australian Army and served in Vietnam. He returned to this country in 1990 and took a lease on a furnished flat in Lancaster Gardens, just off the Bayswater Road."

Ashton wrote swiftly. He still couldn't fathom why Harriet had waited this long to give him the information when it must have been in her possession when she saw him that morning. Nor could he think why she had been pacing up and down the corridor before he'd called her into his office. What she had told him now was very helpful but it hadn't been necessary to do anything underhand to obtain the information. There was, in short, no reason for her to be so secretive about the end result that she could only disclose it to him in private.

"The strange thing is, Neville has made no attempt to contact his sister in Grimsby. He hasn't written, phoned or been to see her. Indeed, she wasn't aware he had returned to this country."

"That is odd."

"What is going on, Peter?"

Ashton looked up from the notes he had been making on his millboard. "Search me. What else have you dug up on George Neville?"

"I am talking about last Thursday evening when I was the duty officer and you were hiding in Frank Warren's office."

"I was doing what?" he spluttered and gave a fair impression of choking with laughter.

"Hiding in Frank's office," she repeated calmly.

"Nonsense. I had just come out of the men's washroom when we bumped into one another in the corridor."

"I saw you in his office. You were standing on the right side of the door with your back to the wall. The lights were on and I saw your reflection in the window – it acted as a mirror."

The only thing to do was keep on denying it. "I'm sorry, Harriet, you are mistaken."

"I know I'm not," she said in a level voice. "And I can guess what you were after in that security cabinet."

"Oh, so now I'm a burglar."

"Frank Warren told me what was in there – blank passports, identity papers, travel documents for every country in Eastern Europe."

"When did you and Frank have this little chat?"

"While you were in Moscow."

Ashton stared at her, his mouth suddenly dry, his heart pumping faster. "While I was in Moscow?" he echoed.

"With Mr Hicks."

"You mean before you officially joined us?"

"But of course. How many times have you been to Moscow?"

She might have kept her voice light and made a joke of it but the fencing was over and in her own quiet way, Harriet was telling him that she knew he'd been back. Whether she could prove it was another matter.

"Have a guess," he said, challenging her.

"I'm not very keen on guessing games."

"Neither am I." Kelso sauntered into the office. "That's something we have in common, Harriet." He smiled at them both in turn. "I'm not interrupting anything, am I, Peter?" he asked.

"Nothing that can't wait," Ashton assured him and stood up. He wondered how long Kelso had been lingering out in the corridor and, more importantly, how much of their conversation he had overheard.

"Well, never mind, this won't take a minute." Kelso advanced farther into the room to return the paper Ashton had submitted to him. "This appreciation of yours is all very well as far as it goes," he continued, "but how do we counter the accusations this Iremonger person has levelled at the Foreign Office?"

"That's their problem, not ours," Ashton said and sat down again. "Our job is to convince the KGB that Mr Yeltsin is going to be very cross with them if they don't find Elena Andrianova."

"I don't think the DG will be entirely happy to take such a hard line. He'll want a more flexible response." Kelso sidled round the desk and stood next to him, his index finger indicating the comments he had scrawled in red ink at the foot of the page. But his eyes weren't on the paper; they were focused surreptitiously on Harriet's exposed thigh. She too had stood up when he'd entered the room and had not been too careful when she had sat down again. The skirt had ridden well above her knees to reveal a tantalising glimpse of black lace. "As you can see, I've made one or two suggestions, Peter," he said, clearing his throat. "Perhaps you would rehash your paper and have it retyped for my signature first thing tomorrow?"

"No problem."

"Good. Well, I'll say goodnight and leave you two to get on with whatever it is you're doing."

Some people know how to make an exit; Kelso was one of those who didn't. He slithered rather than walked out of the room.

"What an unpleasant little man," Harriet murmured.

"He's not my favourite Assistant Director, but I'm told he grows on one." Ashton smiled. "Like poison ivy," he added.

Harriet did not return the smile; instead, she asked him when he was going to answer her question.

"What question?"

"Were you in Moscow last weekend?"

"You don't want to know," he told her.

"Oh, but I do."

"You'll be sorry."

"You let me be the judge of that."

"Well, okay, I was there – illegally I might add."

Harriet closed her eyes briefly. "I'm not going to ask you what you were doing there."

"Good. It might give you nightmares."

"And you were right – I am sorry you told me."

"So what are you going to do about my confession?"

"Nothing. I'm going to forget I asked."

"Why?"

"Because Clifford Peachey, my guide and mentor at MI5, implied you were a good bet. And also because I think you may be on to something. There are a couple of things I haven't told you about George Neville. He was captured by the Viet Cong in August 1971 shortly before the Australian and New Zealand governments announced they were going to withdraw their forces from Vietnam. He remained a prisoner of war until February 1973 when he was released with the first batch of American captives following the agreement to end hostilities."

"How do you know all this?"

"Clifford Peachey obtained the information from the Australian Defence Department in Canberra. The other thing is that there is a huge blank in his life between 1976 when he left Australia purportedly for San Francisco, and 1990 when he returned to this country."

"Be interesting to know how, where and when he met Colin Joyner."

"I imagine it would," Harriet said.

Ashton flipped through his desk diary. "Fancy a day out on Wednesday?" he asked.

"I wouldn't mind. Where are we going?"

"The Training School outside Petersfield. I'm due to give them the once-over."

"And that's close to Liphook where the widow lives."

"Exactly." Ashton stacked the wire filing baskets one on top of the other and locked them away in the safe. "Time we called it a day and went home," he told her.

Ashton put on his trench coat and walked Harriet back to her office, then waited while she slipped into her Burberry raincoat. "Fancy a drink?" he asked as they went on down the corridor towards the lifts.

"Not tonight, another time perhaps."

"Sure." Ashton pressed the call button. "Did old Clifford really give me a good chit?" he asked.

"More or less." A faintly mischievous smile appeared at the corners of her mouth. "Actually, I asked him if you were a good bet and he said not as far as I was concerned."

Chapter 17

Ashton said goodbye to the driver and walked into the booking hall, then waited for the Rover 800 from the Training School, which had dropped him outside the entrance to Petersfield station, to move off before promptly leaving again. Life was getting to be a tiny bit complicated. He had left the flat in Surbiton that morning, motored down to Petersfield in his Vauxhall Cavalier and had subsequently handed the car over to Harriet Egan after meeting her off the fast train from Waterloo. Ten minutes after she had departed for Liphook, the Rover 800 from the Training School had arrived to pick him up.

There were no secret documents to speak of at Amberley Lodge and he had banked on completing the security check long before noon, but he hadn't allowed for the hospitality of the permanent staff. They didn't get too many visitors from either Benbow House or Century House and if they couldn't persuade him to stay for lunch, there was no way he was going to escape without having several drinks with them in the bar. As a result, he reckoned Harriet must have been waiting a good hour for him in the station yard. As he walked towards the Vauxhall Cavalier, he imagined she would not be best pleased with him, a supposition he knew to be correct when she got out of the car and he saw the expression on her face.

"You drive," he told her, then walked round to the nearside and got in.

"It's like that, is it?" she said, stony-faced.

"Like what?"

Harriet closed the door, buckled the seat belt and cranked the engine into life. "I don't need a Breathalyser to know you're probably well over the limit."

"You're right, I have had a couple of drinks . . . well, maybe three. It was difficult to refuse their hospitality.''

He had needed that extra drink after telephoning Hazelwood from the Commandant's office and learning that there was still no news of Elena Andrianova. Either the KGB weren't trying too hard to find her or she had vanished without trace.

"You could have had tomato juice."

"I hate tomato juice," he told her, then, changing the subject, asked if she had had anything to eat.

"I'm not hungry," Harriet informed him.

"Are you just saying that because you're annoyed with me?"

"My name isn't Jill Sheridan," she said meaningfully. "Now do you want to know how I got on?"

"Yes, tell me."

"The Joyners certainly believe in seclusion. Finding their house wasn't easy and when I eventually did, the lady wasn't at home."

"That's a pain."

"I have a feeling she hasn't been around for several days. When no one answered the door, I peeped through the letter box and saw there were quite a few letters and more than one newspaper on the doormat."

"I think I'd like to take a look at the house."

Harriet shifted into gear, released the handbrake and drove out of the car park that fronted the station. "I had a feeling you might say that," she told him.

Fitzroy Court was roughly a mile south of Liphook and six hundred yards back from the main road up a narrow unadopted lane that led to nowhere. The house was set amongst trees on high ground which offered peep views of the golf course. A ten-feet-high privet hedge either side of the wrought-iron gates afforded additional privacy for the Joyners. A gravel drive led up to the house and doubled back on itself encircling an uneven dome-shaped lawn that hadn't been cut since the end of the growing season. Successive owners had added to Fitzroy Court, building on a conservatory and a games room as well as another wing so that the roofline was a series of peaks and troughs.

"Late Edwardian-cum-Thames Valley stockbroker," Harriet said, identifying the styles of architecture for him.

"Is that an expert opinion?"

198

"I worked for an estate agent during the long vacs from university."

"I'm impressed."

"Don't be; all I did was despatch property brochures to would-be buyers." Harriet got out of the car, waited for him to join her, then pointed to the red metal box on the wall above the porch. "As you can see, the burglar alarm was fitted only recently."

"What have we got up there under the eaves? Television cameras?"

"If they are, they've been partially dismantled. However, I did find evidence of an infra-red intruder system in the grounds; there are a number of floodlights under the front hedge and in various bushes around the back which automatically illuminate the house if anyone should break the electronic fence."

The land behind the house sloped away towards the golf course in the distance. The garden was mostly lawn with clumps of rhododendrons scattered about in haphazard fashion. The dilapidated gazebo and dried-up ornamental pond choked with stinging nettles were sad reminders of bygone days when the garden had been well cared for.

Ashton continued on round the house until he reached the gravel drive again, then veered off to have a look at the large detached double garage. Both up-and-over doors were locked and the two windows at the back didn't open. They hadn't been cleaned in light years either, and the interior ledges were covered with dead flies, but despite the dirt and grime it was possible to see inside. Beneath the windows, a workbench took up the whole of the end wall and various garden implements hung from nails driven into the breeze blocks on the left side of the garage. There was also a Suffolk Punch lawnmower, an extending ladder and a lot of empty space.

"Well, we know the Joyners were a two-car family," Ashton said, looking at the sump stains on the concrete floor. "If she went off somewhere with one of them, what did she do with the other vehicle?"

"Perhaps she gave it to her daughter?" Harriet suggested.

"That's the most likely explanation." Ashton returned to the front of the house and peered into the letter box just as Harriet had done when she'd called at the house earlier on. "Looks as if there are three copies of the *Daily Express* on the mat."

"Are there? I didn't stop to count them."

"She cancelled the milk but not the papers."

"It was possibly an oversight," Harriet said.

"Or she was in a tearing hurry; left a note for the milkman in one of the empties but didn't have time to call in at the newsagents."

"Why couldn't she have rung them, Peter? They are bound to be on the telephone and it wouldn't have taken her more than a couple of minutes."

"Maybe she did, maybe they were engaged or the newsagent asked her to call in or confirm the instructions in writing. Your guess is as good as mine. The fact is, she didn't have to do anything about the newspaper delivery."

"What?"

"First thing a burglar looks for is milk on the doorstep because that tells him no one is at home. But the papers come straight through the letter box and end up on the floor because there's no wire basket on the inside to catch them."

There was one further possibility. Frances Joyner might not have thought it worthwhile to cancel the *Daily Express* if she planned on only being away for a day or so.

"Are we finished here?" Harriet asked.

"Yes, we might as well go on back to the office."

"Who's driving?"

"You still are," he told her.

They passed no one in the lane and for once there was a clean break in the traffic when they rejoined the A3 trunk road and headed towards London. Harriet's stomach began to complain when they were on the Guildford bypass and kept on rumbling despite repeated claims that she had had a good breakfast and definitely wasn't hungry. Under cross-examination it transpired that her idea of a good breakfast was a glass of orange juice and one slice of dry toast. It took a bit of doing but he finally managed to persuade her to pull into the Happy Eater service station three miles south of the M25 orbital motorway. After Danish pastries and coffee, Ashton rang Trans Globe from one of the pay phones outside the restaurant.

"Why are you ringing them?" Harriet asked.

"Out of curiosity, and I'm not getting a reply. Okay, I know there could be several rational explanations. Neville could be away on business and his secretary off sick. Debbie Roxburgh could have handed in her notice a week earlier than she had intended and quit last Friday instead of this coming one. And it's possible the Brewer Street Bureau might not have found a suitable replacement yet. But . . ."

"Something tells me we are going to Victoria."

"No, I'll drop you off at the nearest Tube station."

"Not on your life. I'm coming with you."

Calthorpe had to remind himself that Michael Vaughan was only a few weeks away from his twenty-sixth birthday. Except for his fair hair, which was already receding and going thin on top, the Third Secretary, Commerce looked incredibly young for his age. He had read Politics, Philosophy and Economics at New College, Oxford, and had walked away with a first, a distinction he found hard to forget. A small man full of bounce and exceedingly pleased with himself, he never missed an opportunity to allude to this crowning achievement whenever he met anyone for the first time. Calthorpe presumed that immature was an adjective which readily sprang to mind once a year when the counsellor in charge of the commercial attachés was faced with the task of writing his annual confidential report. In his capacity as Head of Station, Moscow, Vaughan was the last person he would have considered for even the most routine Intelligence work, but for this particular task he was the ideal choice.

"The KGB have just found Elena Andrianova," Calthorpe announced abruptly when the junior Commercial Attaché reported to his office.

"Where?"

"In the Piragow Hospital."

"But I thought the hospital had denied all knowledge of her?"

"They did, and the hospital authorities still maintain they have never heard of Elena Andrianova. However, it seems their records show that a young woman called Elena Fedichkina was admitted with similar injuries on Tuesday the twenty-fourth of March."

"Fedichkina was her married name."

"Exactly, Michael."

"But they've got to be lying, haven't they? I mean, why would

Elena have given them her married name when she was in the process of divorcing her husband?" Vaughan's face brightened visibly as a more pleasurable thought occurred to him. "I wonder how Walter Iremonger likes having egg on his face?" he mused. "Serves him right, after what he said about us and our lack of concern." The smirk faded a little. "I take it Iremonger is aware of this development, Hugo?"

Calthorpe nodded. Quennell had lost no time in passing the news on to him and had even extracted a reluctant apology from the AP correspondent. But the Ambassador wasn't satisfied with that, he wanted a good press. His desire to show the world that the embassy had a caring face was the reason why the SIS had been allowed to borrow Vaughan.

"The bloody cheek of that man. To hear him talk, anyone would think Elena Andrianova was a model of propriety instead of a contemptible, money-grubbing spy."

"That's all water under the bridge now, Michael. The Ambassador wants you to see Elena and find out how she is."

"Me visit Elena in hospital?"

"Why not? She worked for you."

"That's all very well but – "

"It's a public relations exercise," Calthorpe said impatiently. "The press corps have been giving the embassy a hard time and you are going to pour oil on troubled waters and similar such clichés. However, your real job is to find out what the hell is going on. I want to know if there is any truth in the hospital's version of events, but don't ask Elena any direct questions. Use the indirect approach, make a lot of small talk about the number of visitors who have been to see her and gradually turn the conversation around to her husband. If she really was admitted under her married name, he should have been one of the first people to visit her in hospital. You see what I'm getting at?"

"Yes, Hugo, you've explained it very succinctly."

"Good." Calthorpe pushed a slip of paper across the desk. "Here's a list of other things I want to know. Think you can handle it?"

"I'm sure I can." Vaughan glanced at the memo, folded it in half and slipped it into the breast pocket of his suit.

"Oh no." Calthorpe wagged a finger at him. "You don't walk out of my office with that in your jacket. You sit down here and commit the list to memory, then I want to see you destroy it. Okay?"

"Understood, Hugo." Vaughan took out the list, carefully read it twice, then fed the slip of paper into the secret waste destructor. "The KGB weren't exactly quick off the mark, were they?" he said when the machine stopped whirring. "I mean, Iremonger tells us on Sunday that she had vanished from the Piragow and it takes them until today to discover she is still there but under a different name. Do you suppose they held back to give the hospital authorities time to cook the books?"

"Answering a question like that is like trying to complete a jigsaw puzzle knowing that a lot of the pieces are missing. It's possible Elena Andrianova was moved from hospital to hospital, but she's unlikely to tell you so straight out. It's her demeanour you have to look out for, how she reacts when you ask her about the sort of medical treatment she has been receiving."

"Don't worry, Hugo, I'll watch her like a hawk."

"Good." Calthorpe nodded dismissively. Then said, "Don't go there empty-handed, take her some little gift."

"I was going to," Vaughan told him plaintively from the doorway.

Calthorpe almost called him back. He wanted to know what protection, if any, the KGB were providing for her, then decided that immature though he was, Vaughan was bright enough to notice what security measures were in force without a special briefing from him. Besides, the whole Andrianova affair was fast becoming an uncharted minefield. It was all very well for Hazelwood back in London to urge him to lean on the KGB but he wasn't in the firing line. On Monday, he had contacted Major General Gurov to persuade the Chief of Police to find Elena Andrianova only to learn that the Criminal Investigation Division had been looking for her since Saturday evening on Major Oleg Lysenko's instructions.

The London Streetfinder showed there were two car parks within walking distance of Arlington House, one near the Victoria coach station in Semley Place, the other off Buckingham Palace Road. With Ashton doing the map reading, they tried each in turn, found they were both chock full and were forced to cruise the back streets looking for a vacant space at the kerbside. Three-quarters of an hour and a gallon of 4-star later, Harriet managed to squeeze the Vauxhall Cavalier into a slot between a Volvo 740 and a Toyota Carola.

"I couldn't have done that," Ashton told her.

"Who are you kidding?"

"No, I mean it, you only had about a foot to play with."

"What is this? A be-kind-to-Harriet-Egan day?"

"Something like that."

Ashton checked the map again before they set off for Arlington Gardens but there were no short cuts and it turned out to be a bit of a route march. At four o'clock in the afternoon, the seven-storey office block was scarcely a hive of activity, which meant the usually busy commissionaire in the lobby wanted to know if he could help them.

"Thanks all the same," Ashton told him, "but I've been here before and know the way."

He ushered Harriet into the lift, pressed the button for the fourth floor as though they were going to see Jerome, Jerome and Bowker, Solicitors and Commissioners for Oaths, then walked the rest of the way up to the top floor. Both offices rented by Trans Globe were locked.

"What now?" Harriet asked him.

"I'd like to have a look inside. Trouble is, both doors look pretty solid."

"I know this is April Fool's Day but you're not thinking of breaking in, are you?"

"Do you have a better idea?" he asked. "You don't think the landlord will lend us a key, do you? And don't tell me to get a search warrant because, apart from the fact that I can't show just cause, the SIS isn't a law enforcement agency."

"This is important, is it?"

"In a word – yes."

"All right, you stand guard."

Harriet went through the contents of her handbag, found a couple of hairpins, then opened her purse and took out the Barclay card. She straightened the hairpins, twisted them together and inserted the crudely fashioned skeleton key into the lock. The piece of plastic had more than one use; slipping the credit card between the door and the frame, she worked it around the lug while agitating the skeleton key with her left hand. At the critical moment, she gave the door a gentle nudge with a knee and sprang the lock.

"I can see you've had a liberal education," Ashton said.

The outer office where he had met Debbie Roxburgh had been stripped bare, so had the inner sanctum where Neville had worked. Everything had gone; desks, chairs, filing cabinets, typewriters, VDUs, printer, computer terminals and fax machine. A couple of lonely telephones on the window ledge and a sheet of scuffed paper on the floor provided the only evidence to show that the rooms had once been occupied by Trans Globe Services.

"I don't like it," Harriet said. "Let's get out of here before someone comes by and notices us."

"Right." Ashton bent down, picked up the sheet of paper and turned it over. "Who the hell are Pacific Northwest Oil and Gas?"

"I don't know. Does it matter?"

"The head office is in Seattle, Washington."

"For goodness' sake, let's go," Harriet said with even more urgency.

"I'm right with you." He folded the paper in half, slipped it into his jacket, then followed Harriet out of the office and closed the door quietly behind him. "We don't know too much about Trans Globe, do we?"

"Not a lot; Clifford Peachey is still working on it."

"I wonder if they are part of some conglomerate like Pacific Northwest Oil and Gas?"

Harriet pressed the call button for the lift. "Have you got anything to connect them other than a blank sheet of crested notepaper?" she asked.

"No. However, I know someone who could find out." He would call Tony Zale, but not over an open line. "I'll have to use the secure satellite link at Century House," he said, thinking it through.

Harriet stepped inside the lift and pushed the button for the ground floor. "What's that you said?"

"Nothing. I was talking to myself. Do you think you could trace Debbie Roxburgh? I doubt the Brewer Street Bureau would give me her address but I reckon you could probably worm it out of them."

"I'll give it a shot. What do you want from Debbie if I do run her to ground? The date she left Trans Globe, what happened to all the office furniture and where did Neville go?"

"You've got it," Ashton told her. "I'd also like you to check with British Telecom to see if Neville paid the phone bill before he moved on. Perhaps you can find out who owns Arlington House and ask them what sort of agreement they had with Trans Globe. Give Beresford and Son a ring and try to discover whether they have sent their bill for Colin Joyner's funeral on to Harold Raeburn and Associates yet."

"This is getting to be quite a shopping list," Harriet said.

Ashton had only just begun. He wanted to know why Neville had chosen Harold Raeburn and Associates and what MI5 made of the People's Law Centre. He rattled off the points as he walked Harriet Egan back to the car, and didn't let up when he took over the wheel and drove her to Benbow House by way of Victoria Street, the Embankment and Blackfriars Bridge. By the time he got around to the problem of how to find out where Mandy Joyner lived, she had already filled two complete pages in her pocket diary.

In bold capitals, Zale wrote the words "FIRST DRAFT" at the top of the page, followed by "Yugoslavia – an assessment of the potential cost of military intervention in human terms", which he then carefully underlined. He assumed that somewhere, someone had been tasked to write the same paper in fiscal terms. The money man had accurate statistical data at his fingertips. There were tables to show how much it would cost to move various combinations of combat and logistic units into an operational theatre x, y or z miles from the home base and the daily tonnage required to maintain them in the field. It didn't matter what force level was committed to what theatre by the Executive with the approval of Congress, the financial wizards could produce a pretty accurate estimate of the cost in terms of dollars and cents.

There were no such tables to enable him to calculate the cost in terms of human lives. You had to take into account the terrain, the morale of the Serbian irregulars, their standard of training, available resources and a hundred other imponderable factors. Historical precedent was the only thing Zale could draw on and the library had provided him with enough material to open a branch of his own. His desk was buried under hardbacks, old War Department papers and photocopies of *Wehrmacht* After Action Reports, courtesy of the German Military-Historical Research Office.

He was sitting on a mass of information and a lot of it was conflicting. There were papers to prove that up to forty Axis divisions had been bogged down in Yugoslavia and equally authentic documents which showed that in 1943, only six German divisions had been employed on anti-partisan operations. And of these divisions, two had been Croatian and a further three had been under strength and manned by elderly, unfit reservists. Making some sense out of that lot was, in Zale's opinion, a job for a historian not a Senior Analyst, Special Intelligence. It most certainly was not the sort of job he'd expected to end up on his desk when he had returned from Moscow.

Zale looked at the rough notes he had already completed, then checked his wristwatch and decided it was time he had a bite to eat. He wasn't hungry, but any excuse would do if it meant he could postpone the awful moment when he would have to commit his thoughts on the Yugoslavian crisis to paper.

"Telephone."

The abrasive voice with the New Jersey accent could only belong to the once-widowed, twice-divorced Mrs Bernice Krueger.

"Telephone," she repeated in an even louder voice, then added, "UK satellite link."

Zale looked up. "For me?" he asked, and knew it was a pretty dumb question because all the other analysts had gone to lunch.

"I don't see anyone else around here," Mrs Krueger told him.

The section only had two cipher-protected telephones with access to the UK satellite link. One terminal was in the Chief Analyst's office while the one for general use was located in the adjoining room which was occupied by Mrs Bernice Krueger, the most intimidating and unlovable PA any section head could have.

"Do we know who's calling?" Zale asked her.

"Some guy called Ashley."

"Sure it wasn't Ashton?"

"Could be – only one way to find out."

"Damn right." Zale picked up the phone, waited pointedly until she took the hint and left, then said, "Hi, Peter, what surprise are you going to spring on me this time?"

"Ever heard of Trans Globe Services?"

"Can't say I have."

"How about Pacific Northwest Oil and Gas in Seattle?"

"Sounds familiar. What's this all about?"

"I think they are linked in some way," Ashton told him. "Before they moved office in a hurry, Trans Globe was doing a lot of barter trade with Russia and we've reason to believe some of it wasn't kosher."

"Mind if I ask a brutal question? What's in it for us?"

"If I'm right, I think we could have a com . . . int . . . est."

"Your voice is breaking up," Zale told him. "The satellite must be going over the horizon."

"I can ca . . . back . . . hour."

"No need, I know what you want," Zale shouted and put the phone down, wondering whom he knew on Capitol Hill who might be able to tell him something about Pacific Northwest Oil and Gas.

Ashton left the communications centre and walked straight into the arms of a security guard who had been waiting for him. Century House had its own internal intelligence system and it seemed Hazelwood had been alerted soon after he'd obtained a visitor's pass from the duty sergeant in the lobby. Turning about, he walked over to the bank of lifts and went on up to the top floor, the eyrie occupied by the DG, his deputy and the Assistant Directors in charge of the Eastern Bloc, African, Asian, Pacific Basin, Middle East and Rest of the World Departments.

There had been one noticeable change since the last time Ashton had been there; someone had placed a "No Smoking" sticker on every door and at tactical intervals throughout the corridor. However, this stricture had had absolutely no effect on Hazelwood, who continued to enjoy his Burma cheroots and appeared to thrive in a smoke-laden atmosphere.

"You wanted to see me, Victor?" he said, tapping on the open door.

Hazelwood looked up from the file he had been reading and nodded. "I thought you would like to know the KGB have found Elena Andrianova, alive and as well as can be expected, I might add."

208

"That is good news."

"I knew you would be pleased." Hazelwood closed the file on his desk and tossed it into the pending tray, then stubbed out his cigar. "You want to come in and shut the door behind you?"

It wasn't exactly a royal command but it was close enough to make little difference. Ashton had also heard the quiet serious tone of voice before and knew something was eating at Victor.

"That was the good news," Hazelwood continued. "This DO letter from Calthorpe contains the bad. This Mr Richard Quennell sounds as though he's too clever for his own good."

After reading the handwritten note, Ashton handed it back. "What do you want from me, Victor? A denial?"

"I don't want to hear anything, Peter, not so much as a word. All I am saying to you is keep a low profile and don't show your head above the parapet."

"I seem to have heard that advice before," Ashton said with a faint smile.

"It doesn't make it any the less valid. All right, I know the DG threw you at Lysenko and you've had a raw deal, but it will come all right in the end. Doesn't matter who wins the general election on the ninth, there is going to be a new face to go with our new image when we set up shop in Vauxhall Cross and you'll be starting with a clean slate. Okay?"

"It will be, if you are right. Meantime, what do you intend to do about Calthorpe's DO?"

"Nothing. Naturally, I can't destroy his letter but at the same time, I am not going to invite dear old Hugo to look into the allegation." Hazelwood opened the ornately carved wooden box and helped himself to another Burma cheroot. "Does that answer your question?"

"Yes, and thank you – "

"Something you should bear in mind," Hazelwood said, cutting him short. "If there should be more bad news from Moscow, we never had this conversation."

Chapter 18

Harriet Egan asked only two things of anyone in authority – a clear directive and the freedom to get on with whatever task it was that she had been given. On that level, Peter Ashton had to be one of the best senior management officers she had worked for. He said what he wanted, didn't change his mind, and didn't look over her shoulder. On the other hand, he was demanding, single-minded and expected other people to have the same cavalier attitude towards the rule book as he had. In the short time she had known Ashton, there had been several occasions when she had positively disliked him, but then he would say or do something and the antagonism would become a thing of the moment, evaporated and forgotten. Some days, like this morning for instance, it was even a pleasure to walk into his office and ask if he could spare her a few minutes of his time.

"You've found Debbie Roxburgh," he said, ruining her entrance.

"More than that, I've had a long talk with her."

"And?"

"She never got a chance to hand in her notice. Last Friday, the day after the funeral, Neville called Debbie into his office and gave her a month's severance pay because Trans Globe was relocating in Manchester. I might add this was news to British Telecom; it seems he told their accounts department that the parent company was in financial difficulties and had decided to close down the UK office."

"Did he settle their bill before leaving?"

Harriet nodded. "Posted a cheque to Telephone House on Monday. Same with London Electricity, only with them he had to get someone in to read the meter on Friday afternoon. Arlington House is owned by White Star Securities. Neville signed a

211

three-year lease for the offices on the seventh floor, which wasn't due for renewal until October '93. However, he took advantage of an escape clause and the agreement was terminated by mutual consent after he approached White Star and advised them that the UK office of Trans Globe was to be closed because of the world-wide recession. He did all this while Frances Joyner and her daughter were in Moscow."

"What about his furnished flat in Lancaster Gardens?"

"He wasn't answering the phone yesterday and there was no sign of life when I went round there last night. This morning, I phoned the property company which owns the place, said I was looking for a larger flat than my present one and had been recommended to try them by George Neville who was one of their tenants. The girl I spoke to was very pleasant and seemed genuinely sorry I hadn't rung her when I had first heard about the vacancy. She went on to tell me that unfortunately the flat had been snapped up by an Arab businessman who was moving in next week. I thought it best not to ask her how much notice Neville had given."

"What else have you got?"

It was, Harriet thought, typical of the man. She had worked her butt off and had explored avenues outside the original brief, but he still wanted more.

"You wanted to know about the office furniture," she said with a weary sigh.

Ashton smiled. "I bet it was rented," he said.

"From Office Suppliers Limited, so were the computers, printers and VDUs." Harriet returned his smile in spite of herself. "I think Neville probably leased his BMW too."

"And the funeral bill?"

"Beresfords have forwarded it to Harold Raeburn and Associates in accordance with the instructions they had received from him. I doubt if probate has been granted yet, but before you ask, I haven't had time to speak to the solicitors. Same goes for my friends in K1."

"What have they got to do with it?" he asked, seemingly in all innocence.

"You were curious to know what the Security Service thought of the People's Law Centre. Remember?"

"So I was." Ashton leaned back in his chair and began

drumming the desk with his right hand as though performing a five-finger exercise on the piano. "This was no panic move," he said presently. "Neville planned everything well in advance."

"All the evidence points to that," she agreed.

"So what did he do with the office correspondence and software? Don't tell me the files were still in the cabinets when the furniture was collected?"

"I think I can guess what's coming," Harriet said weakly.

"Good, saves me explaining what I'd like you to do next. And while you're at it, check with the Post Office to see if he arranged to have the mail redirected from Arlington House and Lancaster Gardens. If he did, get the forwarding address; if he didn't, we'll know he's done the old vanishing act."

"How am I going to persuade the postal authorities to give me that information when it's private and confidential?"

"Oh, I'm sure you'll think of something, Harriet," he said airily.

Harriet protested that that wasn't good enough, but he wasn't listening. There were other things he wanted her to look into and she found herself adding to the original shopping list. Demanding and single-minded, Ashton was all of that and more.

"Do you mind if I ask you an impertinent question?" she said when he finally stopped.

"Why not?" A smile touched his mouth. "So long as you're standing at a safe distance."

The faint smile suggested it was a joke but Harriet didn't care one way or the other. "What will you be doing?" she asked bluntly.

His eyes drifted towards a crowded in-basket. "Well, I might think about clearing that little lot before I go and see Mrs Winnie Joyner. It could be interesting to hear what she has to say about her daughter-in-law."

Harriet pushed a slip of paper across the desk. "You might find this interesting too," she said, and stood up to leave.

"228B Churchill Gardens, SW1 – 071 222 7010." Ashton looked up from the slip of paper. "I don't understand."

"It's the address of a flat owned by the Church Commissioners which I know happens to be going begging at the moment. If you want somewhere to live for the next six months while you are house hunting, you could try ringing that number."

"Thanks. Is Churchill Gardens near where you live?"

"It's not far from Dolphin Square," she admitted, annoyed with herself for blushing.

"In that case, I'll get on to them right away," he said solemnly.

It was the second time Michael Vaughan had been required to visit Elena Andrianova in hospital and he was beginning to resent the way the SIS were using him to run errands for them. He was a commercial attaché; had he wanted to be in the cloak and dagger business, he wouldn't have joined the diplomatic service. But it was Calthorpe's attitude that really niggled him. For reasons he couldn't begin to fathom, Hugo appeared to blame him for Elena Andrianova's treachery. It was ridiculous. How was he supposed to have known that her mother had become a vegetable when she had never mentioned her damned family from one week's end to another?

Thanks to her extra mural activities, he had had to check every letter, document and cable the section had received since last September in order to assess how much damage she could have done. She had not lifted so much as her little finger to assist them, yet here he was fawning over Elena as if she had been one of the embassy's most faithful servants. There was even talk that the Foreign and Commonwealth Office was now prepared to secure a post for her with the British Council when she had recovered from her injuries. Even more remarkable was the pressure which had been exerted on the KGB to afford her maximum protection while she was in the Piragow Hospital.

Wearing a fixed smile, he walked into the ward sister's office on the second floor, which had been misappropriated for Elena. On Wednesday, a muscle-bound militiamen had stood guard outside the door; this morning, there was no obvious bodyguard, only an attractive brown-haired girl sitting by her bedside who looked like one of the models on the front cover of Moscow's newly emergent fashion magazines.

"This is Katya Malinovskaya," Elena said, introducing her. "She doesn't speak any English."

Vaughan smiled and shook hands with the girl. "Are you a friend of Elena Andrianova?" he asked in execrable Russian.

"Katya Malinovskaya is a sergeant in the Criminal Investigation Division," Elena informed him. "It was she who discovered that the hospital authorities had admitted me under my married name."

Vaughan had heard the same story from her less than forty-eight hours ago, how she had been found lying unconscious by some students from Moscow University and the natural confusion that had arisen after the hospital authorities had completed their records from the documents they had found in her handbag. Elena appeared to believe that the more often she repeated the story, the more credible it became.

"Major Lysenko was Katya's superior officer," Elena told him.

"Really?" Vaughan looked at the Russian policewoman with renewed interest.

"Yes. It was Major Lysenko who instructed her to look for me."

"When was this?" he asked.

Elena translated the question for Katya Malinovskaya's benefit, then promptly entered into a long conversation with her before informing him that she had received her instructions on Saturday evening from Major Lysenko personally. Vaughan wondered if Hugo Calthorpe was aware of this, decided that if he was, it would be typical of the old fox not to pass it on when he'd briefed him.

"Katya wants to know if you are the Englishman who ordered her to inform Major Lysenko that he wished to speak to him."

"English? How did Katya know he wasn't an American?"

Elena repeated the question to Katya and got a terse reply which she immediately passed on to him. "Because he said he was English."

Walter Iremonger couldn't have been the mysterious caller; if the AP man had wanted to speak to Lysenko, he would have told the girl who he was.

"What exactly did this man say to Katya Malinovskaya?"

The question sparked off another voluble discussion between the two women which seemed to become more and more heated the longer it went on. His curiosity now thoroughly aroused, Vaughan waited impatiently for an answer. It was some minutes before he got one.

"The man gave her a message," Elena said eventually. "He said, 'Tell the Major the Joyner case isn't closed, tell him the Englishman says so.' "

Vaughan supposed a reporter with a nose for a good crime story might have said something along those lines. But from what Richard Quennell had said about him, Walter Iremonger wasn't a modest and retiring man. The man who had called the KGB headquarters in Dzerzhinsky Square hadn't wanted to identify himself to a third party, but evidently he had expected Lysenko to know who had left a message for him.

"Katya says he threatened her."

"What?"

"The Englishman," Elena said, a touch irritated. "He said if she didn't contact Major Lysenko, the British Embassy would be in touch with Major General Gurov, the Chief of Police, to complain about her lack of co-operation."

That definitely ruled out Iremonger; he was too sensible to threaten her with something he couldn't deliver. Ashton. It had to be Ashton. He had worked with Lysenko on the Joyner case and had shown a touching concern for Elena Andrianova. It was he who had tried to wish her on to the British Council. Hugo Calthorpe hadn't been too impressed with the information he had brought back after his first visit to the hospital. Vaughan fancied he would get a very different reaction from him this time.

The terraced houses in Headstone Road had been built at the end of the nineteenth century, long before the first motor vehicles had appeared on the street. They had started out as two up, two down, with a privy in the back garden and a washroom tacked on to the kitchen. Nearly a hundred years later, there was nose-to-tail street parking, sashcord windows had been replaced by double-glazing, additional bedrooms had mushroomed in the lofts and no two properties were alike. The bay windows in the terraced house occupied by Mrs Winnie Joyner had been removed and the rooms extended so that the small front garden had all but disappeared.

Before leaving the office, Ashton had phoned shortly after two o'clock to ask if it would be convenient to call on her; the prompt way she answered the door when he rang the bell suggested she had been looking out for him. If the thin-lipped smile he received from her on the doorstep hardly softened a generally sour expression, the pot of tea and plate of chocolate biscuits on the oval table in the sitting room provided mute evidence that she had gone to some trouble to make him feel welcome.

"Perhaps you would prefer a cup of coffee, Mr Ashton?"

"No, tea's fine," he assured her, then hastily changed the subject. "I like your garden," he said for want of something better to say.

It was mostly lawn with narrow flowerbeds full of daffodils and narcissi on either side and a vegetable patch at the bottom.

"Henry does it."

"Henry?" Ashton repeated.

"My next-door neighbour; you met him at Colin's funeral."

"So I did. In a way, that's why I'm here this afternoon."

"You told me it had to do with Colin when you rang me."

"It does. The Russian government has made a number of serious allegations regarding Trans Globe Services. They allege the firm was paid cash in advance for kidney dialysis machines which they failed to deliver. To cut a long story short, Colin's business partner, George Neville, claims that your son pocketed the money."

"That's a damned lie."

"I'm sure it is," Ashton said smoothly. "How well do you know Mr Neville?"

"I met him for the first time at the funeral a week ago yesterday."

And had, it seemed, taken an instant dislike to him. Listening to her, it was obvious to Ashton that anyone who was on friendly terms with Frances Joyner was automatically a candidate for her enmity.

"Your daughter-in-law appears to think highly of him," Ashton observed, knowing it would provoke another revealing outburst.

"She would."

There was no mistaking the venom in her voice. In a few brief sentences, he was told that Frances Joyner was a common little tart with the morals of an alley cat who couldn't keep her hands off any good-looking man. The bitch had been unfaithful to her first husband and Winnie wouldn't be the least bit surprised to hear that she had been unfaithful to her son.

"I can't think why Colin wanted to marry that woman. He was doing all right at the club, always had plenty of money in his pocket."

"What club was this?" Ashton asked her.

"Annabel's? Aspinall's?" Winnie pursed her lips. "Something like that. He was a croupier on one of them roulette tables, earned a good salary, enough to buy me this place in 1977. Up until then, we'd had a council house in Wealdstone."

"He obviously thought a lot of you," Ashton said dutifully.

"That's where Colin met her, you know. At the club. She was a member, used to come up to town from Liphook, sit at the roulette table all night and then drive home in the morning."

"How long ago was this?"

"Must be all of ten years now. Sometimes she would stay the night at this flat she had in Knightsbridge. She took Colin there lots of times after they became lovers."

"Can you remember the address?"

"It was somewhere in Hans Crescent. They had to sell it two years ago; things were bad in the building trade and Colin told me they were short of money. Didn't stop her gambling though, and she kept on losing."

Ashton remembered Frances Joyner telling him in Moscow that the timber yard she had inherited from her father had been worth a cool three-quarters of a million after the Inland Revenue had presented their demand for capital transfer tax. He also recalled her claiming that large sums of it had been frittered away by her husband on one failed enterprise after another. If only half of what Winnie Joyner said was true, it was apparent that she hadn't exactly been a model of thrift. But just what her predilection for the roulette table had to do with anything that had happened in Moscow was, however, beyond Ashton.

His name was Howard Eugene Falkenberg, but as he had told Zale the moment they had met, he was Gene to his friends. He was dressed by Brooks Brothers, wore hand-made Italian shoes and knew everybody who was anybody on Capitol Hill, not to mention his home state. He liked to describe himself as the Chief of Staff and certainly, nobody got to see the senior senator for the State of Washington without first going through his office.

A man described in clichés, Falkenberg was said to be razor sharp, a smooth-as-silk operator, the original Mr Fix-it and dozens more, all of which happened to be true. His formidable reputation was founded on the office he ran for the senior senator, which he had been astute enough to staff with a hand-picked team of exceptionally bright and eager young people whose willingness to work all the hours God made were a legend on Capitol Hill.

Zale had called the senator's office on Wednesday afternoon and had asked one of the staffers what she could tell him about Pacific Northwest Oil and Gas in Seattle. Now, here he was, rather less than forty-eight hours later, having lunch with Gene Falkenberg at the Madison on 15th and M Streets. Although the venue had been suggested by Falkenberg, Zale had been left in no doubt that he was expected to pick up the tab. His guest from Capitol Hill had also made it clear that an extended working lunch was out because he could only spare him an hour, which Zale supposed was something of a consolation since it would help keep the expenses down. Or so he had thought before Falkenberg had ordered pâté de foie gras followed by a Châteaubriand with a bottle of Mouton Cadet.

"Okay, Tony, let's get down to business." Falkenberg rested both elbows on the table and leaned forward, shoulders hunched. "First thing the senator wants to know is why the Defense Intelligence Agency should be interested in Pacific Northwest Oil and Gas?"

"We aren't," Zale told him in an equally low voice. "The query was raised by a friendly agency."

"Who are we talking about? The Brits?"

"Yeah, they want to know if it's a conglomerate. They've got their eyes on a possible UK subsidiary trading as Trans Globe Services Incorporated."

"You know who's got more money invested in America than anybody else?"

Zale smiled. "I guess you're going to tell me it's the Brits."

"You guessed right." Falkenberg helped himself to a bread roll and buttered a piece before popping it into his mouth. "Got close on a hundred billion dollars worth of interests, makes the Japanese stake look like peanuts." He removed a crumb from his bottom lip, inspected it closely, then said, "Are you sure this is an official inquiry, Tony? This friendly agency isn't fronting for some UK corporation, is it? Because if there is some kind of deal in the offing, my senator will want to know about it first, especially if it means a whole lot more jobs will go down the tube as a result of a merger."

"There is no deal."

"Uh huh." Falkenberg gazed at him thoughtfully. "I can't tell you how many times I've gotten the same assurance from other guys and discovered different."

"This is legit," Zale told him stonily. "If you don't believe me, that's just too bad."

"Hey, why are we having this spat over an itty-bitty outfit like Pacific Northwest?"

"Are you saying it's not a conglomerate?"

"During World War One, Seattle built more ships than any other US port and was still pretty big in World War Two. One of the largest shipyards is owned by Consolidated Merrill Industries who began to feel the pinch when the Japanese started building supertankers and undercutting everybody."

Salvation for the ailing shipyard appeared to arrive with soaring oil prices following the Arab-Israeli war of '73. Suddenly, an old geological survey indicating potential oil and gas fields south of Cape Flattery began to look very promising, especially as the shipyard had the capacity and the necessary skills to build the drilling platforms and rigs.

Pacific Northwest Oil and Gas had been set up by Consolidated Merrill Industries to drive the whole project. There were two reasons why it had failed. Subsequent exploration of the field had raised doubts that oil was present in sufficient quantities to make its extraction economically worthwhile and OPEC had begun to cut the price per barrel. Pacific Northwest Oil and Gas had shed most of its labour force and had become an oil broker instead of a crude producer.

"They are nothing like as big as the Rotterdam spot market but they still run a pretty sizeable operation."

"What's their turnover?"

"I don't rightly know, Tony." Falkenberg broke off while the waiter placed the foie gras in front of him, then said, "My guesstimate is somewhere between two and three hundred mega bucks."

"And Trans Globe Services?"

"I didn't know they existed until you mentioned them just now."

"Is Pacific Northwest still part of Consolidated Merrill Industries?"

"Yeah. Of course, the real power lies with Pacific's Executive Vice President, Mike Todorvic."

"A good guy?"

"You can count on it. A great fund raiser and a very much respected member of the community."

"How about the company's record?" Zale asked casually.

"What are you getting at?"

"Sanctions busting, trading with South Africa before the Le Klerk government started to dismantle apartheid – that sort of thing."

"You are asking me?" Falkenberg said in exaggerated amazement. "Hell, you are in the Defense Intelligence Agency, you should be telling me."

Zale smiled, hoping to give the impression he knew a lot more than he did. Ashton had given him a bum steer and he was getting nowhere fast. "You heard any whispers about the company being used as a front?"

"Who by?" Falkenberg demanded sharply. "The Mafia?"

"Well, you've got to admit you could launder a hell of a lot of money through a company like Pacific Northwest."

"Is that what they are saying over at Justice? Because if they are, those guys have taken leave of their senses. Todorvic is clean, so are all the people who work for him. Get somebody to check with the IRS if you won't take my word for it."

Zale knew he had handled it badly and tried to explain, then ended up apologising. Only Falkenberg wasn't in a mood to listen to him. It seemed he had committed an unpardonable sin by pointing a finger of suspicion at Pacific Northwest and, by implication, its parent company CMI. The recession had hit the aerospace industry, the demand for lumber was at an all-time low and things were tough enough already in Seattle without the Defense Intelligence Agency gunning for Consolidated Merrill Industries. Long before they went their separate ways, Zale got the impression he hadn't done himself any favours by lunching the senior senator's right-hand man. He also wished to God he had never listened to Ashton.

Abbreviations were meat and drink to the civil service whose

221

policy documents were liberally splattered with them. TGIF was an unofficial one but known throughout Whitehall as 'Thank God it's Friday'. It was equally well observed by the rank and file of the SIS, which was why Benbow House was virtually deserted by the time Ashton returned at ten minutes past five. There was, however, one conscientious officer left on the third floor and he bumped into her when he stepped out of the lift.

"I left a note for you on your desk," Harriet informed him.

"Important?"

"Maybe. I phoned Raeburn Associates this afternoon and spoke to a very helpful if somewhat indiscreet secretary. She thought I was from Beresford and Son and I went along with the assumption. Which is how I learned that Neville had sent them a letter stating that all future instructions would be coming direct from Mrs Joyner."

"Well, I suppose that's in keeping with everything else he has done."

"I told myself the same thing; didn't stop me ringing the house in Liphook though."

"And?"

"A woman answered the phone."

"She's back?"

"Only one way to find out, Peter. You'll have to go down there on Monday."

"You know something?" Ashton said. "I think you deserve a drink."

"I think I deserve one too," Harriet told him.

Chapter 19

Monday began like any other day of the working week for Harriet Egan. When the alarm woke her at ten minutes to seven, she immediately kicked off the duvet and got out of bed, resisting as always the temptation to sneak a few extra minutes between the sheets. She stripped off her nightdress, walked into the bathroom and freshened up under the shower, then towelled herself dry, removed the plastic bathing cap and ran a comb through her hair before donning a silk bathrobe.

Breakfast was the usual glass of orange juice and slice of unbuttered toast which, although not very sustaining, was all she could face in the mornings. Breakfast over, she put the glass and side plate in the dishwasher ready for the weekly cycle on Friday evening and returned to the bedroom. She was still in her underwear when the telephone rang five minutes later. A notion that somebody had dialled the wrong number was dispelled the moment she lifted the extension on the bedside table and found Ashton on the line apologising for disturbing her at such an early hour.

"You haven't," Harriet assured him. A week ago she would have made some tart rejoinder, but a lot could happen in seven days and she saw him now through different eyes. "Where are you calling from?" she asked.

"A phone box not far from you."

"Well, why don't you pop in for a cup of coffee on the way to the office?"

"I don't think that would be a very good idea," he said.

She was more hurt than angered by the curt rejection. That was her first reaction; on second thoughts, she knew Ashton wouldn't have phoned her at this hour of the morning unless it was important. It also occurred to her that he may have used a public call box because he hadn't wanted Jill Sheridan to hear what he had to say.

"What's happened?" she asked.

"There's been some kind of eruption in Moscow and I'm up before the Star Chamber," he told her. "They evidently suspect I've been to Russia without official permission, but it looks as though they can't prove it beyond all reasonable doubt, otherwise I would already be under arrest." Ashton paused. "Did I tell you Frank Warren has also been summoned to Century House?" he asked, suddenly taking a different tack.

"No, you never mentioned his name."

"Well, he has, though I didn't hear it from him. I have a feeling that poor old Frank is a witness, which can only mean they have checked the contents of his security cabinet and discovered that there are a number of deficiencies. I'm not going to make things easy for them by putting my hand up; at the same time, I can't let Frank carry the can for the missing documents." Ashton broke off to feed several coins into the meter, then said, "Which brings me to you. You're the only person who knows I burgled his safe."

Harriet wondered what was coming next. Would he ask her to forget that she had seen him in Frank Warren's office?

"They are bound to question all the duty officers for the past few weeks . . ."

She was right. Ashton wanted her to keep her mouth shut but wasn't quite sure how to put it. "What are you trying to say?" she asked him frostily.

"You've got to look out for yourself, Harriet. Above all, you are not to do anything quixotic on my account."

He thought it was perhaps too late in the day for her to let them know that she had seen him in Frank's office. On the other hand, there was no reason why she shouldn't mention the fact that he had returned to Benbow House after normal office hours the night she had been duty officer. She could also infer that she had thought his behaviour was a little strange at the time considering the Vetting, Security and Technical Services Division was scarcely faced with a backlog of work.

"I'm not happy about this," she told him. "I don't want to be the one who drives the last nail into your coffin."

"Don't worry about it, I'll be okay."

Peter Ashton – the loner and born survivor – a very private and very solitary man. She had got to know him a little better over a drink on Friday evening. Father an insurance salesman, killed in a traffic accident when he was eight, brought up by paternal grandparents after his mother remarried less than a year later. Although he hadn't said so, Harriet was pretty sure that his step-father had wanted nothing to do with him, for young Peter had stayed behind when his mother and her new husband had emigrated to Australia in 1969. It had been far too late to establish a close-knit family relationship when she had suffered a fatal coronary in 1983; somewhere out there in Perth there was a half-sister and -brother he had never seen, never heard from.

"I seem to be running out of change," Ashton said seconds before the phone started bleeping, then the line went dead before she could ask him for the number of the kiosk.

Harriet put the receiver down. She had thought the worst of Ashton and had been proved utterly wrong. Only one other man had ever made her feel deeply ashamed of herself and then it had been for a very different reason. Jeremy Kingsbridge – merchant banker, womaniser *par excellence* and acting major in the Artists' Rifles, the most exclusive regiment in the Territorial Army. There had been a time when she had imagined herself to be in love with him and he with her. She had been twenty-three, four years younger than Jeremy Kingsbridge and gauche enough to want to please him. Why else had she snorted cocaine with all the other very upmarket people at that oh-so-exclusive dinner party in Chelsea? Why else had she refrained from punching her society hostess on the nose when she had got decidedly fresh with her?

Fourteen months ago, a former detective chief superintendent of the Special Branch had revalidated her security clearance. In the course of what was meant to be a very searching interview, he had asked her if she had ever used drugs or experienced a lesbian relationship. She had given him an unequivocal no to both questions and he had evidently believed her. She wondered if Ashton could lie with equal conviction.

Ashton parked the Vauxhall Cavalier in the vacant slot that had belonged to the Assistant Director, Pacific Basin before his fiefdom had been merged with the Rest of the World Department on the first of April. To obtain a visitor's pass for Century House, he printed his name, initials and appointment in block capitals on the buff-coloured form, and in the box headed "Reason for Visit" he was sorely tempted to write "You tell me". On wiser reflection, however, he inserted "Attending Board of Inquiry", then signed and dated the application before presenting it for authentication. When he turned away from the reception desk, he found a worried-looking Frank Warren waiting for him.

"I hope you don't think any of this was my doing?" Warren said in a voice that sounded as if he was masticating a mouthful of food.

"Of course I don't," Ashton assured him. "Matter of fact, I don't know what's going on . . ."

"Neither do I really. All I know is that Roy Kelso summoned me into the office on Sunday afternoon because he wanted to check the contents of my security cabinet." Warren lowered his voice. "I'm afraid I was short of a visa application and a Moscow residential permit."

"Oh yes? What did Roy have to say about that?"

"Very little. Curiously enough, I thought he looked rather pleased that I was unable to account for the missing papers. He asked me if I was satisfied that there were no deficiencies when you last checked the contents, and I said yes." Warren frowned. "They were all there, weren't they, Peter?" he asked in a tone which suggested he wasn't too sure.

"I wouldn't have signed the register if the stock hadn't tallied."

"That's what I told our Assistant Director." Warren inspected the gleaming toecaps of his shoes. "He tried to get me to say that you probably knew the combination to my safe because I had set it by the day, month and year of my birth."

Ashton made no comment. Something had happened in Moscow which had pointed a finger in his direction and Kelso believed he could prove he had made an illegal trip to Russia. It was as simple as that.

"Maybe we should go on up, Frank," he suggested.

With some reluctance, Warren agreed it was time they made a move. He seemed worried that Kelso or the DG himself would see them together when they arrived on the top floor. A hunch that Warren had been told not to speak to him was reinforced when he checked the corridor to make sure no one of any importance was around before he alighted from the lift.

226

"Do me a favour," he said as they parted company outside the executive dining room. "Don't let on that I told you Kelso had been through the contents of my safe. Okay?"

"What are you talking about?" Ashton said, straight-faced. "We haven't seen one another since Friday."

The twentieth floor was a different world, inhabited by people who were seriously rich compared with middle-ranking officers of the SIS. The DG was on seventy-five thousand a year, his deputy received seventy and every assistant director was scratching a living on sixty K. Since no right-minded person could seriously expect the chairman of a large corporation and his fellow directors to bring their own sandwiches into the office, the current DG, in common with his predecessors, could see no reason why the SIS should be the first to establish such a precedent. There being no suitable restaurants in the immediate neighbourhood, the Treasury had reluctantly agreed the need for an executive dining room, which, this morning, was being used as a waiting room for witnesses attending the Board of Inquiry. Unless the proceedings were therefore completed before ten thirty, the DG was unlikely to enjoy his customary lunch subsidised by the taxpayer.

The Board consisted of Hazelwood, Kelso, the DG and his deputy, Stuart Dunglass, who some people believed would succeed him soon after the voters had gone to the polls in three days' time. In contrast to his chief, Dunglass was coolness personified. Kelso was doing his best to ape him but could not disguise the triumphant gleam in his eyes. Hazelwood merely looked glum, possibly because the whole of the top floor with the exception of his own office was a no smoking area and he would be unable to enjoy a Burma cheroot while the Board of Inquiry was in session.

The DG opened the proceedings by reading the convening order which he had personally drafted, then turned the whole thing over to Dunglass and retired to his office. The first witness was the chief archivist of the Eastern Bloc Department who submitted a photocopy of a long cable from Moscow which gave a verbatim account of a conversation Vaughan had had with Katya Malinovskaya of the KGB's Criminal Investigation Division. The second and very reluctant witness was Frank Warren. Given the opportunity to question him after he had

227

finished giving evidence, Ashton declined to do so, as he had with the chief archivist.

"A visa application in triplicate and a residential permit are missing, and you have no questions?" Dunglass raised his eyebrows. "I must say I'm rather surprised."

"The documents were there when I checked them," Ashton told him, "now Frank says they aren't. Why should I doubt his word?"

"Why indeed?" Kelso echoed. "Especially as you know what has happened to them."

"Would you care to enlarge upon that?" Ashton said in a voice only marginally warmer than the polar icecap.

"I would refer you to Mr Vaughan's statement – "

"Since when has the Third Secretary, Commerce been an expert on Intelligence matters?"

Attack had always been the most effective means of defence in Ashton's book and he had few qualms about demolishing the Assistant Director in charge of Administration. Kelso was both the weakest and the most dangerous member of the Board; destroy his credibility and the battle for survival was half won.

"This is the man who couldn't see what was happening right under his very nose," Ashton continued remorselessly. "If he could be caught napping by his none-too-bright secretary, just think of the amount of disinformation the KGB could feed him in the confident expectation that he would swallow every morsel."

"I still find Katya Malinovskaya's allegation entirely believable, especially as it happens to explain why certain travel documents are missing."

Kelso was nothing if not dogged, but he was going it alone. Hazelwood's silence was understandable; Victor was an ally, albeit a passive one, and any questions he might have for him were likely to be of a sympathetic nature. Dunglass, however, was harder to figure. As President of the Board, Ashton would have expected him to steer the inquiry the way he wanted it to go, instead of which, he seemed content to take a back seat. He wondered uneasily if the Deputy DG was playing some sort of waiting game.

"I'm not surprised you are lost for words," Kelso said when Ashton didn't react immediately.

"You're right, I am rather lost for words," Ashton told him.

"I'm surprised you can attach so much importance to a visa application which can be obtained from any travel agent in the country. So one is missing, so what? How can a blank form harm the national interest?"

"That's not the point – "

"Now there I agree with you. We should be asking ourselves what certain members of the KGB were planning to do with Elena Andrianova and why they regard her as such a threat."

Kelso looked to the Deputy DG, hoping he would intervene. When he failed to do so, he attempted to get the inquiry back on track himself. "We are here to investigate – "

"I heard the convening order too," Ashton said, interrupting him. "And I accept that I am ultimately responsible for the missing documents, but that's as far as it goes."

"I think you went all the way to Moscow on those papers."

"Nonsense."

"Because you were in Wales when this mysterious Englishman spoke to Katya Malinovskaya," Dunglass suggested in a quiet but ominous voice.

Ashton winced. The Deputy DG had chosen exactly the right moment to make his presence felt and had then done so with devastating effect. It was pointless chiding himself that he should have anticipated the line Dunglass might take; what he had to do now was perform some fancy footwork and dance his way out of a tight corner.

"That's what I told Miss Egan when she asked me where I was going," he conceded.

"Are you saying you lied to her?"

Ashton nodded. "I didn't think what I planned to do over the weekend was any of her business. We hadn't seen eye to eye from the day she joined my division and I was feeling pretty stroppy when Miss Egan buttonholed me."

"May we know why you and Miss Egan had fallen out?"

Whether it was intentional or not, Hazelwood had thrown him a lifeline. "I had given her a number of tasks which she objected to."

"Such as?"

The opportunity to turn the inquiry around was there and Ashton made the most of it. He started with the premeditated murder of Colin Joyner, then went on to explain the reasons why he had targeted George Neville and decided to investigate the curious business practices of the now defunct UK branch of Trans Globe Services. Without naming Oroblinsky, he told them why he believed a member of the KGB's Criminal Investigation Division had gunned down Major Oleg Lysenko. And throughout the dissertation he returned to Elena Andrianova, reiterating his conviction that knowingly or unknowingly, she held the key which could unlock the whole mystery.

"We are all aware of your touching concern for the Russian lady."

Even though Kelso had aired the snide observation in public before, it had lost none of its abrasive effect on Ashton.

"I share Peter's anxiety," Hazelwood said hastily before Ashton rose to the bait. "Matter of fact, I also happen to think we won't get anything more from her until she is satisfied that her family is safe. That means bringing the mother to England for treatment. Naturally, her father and daughter will have to accompany the patient."

"But Mrs Andrianov is a vegetable," Kelso protested. "Vaughan has been to see her and he says she can't do anything for herself. It's right here in the cable from Moscow."

"So what?"

"Well, the Russians know she is incurable; that's why they'll never let her come here."

"I think they can be persuaded if the approach is made at the highest level. A personal letter from the PM to Yeltsin should do the trick."

"Nonsense. His own people will tell him there is nothing we can do for her."

"Physiotherapy, that's the name of the game, Roy. We may not be able to put Ludmilla Andrianova together again, but we can surely teach her how to feed herself and a few other basic skills. At least, that's what our PM, whoever he is come Friday, should tell friend Boris."

"This is crazy . . ."

It was, Ashton thought, rather like a tennis match with Hazelwood on one side of the net and Kelso on the other. And perhaps aware that his opponent was a vastly superior player, the Assistant Director in charge of Administration and Personnel was becoming more and more desperate the longer each rally went on. Umpire Dunglass sat between them, seemingly not interested in the exchange, his eyes locked on Ashton, watchful and unblinking.

"I'm still waiting to hear where you spent the weekend of the twenty-eighth, twenty-ninth of March, Mr Ashton," he said when finally there was a lull.

"I went down to Kent. I needed some time to myself to sort things out and a friend of mine lent me his cottage near Meopham."

"Does this friend have a name?"

"I can do better than that, I can give you the number of his chambers in Pump Court."

"He's a barrister," Dunglass said in a flat voice.

"One of the best," Ashton told him cheerfully. "Keith's a bit of a crusader, fond of championing the underdog. We met in the TA."

They had been patrol commanders in the same squadron of 23 SAS and had kept in touch over the years. Ashton had been best man at his wedding in 1986, a duty he had performed at short notice when Keith's first choice had fallen by the wayside at the last minute. "You can reach him on 071-289 8216."

"Thank you," Dunglass said and made a note of the number on his scratchpad.

Ashton doubted if the Deputy DG would telephone him personally. The SIS had its own lawyers and Dunglass was likely to go through them, which would give him a chance to get in first. If by any chance they beat him to it, he knew he could rely on Keith to see them off until he had heard his side of the story. It wasn't just wishful thinking; whether Regular or TA, the SAS regiments were noted for their very special esprit de corps, the togetherness which no outsider could hope to penetrate. In any event, Keith was his only hope; no one else could help him without placing themselves in jeopardy, and that most certainly included Harriet as well as Victor.

"Exactly where are we going?" Hazelwood enquired in a tone that implied the proceedings were a farce and he'd had more than enough.

"All the way," Dunglass told him crisply. "You've been

pressing the DG to get Elena Andrianova out of Russia, so let's start with her mother and line up some big names in the medical profession who are willing to perjure themselves about the marvellous treatment awaiting her in London."

Observing their faces, Ashton found it hard to decide who looked the most surprised – Hazelwood or Kelso. He was, in fact, more than a little taken aback himself.

"On second thoughts, that's a job for you, Roy," Dunglass added.

"Me?" Kelso said incredulously.

"Why not? You're the Assistant Director in charge of Administration. In any event, Victor and I will have our work cut out rallying the Foreign Office to the cause."

"What about Ashton?"

It sounded like a heartfelt cry for justice. In seeking to negate it, Ashton went out of his way to be obtuse and answered the question literally.

"I was going to see Frances Joyner," he said. "It could be helpful to know how, why and when her late husband was taken on by Trans Globe."

"I agree with you," Dunglass said, and turned to Kelso. "I presume you can spare him, Roy?"

"What about the Board of Inquiry? Shouldn't we reach a conclusion?"

"We already have. Ashton has admitted he was negligent, so there's nothing more to be said. In due course, I'll let you have an official reprimand in writing, which you can place in his personal file."

It was over. Ashton couldn't believe it, neither could Hazelwood, but their surprise was nothing compared to Kelso who looked as if he was in deep shock. He was still sitting there unseeing, unhearing and lost to the world as they left the executive dining room.

"You've got the luck of the devil," Hazelwood whispered when they were safely outside.

"You don't have to tell me that," Ashton murmured.

"Well, don't run away with the idea that it will never desert you."

That was something he wouldn't do. Maybe Dunglass had meant what he had said and the inquiry wouldn't be reopened at some future date, but he wasn't about to take that chance. Before driving down to Liphook, he would drop into Pump Court and square things with Keith.

Chapter 20

Umbrella held aloft, Harriet waited for a gap in the traffic on Tottenham Court Road, then crossed over and made her way to Gower Street via Torrington Place. It had started raining shortly before she had left the flat for the office and even now, some five hours later, there was no sign of it letting up. The anonymous building in the heart of Bloomsbury which was occupied by the Kremlin Watchers of MI5 had never looked greyer than it did on this miserably wet day.

Folding her umbrella, she walked into the foyer, showed her ID card to the duty sergeant and informed him she had an appointment to see Mr Peachey, then waited patiently by the desk while he checked to make sure she was expected. The fact that she was an old Gower Street hand and the sergeant knew very well who she was counted for nothing. She no longer worked there and how visitors were to be treated was very clearly laid down in standing orders. Harriet did not believe in exceptions to the rule and would have had it no other way.

No one could have been more pleased to see her than Clifford Peachey when she finally made it to his office.

"You're a sight for sore eyes," he told her. "I know it's only just over a fortnight since the last time you dropped in to see me but it seems far longer."

"You say the nicest things, Clifford."

"Only if they're true."

Harriet removed her Burberry raincoat and hung it on the hook behind the door, then turned to face him again. "Nevertheless, it's very good of you to forego your lunch break to see me."

"Nonsense, I haven't given up anything. I don't eat lunch these days." He patted his stomach. "I'm trying to lose weight."

Going on a diet was the last thing Clifford needed to do. There wasn't a spare ounce of flesh anywhere on his body and she thought he had lost too much weight already.

"I'm always asking you for help," Harriet began apologetically.

"We're friends, aren't we?"

"Yes, of course."

"Well then . . .?"

"I was wondering if you had any further information on George Neville?"

"I thought I'd given you a pretty good biography, Harriet."

"You did, but there is a big gap in his life, the fourteen years he spent in America between leaving Australia and returning here. I was hoping you could fill it in."

Peachey took out his pipe and filled the bowl from a tin of Dunhill Standard Mixture, then struck a match and lit up. "I think you're reading too much into the gap," he said between puffs. "It's simply the mathematical difference between 1976 and 1990. He left Australia purportedly for San Francisco three years after being released from a POW camp in North Vietnam and we know when he returned to England on a BA flight from JFK New York. It's only our supposition that he spent the intervening years in the States. Neville could have lived in Canada, Mexico, anywhere you care to name."

"He left England in 1969 but he never changed his nationality," Harriet mused.

"I believe that's what I said in the biographical notes I sent you."

"If he kept his British passport, he would have had to renew it every ten years. Right?"

"Yes."

"So where, when and how often did he do it?"

"I don't know, but I daresay we could make some enquiries if it's important."

"Could you also check him out with the FBI?"

"They'll want to know why we are interested." He gazed at her thoughtfully, pipe clenched between his teeth, a thin wisp of smoke eddying towards the ceiling. "Would you care to tell me what I am going to say to them, Harriet?"

"Remember when I first asked you to dig up what you could on George Neville, I told you he was the UK rep for Trans Globe?"

"As I recall, you also said he was a bit of a liar."

"Well, now he's folded his tent and vanished." She also told him about the sudden demise of Trans Globe in the UK and the reason for believing it was a subsidiary of Pacific Northwest Oil and Gas.

"We're in the middle of a recession, Harriet. Businesses are folding left, right and centre. Why should Trans Globe be an exception? And a letterhead on a blank sheet of paper which you found on the floor is pretty flimsy evidence for concluding that Pacific Northwest Oil and Gas is the parent company."

"You're right, it was."

"Was?" Peachey said quietly. "Why the past tense?"

"My boss isn't in the office today, so I'm covering for him. That's how I saw this telex from someone called Zale in the US Defense Intelligence Agency. Evidently, Peter had asked him to see if there was a tie-in with Trans Globe and the answer he got is a resounding no."

"Does that surprise you?" Peachey shook his head. "It shouldn't. Seems to me Ashton is trying to make a comeback and is clutching at any straw which might persuade his superiors to believe he is on to something."

"I hear what you are saying, Clifford."

"There's something else you should take note of. We are working in a different environment; the Official Secrets Acts have been rewritten, the government has declared there is to be more openness, and both ourselves and the SIS are going to be a lot more accountable than we have been in the past."

"I read the newspapers too," Harriet said quietly.

"Then don't do anything silly in future."

It was Clifford's way of letting her know that he suspected she had burgled the offices of Trans Globe. He was also warning her that if she was caught doing something illegal, the Service would no longer close ranks and protect her.

"I think we have been on the wrong track, Clifford."

"So long as you have learned your lesson, no harm has been done."

"That isn't what I meant. On paper, Trans Globe and Pacific Northwest Oil and Gas are independent of each other; it's Neville who is the connecting link."

"Ashton's really got to you, hasn't he?"

"Don't be ridiculous," she said heatedly.

"I'm sorry, I didn't mean to be so crass."

"That's all right." Harriet smiled. "You're forgiven."

"Suppose you are right about Neville being the connection. How are you going to prove it?"

"I could start with the Passport Office in Petty France and see if they can tell me where and when he renewed his."

"You could," Peachey told her. "On the other hand, it might be better if you left it to me."

There was a "For Sale" notice by the entrance to Fitzroy Court that hadn't been there five days ago. Ashton wasn't surprised to see that, in deciding to put the house on the market, Frances Joyner had chosen one of the biggest estate agents in the south of England. Circling the grass island at the top of the drive, he stopped opposite the front porch some twenty feet from the detached garage. A phone call from Keith's chambers in Pump Court had established that Frances Joyner was at home; the sight of a dark blue Mercedes in the left-hand bay, where the up-and-over door had been left in the raised position, suggested she may have been down to Liphook in the meantime. Braving the rain, Ashton made a dash for the porch and rang the bell. He did not have long to wait before she opened the door to him.

On the few occasions he had met her, Frances Joyner had always looked immaculate. This afternoon, she was no less fashion-conscious than previously, in high-heeled sandals, black flared pants and matching bolero jacket over a blouse with a plunging neckline.

"This is getting to be a habit," she said, "a not unwelcome one, I might add."

Ashton returned her smile and confined himself to a mumbled greeting because there was nothing he could say that wouldn't sound equally coy. She stepped aside to let him into the hall, then closed the door and contrived to brush shoulders as she moved ahead to lead the way into the drawing room.

"I've made us a pot of coffee," she said and waved him to an easy chair.

"That's very kind of you," Ashton told her, "but it really wasn't necessary."

"It was no trouble. How do you like your coffee?"

"Black, please, no sugar."

The ornate silver tray was late nineteenth century and looked out of place against the Georgian coffee-pot, sugar bowl, cream jug and dainty spoons. The Crown Derby cups and saucers were obviously another family heirloom which had been produced for the occasion.

"My father bought the silver at an auction before I was born," she told him. "The Crown Derby belonged to my grandmother."

"It's very beautiful," he said.

"I think so too." A smile softened the hard line of her mouth. "But you didn't drive all the way from London to admire my possessions." The smile slowly faded to be replaced by a puzzled frown which he thought was equally false. "You must think I'm awfully dense, Mr Ashton, but I didn't understand half of what you told me on the phone. Exactly what is the nature of this dispute you say the Russians have with Trans Globe?"

Frances Joyner was cool, far too cool for his liking. There were two reasons why he had rung her before setting off for Liphook. Apart from wanting to make sure she wasn't out when he arrived at the house, he'd hoped the phone call would make her feel apprehensive. Unfortunately, it seemed to have had the opposite effect.

"The Russians claim they put six million dollars up front for kidney dialysis machines which Trans Globe failed to deliver."

The Russians had made no such allegation, but Frances Joyner was not to know that, and it was a fact that Trans Globe had supplied kidney dialysis machines to the Third World; Ashton remembered Debbie Roxburgh telling him so when she had explained the sort of information that was stored in her desk-top computer.

"I'm afraid I can't help you there, Mr Ashton. Colin rarely told me about the deals he made in Moscow. With him, business had either been good or just so-so; that was all he ever had to say on the subject."

"Could he speak the language?"

"Not when he first went to Russia. He used to hire an interpreter; I daresay she gave him the necessary tuition in bed. One thing I will say for Colin, he had an ear for languages, even Russian. I don't suppose he ever spoke it like a native but eventually he could make himself understood."

"After how long?"

"I'm not sure." She picked up the coffee-pot, then leaned forward and refilled his cup. "Colin first went to Moscow in September '89 and spent a week examining what sort of business he could do with the Russians as a result of Perestroika."

After that, Joyner had made between five and six trips a year to the former Soviet Union, each lasting a minimum of four days. In between these forays, he had toured England and Wales buying up bankrupt stock from the Official Receiver, which he had subsequently sold to the Russians at a vastly inflated figure.

"Of course, being Colin, he sometimes got his fingers burned and made a loss. It was a good thing when George Neville offered him a job on the side."

"When did your husband meet him?"

"Oh, sometime in January last year. They were staying at the same hotel in Leningrad."

"And shortly afterwards they became partners?" Ashton suggested.

She laughed as though he had made a huge joke. "Oh dear me, no," she spluttered. "George had more sense than that. Colin was strictly on a commission basis. They would meet from time to time over lunch and George would give him his cut."

Ashton thought the arrangement would explain why Debbie Roxburgh had never heard of Joyner. It was likely none of her predecessors had heard of him either. He noted too that Frances Joyner appeared to be on more than nodding terms with George Neville.

"Colin was a sort of tipster," she continued. "He kept his ear to the ground and let George know what capital and consumer durables were in demand. You could also say he was a roving paymaster for Trans Globe. Some of the vendors wanted their invoices settled in cash, others were content to have the money channelled into a Swiss bank account, a few even wanted to be paid off with bearer bonds. It may not be the way we do business in this country, but the Russians are new to capitalism and they make their own rules."

He wondered who had told her that. Not her late husband; only a few moments ago she had told him he rarely said anything about his business trips to Moscow. That left the UK rep of Trans Globe.

"How well do you know George Neville?" Ashton enquired casually.

"I like to think we are good friends."

There had been a momentary hesitation before Frances Joyner had answered, as if she had tried to weigh up how much he already knew about their relationship.

"Did Mr Neville ever tell you why he had offered Colin a part-time job?"

"Not in so many words, but from what George did say, I gathered he had his hands full elsewhere in Europe and needed someone who could speak the language to keep an eye on things in Russia. My guess is Colin made quite an impression on him when they met in Leningrad and he was taken in by his patter."

And then again, maybe Neville had had an ulterior motive for employing her husband. Some of the monetary transactions struck Ashton as decidedly risky and he could understand why Neville might want to use a middle man in order to distance himself from any unpleasantness. And since he was in business on his own account, Colin Joyner was the perfect front. It was even possible that unwittingly, he had made the supreme sacrifice for Neville.

"Why are you asking me all these personal questions, Mr Ashton?"

"I was hoping you might be able to tell me where he is."

"Where who is?" she countered.

"Mr Neville. The UK branch of Trans Globe Services has gone out of business."

"I don't believe it."

"Try ringing his office then; you won't get an answer because the phone has been cut off. The premises in Arlington House have been vacated and all the furniture returned to the rental agency. The girl who worked for him was given to understand that the firm was relocating in Manchester, but the landlords were told that the UK branch was being closed because of the worldwide recession. Mr Neville has also moved out of his furnished flat in Lancaster Gardens without leaving a forwarding address."

"My God, when did all this happen?"

"It would appear that some of the arrangements were made while you and your daughter were in Moscow."

"I think I need something a little stronger than coffee." Frances Joyner got up, walked over to the drinks cupboard near the fireplace and crouched in front of it, her back towards Ashton. The black toreador pants were skin tight and emphasised the rounded contours of her buttocks. "I'm going to have a whisky and soda," she announced. "Will you join me, Mr Ashton?"

"It's kind of you to ask but I don't think I should. I'm driving."

Still crouching, she half turned to look at him over her shoulder. "Please change your mind, I hate drinking alone."

"Well, maybe a weak one."

"How weak?"

"Just colour the soda water," he told her.

She took out a couple of crystal tumblers and stood up. "When did you learn that Trans Globe had folded?" she asked.

"Almost a week ago. I tried to contact you several times but had no luck."

"I was in France, house hunting. Perhaps it's just as well I didn't find anything with this Russian business hanging over me." She mixed their drinks, brought them over to the low table and leaned forward, offering Ashton more than a passing glimpse of her bosom as she placed his glass in front of him. "I couldn't be held liable for the money the Russians claim they're owed, could I?"

"No chance."

"Good. It would be pretty ironic if I was, considering that Colin was owed two thousand pounds commission from his previous trip to Moscow."

"Do you mind if I ask you a personal question?"

"Why not?" She flashed him another brilliant smile. "What else have you been doing thus far?"

"Why did Mr Neville make all the arrangements for your husband's funeral?"

"Because he offered to do so. I don't know why – perhaps it was out of kindness or a sense of duty, or maybe he had a guilty conscience about something."

He thought Frances Joyner might leave it at that but it was as if the drink had loosened her tongue and once started, she needed no further prompting from him. Neville had gone to Beresford and Son because Winnie Joyner had wanted her son's ashes scattered on his father's grave and they were the biggest funeral directors in that part of London. She hadn't asked why he had briefed Harold Raeburn and Associates to handle the probate but could make a shrewd guess.

"Colin had opened accounts with several different banks in town. Of course, he never said anything to me, but I wouldn't mind betting he was hiding the money he had made in Russia from the Inland Revenue. My solicitor is a bit of an old fuddy-duddy and everything has to be above board where he is concerned."

Although she hadn't said as much, the inference was obvious. Unlike the family firm, the People's Law Centre was not exactly pro Establishment and the lawyers were unlikely to feel it was their duty to do the work of Her Majesty's Inspector of Taxes. They would merely accept the client's word and take steps to ensure they could not be accused of participating in tax evasion.

"Do you know anything about probate, Mr Ashton – like how long it takes?"

"I think you can reckon on a couple of months provided there are no complications, but don't quote me."

"Well, it doesn't really matter. With any luck, I'll be living in France long before then."

"Don't tell me you've found a buyer for this house already?"

"In this economic climate? You've got to be joking, Mr Ashton."

"You could be in for a long wait then."

"Not me."

Frances Joyner had no intention of hanging on until the house was sold, she was getting out while the going was good. With the Labour Party looking set to win the election, she dreaded the penal rates of taxation which she believed would follow once they were in office. If that wasn't reason enough to leave the country, the bottom had fallen out of the property market and there was no telling when it would recover. Consequently, small builders everywhere were going bankrupt or teetering on the edge of·it and it was getting more and more difficult to find work for the central heating side of the business. Even the timber yard was barely paying its way.

"Anyway, you didn't come here to listen to my problems," she said with a deep sigh.

Ashton inclined his head. "Actually," he said, "what you had to say was very interesting."

"It was?" She raised her eyebrows. "Well, you do surprise me."

"And what you were able to tell me about Mr Neville was equally illuminating."

Frances Joyner didn't know what to make of that either, but she didn't appear to be the least bit worried when she saw Ashton out of the house and waved him goodbye as he drove off. "Hard as nails"; he recalled the consular officer in Moscow describing mother and daughter in those terms and could think of none more apt.

Ashton picked up the A3 trunk road north of Liphook and headed back to London in the rain. As he had done on the previous occasion, he broke the journey at the Happy Eater service station to use the pay phone outside the restaurant. This time, he rang Benbow House and told Hicks to hang on for him at the office.

Kelso thought it was a good job he wasn't a betting man. Had a book been opened on the likelihood of the Foreign Office going to bat for the Andrianov family, he would have wagered a month's salary that they would do nothing of the kind. But here he was back at Century House for the second time in a day and it was just as well he had been wise enough to do some of the groundwork with the medical profession. Although the Russians might yet resist the blandishments of Her Majesty's Ambassador Extraordinary and Plenipotentiary in Moscow, it wasn't something he could count on.

"These two leading neurologists you've spoken to," Dunglass said, looking up from the sheet of paper he had passed to him across the table. "I presume they are aware of Ludmilla Andrianova's condition?"

"They know she is a vegetable."

"And they are still quite happy for us to use their names, Roy?"

"So long as we stick to the script they dictated to me. They have their international reputations to consider, so we mustn't lead the Russians to believe they can work miracles. The same proviso applies to the other specialists I've recruited."

"What exactly have these neurologists agreed to do?" Hazelwood demanded.

"They are prepared to examine her."

"And?"

Kelso clenched his fists under the table where they were safely out of sight. Only a few hours ago, Ashton had sat in this very same chair facing his inquisitors. Now it was his turn and he didn't like it. He especially resented the fact that the Deputy DG appeared quite happy to allow Hazelwood to take over the meeting.

"That's as far as they will go," he snapped.

"Someone has got to go through the motions of treating Ludmilla Andrianova. We can't just put her in a hospital and walk away." Hazelwood again and twice as abrasive.

"I've been on to the MoD," Kelso told him abruptly, "and the army has agreed to lend us one of their top physiotherapists."

"And he's willing to take his coat off?"

"I don't know; it's up to the Director General, Medical Services to find someone who is."

"Quite so." Dunglass placed the list of medical specialists to one side. "Have you been on to any hospitals yet, Roy?" he asked.

Grateful for his intervention in what was fast heading for a heated argument, Kelso told the Deputy DG of the tentative arrangements he had made with the Royal Masonic. The hospital was outside the National Health Service and a private room was going to cost them, but the location was far enough removed from Century House to allay any suspicions the Russians might entertain while still being reasonably close to the centre of London.

"What about accommodation for the other members of the Andrianov family?"

"I have a list of properties in Ravenscourt Park near the hospital which have been repossessed by various building societies." Kelso smiled, confident he had done his homework and would not be found wanting. "They were originally priced between two hundred and twenty-five and three hundred thousand, but I'm sure we could get one for a third of the asking price."

"You can go up to a hundred thousand. Get Hicks to install all the necessary defences."

"Right."

"You've done a great job, Roy," Dunglass told him.

And then it was Hazelwood's turn to jump through the hoop.

"I'm a little short of Russian speakers," he began.

"And you'd like to borrow Ashton?"

"His name was on the tip of my tongue," Hazelwood confessed.

"Request denied," Dunglass said curtly. "I'm not allowing him anywhere near Elena Andrianova."

It was easily the best news Kelso had heard all day and he made no attempt to conceal his delight.

Hicks told himself he would give it another five minutes and then he was off home, no matter what. It was, he knew, an idle threat. Had Kelso asked him to stay on, he wouldn't have thought twice about leaving, but you didn't take liberties with Ashton. It wasn't necessary to cross swords with him to know that. He stretched out his legs and gazed at the girlie calendar displayed on the wall of his office. April was a striking redhead with unbelievably long legs and a pair of tits that looked as if they had been sculptured in marble. The artist, whose creation she was, had clothed her in skimpy black underwear which left very little to the imagination. He supposed her face was meant to look sultry and full of promise, but there was no character in it, unlike Harriet Egan's. Now there was a real tasty bit of goods. Unfortunately, like the girl in the calendar, she was unobtainable, but it didn't hurt to dream. He was still fantasising when Ashton walked into the office.

"Those photographs you took at the funeral," Ashton said, getting straight to the point, "have you still got the negatives?"

"Yeah, in the filing cabinet behind me." Hicks got up from the desk and fetched a brown envelope from the top drawer. "You want me to run off some more prints of Neville?"

"No." Ashton opened the envelope, took out the negatives and held each strip of four up to the light. "It's Mrs Joyner I'm interested in."

"Which one?"

"The dyed blonde. Think you can do anything with the last negative of this strip?"

Ashton had taken him to Breakespear Crematorium for the

express purpose of photographing George Neville and if he said so himself, he'd done a pretty good job. Because he hadn't been concerned to capture her image at the time, Frances Joyner was invariably on the periphery of each exposure. The exception was the long shot he had taken of Neville in conversation with the funeral director. The blonde and her sulky-looking daughter had been walking towards the chapel when the old woman with the walking stick had called out to her and she had turned around just as he'd pressed the button. Although she was still on the edge of the picture, he had caught her looking straight into the camera.

"What do you have in mind?" Hicks asked him. "An enlargement of her head and shoulders?"

"Yes, something in the region of four inches by five. But I want her photograph to be as clear as you can make it. Nothing grainy, otherwise people are going to say they're not sure."

"What people?"

"The occupants of a certain block of flats in Lancaster Gardens."

"I don't get it."

"It's where Neville used to live," Ashton told him.

Chapter 21

Ashton turned the corner into Dolphin Square and immediately walked a little faster. He had got into the habit of calling for Harriet Egan on his way to the office since moving into the flat owned by the Church Commissioners in Churchill Gardens some two weeks after the general election. In a matter of days, it had become such a well-established routine that she knew almost to the minute when to expect him and would have a pot of coffee waiting. This morning, he barely had time to press the buzzer before Harriet tripped the electronic lock on the front door. Entering the hall, he went on up to the apartment she rented on the top floor and found her waiting for him on the landing. For once, the welcoming smile was missing.

"I've just had Roy Kelso on the phone," she said in a tight voice.

"I thought you looked down in the mouth," Ashton said with a smile. "Now I know why."

"Do you? Then perhaps you'll have a quiet word with our esteemed Assistant Director and explain to him in words of one syllable that you do not live here."

Ashton followed her into the flat and closed the door behind him. "What exactly did Kelso say to you?" he asked.

"He said there were matters he needed to discuss with you and Hicks."

"And that made you angry?"

"No, of course it didn't." Harriet went into the kitchen, unplugged the percolator and poured him a mug of very strong black coffee. "I don't know if I'm imagining it," she said, "but just lately Kelso seems to go out of his way to needle me. Take this morning, for instance; his excuse was that, having failed to get an answer from you, he had rung me. When I told him you

249

weren't here yet, he managed to sound incredulous."

"When was this?"

"Seven forty-five, maybe ten minutes to eight."

At least twenty minutes ago; twice as long in fact as it had taken him to walk from Churchill Gardens to Dolphin Square. Kelso hadn't tried to contact him at home, the cretin had phoned Harriet a good ten minutes before he had left the flat.

"You'd better phone him at home, Peter; he said it was important."

"If Hicks has been playing him up again, I'll straighten him out in my own good time, after I've been to the flat in Lancaster Gardens."

"I can see Mr Chang Li Xian," Harriet said. "It's not something you have to attend to personally. I mean, all I've got to do is show him a photograph."

Chang Li Xian lived in the same apartment house as George Neville and was the one resident Ashton hadn't met. The Chinese man had left for Hong Kong on an extended business trip several days before Ashton had gone to Lancaster Gardens. According to the daily help, Chang Li Xian was due to return that morning. Whether he would be able to help him was questionable. If none of the other residents who had looked at her photograph could recall seeing Frances Joyner, why should Chang Li Xian have encountered her, especially since his flat was directly above the one Neville had occupied? Experience however had taught Ashton that the element of chance was a factor only a fool would discount.

"What's the problem?" Harriet demanded. "Don't you trust me?"

"Of course I do. It's Kelso I don't trust. I have this itchy feeling he's got something up his sleeve."

"There's only one way to find out."

"You're right."

Ashton finished his coffee, picked up the extension in the kitchen and rang Kelso at home. The number had barely started to ring out when he answered the phone and immediately began to act the part of the crisp and effective Head of Department.

"Don't bother to go into the office," Kelso told him. "I'm going straight to Hammersmith and will meet you there at 08.45 hours. I've already informed Hicks."

"What's up?"

"You surely don't expect me to tell you over an open line," Kelso said and hung up on him.

Ashton replaced the phone and turned to face Harriet. "Now, there was one very excited man," he said. "I imagine half the thrill must have come from knowing something I didn't and keeping it to himself."

"Are you going to do the same?"

"No. Hicks and I are to meet him at the house the department purchased in Rylett Close." Ashton reached inside his jacket and took out the enlarged photograph of Frances Joyner. "I think you had better have this," he said.

Eighty years ago, when newly built, the semi-detached house in Rylett Close had cost the first owner three hundred and fifty pounds; in 1988 it had changed hands for two hundred thousand. The property had been repossessed by the building society three years later when the young couple who had purchased it on a hundred per cent mortgage had fallen seriously in arrears with their repayments after both had been made redundant. Kelso had bought it on behalf of the SIS for a mere sixty-five thousand, which was considerably less than he had anticipated. Furthermore, the transaction had been completed in the record time of six working days, a feat that had given the solicitors a few headaches.

The morning the vendors had released the keys to the property, Hicks had moved into the house to install the latest high-tech gadgetry. No building was ever impregnable but he had come very close to converting number 84 Rylett Close into a veritable fortress. The sentries were the television cameras mounted under the eaves, which covered the front, back and east side of the house, while the shared wall with the other semi-detached was protected by audio sensors. The external line of defence was an infra-red intruder system which triggered a flashing light on the monitor screen in the basement whenever the invisible fence was broken. The innermost defence was a sophisticated burglar alarm connected to Hammersmith Police Station.

Even though it wasn't the first time Ashton had been to Rylett Close, Hicks insisted on giving him the full guided tour of the property before Kelso arrived on the scene. His motive for doing so was transparently clear. Should the Assistant Director be tempted to criticise his workmanship, he wanted to say that Ashton had inspected the equipment he'd installed and was perfectly satisfied. Hicks needn't have bothered; when Kelso finally arrived on the scene some twenty minutes late, he was far more interested in the soft furnishings than in the electronic hardware. Like some fussy hausfrau, he simply went from room to room checking the curtains, lampshades, carpets and furniture to make sure everything was spick and span for their guests.

"We go operational this evening," he announced.

"What?"

"The Andrianovs, Peter; they are arriving on British Airways Flight BA873 this evening. Gets into Heathrow at 18.25 hours."

A fortnight ago, the Russians had agreed in principle that Ludmilla Andrianova could go to London for treatment accompanied by her husband and granddaughter. Since then, there had been no further word from Moscow. Now, suddenly, they were on the way. It was, Ashton thought, a typical example of the old stop-go routine, proof that very little had changed for all the talk of Glasnost and Perestroika.

"When did you hear this?" he asked.

"Round about eleven last night. The duty officer at Century House rang the Deputy DG to inform him there was a Personal Immediate signal in from Head of Station, Moscow and in due course Stuart got in touch with me."

"And Elena? What did Hugo Calthorpe have to say about her?"

"She's still in hospital but should be discharged any day now."

"Will the authorities give her an exit visa?"

"Well, that remains to be seen."

It was the kind of evasive answer Ashton had come to expect from Kelso. After three weeks on fracture boards, most people who had sustained a cracked pelvis were up and moving about again. Elena was a healthy young woman and it was hard to believe she would take more than twice as long to recover. On the other hand, he could well believe the KGB had told the hospital authorities to detain her indefinitely.

"We're not going to get anywhere without Elena."

"Let's take one step at a time, shall we?" Kelso said irritably.

Number 84 Rylett Close was a one-off. It had been acquired

because it was situated within easy walking distance of the Royal Masonic Hospital and all the other safe houses owned by the SIS were out in the country miles away from London. In addition to the purchase price, Ashton calculated they must have spent at least six thousand on furnishing the property to a reasonable standard. There were other expenses which would surface later. The air fares would total a minimum of eight hundred and there was no computing the hospital bills which, like everything else, would be charged to public funds. Unless they could get at Elena, it would all be money down the drain and, as usual, the taxpayer would be the loser.

"I will meet the Andrianovs at Heathrow but I shall need your services, Peter." Kelso laughed, striking a false note of bonhomie. "I'm afraid my Russian is limited to *da* and *nyet*."

"Has someone had a change of heart?" Ashton asked him.

"I don't know what you mean."

"I think you do." When the Russians had indicated they were prepared to let the Andrianovs go to England, Hazelwood had been the first to let him know the good news. He had also told Ashton unofficially that the Deputy DG had stated that on no account would he be allowed to meet Elena and her family. "Have you spoken to Mr Dunglass about this?" he added in case the penny hadn't dropped with Kelso.

"Of course I have."

"And he is happy about it?"

"Stuart raised no objections." Kelso glanced at his wristwatch. "Time I was going," he said and edged past Hicks towards the hall. "We'll use an official car and leave from the office at 17.00 hours."

"Right." Ashton followed him out into the hall. "Can I cadge a lift back to town?"

" 'Fraid not, Peter. I want you to hang on here until the provisions arrive." The mechanical smile made another brief appearance. "We can't let the Andrianovs think we're on starvation rations over here, can we?"

"And what do you want me to do?" Hicks demanded aggressively.

"I expect you to make sure all the domestic appliances are in good working order," Kelso told him, and stalked out of the house.

★ ★ ★

Spring had finally come to Moscow. The last traces of impacted snow had vanished from the forests and under the hedges in the parks, the sky was no longer overcast and the sunlight was actually warm. But it wasn't just the fine weather that lifted Michael Vaughan and made him feel good. With any luck, this would be the last time he would play nursemaid to the wretched Andrianovs. No one would be more relieved than he when the family left the departure lounge at Sheremetyevo 2 to board the British Airways Boeing 767 to London. Unfortunately, there was one last chore he had to do before that happy event came to pass.

Although the Piragow Hospital was not on the way to the airport, Konstantin Kirillovich had insisted on saying goodbye to his daughter before leaving Moscow and he had no option but to accommodate the Russian. The Embassy had provided a transit van for the journey because it was the only vehicle capable of transporting a patient in a wheelchair. It was not, however, equipped with a powered loading platform and he and Konstantin Kirillovich would never have been able to lift Ludmilla and the wheelchair into the back without the assistance of the driver. Vaughan just hoped the old man wouldn't insist on taking his wife into the hospital to see Elena.

They left the Garden Ring at the Hotel Warsaw and made a right turn into Lenin Prospekt. The hospital was the fourth turning on the right; tripping the nearside indicator, the driver wheeled into the approach road and motored on down to the main entrance. All the parking spaces were taken, but that didn't bother him. With infinite faith in the CD plates on his vehicle, he parked across the back of two limousines which obviously belonged to senior members of the hospital management.

The altercation with the hall porter, who cared nothing for diplomatic privileges, started while Vaughan was still in the van. It became even more heated when the driver got out and was joined by Konstantin Kirillovich. With the instinct born of a true Foreign Office representative, Vaughan disassociated himself from the shouting match and became instead an interested spectator on the sidelines. The dispute was finally resolved by the driver, who agreed to move his van some twelve to fifteen feet so that the expensive foreign limousines were no longer obstructed. That it now blocked two rusting Ladas was of no consequence since they apparently belonged to two lowly interns.

"Is everyone happy now?" Vaughan asked in appalling Russian when peace was restored.

"We wish to see Elena Andrianova," Konstantin Kirillovich informed him stiffly.

"Yes, of course. Shall we go?"

"Ludmilla wants to say goodbye to her daughter."

How the old woman had been able to communicate any such desire was beyond Vaughan but it was more than his career was worth to make an issue of it. With a fixed smile, he helped Konstantin Kirillovich and the driver to lift the wheelchair out of the transit van and push it up the ramp into the building. Once inside, there was a ten-minute delay before the lift responded to the call button. When it did arrive, Vaughan discovered there was only sufficient room for Ludmilla, the wheelchair, Konstantin Kirillovich and granddaughter Vera. Ever the diplomat, he waited until the doors had closed before he gave vent to his feelings with a choice collection of expletives. His anger then slightly mollified, he climbed the stairs to the fourth floor where Elena had a small room to herself.

Elena had acquired a new watchdog. The attractive Katya Malinovskaya had been replaced by a hulk with a lumpy face and a short muscular neck which barely surfaced above the ox-like shoulders. He had fists the size of hams and the buttons on the jacket of his brown pinstripe suit looked as if they were about to pop off at any moment. Vaughan took one look at him and decided the Russian was not the sort of man he would care to encounter on a dark night in a lonely place, or in broad daylight for that matter.

"I'm from the British Embassy," he told the KGB man, then pointed to the door of Elena's room and explained that he was with the Andrianov family.

"Papers," the Russian grunted and remained seated on his chair out in the corridor.

Vaughan produced his passport, Moscow driving permit and a thin smile. "Are you always this charming?" he asked in English.

Whether he had understood him or not, the Russian spent an inordinate amount of time examining every page between the stiff covers of his passport before he allowed him into the room.

Elena was sitting up in bed. The cage which had kept the weight of the bedclothes off her legs had been dispensed with a fortnight or so ago and she had seemed in pretty good shape when Vaughan had last seen her. This morning, however, she looked like death warmed over and there were beads of perspiration on her face. Because the chart at the foot of the bed indicated that her temperature was normal, he assumed it was that certain time of the month and she was having a particularly bad period.

Satisfied with his diagnosis, Vaughan turned his thoughts to other matters. In Moscow, it was advisable to check in three hours before the scheduled departure and it was going to be a close-run thing if the family leave-taking went on much longer. He wondered if Ludmilla was incontinent and could envisage all kinds of problems if she was. The whole rigmarole of boarding a plane from Sheremetyevo 2 was something of a nightmare at the best of times. The Andrianov family practically guaranteed it would be a real horror story on this occasion, one that he was averse to prolonging a minute longer than necessary.

"It's time we were moving on," Vaughan said abruptly, then grabbed the wheelchair and pointed it towards the door.

"You are in too much of a hurry," Konstantin Kirillovich told him with great dignity. "Ludmilla hasn't said goodbye to her daughter yet."

It was a pantomime. Andrianov manoeuvred the chair backwards and forwards until it was close enough to the bed for Elena to lean forward and peck her mother on the cheek. Then she hugged and kissed Vera, did the same with her father and would have gone on embracing the pair of them alternately if he hadn't intervened and shooed the family out of the room.

"Mr Vaughan – please."

Her voice was low but insistent and oddly compelling. Though reluctant to do so, Vaughan returned to her bedside.

"Yes? What is it?" he asked, barely able to conceal his impatience.

"That man out in the corridor . . ." Elena said in a conspiratorial whisper.

"What about him?"

"His name is Oroblinsky, Sergeant Oroblinsky."

"Yes?"

"He is a very bad man." Elena reached for his hand and squeezed it. "You tell Mr Ashton, he will understand."

★ ★ ★

256

Harriet listened to the footsteps drawing nearer and knew it was Ashton before he walked into her office.

"Mr Chang Li Xian is back," she told him before he had a chance to ask her. "I saw your Hong Kong businessman around eleven this morning and showed him the photograph of Frances Joyner. He is pretty sure she is the woman he saw with Neville on several occasions."

"How long ago was this?"

"He couldn't really say, but it was some months back. One time he bumped into her on the landing when he was leaving for his London office."

"The inference being that she had spent the night with Neville."

Harriet thought Ashton could hardly have been less enthusiastic had she told him that Chang Li Xian hadn't seen her. He had wondered if there was anything between Neville and Frances Joyner other than a casual acquaintanceship; she had returned from Lancaster Gardens with as good as proof that they were lovers and now it seemed he was no longer interested. It simply didn't make sense.

"I wonder how much Mandy knows?"

"You can forget about that young lady," Harriet told him bluntly. "We don't have an address for her in London and I don't see how we are going to find out where she is living. She has never come to the notice of the police, not even for a minor traffic violation, and we haven't the faintest idea what she does to earn her keep. And if you're thinking we can trace Mandy through her National Insurance number, you can put that idea on the back burner. We would have to know her date and place of birth before we could ask the Department of Social Security to assist us."

"Okay, you win."

He made it seem they had been engaged in a contest of some kind, which was stupid because she had only been doing what he'd asked of her.

"You wanted to know where and when Neville renewed his British passport," she said, changing the subject.

"So I did. What have you got?"

"Neville was issued with a new passport by the British Consul in San Francisco two years after he'd arrived in America. This

257

was in 1978; ten years later he obtained another one, this time from the representative of the British High Commission in Victoria, British Columbia."

"I'm not sure where that gets us," Ashton said.

She wasn't looking for praise but a polite thank you would not have come amiss. "If you really want to needle me, try poking a stick in my eye," she blurted out.

"What?"

"How do you suppose I got all this information?" Harriet demanded angrily. "Have you any idea how many favours I've asked of Clifford Peachey. You take everything for granted and it just isn't good enough . . ."

She never got to finish the sentence. Eyes widening, she watched Ashton walk round the desk and was still wondering what he was up to when he gently lifted her to her feet and kissed her. She placed a hand against his chest, thought about pushing him away only to find herself responding.

"Why did you do that?" she asked when Ashton released her.

"I'm sorry, I shouldn't have."

"I didn't say I didn't like it." She looked up, expecting to see a smile but he merely looked preoccupied. "Something's gone wrong, hasn't it? Come on, tell me what it is."

"Kelso wants me to meet the Andrianovs at Heathrow when they arrive this evening and I can't get out of it. I'm the sole linguist in the Administrative Department and the Russian Desk is only interested in questioning Elena."

"And officially you've never seen Konstantin Kirillovich before."

"Yes. Can you imagine what Kelso will make of it if Elena's father greets me like a long-lost friend?"

"So what are you going to do, Peter?"

"Hope for the best, I suppose," Ashton said with a wry smile. "Trouble is, it gets harder to differentiate between friends and enemies these days."

Chapter 22

The crowd waiting to meet relatives, friends and business acquaintances in Terminal 1 was, Ashton estimated, large enough to fill a European Airbus several times over. The crush had nothing to do with adverse weather conditions over Europe, a lightning strike by air traffic controllers in France or any other happenstance. It so happened that Flight BA873 from Moscow arrived at 18.25 hours together with a Finnair plane from Helsinki, the Supershuttle from Manchester and yet another British Airways flight from Leipzig via Hanover. It was immediately preceded by an Aer Lingus 737 at 18.20 from Cork and was followed at 18.30 by BA955 from Munich. Similar flight patterns were to be found in the other three terminals at Heathrow and were merely a symptom of the busiest airport in the world.

Kelso had added to the congestion both inside and outside the building with the reception committee he had organised to meet the Andrianovs. To transport the family to Hammersmith, he had laid on an ambulance, a government limousine and an escort of three hard-nosed men in a Rover 800. This small convoy was now parked nose to tail on the first lane immediately outside the exit where it impeded the traffic, much to the annoyance of numerous bus and taxi drivers. The reception committee itself was causing nothing like the same problems inside the terminal building but its composition was still too big for Ashton's liking.

He could understand why Kelso should have wanted the paramedic to be present and the chauffeur was obviously there to help the Andrianovs with their baggage, but the role of the third man was less clear. Like his two companions in the Rover, he was police Special Branch and used to working hand in glove with MI5, the Security Service. He was the eyes and ears of the Kremlin Watchers and it was by no means obvious to Ashton who he was watching tonight. If Kelso seriously believed the Andrianovs were at risk, then the ambulance, limousine and escort should have been waiting for them on the apron. Instead of putting them through Immigration and Customs, they should have been taken straight off the plane and whisked out of the airport. As it was, Ashton had a nasty feeling the Special Branch man was nicely placed to observe Konstantin Kirillovich's reaction when he spotted him amongst the crowd.

Kelso would be in a position to reopen the Board of Inquiry and no one would be able to accuse him of waging a personal vendetta because this time he would have an independent witness, and who was better than a police officer without an axe to grind? With a fresh influx of travellers beginning to surge into the arrivals hall from the direction of Customs, Ashton knew he was in deep trouble unless he could pull a fast one.

The chauffeur was standing next to him holding a piece of cardboard against his chest with the words MR ANDRIANOV printed on it in block capitals with a biro. Reaching across, Ashton snatched the piece of cardboard from him and held it aloft.

"What the hell are you playing at?" Kelso demanded angrily.

"I'm trying to reassure Konstantin Kirillovich. Elena will have told him what I look like and I want to draw attention to myself. Okay?"

"No, it's not okay. Now give it back to the chauffeur."

"Don't be stupid all your life," Ashton rasped. "When Konstantin Kirillovich comes through into the hall, the first thing he is going to see is this notice, then he'll recognise me and know he is safe."

Ashton moved forward to the rope barrier, side-stepped one pace to his right and used a shoulder to ease Kelso out of the way and thereby restrict his view. The number of travellers spilling out into the hall dried up for a few brief moments, then surged again. The column was headed by a group of holiday-makers returning from Moscow, the name of the tour operator who'd organised the trip prominently displayed on the tags attached to their bags. Behind them, immobile in her wheelchair came Ludmilla Andrianova with a member of the airport staff in attendance. One of the cabin crew led Vera by the hand while a bemused-looking Konstantin Kirillovich walked beside his granddaughter pushing a baggage cart. The instant he spotted Ashton in the crowd, his face creased in a smile. It subsequently faded and was replaced by a puzzled expression when Ashton spoke to him in Russian in a way which suggested they were strangers meeting for the first time.

"This way, Mr Andrianov," he said, pointing to the gap in the rope barrier to his left.

"You will be waiting for us there?" Konstantin Kirillovich asked.

"We all will," Ashton told him. "Mr Kelso, myself and the chauffeur."

The omission of the Special Branch officer had been deliberate, but nothing came of it; if he did understand Russian, he was cute enough not to show it. Unfortunately, Konstantin Kirillovich was incapable of such subtlety; once clear of the crowd of onlookers, he advanced on Ashton and embraced him fervently.

"Touching," Kelso observed acidly, "very touching."

"This is my superior officer," Ashton said, disengaging himself from the bear-like hug. "He made all this possible. It's him you should be thanking, not me."

The diversion worked. Before Kelso could ask what he had said to Andrianov, the Russian was embracing him to express his gratitude.

"Get him off," Kelso hissed. "Will you kindly get him off me?"

"I'm doing my best," Ashton told him, "but we are dealing with a very demonstrative man and we don't want to offend him, do we?" He tapped the Russian on the shoulder and smiled broadly. "Time we were moving on, Konstantin Kirillovich," he said cheerfully, "we're only causing a log jam here."

Leaving the chauffeur to take charge of the baggage cart, Ashton steered the old man and his granddaughter towards the exit. The paramedic tagged on behind with Ludmilla, Kelso and the Special Branch officer. There was a slight hiccup when Andrianov indicated that he wished to travel in the ambulance with his wife, but Ashton was able to persuade him there was no room for his granddaughter and it wouldn't be right to leave her with strangers.

"I promise you it is going to be all right," he assured him as the convoy moved off. "We shall be following the ambulance all the way to the hospital and you can stay with Ludmilla while she is being admitted."

"I sleep at the hospital," Konstantin Kirillovich announced and nodded to himself as though it was all settled.

"No, I'm afraid you can't do that," Ashton said. "We have this house for you which is only a short walk away."

"I want to stay with Ludmilla."

Kelso twisted round to face them both. "Is there a problem?" he asked.

"Nothing I can't handle."

"I'm sure you're right, but I would still like to know what is bothering him."

"He doesn't want to move into Rylett Close," Ashton said, then resumed his conversation with Konstantin Kirillovich in Russian. "Do you have any idea what time it is in Moscow?" he asked.

"Same as here."

"No, it's ten to ten over there. Moscow is three hours ahead of us and your granddaughter looks as if she is ready for bed. The hospital is only expecting Ludmilla and there is nowhere for you and Vera to sleep. Now, why don't you stay at the house tonight and we'll talk about it in the morning?"

"You will be there the whole time?"

"If that's what you want."

"Then I am happy to do as you ask," Andrianov told him gravely.

"It's all settled, Roy," Ashton said wearily. "I'm spending the night with them."

"Good." Kelso took out his cellphone, punched up the number for Century House and informed the duty officer that their package had arrived intact.

Hazelwood had only intended to stay on at the office until he received confirmation that the Andrianovs had arrived safely. He was still there now because Dunglass had caught him just as he was about to leave and asked that he should wait for the cipher clerks to decode an emergency Top Secret cable from Moscow.

There was an old adage which maintained that the security of a coded message was entirely dependent on the length of the clear text to be encoded. Apart from making the job of a hostile intercept station that much easier, the almost inevitable repetition of certain key words in a long signal was a godsend for the codebreakers. Early on in their careers, Hazelwood and Calthorpe had worked for a department head who'd had the mnemonic KISS for Keep It Short and Simple prominently displayed on his desk. It was an exhortation Hazelwood had taken to heart but one which Head of Station, Moscow seemed to have forgotten on this occasion. The signal he had despatched to London was the equivalent of a newsletter and took close on an hour to decipher.

"Have you heard of this Sergeant Oroblinsky?" Dunglass asked when he'd read the cable.

Hazelwood nodded. "Ashton told me about him. He's with the KGB's Criminal Investigation Division and was on the Joyner case. His superior officer at the time was Major Oleg Lysenko."

"Who subsequently died from two gunshot wounds in the head?"

"That's the man, Stuart."

"What else do we know about Oroblinsky?"

Hazelwood suspected he was in for a long session with the Deputy DG and shifted uncomfortably in his chair. He would have given anything for a Burma cheroot but Dunglass was one of the most rabid non-smokers on the top floor and there was no way he would allow him to light up in his office.

"The men who murdered Colin Joyner and Nina Golodkinova were killed in a shoot-out at the public bath house in the Nagatino District of Moscow. Oroblinsky led the assault team who stormed the building and there are grounds for thinking he was determined not to take them alive."

"Who says so?"

"Ashton." Hazelwood cleared his throat. "He believes it was a set-up. Oroblinsky might not have organised it but he was definitely the executioner."

Dunglass left his desk, went over to the window and stood there gazing down at the labyrinth of railtracks outside Waterloo station, hands clasped behind his back. "Elena Andrianova seems to be terrified of him, Victor."

"Yes."

" 'He is a very bad man. You tell Mr Ashton, he will understand.' That's what she said to Vaughan, and I'd like to

263

know what is behind it. Is she trying to pressure Ashton? Or, to put it more crudely, does she have something on him?"

"Like what?"

"The Chief is leaving at the end of the month and I'm moving into his chair on Monday the first of June."

Hazelwood blinked, momentarily thrown by a statement that had nothing to do with the question that had just been raised. To heads of departments, the DG was either The Chief or more simply The Director. In common with many others, he had been prepared to bet that Dunglass would be the next Head of the SIS and the only real surprise was that the government had waited so long after the election to confirm his appointment.

"My congratulations, Stuart," he said.

Dunglass turned about. "Well, actually it's mutual – you're going to be my deputy."

From Head of the Russian Desk to Deputy Director General in the space of eighteen months was hard to take in. Although he was not lacking in ambition, the promotion to the number two spot had been beyond his wildest dreams. He wondered what Alice would say when she heard the news.

"I'm speechless," he told Dunglass. "I don't know how to thank you, but I do know we can do a good job together."

"I think so too, Victor, and there is no getting away from the fact that I need someone with your background. Whatever the politicians might like to think, peace has not broken out in the former Communist Bloc. If anything, the break-up of the Soviet Union has led to a much more volatile and potentially dangerous situation."

Hazelwood wouldn't argue with that analysis, and Stuart wasn't being smarmy when he'd said he needed him. All his practical experience in the field had been gained in the Far East, which was why some people referred to him as "Jungle Jim" behind his back.

"The thing is, I have to be sure of your judgement," Dunglass continued, "so think carefully before you answer this question."

"Which is?"

"What am I to make of Ashton, Victor?"

Hazelwood supposed his promotion to Deputy DG could hinge on how he answered the question but he didn't let the possibility influence his reply. He could have made a speech emphasising

264

Ashton's strong points and his many fine qualities. But he didn't; instead, he put it simply and succinctly.

"If it was within my gift, I would give him the Russian Desk."

"So what message was Elena Andrianova trying to convey?"

"I think certain people guessed that Konstantin Kirillovich would insist on saying goodbye to his daughter before he left Moscow, and Oroblinsky was there to make sure she didn't use her father as a courier. It could be he was one of the men who put her in hospital in the first place."

"You've no reason to believe Ashton has seen Elena Andrianova since he interrogated her in Vaughan's office, have you, Victor?"

There was a personal letter from Hugo Calthorpe on his demi-official file which suggested exactly that, but he had said nothing about it at the Board of Inquiry and he didn't propose to do so now. Apart from his commitment to Ashton, he was also aware that it was a little late in the day to be thinking how he could save his own skin.

"None whatever," Hazelwood said firmly. "I know there have been a number of rumours floating around Moscow but you can trace all of them back to Dzerzhinsky Square. I also happen to think the KGB have been busy throwing dust in our eyes."

Dunglass returned to his desk, stacked the filing trays one on top of the other and locked them away in his safe. "It's time we stopped chasing our tails," he said. "Our job is to extract Elena Andrianova from their clutches any way we can. I'll keep pressuring the Foreign Office, meantime you'd better have something up your sleeve in case the Russians prove awkward."

"We're talking dirty tricks?"

"Is there any other kind?" Dunglass shepherded him towards the door, then looked back to satisfy himself that the duty officer would not find anything amiss when he checked the office. "I think it's time you and I called it a day," he said.

It was, Hazelwood thought, one of those enigmatic remarks that could be taken several ways.

Measured from door to door, 84 Rylett Close was approximately six hundred yards from the Royal Masonic Hospital provided you took the alleyway below the railway embankment as a quick cut to Goldhawk Road. They did the short journey by car because six-year-old Vera Fedichkina was practically asleep on her feet by the time Ludmilla Andrianova had been settled into her private room. Kelso also believed in playing it safe; the night had drawn in, there was no moon to speak of and the pedestrian alleyway was badly lit. If there was going to be any unpleasantness, the quick cut to Goldhawk Road was an ideal spot for it.

That it would have been a lot easier for the KGB to neutralise the Andrianovs had the family remained in Moscow was beside the point as far as Kelso was concerned. Attention to detail was his guiding principle and he was confident that no one could ever accuse him of having failed to anticipate a problem. There was some justification for his proud boast; apart from turning 84 Rylett Close into a fortress and providing a well-stocked larder for the family, he had also found a housekeeper for them. Her name was Ruth. The widow of a former officer in the SIS, she too had been a member of the Secret Intelligence Service and had retained her security clearance long after she had officially retired from the firm.

"Well, that's it," Kelso said after Ruth had taken the little girl up to her room. "I don't think I've overlooked anything. Special Branch have left a nightwatchman down in the basement, so you can sleep easy tonight."

Ashton followed him out of the house. "Is someone going to relieve me tomorrow?" he asked.

"Perhaps."

"I'm going to need a change of clothes – clean shirt, socks, stuff like that. And my shaving tackle."

"I'm sure Miss Egan will be only too happy to assist you there."

"Just what are you inferring, Roy?"

"Nothing." Kelso shot him a hasty smile. "I merely thought she would be willing to pop round to your place in Churchill Gardens and collect whatever you need."

Ashton hesitated. He remembered the evening the Assistant Director had undressed Harriet with his eyes when she had been wearing the charcoal grey suit with the short skirt. He could picture her distaste when Kelso pitched up on her doorstep, but then decided she was quite capable of dealing with him.

"She'll need these," Ashton said and gave Kelso the keys to his flat. "I'll phone Harriet and warn her to expect you."

"Yes, you do that." Kelso looked towards the chauffeur who was waiting patiently for him ready to open the rear door of the limousine. "Be with you in a minute," he called out, then faced Ashton again. "Our Russian guest seems to think the world of you. Anyone observing the way he embraced you at the airport would think you two were old friends."

"Like I already said, he must have recognised me from Elena's description. Anyway, if you had been holding the card, he would probably have embraced you first."

"I doubt it," Kelso said triumphantly. "You see, his name wasn't printed in the Cyrillic alphabet."

It was a bad moment. Ashton hadn't looked at the card when he had grabbed it and didn't know if Kelso was bluffing.

"Elena is a graduate of the Lenin Institute of Foreign Languages," he said, feeling his way. "I naturally assumed it had already occurred to you that when she collected her diploma she would have shown her proud father how to write the family name in English."

The self-satisfied smirk died on Kelso's face. "I might have guessed you would have a plausible explanation," he said curtly, then turned and walked away.

Ashton watched him get into the limousine and waited until he and the Special Branch escort in the Rover 800 drove off before he went back into the house. Kelso hadn't accepted the explanation but even though he had an independent witness to the scene at the airport, he still didn't have any concrete evidence to put before the DG. How long that happy situation would last was problematical in the extreme. Hicks hadn't simply turned number 84 Rylett Close into a fortress, he had also bugged the place from top to bottom so that they could eavesdrop on Elena Andrianova when, or if ever, she was reunited with her family. Somehow, he would have to warn Konstantin Kirillovich in case he let the cat out of the bag.

Among his fellow senior analysts at the Defense Intelligence Agency, Tony Zale was now known as the King of the Balkans. It was not an accolade he had sought or wished to retain. He had acquired it as a result of a chance assignment when he had been required to write a paper assessing the potential cost of military intervention in Yugoslavia. When he had printed the words

"FIRST DRAFT" at the head of a sheet of foolscap, what he had known about that sad country could have been encapsulated in a short paragraph. By the time he had submitted the final published version, he had become an authority on the Balkans.

His knowledge of the region had been acquired from books, newspaper cuttings, old newsreels, TV documentaries and back copies of *National Geographic*. He had also raided the historical archives and had read everything the Office of Strategic Services and the British Special Operations Executive had to say about the activities of Tito's partisans and the Serbian Chetniks during the Second World War. But he had never set foot in Albania, Greece, Bulgaria or Romania, much less Yugoslavia, which made him feel something of a fraud.

A profound hope that he would not be required to write another assessment had evaporated on April 5, the day after the Muslims and Croats of Bosnia Herzegovina had voted for independence in a referendum boycotted by the Bosnian Serbs who made up thirty-one per cent of the population. The new civil war had inevitably led to calls for further assessments. Life had been much more simple two months ago when he had been analysing the movement of freight trains through Romania. Although someone else now had that job, a copy of the weekly survey report was passed to him for information and he had been pleased to see that the liaison visit which he and the other members of the Defense Intelligence Agency team had made to Moscow appeared to have paid off. There was solid evidence that the arms embargo imposed by the UN was now being rigorously enforced and nothing was getting through to Belgrade by rail.

The one remaining loophole was the Danube. For the hundred and ninety miles west of Velika Gradište, where the river ceased to mark the frontier with Romania, to the Hungarian border, the Danube passed through Serbian territory unpoliced by UN observers. There was therefore no way of knowing whether a barge from Galaţi in Moldavia or Izmail in the Ukraine loaded with goods destined for Vienna actually delivered the cargo it had started out with. The same applied to barges heading downstream to the Black Sea.

The Danube however was not a factor Zale needed to take into account. No tributary of the river flowed through Bosnia Herzegovina and by all accounts, the Yugoslav National Army had left the Bosnian Serbs with enough arms and ammunition to keep them going for ten years when they had withdrawn from the Republic. Although the Muslim population outnumbered the Serbs by almost six hundred thousand, they were poorly equipped and hopelessly outgunned. So far, the Croat minority were fighting alongside the Muslims, but the State Department suspected that in the not-too-distant future, the Croats and Serbs might decide to carve up the Republic between them. Zale was prepared to bet that if American troops were sent into Bosnia Herzegovina, it wouldn't be long before they were being shot at by Muslims, Serbs and Croats. It was that kind of situation.

"You want to see the latest poop in the newspapers?"

Zale recognised the abrasive voice with the New Jersey accent and didn't bother to look up when the folder landed on his desk. "Thanks, Bernice," he said.

"You're welcome."

Two cups of coffee and several sheets of crumpled foolscap later, Zale got round to the folder and went through the clippings to see if there was anything that would help him update his latest assessment of the military situation in Bosnia Herzegovina. A blurred photograph of a rangy, bearded figure in combat fatigues caught his eye and he read the accompanying article with interest. Under the heading "White Eagle – Scourge of the Muslims", there was a thumbnail biography of a Serbian irregular whose parents had been murdered by Croats serving in the locally recruited *Waffen SS* during the Second World War. In the late summer of '91, he had extracted a terrible revenge for that wartime atrocity and was reputed to have personally killed over a hundred and fifty men, women and children in an ethnic cleansing operation around Vukovar in Croatia. Now he and his band of irregulars were thought to be moving south on Sarajevo.

The name of the man who called himself the White Eagle was said to be Slobodon Todordzic. Zale thought it sounded familiar but couldn't place it at first, then the penny dropped and he wondered if the Serbian gunman was in any way related to Mike Todorvic, Executive Vice President of Pacific Northwest Oil and Gas.

269

Chapter 23

The dining room was at the back of the house next to the kitchen. French windows opened on to a garden that had been sadly neglected by the previous owners of 84 Rylett Close once they knew the building society was going to repossess their home. In a few short weeks, the flowerbeds had become choked with dock, groundsel, dandelions and sundry other weeds while the lawn now resembled a hayfield. Konstantin Kirillovich however was much too preoccupied to care what the garden looked like or do more than pick at the breakfast of sausage, cheese and buckwheat pancakes with soured cream which Ruth had prepared, hoping to make him feel at home.

Ashton thought it was one of life's little ironies that the SIS had probably made him feel that he had never left Russia. Last night, while making small talk, he had passed Konstantin Kirillovich a series of notes warning him not to say anything that might indicate they had met before in Moscow. "The walls have ears," he had printed in bold letters, and the old man had been smart enough to catch on. But of course, if like Konstantin Kirillovich, you were sixty-four years old, you knew all about Stalin and Beria and the Secret Police. And it was just a little disappointing to find that in England apparently you also had to be careful what you said and to whom.

"Something on your mind, Konstantin Kirillovich?" he asked.

"It is safe to talk here?"

"Of course it is, you're in England now."

"But you also have KGB. Yes?"

"I wouldn't put it quite like that but yes, we do have a security service."

"And you are officer with English KGB, Mr Ashton?"

271

"Didn't Elena Andrianova tell you? I'm a Queen's Messenger, I deliver confidential papers from the Foreign Office to embassies all over the world."

"And you always tell the truth?"

Ashton went over to the sideboard and refilled his cup from the percolator on the hot plate. Even if the Special Branch man in the basement didn't understand the language, the Russian experts at Century House would sit up and take notice when they listened to the tape.

"I try to," he said carefully.

"Well then, Mr Ashton, tell me what the doctors can do for Ludmilla. Can they cure her?"

There was, he decided, nothing to be gained by lying to the old man. Konstantin Kirillovich was not a fool and would know when someone was trying to pull the wool over his eyes.

"No, they can't," he said, "but there is an outside chance that the physiotherapist can make her less dependent."

"I thank you for your honesty."

Konstantin Kirillovich picked at the buckwheat pancake, ate another mouthful, then laid his fork down and pushed the plate aside before lighting a black cigarette with a pungent odour. Vera looked at her grandfather with round eyes, announced she had finished and was going upstairs to play with the dolls Ruth had given her.

"When can I see Ludmilla?" the old man asked after she had left the room.

"Hospital visiting hours are from two to four thirty and again from six to nine in the evening." Ashton smiled. "I'll walk you over there this afternoon."

"There is danger?"

"No, it's just a routine precaution."

"Ah yes." The old man nodded sagely. "And when will you be sending us back to Moscow?" he asked.

"We are not going to send you anywhere. How long you want to stay in this country is entirely up to you. There's no need to rush things. In fact, why don't you wait until Elena arrives and then talk it over with her?"

"I do not think they will allow Elena to come here."

"Why would they stop her? The Russian government has been very co-operative so far."

"The KGB doesn't listen to Mr Yeltsin." Konstantin Kirillov-ich flicked his cigarette over the plate, depositing ash on the half-eaten pancake. "This man who came to the flat told me so."

"What man?"

"He did not give me his name, Mr Ashton, but I am not likely to forget him."

The stranger had had the build of a circus strong man, thick neck, broad shoulders, powerful chest, muscular biceps and the biggest pair of hands Konstantin Kirillovich had ever seen. Ashton thought the description fitted Oroblinsky like a glove.

"One side of his jaw was swollen."

The clincher was the facial injury he had inflicted on the sergeant when he had butted him under the jaw. "What exactly did he say to you?" Ashton asked.

"He said the British were making a lot of fuss about Elena and claimed she was missing, which was a lie because the KGB had traced her to the Piragow Hospital where she had been admitted under her married name. I said he was mistaken but he wouldn't hear of it and then he threatened that the KGB would make trouble for me if I persisted with my story."

There were any number of questions Ashton wanted to ask the old man but the room was bugged and he couldn't risk pursuing the matter in case the Russian inadvertently betrayed him. One thing however was crystal clear and there was no need to look to Konstantin Kirillovich for confirmation. Barely four days after he had murdered his superior officer, Oroblinsky had called at the flat to warn Andrianov to keep his mouth shut. That could only mean that certain people in Moscow had decided the sergeant was expendable. It also probably meant that Oroblinsky didn't know who he was working for because you didn't throw a man to the wolves who could implicate you if he was caught.

"He was there at the hospital yesterday when I said goodbye to Elena."

That settled it. Any pressure the Foreign Office tried to apply to unite the family could well have fatal consequences for Andrianov's daughter.

"Tell me something," said Ashton. "How much does Elena mean to you?"

"I'd willingly give my life for her."

Most Russians had an overdeveloped sense of the dramatic,

but in this instance he knew Konstantin Kirillovich meant every word.

"Why do you ask?"

Ashton found the old man a glass ashtray before he stubbed his cigarette out on the breakfast plate. "No special reason." He glanced pointedly at his wristwatch. "It's time I called the office to see what plans they have for us today," he said. "You want to go into the front room and watch TV while I'm on the phone?"

"I don't think so."

"The radio then; it's tuned to the World Service beamed at Russia."

Leaving him to make up his own mind what to do, Ashton went down into the basement and had the Special Branch man play back part of the conversation he'd just had with Konstantin Kirillovich. Then he put a call through to Century House and spoke to Hazelwood and suggested he should make a flying visit to Rylett Close.

"Of course, you could wait for the tape to be transcribed, but I wouldn't advise it."

Hazelwood said he took his point and would be with him inside the hour.

Hazelwood wasn't in the best of tempers when he turned the corner into Rylett Close. "Morning Prayers", the daily routine whereby heads of operational departments summarised the Intelligence reports that had been received during silent hours for the benefit of the DG and his deputy, had run well over time. There had been other contributory irritations to put him in a foul mood. After the wretched transport officer had been unable to provide him with an official car, he'd had to travel by the Underground and had been further delayed by a train failure between Gloucester Road and Earls Court on the District Line.

He stopped outside number 84, pushed the gate open and strode up the front path and was met at the door by Ashton who had obviously been keeping an eye out for him. He was momentarily taken aback by the scruffy appearance of his former protégé; Ashton hadn't shaved, his shirt appeared to have been retrieved from the linen basket before it could be put into the wash and the creases had fallen out of his slacks.

"Where did you spend last night?" he demanded. "Under the nearest hedge?"

"The laundry service around here isn't what it should be."

"What?"

"I was hoping Harriet Egan would have delivered some clean clothes for me before this." Ashton stepped aside. "You want to go through to the dining room at the back? Konstantin Kirillovich is fiddling around with the radio in the front parlour."

Hazelwood preceded him down the hall, caught a glimpse of Ruth in the kitchen and waved to her before entering the dining room. He had known Ruth's husband well and could recall the sense of shock and outrage he'd felt when he'd learned that two Provo gunmen had murdered him in cold blood as he left his flat overlooking the Tivoli Gardens in Copenhagen. It had happened eight years ago, yet it seemed like only yesterday. And the worst part was knowing his killers were still walking free, heroes who had passed into Irish mythology after putting nine rounds into the head of their unarmed victim while he lay dying on the pavement at their feet.

"I hope to God this is important," he snarled, venting his rage on Ashton.

"I think it is. You see, there is this man Oroblinsky, and if we make one false move, he is going to take out Elena."

Hazelwood was tempted to stop him before he went any further. There was, he believed, nothing Ashton could tell him about the militia sergeant, CID investigator, KGB agent or whatever he liked to call himself, that he hadn't already learned from Head of Station, Moscow. He kept silent and permitted Ashton to finish because he wasn't aware the sergeant had called on the Andrianovs and had threatened the old man.

"I don't understand why the KGB have been so incompetent," Hazelwood said. "First, they beat up Elena Andrianova badly enough to put her in hospital, then they move her around when somehow they hear a foreign correspondent wants to interview her, and then suddenly she reappears in the same hospital, this time under her married name. If they believe she is that dangerous, why the hell didn't they put her away for good?"

"We're not talking about the whole monolithic organisation, Victor; we are dealing with a faction, a group of men who are acting illegally and are constantly looking over their shoulders. They are indecisive in an emergency and they panic."

Ashton knew more than he was disclosing. Kelso had been right all along; Peter had made an unauthorised trip to Moscow. But he wasn't about to open that particular can of worms again, nor did he intend to inform Dunglass off the record.

"These people have got to be holding Elena against her will," Ashton continued. "I mean, have you ever known anyone with a fractured pelvis to spend almost eight weeks in hospital?"

"No, I can't say I have."

"Yes, well, Elena will continue to need police protection after she has been discharged, so the first thing we have to do is keep Oroblinsky away from her. We don't want anyone around her she doesn't trust."

"Do you have someone in mind, Peter?"

"Vaughan seemed to think she liked this Katya whats-hername . . ."

"Malinovskaya," Hazelwood said, then smiled wryly. Ten to one, Ashton had known her last name but he had tricked him into supplying it. Clever bastard, he thought.

"Malinovskaya. Right. Well, she can't be on duty round the clock, day in, day out. We should ask Major General Gurov to detail his best officers to help her look after Elena, people he can trust implicitly."

"You're asking a lot."

"He owes us a favour, Victor. And Vaughan should stop visiting her regardless of whether she is still in the Piragow or has been discharged and is living at home."

"Just where is all this leading?"

"If it took the embassy fourteen days to obtain exit visas for her parents and daughter, what chance do they have of getting one for Elena quicker than that?"

"None whatever."

"But it could be a different story if Konstantin Kirillovich were dying. With the embassy applying a little judicious pressure on the official who granted the family exit visas, she would be on the first plane out of Moscow."

"Are you telling me her father is a very sick man?"

"No, but he soon could be . . ."

Hazelwood told him he didn't want to hear another word, only to find himself listening to Ashton. He started out thinking it was the craziest idea anyone in the SIS had ever propounded in his presence but gradually came round to the view that it could work. He disliked the concept however because it was unethical, and he said so loud and clear.

"Konstantin Kirillovich will do anything for his daughter. I've told him there are risks but he is still happy to – "

"Happy is not the adjective I would have chosen," Hazelwood said, interrupting him.

"Okay, how about prepared? Let's say he is still prepared to put his life on the line for her. If you don't believe me, ask him yourself. All you've got to do is go next door."

"Don't think I won't when I can get hold of a neutral interpreter."

"Just don't take too long over it, Victor. Time is a luxury we can't afford."

"This can't be done at the drop of a hat. Head of Station, Moscow and the Ambassador will have to be briefed, not to mention the Foreign Office."

"Whatever you do, don't send a cable to Moscow," Ashton said tersely. "We don't want the Russian Intercept Service capturing it on tape. Use a courier instead."

"Meaning you, I suppose?"

"No way. Oroblinsky knows my face. Get a genuine Queen's Messenger."

"You think they grow on trees? There are only thirty-three of them to cover the entire world."

"All right, what about someone from the Russian Desk?"

"Out of the question," Hazelwood snapped, disliking the feeling that he was being put through the mincer by a subordinate.

"Harriet Egan then. Got anything against using her?"

"Are you serious?"

"Never more so. Harriet's a very competent operator and she can look after herself."

"Maybe so, but would she be willing to do it?"

"Yes, I'm sure she would."

"I don't know, Peter." Hazelwood shook his head doubtfully. "I mean, even if she agrees, there's the question of getting her a visa, and that takes time."

x

277

"Frank Warren's got a cabinet full of them – if necessary, use one of those."

"My God," Hazelwood gaped at the younger man, "you really are something."

Harriet picked up the paperknife and slit open the envelope. The letter from the Inspector of Taxes had been sent to Gower Street where it had languished in the post room for a whole week before anyone thought to redirect it to Benbow House. It would probably still be there now had she not rung the Inspector to find out when he expected to complete the investigation which she had asked for the day after Ashton had returned from Liphook with the news that Fitzroy Court was up for sale. A further phone call, this time to Gower Street, had led to the letter appearing on her desk an hour later, courtesy of the Special Delivery Service as opposed to the Post Office.

The Inspector had taken what measures he could to protect himself. The letter was undated, unsigned and had not been given either a reference or a file number. By way of an additional precaution, he had also typed it himself, obviously two-fingered and with a host of careless errors. Although there was no mention of Frances Joyner from first to last, the fact remained that any reporter worth his or her salt wouldn't find it an impossible task to discover who the assessment referred to.

From her guarded conversation with the Inspector, Harriet already knew the lady was in deep trouble; the letter simply spelt it out in considerably more detail. In order to pay her tax bill for the financial year 1990/1991, Frances Joyner had had to sell a considerable number of shares which, in turn, had led to an assessment for capital gains amounting to sixteen thousand pounds. This sum had then been added to a demand for eighteen thousand and ninety-four pounds income tax for the year 91/92. As she had been unable to pay the combined amount in one lump sum, her accountants had asked if it could be recovered in two equal instalments, a plea which the Inland Revenue had finally accepted with considerable reluctance.

Thus far, only the first instalment had been received by Her Majesty's Collector of Taxes and interest at two per cent above base rate had been accruing on the outstanding balance since the first of October 1991. The Inspector added that he had reason to believe she had had to realise further investments in order to meet the initial payment, and while it was still early days yet, he looked forward with interest to seeing her tax return for 1992/ 1993.

The letter was highly incriminating and would have serious consequences for the author if it fell into the wrong hands. Although there was no specific request that it should be destroyed after perusal, there was an understanding that it would not be held on file. Harriet walked over to the secret waste destructor, fed the letter into the shredder and returned to her desk. The zipper bag on the floor, which contained the clothes she had packed for Ashton, caught her eye and made her feel guilty, but not for long. Frances Joyner was in hock to the Inland Revenue up to her eyebrows, yet there she was looking for a tax haven in France. There was a smell of bad fish about the whole business; lifting the phone, Harriet rang the house in Liphook and got an unobtainable signal. A subsequent call to British Telecom established that the number had been disconnected.

The widow had left the family home; there was not the slightest doubt of that in Harriet's mind but without some sort of supporting evidence, it was no more than a hunch. Ashton had told her that Frances Joyner had put the sale of Fitzroy Court in the hands of one of the biggest estate agents in the south of England. Leaving the office briefly, she collected the Yellow Pages for Surrey, Hampshire and West Sussex from the library, then started by checking to see how many branches of Fox and Sons there were within a twenty-mile radius of Liphook. It took only two calls to find the right office.

"I'm looking for a five- or six-bedroom house in the Liphook area," she told the office manager, "and a friend of mine suggested I should look at Fitzroy Court."

The man was very apologetic. The house, he informed her with real regret, had been sold less than a week ago, subject of course to exchange of contracts.

"Never mind," Harriet said cheerfully. "I probably couldn't have afforded it anyway."

"Oh, I think you could have done; it went for a hundred and twenty-five thousand, well below its market value even in these depressed times. The people who bought the house are going to turn it into an old people's home."

"Really?" Harriet frowned, wondering how she was going to end the conversation.

"I have several other properties in the area which I think might interest you, Mrs – ?"

"Neville, Mrs George Neville," she told him quickly. "And yes, please do send me some brochures. My address is Flat 2, 26 Lancaster Gardens, London W2 3EP."

She repeated the name and address, thanked the office manager for being so helpful and finally managed to put the phone down on him. Frances Joyner had evidently taken what she could get for Fitzroy Court because she wanted a quick sale in order to get the Inland Revenue off her back before she left the country. She could give her accountants power of attorney so that they could sign the exchange of contracts on her behalf and then there was absolutely nothing to stop her leaving on the first available flight to Timbuktu or wherever else she chose to go.

Harriet lifted the phone again and rang Clifford Peachey. For the next twenty minutes, she argued, cajoled, begged, urged and pleaded with her former colleague until she finally wore him down and he agreed to run a check with all airlines using Heathrow and Gatwick.

"How many countries are you interested in?" Peachey asked wearily.

"The whole European Community plus – "

"Forget it. Pick any four – that's your lot, Harriet."

"All right – let's make it France, Germany, Italy and, oh yes, Switzerland."

"That sounds a reasonable selection," Peachey said and hung up.

Harriet replaced the phone, looked at the number of enhanced positive vetting cases awaiting her attention in the in-tray and decided she had better put her nose to the grindstone. There were three cases for initial EPV clearance, all of them relating to undergraduates who were being recruited into the Service direct from university. Two were straightforward, one wasn't, and on paper, he happened to be the best candidate. Unfortunately, an independent referee had said he suspected the candidate had homosexual tendencies, something the candidate himself had confirmed on re-interview. It was something he was afraid to disclose to his father whom he both admired and respected but who, he said, also had very old-fashioned ideas about homosexuals. It was a situation ripe for blackmail and this made him unsuitable for clearance. Harriet was in the middle of writing a memo to this effect when Ashton walked into her office.

"Oh my God." She glanced at the zipper bag on the floor, then looked up flushing. "I'm sorry, Peter, I was so busy, I completely forgot – "

"It's okay," he told her.

"Roy Kelso said he would get me a car from the pool, so I came into the office, then it turned out he couldn't and – "

"It's okay," he repeated. "I bought myself a throwaway razor and a can of shaving cream."

Ashton, she had to admit, looked reasonably presentable. "I wasn't expecting you to come into the office . . ."

"There have been some changes. One of Hazelwood's team is nurse-maiding Konstantin Kirillovich now."

"That's good," she said vaguely.

"How do you feel about going to Moscow?" he asked.

"What?" She looked up, startled. There were a dozen or more questions on the tip of her tongue but she didn't have to ask a single one. In a few brief sentences, Ashton told her what had to be done and why she was in the frame. "I'll do it," she told him.

"You're sure? You might have to go in with a false visa."

"I'll still do it."

The phone rang before he could think of some other reason which might cause her to have second thoughts. Lifting the receiver, Harriet found she had Clifford Peachey on the line. She grabbed a pencil, made a few notes on her scratchpad, then thanked him profusely before hanging up.

"Frances Joyner has flown the coop," she announced triumphantly. "She flew to Geneva this Monday on British Airways flight BA728."

The news didn't seem to excite Ashton, not even when she told him about the running battle the Inland Revenue were having with Frances Joyner and the precarious state of her finances.

"Don't you see the connection, Peter? Geneva is the European headquarters of Trans Globe Services. She's gone to meet Neville."

"Maybe."

"What do you mean – maybe?"

"I mean it's too neat," Ashton said. "How do we know she hasn't moved on from there?"

From the hotel bedroom on the fifth floor, Frances Joyner could see the Bosphorus, or more accurately, the pinpoints of lights from ships bound for the Black Sea or the Sea of Marmara. She had flown into Istanbul by Swissair departing Zurich at noon. On arrival, she had checked into the Hilton and had dined alone. The phone call she had been expecting all evening came through at seven minutes to eleven.

"Guess who?" said the voice.

"Hello, George," she said coolly. "You certainly took your time."

"Well, that's business. You had a good trip?"

"Of course. How about you?"

"Couldn't be better. Everything's set, I collect the money from the bank at one thirty. I'll meet you outside the Blue Mosque half an hour later. Okay?"

"That's fine by me."

"See you then. Goodnight, Frances."

"Goodnight, George." She put the phone down with a very satisfied smile. Tomorrow she would receive the second and final instalment; tomorrow she would be a very rich woman.

Chapter 24

Ashton walked into Benbow House, showed his ID card to the security guard on duty inside the hall and took one of the rickety lifts up to his office. He had been to Heathrow to see Harriet off on the British Airways flight to Moscow and the experience of saying *au revoir* to her had left him with a strangely empty feeling. He supposed there must have been a time when Jill Sheridan had had the same effect on him whenever they were temporarily parted, but he was damned if he could remember it now.

He stood there long after Harriet had disappeared from view to go through the security check before proceeding to the departure lounge. Tall, slim and elegant in a tan-coloured summer suit; Christ, she looked bloody marvellous even when you couldn't see her face.

Ashton cupped a hand over his mouth, stifling a yawn. He had had precious little sleep in the last twenty-four hours, but who was complaining? Harriet had invited him round for supper because Hazelwood had jacked everything up quicker than either of them had expected and there were scores of questions she had wanted to ask him about Moscow. By the time he had finished telling her about the various embassy people she would meet and what to do or what not to do should she come up against the KGB, it was well past one o'clock in the morning. A cup of coffee and a last nightcap had accounted for a further hour and then when he had finally been about to leave for his place, she had suggested he stay the night.

The lift stopped a good few inches above the floor, then descended to the appropriate level with a jolt the way it always did. Ashton opened the gate, stepped out into the corridor and walked towards his office and the unmistakable aroma of a

Burma cheroot. Hazelwood was seated behind the desk, doing little sums on a piece of scrap paper, apparently calculating the face value of his shares from the FT Index in the *Daily Telegraph*. Because there was no sign of the cheroot he had been smoking, Ashton suspected he had stubbed it out in the metal wastebin.

"Did Harriet get off all right?" Hazelwood asked without looking up.

"Yes, no problem."

"The FT Index is up twelve point four and yet I am down by a hundred and thirty-odd quid on the day before. Can you explain that, Peter?"

"You must have invested in the wrong companies."

Hazelwood folded the newspaper in four and dumped it in the wastebin. "Tell me I'm not buying a pig in a poke with Elena Andrianova. I mean, there is more to this business than gang warfare between a mix of hoodlums and racketeers on the streets of Moscow, isn't there?"

"You surely don't need me to tell you it's a different world out there since the Wall came down?" Ashton leaned against the filing cabinet, folded his arms across his chest. "The days when it was simply us against them are gone. The division has got a little blurred and, yes, sometimes it is hard to distinguish between the KGB and the local *Mafiozniki*. But if they are trading in the munitions of war, does it matter whether it's all part of some complicated political game plan hatched by the Kremlin or they are simply in it for the money? The effect is the same; somewhere a minor conflict grows into a war and the world becomes even more unsafe. I don't think our role has changed; it's still our job to find out what's going on."

"I dare say you're right," Hazelwood agreed without too much conviction.

"Then you'll understand why I'd like someone to have a look at the European head office of Trans Globe in Geneva."

"What do you expect to find there?"

"Nothing much," Ashton told him. "I suspect it's a poste restante."

Hazelwood found a memo slip in the top drawer of the desk. "You got an address for this place?" he asked.

"Rue Chaponniere, 128."

"All right, I'll cable the office of the Consulate General and see what he knows about Trans Globe. Just don't expect him to burgle the place; he's Foreign Office . . ."

"Well, I certainly wouldn't want him to get his hands dirty, but when can we expect to hear something from him?"

"Tomorrow, perhaps the day after." Hazelwood dipped into his jacket pocket, took out a small tin and placed it on the desk. "We could do with a little privacy," he said pointedly.

Ashton took the hint and closed the door. "I see you've got the cocktail, Victor."

"Yes, we're going for Monday."

Ashton reckoned the timing was about right. Harriet would return from Moscow tomorrow evening and then the weekend would be upon them. Konstantin Kirillovich would suffer a near-fatal coronary approximately sixty hours after her liaison visit, which would be enough to allay any suspicions the Russians might initially entertain when they first heard the news.

"You're back on duty nurse-maiding the Andrianovs as from 18.00 hours on Sunday."

"Fine."

"And before you go ahead, I want you to get a disclaimer in writing from Elena's father. We don't want any comebacks on this one."

Ashton stared at the tin box. "Are you telling me that cocktail could be lethal?"

"Of course I'm not," Hazelwood said testily. "But when you stick that hypodermic needle into him, he will go out like a light a few seconds later. If he cracks his skull open in the process, it could be permanent."

Tour A in the brochure produced by Kentur Travel Limited was called "The Big Three". The opening paragraph invited the potential client to "Start with your private guide and motorcoach to drive across the Galata Bridge over the Golden Horn to the Blue Mosque, the jewel among the Muslim places of worship and the only mosque in the world with six minarets." However, Frances Joyner had no plans to visit either Topkapi Palace or the Grand Bazaar, which were the other two star attractions of the tour, nor did she need the services of a guide. This was not her first time in Istanbul; she had spent a week there with her first husband and had been to the Blue Mosque before.

Frances Joyner also knew what the traffic was like in the city and allowed a good forty minutes for the journey across town. Shortly after one fifteen, she walked out of the hotel, asked the doorman to hail her a cab from the rank and tipped him a hundred Turkish lire for his trouble. The taxi was a locally manufactured Peugeot which, like its cantankerous owner, had seen better days. Leaving the hotel, the Turk made a right turn outside the grounds and went on down the hill past the university and the Iönöu football stadium, then made another right turn at the bottom opposite the Dolmabahçe Palace and headed towards the Galata Bridge over the Golden Horn.

The driver weaved in and out of the traffic, right hand on the steering wheel, left arm resting on the door, the horn supplementing a non-stop flow of invective directed at the other road users. The tactic worked well enough until they came to the bridge where a solid mass of vehicles double-banked nose to tail in both directions brought them virtually to a standstill. Thereafter it was stop-go all the way across so that even the lame and the blind overtook them. Still crawling forward at a snail's pace, the driver squeezed his way round the traffic island on the far side and somehow managed to get into second gear beyond the Spice Market.

An ambulance roared past on the wrong side of the road, siren warbling, lights flashing. The driver tripped his indicator and followed it, crossing the double white line in order to do so. The same idea occurred to just about every other motorist in the outside lane. Frances Joyner braced herself against the seat and hung on to the panic strap for dear life. The speedo needle climbed rapidly, past forty, past fifty. With the open window on the left side acting like a wind tunnel, a continuous blast of hot air buffeted her in the face. The ambulance shifted back on to the correct side of the highway and gradually edged across into the inside lane before making a right turn. No one, however, was prepared to give way when her cab driver attempted to follow suit and she died a thousand deaths before he found a gap big enough to slide into. She heaved a huge sigh of relief when a few minutes later, he left the Kennedy Highway and passed under a low railway bridge to follow a corkscrew, uphill route to the Blue Mosque through narrow one-way streets.

Neville found her shortly after she had paid off the cab driver.

He came up behind her from out of nowhere, unseen and unheard until he said, "Hello."

"The car's over there." He pointed towards the Basilica of St Sophia.

Neville had dressed casually, deep blue silk shirt open at the neck, pale grey linen slacks, brown slip-on shoes. He was also empty-handed.

"Where is the money?" she asked.

"In the car," he told her, grinning.

"You're crazy, George. What would you do if someone stole the vehicle?"

"They won't. I've got the keys and the driver is standing guard."

He reached for her right hand and held on to it. His grip was more arresting than affectionate and she found herself taking quick little steps to keep up with him as he strode across the square.

The driver was short, muscular and dressed in black from head to toe. He had dark hair, a round face and a broad smile, which showed off his teeth to advantage. His eyes and most of his cheekbones were hidden behind a large pair of sunglasses. Neville threw him the car keys while they were still some distance from the elderly Volvo 144 and he caught them one-handed. The smile was there when he unlocked the offside front door and it was as wide as ever when he reappeared after ducking the upper half of his body inside the Volvo to release the catches on the other three doors.

"Mind your head," Neville said as he ushered her into the back.

The car was like an oven inside but she hardly noticed the heat. Lying on the back seat next to her was a brand-new leather attaché case fitted with the sort of dainty combination locks that even amateur thieves regarded as a joke.

"What's the combination?" she asked when Neville joined her in the back.

"Zero four seven, same as your age."

"That's not very gallant of you, George."

"Oh, I think you'll forgive me after you've looked inside."

She set the combination, snapped the locks and opened the attaché case. It was, she guessed, roughly eighteen inches by twelve and some six inches deep. The case was packed to the brim with hundred-dollar bills neatly done up in Cellophane packets.

"How much is here?" she asked in a throaty whisper.

"Each packet contains a hundred thousand. But don't bother to count it; we're trading this lot in for bearer bonds."

"Now, just a minute – "

"No, you listen to me, Frances. It's okay to transfer funds from one Swiss bank to another, but walk into your local Crédit Suisse with that little lot and a few eyebrows are going to register surprise. On the other hand, no one is going to take a blind bit of notice if you turn over the equivalent in bearer bonds for safe keeping. As far as the bank is concerned, they are assets you have acquired over the years and you don't have to prove they are yours; possession really is ten-tenths of the law."

She glanced left and right. They had left the maze of narrow back streets behind them now and appeared to be heading out of town on a main road. It was a part of the city she didn't recognise.

"Where are we going, George?"

"To see a man about some bearer bonds."

"I know that, but where are we going?"

"Across the Bosphorus into Asia Minor."

"Will the banks still be open?"

Neville laughed softly. "We're not going to a bank," he said. "These bonds have been stolen."

"What?"

"Does that shock you?" He placed a hand on her leg. "Where do you think those dollar bills you're nursing on your lap came from if they weren't stolen from somebody in the first place? Same goes for the first payment you received."

They picked up the E5 motorway and crossed the Golden Horn. Away to her right she could see the Ataturk and Galata Bridges. The driver kept his foot down, pushing the ancient Volvo towards seventy as they sped through the suburb of Talatpasa.

"Go on, admit it, you find the whole idea exciting."

What was exciting was the way he gently slid his hand between her thighs and began to caress her. The knowledge that the driver couldn't see what George was doing to her with the attaché case on her lap added a little extra spice to the foreplay. She opened her legs a little wider and looked straight ahead, her lips parted and breathing quickly, the perspiration from her forehead trickling down her face.

The motorway climbed up to the high bridge and then they were over the Bosphorus. A sign on the far side said, 'Welcome to Asia Minor' in Turkish, German and English.

The journey could not have been less eventful. The plane had taken off on time from Heathrow and had arrived at Sheremetyevo Airport five minutes ahead of schedule. Contrary to what she had been led to expect by Ashton, she had sailed through Customs and Immigration and the embassy had sent a limousine to pick her up from the airport, though to be fair, he hadn't suggested they wouldn't. If Peter had given her a bum steer in some respects, his description of Hugo Calthorpe couldn't be faulted. 'Only forty-five,' he'd told her, 'but looks older and sports a moustache which is a good deal more luxuriant than his light brown hair. He's also at least three inches shorter than you and some five pounds lighter.' She could have done without the height and weight comparisons but she knew who was Head of Station, Moscow, the moment she walked into the secure conference room located in the basement of the embassy.

The same went for Richard Quennell, the First Secretary. Forty, tall, handsome, snappy dresser, highly intelligent; a rising star in the Foreign Office and fully aware of it. Hazelwood had given her to understand that the diplomatic side would be represented by Head of Chancery but she guessed he was indisposed or something before Quennell introduced himself and apologised for the absence of his superior.

"Actually, Miss Egan, I probably know more about this business than he does," Quennell said, holding on to her hand a fraction longer than was strictly necessary.

"Good, that should save us a bit of time." Harriet looked to Hugo Calthorpe. "Can we talk freely in here?" she asked.

"This place is a hundred per cent safe," he assured her. "It is really a room within a room. All the sections were flown out by British Airways and no Russian was allowed within a hundred metres of the palletised loads. The prefabricated room was then erected by the embassy's security officer with a couple of hired hands from London."

Locally employed personnel were, of course, denied access to that particular part of the basement and Hicks had given the room a clean bill of health when he had swept it with an electronic emission detector a little over two months ago.

"Is there anything else I can tell you?" Calthorpe enquired.

"Only where Elena Andrianova is now?"

"She was discharged from hospital yesterday," Quennell said, beating Calthorpe to it by a short head.

Exactly twenty-four hours after her parents and daughter had arrived in England; Harriet thought that was just a little too convenient. "Has anyone been in touch with her since then?" she asked.

"Michael Vaughan telephoned this morning to see how she was."

"Was anyone with her?"

"Not as far as we know," Quennell said.

"No police protection?"

"So it would seem."

Another thought occurred to Harriet. "Did Mr Vaughan have any forewarning that Elena was going to be discharged?"

"No, Michael only learned that when he went to visit her last night and was told she had been sent home."

It didn't look good. Elena was alone in the flat and could meet with a fatal injury any time Oroblinsky chose to break in. And who in Moscow would question her sudden demise? If Russia was anything like England, there were more accidental deaths in the home than anywhere else.

"A number of people are going to be very unhappy if anything happens to Elena."

"I hear what you say, Miss Egan, but there's not a lot we can do about it."

"There's also a feeling that Major General Gurov owes us the odd favour."

"He probably does." Quennell smiled. "But that is Hugo's department, not mine."

"I can pull a few strings," Calthorpe told her. "Naturally, the General will want to know how long we expect him to provide Elena Andrianova with a bodyguard."

"Until he is satisfied she is not in danger. That will put the onus for her safety on him."

"And between ourselves?"

"Elena Andrianova will become a diplomatic problem early next week."

"May we know the reason why?" Quennell asked.

"Her father is not a well man," Harriet said cautiously.

"And suddenly we shall have a compassionate case on our hands. Correct?"

"Yes."

Harriet didn't elaborate. The Foreign Office hadn't wanted to know the medical details and she very much doubted if Quennell did either. What mattered was the action the embassy officials were required to take when they learned that Konstantin Kirillovich had been placed on the Dangerously Ill list.

"The Foreign Ministry in Moscow will receive the news from the Russian Ambassador in London," Harriet continued. "At the same time, a cable will be sent to the consular officer here informing him that Andrianov has been asking for his daughter. We would then like you to do everything possible to persuade the appropriate officials to give Elena an exit visa."

"Suppose they refuse?"

"They are going to look pretty bad if they do that, aren't they, Mr Quennell? Konstantin Kirillovich is dangerously ill in one hospital, his comatose wife is receiving treatment in another. Who is looking after six-year-old Vera?"

"Even so, they may not be moved. What will you people in London do then?"

"I don't know," Harriet confessed. "But if Elena is refused a visa, I think whoever controls Sergeant Oroblinsky will give him the green light to snuff her out." She looked long and hard at Calthorpe. "That's why Elena needs police protection, that's why Major General Gurov should only detail those officers he would trust with his own life, officers like Katya Malinovskaya."

If Bosnia Herzegovina had become the number one trouble spot, Zale figured his desk had become the repository for every newspaper clipping and photograph on the subject. Most of the stuff was junk, but it kept on coming and threatened to overwhelm him. He picked up the latest batch of glossy prints Bernice Kreuger had unloaded on him and began sorting through them, dumping those he thought were of little interest straight into the waste sack which he now kept permanently by his desk.

These days the Serbian gunman Slobodon Todordzic, a.k.a. the White Eagle, was getting the kind of exposure Hollywood stars dreamed of. Sifting through the photographs, he found half a dozen more of the self-styled resistance leader. All of them were carefully posed in a way that would have been laughable had there not been so much blood on his hands. Slobodon Todordzic in black beret, khaki shirt, knee-length riding breeches, thick woollen socks and stout boots, a Kalashnikov AK47 assault rifle in one hand, a brace of heavy automatic pistols in open holsters and four grenades dangling from the leather belt around his waist.

"Shit kicker." Zale ripped the offending photographs in half and stuffed them into the paper sack. "Goddamned mother-fucking shit kicker."

"Mr Zale."

He looked up guiltily, wondered if the whole office had heard him.

"UK satellite link," Bernice Kreuger yelled from the far end of the room. "Your friend, Asston."

"His name is Ashton." Sometimes he thought the once-widowed, twice-divorced feminist from New Jersey deliberately went out of her way to needle him. Grim-faced, he walked into her office and picked up the phone. "Hi, Peter," he said tersely, "what can I do for you?"

"Remember the conversation we had about Trans Globe some time back?"

"We're not going down that road again, are we?"

"Not exactly. We're interested in a wheeler-dealer called George Neville, an Englishman, served in Vietnam with the Australian Army, then went to San Francisco in 1973 and spent the next seventeen years on the West Coast before coming to London. We are curious to know if he was ever employed by Pacific Northwest Oil and Gas."

"Jesus. What the hell is this?"

"We've been looking at things the wrong way round; it's the man who is the connecting link between Trans Globe and Pacific Northwest. At least, that's what Harriet Egan thinks."

"Who's she?"

"One very bright lady."

There was a lot more speculation and it was hard to decide

whose theory he was listening to, Ashton's or the ultra bright Harriet Egan, but some of it made sense. The business hook-up wasn't the only thing the SIS had got back to front; the KGB was no longer the sword and shield of the USSR, elements within its ranks were now indistinguishable from the *Mafiozniki*. If the money was right, there was nothing they wouldn't provide.

"Oil and gas," Ashton said, winding up, "They're the sinews of war, Tony."

"Yeah. What about this Neville guy? What's his racket?"

"He's done a lot of business in Moscow. We believe his middle man short-changed the suppliers and got himself ventilated as a warning to others."

"Ventilated?"

"Someone gave him a fatal headache with a Makarov."

"Oh, right."

"So what do you reckon?"

"I'll get back to you, if or when I have something," Zale said and broke the connection.

Mike Todorvic and Slobodon Todordzic – could be they were related. When America had been the melting pot of Europe in the late nineteenth century, the Immigration officials on Ellis Island hadn't been too fussy how they spelled the names of the people they were processing. Maybe the great-grandfather of the Executive Vice President of Pacific Northwest Oil and Gas had been called Todordzic in the old country?

"You all through now?" Bernice Kreuger rasped. "Because if you are, I'd like my office back."

"You know something?" Zale leaned across the desk, put his face close to hers. "I'd like you to button your lip and get me on a plane to Seattle Friday morning, returning Sunday evening."

Frances Joyner began the last leg of her journey lying on the floor in the back of a battered transit van, but she wasn't complaining. The men who had slashed her dress from neck to hemline and ripped off her bra had also cut her throat from ear to ear.

Chapter 25

Her Majesty's Consul General in Geneva was not best pleased. The cable addressed to his office had been received in a slightly corrupted form and he had wasted valuable time trying to discover the name of the person who was interested in the European headquarters of Trans Globe Services Incorporated.

"Well, you've got the right man now," Ashton told him.

"The cable advised me to contact a Mr Haston and of course there is no such name in the staff list. As a result, I was passed from one Foreign Office department to another before someone suggested I should try you."

Tough, Ashton thought, but it wasn't his fault that some operator had scrambled his surname. "I hope you didn't have as much trouble with Trans Globe," he said diplomatically.

The Consul, it transpired, had encountered no difficulties. Trans Globe had vacated their office at 128 rue Chaponniere even though according to the concierge the firm had paid a year's rent in advance sometime during the first week in January. The Consul had also been told that the office had only been open two or three days each month at roughly fortnightly intervals.

"It would appear that Trans Globe was pretty much a one-man operation. The company didn't employ any clerks, typists or secretaries and received very little mail." The Consul General paused, then said, "Does that make any sense to you?"

"It's more or less what I had anticipated," Ashton told him.

He laid it on with a trowel when he told the Consul that without his help it would only have been a theory and was suitably grateful. A little praise was good for everyone's ego and it enabled Ashton to end the conversation before Her Britannic Majesty's representative in Geneva got too curious.

The European head office had been a decoy to obscure the real activities of Trans Globe. Twice, perhaps three times a month, Neville had gone to Geneva to feed information into the mainframe computer located at the rue Chaponniere address. It was this so-called data bank, which Debbie Roxburgh had mentioned, that had led the temps he engaged from the Brewer Street Bureau to believe they were working for an international consortium. They had run the legitimate side of the business and held the fort for him in his absence while he was in Geneva updating the files and paying any banker's drafts which had arrived in the mail into a numbered account.

Neville was a sanctions buster and Joyner had been his bagman, the courier who had kept the suppliers sweet with payments in hard currencies. Sometime towards the end of last year, Neville had entered into an intimate relationship with Frances Joyner who had given him a lot of bad ideas after he had bedded her a few times and found it highly enjoyable. After playing it straight with the Russians, Neville had suddenly ripped them off and had left Colin Joyner to take the fall. But for Elena Andrianova's involvement, it would have been just one more sordid crime that had become commonplace in Moscow; she gave Joyner's murder a wider dimension and turned it into a conspiracy.

Ashton picked up the phone and rang Gower Street. When the switchboard operator answered, she merely gave the office number, which was standard procedure. He also knew that she would deny all knowledge of Clifford Peachey when he didn't tell her which extension he wanted. Before she could go into that routine, he gave her his name and own telephone number and left a message for the MI5 man to ring him back a.s.a.p. A few minutes later, he had Peachey on the line trying to recall exactly when it was they had last met.

"I need a favour," Ashton told him once they had got that sorted out.

"Seems to me I've been doing you people quite a number of favours at Harriet's behest."

"If it's any consolation, you would probably have found yourself talking to her this morning if she hadn't been elsewhere."

"I'm listening," Peachey said with the resigned tones of martyrdom.

"You traced Frances Joyner to Geneva, now I want to know if she has moved on and, if so, where to."

"Have you any idea what that will entail?"

"I know there's no way you can trace her if she went by car or train. Just concentrate on Basle, Berne, Geneva and Zurich airports, Swissair departures only, from the date she arrived in the country. Okay?"

"It's a bit of a long shot, isn't it?"

He didn't need Peachey to tell him the obvious. "Will you do it?" he asked.

"Why not? Shouldn't take long."

Ashton thanked him and hung up. If they did discover the present whereabouts of Frances Joyner, it was possible Neville wouldn't be far away. And Neville was the only person who could point a finger at the KGB people he had been dealing with. He hoped Peachey was right and that it wouldn't be long before he came up with some sort of answer. Meantime, there was a full in-tray demanding his attention, beginning with a memo from Kelso reminding him the usual certificate stating that the controlled stores had been checked and found correct or otherwise was due on the thirtieth of the month.

The goatherd came from a small village ten kilometres beyond the outskirts of Kanlica on the Bosphorus. He was twelve years old, illiterate and blind in one eye as a result of glaucoma. He could, however, see well enough out of the other one to tell the difference between a mangy dog and a jackal at a distance of some four hundred metres. Jackals usually hunted for food in packs and were rarely observed in broad daylight; this one was a lone scavenger and had found something near a culvert under the road. As he drew nearer, the goatherd noticed the swarm of flies and knew there was a body.

Although the lower half of the torso was inside the dried-up culvert, the boy didn't have to look very far to discover how the woman had died. She was a foreigner, an infidel with yellow hair, and someone had cut her throat with a knife from ear to ear. The blood around the jagged, uneven wound had turned black, unlike the gore on the chest where the jackal had already devoured one breast.

The gruesome sight and sickly smell of putrefying flesh had no effect on the goatherd; he had seen death before in all its forms and was not at all squeamish. He bent down, grabbed hold of both arms and pulled the body clear of the culvert. The dead woman did not have any rings on her fingers but her shoes looked expensive and he quickly removed them. Hoping to find something else of value, he peered inside the culvert and saw a handbag. To reach it, he had to crawl inside the pipe.

Although the handbag was made of leather, no shopkeeper in Kanlica would give him much for it when the strap was broken and the clasps wouldn't close properly. The contents were equally disappointing – no purse, no wallet, no trinkets, only a comb, a pair of nail scissors, a mirror, compact, lipstick, handkerchief and other woman's things he hadn't seen before.

He put the handbag back where he had found it, looked for a small fold in the ground not too far away from the body and hid the shoes under a small pile of stones before walking back down the road towards his village to report the matter to the Headman. He did so, not out of a sense of civic duty which was an alien concept to him, but in the hope of a reward and the sure knowledge that the police would only give the village a hard time if he didn't.

According to the Rand McNally map Zale bought from a bookshop in the terminal building at Seattle-Tacoma International Airport, the 1980 census showed that the population of the metro area totalled 2,077,100 which he thought was a nice round number. The average temperature ranged from forty-one degrees Fahrenheit in January to sixty-six in July. It also rained a lot, so much so that people tended to rust as opposed to acquiring a suntan in summer, or so the local wags liked to tell it.

Outside the terminal, he passed up a limo in favour of a taxicab for the fourteen-mile drive into downtown Seattle. It was by no means certain that the Defense Intelligence Agency would reimburse him for the trip but if eventually they did agree to fund it, any item on the expense sheet which smacked of luxury would get the thumbs down and he didn't want to find himself too heavily out of pocket. For the same reason, checking into the best hotel in Seattle was also a no-no and he asked the cab driver if he could recommend a modest place to stay in town.

The Mandrake down by the harbour off State Highway 99

certainly fell into that category, but one look at the neighbourhood with its derelicts and winos sleeping rough under the arches
by the waterfront streetcar tracks was enough to convince him
that some economies were not worth the candle. He went
upmarket instead and checked into the Westin hotel on Fifth
Avenue, then picked up another cab to keep a pre-arranged
appointment with FBI Agent William G. McMurtrie in the
Federal Building.

Zale wanted to be sure of his facts before he confronted
Todorvic; what he had been given by Ashton was the most
tenuous circumstantial evidence that didn't bear looking at twice.
His own suspicions were based on even flimsier grounds, a gut
feeling that the Serbian war machine would have ground to a halt
long ago but for outside help, and the possibility of a family blood
tie between the "White Eagle" and the Executive Vice President
of Pacific Northwest Oil and Gas. George Neville was the key
which would unlock all doors, but none of the State or Federal
government departments would give him the information he
needed. At the end of the day, he was simply a Special Intelligence analyst. Only the FBI could obtain what he wanted, and
within a few minutes of their meeting, it became apparent that
Agent William G. McMurtrie was extremely reluctant to extend
him a helping hand.

"You got something against Mr Todorvic?" he demanded
aggressively.

It was the second time someone had accused him of pursuing a
vendetta against the Executive Vice President, Pacific Northwest
and Consolidated Merrill Industries. He wondered if Howard
Eugene Falkenberg, the Chief of Staff to the senior senator from
Washington, had had a word with the local FBI office shortly
after their disastrous lunch at the Madison.

"I'm not after Mr Todorvic," Zale told him just as belliger-
ently. "All I want to know is if a guy called George Neville was
ever employed by his corporation."

"Why don't you ask Personnel at Pacific Northwest?"

"And what am I going to say to them that can't be taken the
wrong way? No, this has to come from a neutral source – the IRS,
Social Security or whatever."

"So go see them."

McMurtrie did not conform to the stereotype image of the FBI agent. Far from being young, clean-cut, alert, intelligent and other such flattering adjectives, he was middle-aged, fat, bald, complacent and seemingly indolent. He was not the sort of person Zale warmed to but when you wanted someone to do a favour, it wasn't politic to show your dislike.

"I don't have the necessary clout, Mr McMurtrie; they would simply show me the door."

"Tough."

Zale gritted his teeth but somehow managed to keep smiling. "Which means I go back empty-handed and we start all over, this time at the highest level. It won't do me a power of good – how's your reputation at the Bureau?"

McMurtrie thought about it, a process that involved a number of facial contortions. "What's this Neville character supposed to have done?" he asked finally.

"He's a commodity broker," Zale told him. "Does a lot of business with the Russians, none of it strictly legit. His partner got iced in Moscow a couple of months ago."

"Are you suggesting Mr Todorvic is involved with this guy?"

"No way. Neville returned to England in 1990."

"He's a Brit?"

"Yeah, born in Grimsby on March eighth 1948 . . ."

"Hold it a minute." McMurtrie took a biro from the miniature toby jug on his desk and printed something in capital letters on a scratchpad. "Okay," he said, looking up, "let's have those details again."

Zale repeated the date and place of birth, then went on to disclose everything Ashton had told him about Neville's life history. There was a lot to be gained from the fact that the Englishman had been captured by the Viet Cong while serving in Vietnam with the Australian Army and he used it as bait to hook McMurtrie. It led to a series of questions, culminating in the obvious.

"He might have been in San Francisco from '76 to '78," McMurtrie said, "but how do you know he was even in this neck of the woods?"

"Because he applied for a new passport at the ten-year point in 1988. To get one, he had to make a couple of trips to Victoria BC where he saw the representative of the British High Commissioner."

"And?"

"Neville told him he was living in Seattle and gave an address in Magnolia," Zale said, lying in his teeth.

There was a longish silence, then McMurtrie nodded. "Leave it with me," he said.

"For how long?"

"In a hurry, are you?"

"I'm not one for watching the grass grow under my feet," Zale said.

"Tell you what you do. Go take a look at this lovely city of ours, see some of the attractions like the Seattle Aquarium and the Space Needle, and call me back in an hour or so. Maybe I'll have something for you by then."

"Thanks."

"You may need this," McMurtrie said and gave him a map of the downtown area.

It started raining soon after Zale had flagged down a cab outside the Federal Building. He killed some time in the revolving restaurant on top of the Space Needle eating a light meal he didn't need, then went on up to the observation deck to kill some more. He called the FBI office at three o'clock from a pay phone, then again one hour later. At five, McMurtrie was able to confirm that George Neville had indeed been employed by Pacific Northwest from January 1984 to inclusive December thirty-first 1989. It seemed Ashton hadn't given him such a bum steer after all.

The offices of Pacific Northwest Oil and Gas occupied the entire seventh floor of the Merrill Building on Virginia Street and Second Avenue. Zale got there a few minutes after five thirty with no great hopes of catching the Executive Vice President before he went home. The receptionist on the front desk shared his opinion but she rang Todorvic's personal assistant on the off chance and was equally surprised when he readily agreed to see him.

Michael Todorvic was in his fifties, had a full head of iron-grey hair and the physique of a man half his age who worked outdoors in all weathers. He wore expensive suits and handmade Italian shoes but still managed to give the impression that he didn't give two hoots about his appearance. He was friendly, good humoured and had charisma. It was easy to

301

see why he commanded the loyalty and affection of his staff. He was also quick to establish himself on first name terms.

"It's a pleasure to make your acquaintance, Tony," he said and sounded as though he meant it. "I don't think I've met anyone from the Defense Intelligence Agency before."

"Well, I know I haven't met an oil baron before," Zale told him.

"I've been called many things in my time but an oil baron I'm not. Wish I was though." He smiled. "Mac tells me you're anxious to trace George Neville."

"Mac?"

"Bill McMurtrie."

Zale could understand now why he had had to wait so long for the information. McMurtrie had held it back until he'd contacted the Head of Pacific Northwest and told him what was going down. The Seattle office of the FBI obviously saw it as their duty to protect Todorvic from outside interference; anyone else in his position would have used this special relationship to intimidate him, but evidently that wasn't his style.

"We'd certainly like to interview Mr Neville," Zale said. "I don't suppose you happen to know his present whereabouts, Mr Todorvic?"

"Mike."

"Mike." Zale repeated dutifully.

"I'd like to help, Tony, but we haven't heard from George since he left us nearly two and a half years ago. I don't mind telling you I was sorry to see him go. Best damn broker we had, knew the oil business from A to Z."

"Any idea why he left?"

"George wanted to go into business on his own account. He kept talking about the European Community and the effect the single market was going to have when it started up in '93. And how he figured it was going to be the opportunity of a lifetime."

"I guess things didn't work out for him," Zale said, then added, "Mike."

"Yeah? What happened?"

"He set up as a commodity broker trading under the name of Trans Globe Services Incorporated. It went down the tube a couple of weeks ago."

"I'm really sorry to hear that." Todorvic pointed a stubby

finger at him. "Listen, if you run across George, you tell him he can have his old job back any time he cares to touch base. You hear, Tony?"

"You seem to have a high regard for him."

"Damn right. Mac says he is supposed to have pulled some shady deals with the Russians, but that's got to be horseshit."

"No reservations then?"

Todorvic hesitated. "Well, there was one thing that puzzled me. See, George was almost forty-two when he left the company and I could never figure out why he didn't have a wife and family because he was a pretty good-looking guy, very personable too."

"Maybe he's gay?"

"If he is, I'm the faggot of the year with four kids aged twenty-five on down to sixteen to prove it. No, George is the kind of adopted son America can be proud of."

"Except he's British."

"No, you've got it wrong, Tony. I've seen his passport, that's why he didn't need a work permit. Besides, the US of A doesn't recognise dual nationality."

"Nevertheless, Neville obtained a new British Passport in 1988. It was issued by the High Commission in Victoria BC. He collected it personally."

"Jesus."

"You didn't know he had been to Canada?"

"Sure I did, he was always crossing the border on hunting trips. He's a great outdoor man, was always spending weekends camping out in the Cascades. Used to take his vacations in the Rockies. But what you're telling me, Tony, is something different. Seems I hardly knew him at all."

"It happens."

"What are these shady deals you say he's been doing with the Russians?"

"Buying arms for the Serbian irregulars."

"I don't know how the sonofabitch could dirty his hands like that." Todorvic shook his head. "It's a damned good thing he's gone broke."

"He'll start up again when he finds another backer."

"Then you'll have to put him away." Todorvic broke off, called his PA on the intercom and told her to have his limousine ready in ten minutes. "Sorry about that, Tony," he apologised, "but we've got some people coming to dinner this evening and Elaine is going to be pretty upset if I am home late."

"It's very good of you to have spared me the time – Mike."

"Think nothing of it. Can I drop you someplace when I leave?"

"No, that's okay . . . really." Zale found himself shaking hands before being gently ushered towards the door.

"Where are you staying?"

"The Westin."

"Nice place, one of the best hotels in town. See Diane on the way out and tell her I said to get you a cab."

"Well, that's very kind of you but . . ."

"No buts – okay?" Todorvic smiled, pumped his hand again with a vice-like grip. "One other thing," he said, "don't hesitate to get back to me if there's any way I can help you nail that bastard."

Zale said he would be sure to do that, nodded goodbye to the PA as he passed through her office and rode the elevator down to the ground floor.

It had just stopped raining and there was a rainbow of sorts even though the sky was still largely overcast. And that just about summed things up as far as he was concerned. Either Todorvic was the best damned actor who had never put on greasepaint or else he was squeaky clean. Zale couldn't make up his mind which of the two possibilities applied.

The bird was in full song, trilling loud enough to wake the dead. Ashton reluctantly opened one eye, couldn't think why the dawn chorus should have started up when it was still dark, then realised it was the telephone. He rolled over on to his right side, groped for the phone and promptly fell out of bed.

"Good God," Harriet said in a pained voice. "What the hell are you doing on the floor?"

"Trying to answer the phone."

"It's my side," she said and switched on the light.

He had taken most of the duvet with him, leaving Harriet with just one tiny corner which barely covered her knees. He climbed back into the narrow bed, snuggled up to her and received a sharp elbow in the stomach for his pains.

"Duty officer – for you," she hissed and handed over the phone.

304

The duty officer at Century House started talking before Ashton could put the receiver to his ear. It seemed there had been some minor hiccup in the communications centre and the signal from the Consul General in Istanbul had been placed on the wrong pile. Hence, it had been overlooked for which he was full of apologies.

"Never mind all that," Ashton told him. "What's in the cable?"

"Well, you were right; Mrs Joyner did arrive on the Swissair flight from Zurich the day before yesterday."

The information had come from Clifford Peachey, but that was beside the point. The important thing was that she had been traced to the Hilton.

"Trouble is, she's now missing."

"What?"

"None of the hotel staff have seen her since lunchtime on Thursday."

"Maybe she has moved on without paying her bill?"

"If she has, she left all her clothes behind."

"That's interesting," Ashton said in a neutral voice, then told the duty officer to fire off a signal to Istanbul requesting Her Majesty's representative to keep them fully informed of developments. As soon as he had finished, Harriet took the phone off him and put it down.

"You want to tell me how the duty officer knew where to find you?" she asked sweetly.

"I gave him your number," Ashton told her.

"When was this?"

"Before I left the office to meet you off the plane from Moscow."

"That was bloody presumptuous of you."

"Oh, I don't know, I'm here, aren't I?" he said cheerfully and got another dig, this time lower down.

Usually, Todorvic rode up front with the chauffeur on the way home from the office; this evening, he sat in the back of the stretch limousine, silent, brooding. This desire to be left in peace was not a sudden aberration; the chauffeur had known other evenings when he had wanted to withdraw into his shell after a bad day at the office. From the Merrill Building, the chauffeur headed north to West Mercer Street, picked up Interstate 5 and stayed with it as far as the intersection with State Highway 520. They drove on through Montlake, across Foster Island and over Lake Washington into King County by the Evergreen Point floating bridge. When Todorvic said goodnight to the chauffeur outside the large six-bedroom property by the lake shore on Waverly Avenue, it was the only exchange they'd had throughout the fourteen-mile journey.

Todorvic let himself into the house and went straight into the den without first calling out to Elaine, his wife. He unlocked the top drawer of the desk and took out the large white envelope which was hidden under a wad of crested writing paper. Bearing a London postmark, it contained three photographs taken inside a mortician's chapel of rest and a small clipping from an English newspaper. The dead man had paid a hell of a price for the eight million dollars he had embezzled from the Russians. He had been shot through the head and a large piece of the skull above the right eye had been destroyed by the bullet when it had exited. Todorvic tore the prints in half and half again, then carefully arranged the pieces in a heavy glass ashtray and set fire to them, destroying the only hard evidence that linked him currently to George Neville.

Chapter 26

The fillet steaks were thick, juicy and sizzling on the grill above the glowing charcoal, as were the king-size Pacific prawns. Todorvic figured the barbecue would be ready in a few minutes and cast a professional eye over the table on the patio to make sure nothing had been overlooked. Salad, French dressing, Thousand Island, garlic bread and two bottles of Chardonnay from the Glen Ellen winery in the Sonoma Valley for those who didn't like red wine; he smiled to himself, content that everything was to hand.

It was a typical Sunday evening get-together – a couple of neighbours, the head of accounts with his new wife and the whole family with the exception of Greg, his eldest son. Greg was a navy pilot serving on the carrier *Nimitz* and Todorvic was immensely proud of him, but then what father wouldn't be? He looked round the yard at his family and friends with a deep sense of satisfaction; this is nice, he thought, and felt good until sixteen-year-old Kirsten spoilt the idyll for him.

"Telephone for you, Dad," she told him, appearing from the living room.

"Yeah? Who wants me, honey?"

"A Mr Neville, says he's an old friend."

His heart skipped a beat and his body temperature seemed to plummet as if he had walked into a cold store stark naked. "You want to keep an eye on the steaks, Kirsty?"

"Sure, Dad. What's the matter with your voice? Sounds all croaky."

He cleared his throat. "Must have got a lungful of smoke," he said, then went into the house.

Kirsten had answered the phone in the living room and it was too risky to take the call on that extension when people were

307

walking in and out from the patio. He lifted the receiver and told Neville to hang on while he went on through to the den. Once there, he repeated the process in reverse, this time returning to the living room to hang up the extension before picking up the phone in the den again.

"Where are you calling from?" Todorvic asked him bluntly.

"The airport. Just got in from Chicago, been travelling since Friday . . ."

Todorvic half listened to an itinerary that sounded like a world tour – Ankara, Rome, Frankfurt and then Chicago by Turkish Airlines, Alitalia, Lufthansa and United. Neville made it sound as though he had been on a business trip which, in a way, he had. Todorvic, however, paid little attention to the monologue; his thoughts were centred on Tony Zale and the harm he could do him. It was always dangerous to underestimate a potential adversary and maybe he had been a little too complacent about the way he had handled the young Intelligence officer on Friday evening. What if Zale had seen through his little act? What if he had got a wire tap on the house, legal or otherwise? The possibility scared the hell out of him. Then he heard Neville say that he had sorted out the problem they'd had with the suppliers and knew he had to get him off the phone before they were both hopelessly compromised.

"I'm sure you did a swell job – " Todorvic began, only to be interrupted before he could finish the sentence.

"Naturally, it wasn't possible to recover all the money that was owing but I managed to recoup enough to keep the clients sweet."

Neville was being cautious, something that was almost second nature to him, but if their conversation was being recorded, the veiled speech wouldn't fool Zale. "We'll have to continue this some other time," he said abruptly. "Right now, I'm kind of busy entertaining half the neighbourhood to a barbecue."

"Sure. You want me to come into the office tomorrow?"

It was the last place he wanted to see Neville. If they were going to meet face to face, it would have to be a long, long way from Seattle.

"I'm going to be tied up with board meetings all next week," Todorvic told him. "This recession is biting and we're facing a lot of competition from some people on the East Coast who'd like to move in on our markets." He ran a hand through his hair, wondered what else he had to say before Neville caught on. "I tell you, it's a real battle for survival," he added.

"And you are being forced to contract?"

"No, but we can't afford to take any risks in this climate."

"So when do I get to see you?"

"Well, we're planning to spend next weekend in the Selkirk Mountains at Rogers Pass. Why don't we get together up there on Saturday evening, say around five thirty? Elaine won't mind us talking business so long as we don't take all night over it."

"Sounds great to me," Neville said after a pause. "I guess I can reschedule my trip to Edmonton."

"Good. I'll see you then, okay?"

"Sure."

Todorvic put the phone down, his hand shaking. He had got the message across; Neville had read the danger signals and would go to ground, that was the important thing. There was no family haunt in the Selkirks but there was a diner up at Rogers Pass they had used before, and Neville would be waiting for him there next Saturday.

Todorvic found a glass in the drinks cabinet, poured himself a large bourbon from a bottle of Jack Daniel's and downed it in one. A warm glow spread through his belly and presently his hands stopped shaking. Calmer now, he left the den to join his family and friends on the patio.

Ashton and Konstantin Kirillovich left the house in Rylett Close, crossed Goldhawk Road and took the quick cut below the railway embankment which led them past the Royal Masonic Hospital into Ravenscourt Park. May was ending as it had begun, hot and sunny, but only the old and the unemployed had the leisure time to enjoy it. The rush hour was over, the young were in school and most housewives were far too busy to go walking in the park.

"You don't have to do this," Ashton said quietly. "Elena is under police protection, guarded by officers who can be trusted, so it's not likely anyone will try to harm her. And, in time, the embassy can probably talk the authorities into granting her an exit visa."

"I said I would do it," Konstantin Kirillovich told him, "and I am not the sort of man to go back on his word."

"No one is going to accuse you of that. There are risks . . ."

"So you have said many times before and I have listened to you with great respect, but now is the time to act."

"Look . . ."

"I do not wish to hear any more arguments, just do it."

Konstantin Kirillovich was one of the most obstinate of men and as Ashton had cause to know, no one could be more stubborn once his mind was made up. Maybe the old man would not have been quite so fearless if he had got him to sign the disclaimer as Hazelwood had wanted. But he hadn't, and furthermore, never would be able to bring himself to do that. If anything went wrong, the family deserved to be compensated. It was one of the reasons why he had never spoken of the risks inside the house where the hidden microphones could pick up their conversation.

"You are very silent, Mr Ashton."

"Sorry, I was thinking."

"You are worried perhaps?"

"No. No, it's going to be all right."

"I do not wish you to tell me when it will happen."

"Whatever you say," Ashton murmured.

They reached the gates at the far end of the park, turned right on the road outside and passed under the railway bridge on their way up to King Street. An elderly man emerged from the betting shop at the top on the right, a young mother wheeling a pushchair passed them heading in the opposite direction. No one else was on the street, no one appeared to be watching them from the terraced houses on either side. They walked on towards the first shop in a small precinct, a former hardware store that had gone into liquidation and whose premises were now available to rent. Beyond that, there was a newsagent, then a mini market on the corner. Behind him, Ashton heard a train clatter over the bridge and knew he had to act before any passengers descended to street level.

Konstantin Kirillovich had dispensed with a jacket and had rolled up his shirtsleeves, making it easy for Ashton to hit the main artery. The hypodermic was spring loaded and modelled on the lines of the self-injection kit produced for the armed forces to enable personnel exposed to a nerve agent to pump themselves with an antidote to counteract the effects on the nervous system. Aiming the hypodermic at the target, Ashton pressed the release catch and the spring did the rest, driving the needle into the vein and emptying the syringe automatically.

He slipped the hypodermic into his trouser pocket and tried to grab hold of Andrianov before the poison had time to act, but somehow the old man eluded his grasp and staggered on past the newsagent, weaving about like a drunk. Although he managed to catch hold of a wrist at the second attempt, Konstantin Kirillovich was already on the way down and they hit the ground together outside Ranjit Patel's mini market. Ashton managed to break the fall with his free hand, but the old man was now unconscious and physically unable to do anything. He landed face down and started bleeding from the mouth, nose and forehead where the raised lip of a paving stone had caught him. Before Ashton could render first aid, the Indian shopkeeper ran out of the mini market and attacked him with a broom handle under the impression that he was a mugger. He raised an arm, warded off a blow aimed at his head, then grabbed hold of the handle and wrenched the broom from the shopkeeper's grasp.

"What the hell's the matter with you?" he roared. "This man is having a heart attack. For God's sake, ring for an ambulance."

Ashton shoved the broom at him and crouched beside Konstantin Kirillovich. In the space of a few minutes, a small crowd had gathered round the old man, which meant that he received any amount of unsolicited medical advice. He didn't need anyone to tell him that Andrianov didn't look too good but even though the blood on his face obviously made Konstantin Kirillovich look worse than perhaps he was, his pallor gave him cause for concern. He wiped the blood from his face with a handkerchief and started to give him mouth to mouth resuscitation.

The police were the first to respond to the emergency and an onlooker in the crowd told one of the PCs that the victim had been attacked in broad daylight. Consequently, when the ambulance arrived on the scene a few minutes later, Ashton was not allowed to accompany Konstantin Kirillovich to hospital. No matter how many times the Indian shopkeeper explained that it had all been a mistake, the police still wanted a statement and the more Ashton protested, the more determined they became.

He was taken to Hammersmith police station where his ID card made a lasting impression on the desk sergeant who permitted him to keep phoning Century House until he raised Hazelwood.

After that, things began to look up. Instead of taking a statement, the police checked the local hospitals, then provided a car to take him to the Intensive Care Unit at Hammersmith General.

The doctors who had examined Konstantin Kirillovich were not a hundred per cent convinced he'd had a heart attack and were more concerned that he might have fractured his skull than they were about a possible coronary. However, in this case and in view of his age and the fact that he had been unconscious on admission, they were not taking any chances and his condition was being closely monitored. At that stage, the hospital authorities saw no reason to put him on the Dangerously Ill list. They changed their minds at ten eighteen, sixty-five minutes after Andrianov had collapsed outside Ranjit Patel's mini market. Konstantin Kirillovich's condition had not deteriorated; it was the pressure exerted by the Foreign Office through the Regional Health Authority which had persuaded them to have second thoughts. Kelso's arrival with an entourage of friendly consultants was the ultimate sanction.

"You can go now," he told Ashton loftily. "We are expecting the Minister Counsellor from the Russian Embassy at any moment."

"Right."

"You'd better see the granddaughter and tell her what has happened."

Only Kelso could have referred to six-year-old Vera as "the granddaughter", relegating the child to a mere appendage in the scheme of things.

"Of course I was planning to," Ashton said curtly.

He did not add that he had no idea what he was going to say to the little girl who had already been through so much in her short life.

"Oh, and one other thing," Kelso said as he turned to leave. "We've had another cable from Istanbul. Looks as if your Mrs Joyner may have been murdered. The body of a European woman answering to her description was found outside Kanlica on Friday. The throat had been cut."

"What about Neville?"

"There's been no word on him. But if he did have anything to do with her murder, it's police business, not ours." Kelso paused, then offered a glimpse of the blinding obvious. "We are an

312

Intelligence gathering organisation," he said peevishly, "not a law enforcement agency. I think you sometimes lose sight of that."

Elena Andrianova felt safe whenever Katya Malinovskaya was on duty; when her relief took over, she was on tenterhooks for the next twenty-four hours until the twenty-eight-year-old KGB officer came on shift again. The man who spelled Katya was in his forties and had sleek black hair which he combed straight back without a parting. Although he had behaved himself so far, he made Elena nervous the way she sometimes caught him looking at her with his deep-set hooded eyes as if he were sizing up his chances. Whenever he was on watch, she made a point of dressing as dowdily as possible to put him off.

She changed now into a pair of loose-fitting slacks and a much-darned sweater that was at least one size too big for her because the shifts changed at 16.00 hours and Katya Malinovskaya was about to be relieved by the KGB's would-be Lothario. Elena checked her appearance in the mirror, removed the last traces of lipstick from her mouth with a handkerchief, then returned to the living room.

"How do I look?" she asked.

"Dowdy," Katya told her. "No man would give you a second glance."

"Except perhaps your colleague?"

"If he condescends to appear."

"It's not four o'clock yet."

"He is supposed to be here ten minutes before the shift changes." Katya went over to the phone and lifted the receiver. After dialling the area code for the Criminal Investigation Division, she began to jiggle the hook as if trying to raise the operator. "That's funny," she muttered, frowning.

"What is?"

"The phone's dead."

"Perhaps there's a fault on the line," Elena suggested.

"No, it's completely dead." Katya held the receiver out to her. "Listen for yourself."

Elena took the handset reluctantly and held the receiver to her left ear. There was no rushing noise or the queer sort of warble she remembered hearing at other times when the phone had been temporarily out of order; instead, there was just a total nerve-racking silence. Behind her, Katya put the security chain on the door, then unzipped her handbag and took out a small semi-automatic pistol.

"What are you doing?" Elena asked nervously.

"What does it look like?" Katya pulled the slide back and jacked a round into the breach of the automatic, then applied the safety catch. "Who else has got a phone in this block of flats?"

"There's a woman doctor on the ground floor, she might have one."

"Let's hope you're right."

"You're not planning to leave me up here alone, are you?"

"Lock the door after me, put the chain on and look through the peephole before you let anyone in."

The peephole and the security chain were botched jobs that had been hurriedly done by a ham-fisted workman the KGB had sent when they had decided she was at risk some twenty-four hours after the hospital had sent her home. She had no faith in either security measure. The view through the peephole was restricted and the chain wouldn't stop a bull like Sergeant Oroblinsky.

"No." Elena shook her head. "No, I won't let you go."

"Don't be ridiculous, you won't come to any harm."

"How do you know?"

"Look, there's undoubtedly a rational explanation for the phone being cut off but we shouldn't take any unnecessary risks . . ."

"Then don't leave me," Elena said desperately.

"You'll be all right."

Katya gave her the automatic, told Elena that all she had to do was push the safety catch forward, point the gun at the target and keep squeezing the trigger. The young KGB sergeant removed the chain, unlocked the door and stepped out onto the landing.

Elena closed the door and turned the key. That was the easy part; sliding the lug at the end of the security chain into the guide rails called for a steady hand and she couldn't stop shaking. Her heart started palpitating and in her terror she mewled like a new-born kitten.

Katya pressed the call button one more time before giving it up as a bad job. The apartment house was served by two lifts, both of which, according to the indicators, were stuck on the ground floor. From past experience, she had learned this was not unusual, but that didn't make it any less of a bind. Anxious not to leave Elena alone a minute longer than necessary, she ran down each flight, taking the steps two at a time in her low-heeled shoes.

Fourth floor, third, second; right hand on the steel banisters to steady herself, she ran down the stairs, gathering momentum the whole time. There was nothing sinister about a fault on the line; as every Muscovite knew, the telephone system was not a hundred per cent reliable these days and individual subscribers were frequently cut off. Unfortunately, Elena Andrianova was a highly strung, neurotic woman who was terrified of her own shadow and whose fear was contagious. They were not in danger, it was all in her mind. Katya Malinovskaya drew comfort from that thought until she reached the ground floor and came face to face with Sergeant Oroblinsky.

He had his back to the entrance and was nicely placed to intercept her if she attempted to run out into the street. Wheeling right, Katya darted towards the lifts, saw the wedges he had jammed under the doors and realised she had made a terrible mistake. Before she could cry out, a meaty hand closed over her mouth, then a knife went into her back and the world suddenly became a dark and painful place.

A few days ago, Vaughan had been congratulating himself that he had seen the last of the Andrianovs. Now, thanks to intense diplomatic activity in London and Moscow, he was once more on his way to Rusanova Prospekt. Shortly after midday, Moscow time, Konstantin Kirillovich had been rushed to hospital after collapsing in the street; barely four hours later, his daughter had been granted an exit visa. Old timers in the embassy could not recall an occasion when officials of the Foreign and Interior Ministries had been quite so helpful, even allowing for Glasnost, Perestroika and all the other current buzz words.

Hugo Calthorpe, however, continued to live in the past and refused to prejudice the security of the SIS officers on the diplomatic staff. Their identities had to be concealed despite the radically different political climate, which was why he was still running errands for them. Thanks to a defunct telephone, he had also been landed with the unenviable task of informing Elena Andrianova that her father was dangerously ill in hospital. It was a job Vaughan would gladly have passed on to any one of the other three occupants of the embassy's Rover 850 – Feliks, the locally employed chauffeur, the myopic liaison officer from the Ministry of the Interior, or the KGB officer who was due to relieve Sergeant Katya Malinovskaya. The trouble was, Elena Andrianova wouldn't believe the news unless she heard it from him.

Vaughan sighed deeply, looked out of the car window. They were heading north on the Mira Prospekt and were approaching the Cosmos Hotel. From there, it would take them approximately five minutes to reach Rusanova Prospekt in the Babuskin District.

Chapter 27

Oroblinsky forced the control panel in the far lift with his bloodstained knife and pulled the fuse from the box. Moving to the other elevator, he retrieved the wedges he had shoved under both doors and hit the button for the fifth floor. Order, counter order, disorder; there was more than a grain of truth in that old maxim. They should have buried Elena Andrianova the day she had lost her job at the British Embassy, but that idea had been vetoed by the faceless men in the First Chief Directorate. They'd argued that such an extreme measure would alert the British, and so they had settled for intimidation instead.

But life was never that simple and there was always a rogue factor; they hadn't allowed for an Englishman called Ashton. He had traced Elena Andrianova to the Piragow Hospital and, as a result, had triggered a deluge of conflicting orders. "Hide the bitch in a psychiatric hospital – get rid of her – no, don't do that, return her to the Piragow and get the hospital to admit the woman under her married name." Shit, there had been times when he hadn't known his elbow from his arse. It was unbelievable, but those morons had passed up yet another opportunity to deal with her once and for all after she had been discharged from hospital. For twenty-four hours she had been alone in the flat but of course that had been much too easy; they had to wait until the situation was about as unfavourable as it could be before they gave the order to kill her.

A sudden decision conveyed by an anonymous voice on the telephone he'd heard many times before. No explanation, just a terse order and a warning that he'd only got an hour in which to carry it out. He'd had to put both lifts temporarily out of action while he cut the line to the Andrianovs' apartment and then Katya Malinovskaya had come running before he'd time to do anything else. When you'd served together in the same squad as long as they had, you didn't need to see her face; he had recognised Katya by the sound of her footsteps on the stairs long before she had appeared in view.

The lift bumped to a stop at the fifth floor, a few moments later the automatic doors opened sluggishly. Oroblinsky bent down, shoved a wedge under the nearest door to prevent it closing and then moved out onto the landing. No one above or below the fifth floor could now call for the one car that was still in action and he had the means to make a quick getaway once the job had been done.

There were sixty housing units on each floor of the block and he would have a problem if any of the occupants on the fifth appeared on the landing at the wrong moment. In that event, there were two possible solutions. He could either produce his KGB ID card and order the interlopers to back off or he could shoot anyone who argued the toss with him and drop the body down the lift shaft. Either way he would be finished, yet he couldn't turn his back on Elena Andrianova without signing his own death warrant. Maybe he couldn't identify the clique who were running him, but he could point a finger in their direction and they wouldn't allow that.

The Andrianovs lived in apartment 1258 and he knew exactly how much of the landing could be seen through the peephole. Keeping outside the field of vision, he moved across the open space and positioned himself on the left side of the door, his back to the wall. He drew the 9mm Makarov automatic pistol from his shoulder holster, reached into his jacket pocket for the noise suppressor and locked it onto the specially adapted barrel. Then he loaded the pistol and pressed the doorbell with his free hand.

"It's only me – Katya," he said, in what he thought was a fair imitation of her voice.

He listened for the sound of footsteps, thought he heard Elena coming towards the door and moved sideways to place himself in front of the spyhole before he opened fire. A hole appeared in the door and a bullet passed close to his head a split second before a cannon boomed inside the apartment. Round after round came through the door, splintering the woodwork, and suddenly there was this searing pain below his left ribcage. The impact dumped him on the floor and for some moments he sat

318

there staring in disbelief at the warm stain that was beginning to spread all down his left side.

"You bitch," he said hoarsely. "You shot me, you fucking bitch."

He raised the automatic, aimed it at the door and, squeezing the trigger, managed to hit the wall. The world was already revolving like a carousel and an insistent voice inside his head urged him to get the hell away before he passed out.

Oroblinsky crawled into the lift, removed the wedge that was holding the door open and levered himself up on to his feet. He hit the button for the ground floor, but the lift responded to an earlier call and began to ascend. It went past the next two floors and stopped at the eighth where he was confronted by a sea of faces.

"Back." He threatened them with the pistol. "You hear what I said," he croaked. "Get back."

Nobody seemed inclined to take him seriously; deciding there was only one way to enforce the order, Oroblinsky shot an old man, then fired again into the crowd, downing two women with a single round. There was a stunned silence, then everyone started screaming as they ran for cover. He hit the button again, and this time the car began to descend.

Katya rose slowly to the surface until her head was just above the water. She couldn't breathe properly, there was a tight band around her chest and her lungs felt as if they were bursting. Fearful of drowning, she tried to heave herself out of the water and promptly fell back, coughing and spluttering. She put a hand to her nose and mouth to keep out the water, only to find that her fingers came away sticky with blood. Then suddenly everything fell into place and she realised that Oroblinsky had dumped her in the stairwell behind the lift shaft where the communal litter bins were kept for the residents on the ground floor.

She reached out, grabbed hold of the metal handle on the side of the nearest bin and used it to haul herself up on to her feet. Bent double and coughing blood, she inched her way round the lift shaft, leaning against it for support. One of the women waiting for the lift, who was old enough to be somebody's *babushka*, called her a drunken cow as she lurched past them.

Katya didn't care, her one aim was to reach the street and call for assistance from a pay phone.

She staggered on towards the entrance and put out a hand to push the swing doors open long before she was within touching distance. Behind her, a woman screamed in terror and provoked an hysterical reaction from others in the crowd of onlookers. Above the din, she heard a man swearing and was amazed that the sight of blood should cause so much alarm. Then she looked back over her shoulder, saw Oroblinsky deliberately execute a man who was already lying on the ground, and shared their fear. She collided with the swing door, somehow found enough strength to push it open, and reeled out of the apartment house almost into the arms of her relief. She wanted to ask where the hell he'd been when she had needed him but the words simply gurgled in her mouth.

To Vaughan everything seemed to be happening in slow motion. He saw Katya Malinovskaya lurching towards them, pink froth bubbling from her open mouth, watched her trip and fall on to her face as she missed the outstretched arms of their KGB escort, then stared dumbfounded at the bull-like figure of Oroblinsky standing motionless outside the entrance to the apartment house, leaking blood onto the concrete path. He was, Vaughan noted, wearing the now familiar brown pinstripe suit which today looked even more rumpled than usual. He heard the sergeant greet his fellow officer by name and smile inanely before he slowly raised the pistol he was holding in his right hand.

Suddenly, everything began to move at fast forward speed. The vacant grin disappeared from Oroblinsky's mouth under two hammer blows to the chest, which knocked him off his feet to land backwards on the path, his head towards the entrance. Out in the open, the pistol shots sounded no louder than a couple of firecrackers; they were, however, a great deal more lethal. The whole of Oroblinsky's shirtfront was one large brownish-red stain and a sluggish meandering stream began to appear from beneath him.

"We go now," Feliks said, tugging at his sleeve. "This is bad, very bad."

Vaughan rounded on the embassy chauffeur. "Now you listen to me," he snapped. "You will wait here. If you leave before I return, you will be dismissed. That's a promise."

He turned away, grabbed hold of the liaison officer from the Ministry of the Interior and dragged him into the apartment house. Calthorpe had told him to put Elena Andrianova on a plane to England and that was exactly what he intended to do, provided she was still alive. One look at the milling crowd in the entrance hall convinced Vaughan they should forget the lifts and take to the stairs. Confident of his fitness, he started at the double and wasted a lot of breath urging the myopic liaison officer to keep up with him. He began to hurt before they reached the fourth floor and, giving up on the Russian, he went on alone, breathing heavily, his heart beginning to pound in overdrive. When he started to climb the last flight, his legs felt as though they didn't belong to him and he was forced to take a breather on the landing.

The door to the Andrianovs' flat had almost as many holes in it as a colander. Another one appeared when he pressed the bell and called out to her, the wood splintering four inches from his head on a level with his left eye. An angry bee buzzed past him, glanced off the far wall and went on ricocheting until its energy was spent. He didn't know what calibre weapon she had but it sounded like a howitzer.

"For God's sake, Elena," he yelled, "it's me, Mr Vaughan."

Rather late in the day, it dawned on him that it would be a good idea to move away from the door in case she opened fire again. Like a crab scuttling for cover under a rock, he moved sideways and flattened himself against the wall.

"Did you hear what I said, Elena?" he shouted. "It's me, Mr Vaughan. It's all over, you're safe now. Okay?"

There was no answer. All he could hear was the heavy breathing of the liaison officer who had finally made it to the fifth floor.

"I think she no understand you," the Russian said in rudimentary English. "Perhaps I speak to lady in her own language?"

Vaughan could imagine what sort of reaction that was likely to provoke. If she had any ammunition left, there would be a few more holes in the door. "*Nyet, nyet.*" He toyed with the idea of explaining why it was not a good idea, then decided his vocabulary wasn't up to it. "It's me, Elena," he yelled at the top of his voice. "Please let me in, I have something to tell you."

He heard the lock turn, then a hinge squeaked and the door slowly opened. Emboldened by his apparent success, Vaughan put his head round the door frame and found himself looking into the ugly snout of a pistol.

"Do you mind not pointing that thing at me?" he requested in a voice that quavered like an amateur contralto striving to reach a top note way above her range.

Elena closed the door in his face to remove the security chain, then invited him to come in. She was, he thought, in a dreadful state. Ashen-faced, sweating and trembling as if she had a fever, she was barely in control of herself and was liable to throw a wobbly if she were put under further stress. Given that possibility, Vaughan was damned if he was going to tell her that Konstantin Kirillovich was dangerously ill in hospital. Relieving her of the automatic pistol, he placed it on top of the TV.

"We have some good news for you," he announced and pointed to the liaison officer. "This gentleman is from the Ministry of the Interior and we are going to take you to the airport."

"Airport?"

"You've been granted an exit visa and you are flying to England to join your parents and daughter."

Elena stared at him blankly. He could see she wasn't taking it in; everything he had told her had gone straight over her head.

"Have you got anything to drink in the flat?" he asked.

Elena didn't answer. Rather than repeat the question, Vaughan went through all the cupboards and found a three-parts empty bottle of vodka in the cabinet above the kitchen sink at the far end of the living room. He poured a large measure into a cup, then folded her hands around the vessel.

"Here, drink this," he told her, "it will make you feel better."

Her teeth chattered on the rim of the teacup and some of the vodka ran down her chin, but she managed to swallow most of it. The liquor burned her throat, brought tears to Elena's eyes and made her cough and splutter, but at least the old adrenalin was flowing again.

She still looked terrible, of course, a frump in baggy trousers and a sweater that even a rag-and-bone man wouldn't have bothered with, but there was no time for her to change into anything halfway decent, let alone pack a suitcase. Vaughan knew he had to get her out of the flat and on to a plane before the Ministry of the Interior learned what had happened in Rusanova Prospekt.

He picked up a handbag that was lying in the seat of an armchair. "Yours?" he asked.

"*Da* – yes."

Two words, one Russian, one English; things were definitely improving.

"Good, let's go. You too, Igor."

"The police, Mr Vaughan." The liaison officer placed a restraining hand on his arm. "They will have questions."

It was exactly what Vaughan had feared. Naturally the police would have questions, hundreds and hundreds of them, and Elena would never be allowed to leave the country once they got their hands on her.

"Now you listen to me," Vaughan said in execrable Russian, "Elena Andrianova has been granted an exit permit and you and I are going to put her on a plane."

"I don't think – " the liaison officer began.

"It doesn't matter what you think, I'm telling you Mr Yeltsin is going to be pretty unhappy if you are responsible for a diplomatic incident. Now, let's go."

Vaughan seized the two Russians by the arm and hustled them out of the flat. Knowing how unreliable the lifts were, he ran them downstairs and out into the street, past the ambulances and police cars which had arrived on the scene. The Rover 850 was parked by the kerbside opposite the entrance to the block of flats. Long before they got there, Feliks had the engine running and the nearside doors open.

Zale wished he had never listened to Ashton. Not only had the weekend in Seattle been a complete waste of time, it had also won him no friends in the local field office of the FBI. Michael Todorvic was a highly respected member of the community and pure as the driven snow. He had freely admitted that George Neville had worked for Pacific Northwest Oil and Gas but they had parted company nearly two and a half years ago and there was no reason to suppose he was lying.

There was a Serbian connection. In 1908 his grandfather had arrived in America from Belgrade with little more than the clothes on his back. Zale had spent the whole of Saturday morning in the library of Seattle's *Post-Intelligencer* reading up on the family in back issues of the newspaper and had come across a profile of Michael Todorvic when he had been appointed Executive Vice President of the corporation in 1977 at the age of thirty-nine. So it was pointless for Ashton to waste time and money on a satellite call in a last-ditch attempt to smear the guy.

"You don't know him like I do," he told Ashton. "He's a hundred per cent all-American hero, voted the guy most likely to succeed in High School, quarterback Washington State, Phi Beta Gamma fraternity, ROTC – you name it, he did it. Got a Distinguished Service medal and a Silver Star in Korea and picked up a Purple Heart. He's the great untouchable."

"Then he should choose his friends more carefully; George Neville is a murderer."

"So you told me a few minutes ago. But where is your proof that Todorvic was involved?"

They were going over the same ground again. Ashton was nothing if not persistent, he kept hammering the same point in the belief that he would eventually get his own way by process of attrition.

"I believe he's back in the States, Tony."

"Yeah, yeah." Bernice Kreuger was making circles in the air with an index finger like some goddamn TV director urging an interviewer to wrap it up. It might be twenty after five in London but it was only noon here and clearly she was getting hungry.

"All I am asking is for you – "

"You don't have a shred of proof that Neville is back in the States."

"He had that woman murdered."

"Okay, Peter, if you want the Federal Bureau to check with the Immigration authorities, you get your Scotland Yard to ask for their assistance. I don't want to know." Zale paused. "I'm sorry, but that's the way it is," he added and put the phone down.

Bernice Kreuger was smiling as if in her opinion he had done something right for once. He felt pretty bad about hanging up on Ashton; her approval made it even worse.

The date time group of the first cable from Moscow showed that it had been despatched at 13.55 hours Greenwich Mean Time.

Given a signals precedence of "Immediate", it was unclassified, addressed to FCO London for attention Secretary of State, Foreign Affairs, copy to Consul General, Paris. It read:

> Elena Andrianova granted exit visa on compassionate grounds departed for London via Paris on Air France AF924 at 17.10 hours Moscow time. Please arrange Consul General to meet subject on arrival Charles de Gaulle Airport. Onward movement from Paris NOT repeat NOT confirmed this end. Suggest either British Airways BA323 departing 20.35 or Air France AF824 leaving five minutes earlier. Grateful you info all concerned.

The second cable was despatched some three and a quarter hours later; it carried a Top Secret security classification and was considerably longer. Even though a high-grade cipher had been used to encode the text, the originator had been careful not to identify the subject by name and no reference was made to the previous message. The signals precedence of "Emergency" ensured the communications centre delivered it piecemeal to Hazelwood as each page was decoded. The content was such that he in turn walked it down the corridor to the Deputy DG as soon as the entire text was to hand.

"Now we know why Elena was put on a plane to Paris rather than the direct British Airways flight to London which departed fifteen minutes later."

"Quite." Dunglass looked up from the signal. "Vaughan did a good job; if he had waited for the later flight, the police might have detained her."

"The Foreign Office isn't too happy; she's a material witness and the Russians will obviously want to question her."

"Fine. Major General Gurov can always send one of his investigators to London. We'll certainly make her available, but she isn't going back."

"That's what I told them," Hazelwood said.

"Good. Do we have details of her onward flight from Paris yet?"

"Yes, British Airways – arrives Terminal 4 at 20.45 hours. Roy Kelso will meet her off the plane." Hazelwood paused, wondered how he was going to persuade the future DG to change his mind about Ashton. "Elena hasn't been told that her father is in hospital," he said, opting for the oblique approach.

"I've read the cable too," Dunglass said quietly. "But it's not a problem, is it? I mean, it's not as if her father is dangerously ill."

"The news is still going to come as a shock and she has had a pretty stressful time of it today. Someone gave Oroblinsky express orders to kill her and he damn nearly succeeded."

"What are you leading up to, Victor?"

"The point is, she is in a highly emotional state and I think there ought to be at least one familiar face in the reception committee."

"Meaning Ashton, I presume?"

"Yes. Look, I know you don't want him to interrogate her but she doesn't know anyone but Ashton over here, and frankly, Roy is the last person to tell Elena what her father is doing in hospital."

"All right."

"If Ashton is there to prepare her, my people will have a much easier task – "

"You've made your point, Victor."

"She may even start to confide in him . . ." Hazelwood stopped in mid-sentence. "What did you say just then?" he asked.

"I withdraw my objections, you can have Ashton." Dunglass smiled. "I don't imagine it will come as a big surprise to him."

Neville left the outskirts of Windemere behind him and continued north on Provincial Highway 95 towards Rogers Pass. He had set off from Seattle at eight o'clock that morning in a four-seater Piper Turbo Arrow 4 he'd chartered from Airspeed at Renton Airport. Four hundred miles and two hours twenty minutes later, he had landed at Kimberley where he had rented the Ford Tempo he was driving. The backpack, bivouac, sleeping bag, provisions and hexamine cooker in the trunk of the car had been purchased from a sports and camping store on Main Street; the plaid shirt, corduroys, thick socks and heavy-duty walking shoes were from a men's outfitters in the same town.

He planned to branch off onto Provincial Highway 93 south of Edgewater and spend the next three days trekking in the Banff

326

National Park around Lake Louise. On Friday morning he would collect the Ford from the parking lot of the motel where he was staying tonight and make his way to Rogers Pass on the Trans-Canada Highway. Another night in a different motel and he would be ready for the face-to-face with Mike Todorvic the following evening.

It was not something he was looking forward to; the American had sounded edgy when he had phoned him at home yesterday evening and he had a funny feeling that his nervousness had something to do with Ashton. Of course it was illogical; he couldn't see how Ashton could have zeroed in on the Executive Vice President of Pacific Northwest Oil and Gas even though the bastard had been sniffing round the Trans Globe offices in Arlington House. Maybe one of the oilmen in the First Chief Directorate had tipped off the SIS? No, that couldn't be right; the suppliers believed they had been ripped off by Colin Joyner and he had delivered his head on a platter. Not only that, he had returned the missing two million dollars and out of sheer gratitude, they had taken care of Frances Joyner.

Perhaps Todorvic hadn't been nervous? What if the American had been uptight because he had learned that he had been ripped off to the tune of seven and a half million? So who had told him? The Serbians? Hell, they had no idea how many barrels of oil Todorvic had paid for. They took whatever came up the Danube and were grateful for every drip. Maybe there was going to be an internal audit and Mike was worried the accountants might uncover certain irregularities? What the hell did it matter? He had covered his back and there was no way Todorvic could harm him. If the American wanted to pull out, he would simply tell the suppliers he either found a new backer or they called it a day. And if the worst did come to the worst, there was always the nest egg of five million in the numbered account in Zurich to fall back on.

Neville tripped the indicator and turned off on to Highway 93. Twenty minutes later, he stopped for a late, late lunch at a diner in Radium Hot Springs.

When Konstantin Kirillovich and Ludmilla Andrianov had arrived at Heathrow with granddaughter, Vera, they had been escorted through Immigration and Customs by one of the airport staff and a member of the cabin crew. Things were different this time round; instead of waiting for Elena in the arrivals hall, Ashton and Kelso were there to meet her the moment she stepped off the plane.

If he hadn't known better, Ashton would have said Elena was a down-and-out bag lady. The sweater she was wearing looked as if it should have been consigned to the dustbin long ago and the voluminous slacks could have accommodated a woman twice her size. Her eyes had the glazed expression of a confirmed alcoholic whose sole interest in life lay in obtaining the wherewithal for the next drink. There was no sudden transformation when she spotted him, merely a faint smile of recognition.

"You'll need to walk on eggshells with that one," Kelso observed in a whispered aside. "Be careful what you say to her."

"I intend to."

Ashton went forward to meet her, introduced Kelso, then took Elena by the arm and steered her towards Immigration, making small talk the whole time, mostly about Vera. There was, however, a limit to how long he could avoid mentioning Konstantin Kirillovich and inevitably Elena wanted to know where he was.

"In bed," Ashton told her, "like Vera. They've had an exhausting day."

There was a semblance of truth in what he'd told her. Both of them were exhausted, Konstantin Kirillovich as a result of the drug-induced coma, Vera who had become hysterical when her grandfather had failed to return from a walk in the park. And both were in bed, albeit in separate locations. He kept up the pretence that all was well until she was safely in the Rover limousine and they were on the way to 84 Rylett Close. Then he lifted the veil.

"Your father made this possible," Ashton told her. "Your being here I mean."

Elena gazed at him apprehensively. "I don't understand," she said in a low nervous voice.

"We faked a heart attack. I'm not sure whether your fellow countrymen at the Russian Embassy were completely taken in by the charade, but they went along with it. Money talks, you know, and Mr Yeltsin wants all the credit he can get. My guess is the Foreign Office offered Moscow a number of financial inducements and your exit visa was one of the gestures made in return." Ashton reached out for one of her hands and squeezed it gently. "The thing is, Konstantin Kirillovich sustained a nasty bump on the head when he passed out in the street. Your father is going to be okay but right now, he is in hospital."

"Oh my God."

He thought it strange that someone who had been brought up as an atheist and had never been inside a church should immediately turn to God in adversity, but he had seen it happen before.

"It's nothing to worry about," Ashton assured her. "Konstantin Kirillovich will be up and about in a day or two, you see if I'm not right. Meantime, you are no longer in danger; that's the most important thing to have come out of all this." Ashton paused, gave her time to digest what he had just said, then started to bring a little pressure to bear. "Take it from me, no one is going to harm you so long as you're in London."

"How long can I stay in England?"

He was afraid Kelso would tell her she could apply for political asylum and jumped in first. They would get ten times more out of Elena while she was still feeling vulnerable than ever they would if she believed the sword of Damocles was no longer hanging above her head.

"Naturally we shan't send you back until we believe it is safe to do so." He paused again to let the implication sink in, then planted a seed of doubt. "Of course we shall need your help to make a valid judgement of the situation."

"My help?" she repeated blankly.

"You'll have to tell us exactly what it was 'Mikhail' wanted from you."

"Ah . . ."

Elena understood what he wanted but she didn't say anything, merely stared straight ahead, eyes riveted on the chauffeur in front as though in a trance.

"Remember what you told me in Moscow?" Ashton said quietly. "You said he was interested in the price of gold and silver bullion on the London market and the future quotas for oil and gas, but there has to be more to it than that."

He wondered if he should point out to Elena that a lot of people had gone out on a limb to save her neck but that smacked too much of bullying and he couldn't bring himself to do it.

"Trans Globe," Elena murmured.

"What was that?" Kelso asked.

"Mikhail," she said in a louder voice. "He wanted me to look out for any commercial cables from London which mentioned Trans Globe and Pacific Northwest . . ."

Ashton leaned back in the seat and smiled to himself in the darkness. Elena had finally dotted all the i's and crossed every t for him. No more prevarications, no more excuses; the FBI would have every reason now to look for Neville. As soon as they arrived at Rylett Close he would call Zale and set the wheels in motion.

Chapter 28

Ashton checked to make sure he had answered all the questions and placed a tick in the appropriate boxes on the reverse side of the US Customs and Immigration declaration before slipping the form between the covers of his passport. It had taken the FBI a little over forty-eight hours to come up with the information that Neville had arrived in Chicago by Lufthansa from Frankfurt and had stayed one night at the Holiday Inn near O'Hare Airport before boarding a United Airlines flight to Seattle on Sunday, May the twenty-fourth. Thereafter, Neville had become inconspicuous; his name hadn't appeared on any hotel register, he hadn't been near Hertz or any of the other rental agencies in town and according to their records, none of the airlines using Boeing/King County International, Renton Municipal or Seattle-Tacoma International Airport had sold him a plane ticket.

Two notes on a gong made Ashton look up at the illuminated signs in the panel above his head; adjusting his seat to the upright position, he fastened the seat belt across his lap. Middle-ranking civil servants were not entitled to go first class; officers of his seniority were, however, allowed to travel Club World but only on British Airways. Although on a BA flight, he had ended up in the World Traveller or economy class because all the seats in the other section had been taken by the time he'd booked. After nine and three-quarter hours in the air and almost another two on the ground at Chicago, both legs were now one big ache.

At 17.00 hours, Flight BA085 touched down exactly on time at Seattle-Tacoma International Airport. Some fifteen minutes later, Ashton cleared Immigration, collected his bag from the carousel and passed through Customs to find Zale waiting for him in the concourse.

"It's good to see you again, Tony," he said and presented the

American with a bottle of Glenfiddich he'd bought in the duty-free at Heathrow.

"You shouldn't have." Zale smiled. "But I'm glad you did; there's nothing like a fine malt whisky to put even the most ornery of men in a good mood. And I have to say Mr William G. McMurtrie is one contrary s.o.b."

"Don't tell me," Ashton said, "he's the FBI agent you've been dealing with?"

"You got it. He's in charge of the local field office." Zale steered him out of the terminal building and signalled a cab from the rank. "You're staying at the Roosevelt; we'll drop your bag off at the hotel, then go see him in his office."

"Right. Any further word on Neville?"

"No. If he's still in Seattle, he must be using a different name and settling his bills in cash. Personally, I think he's moved on."

"Neville leaves a trail all the way from Chicago to here and then suddenly he disappears. What does that suggest to you, Tony?"

"I don't know, you tell me."

The taxi driver didn't appear to be listening to their conversation but Ashton thought it best to assume he could overhear them. Having been told that Todorvic was a well-known and much respected member of the community whose photograph frequently appeared in Seattle's *Post-Intelligencer*, he chose his words with care.

"I think he contacted our friend on Sunday evening and was told to lose himself."

"You're guessing."

"Of course I am, but it fits."

"Have you got that deposition with you?"

"In here, signed and witnessed." Ashton patted the briefcase on the back seat between them. "I've also got a cassette which is compatible with an American VCR."

The day after her arrival in the UK, Elena Andrianova had been questioned at length by officers from the Russian Desk. In the course of a four-hour interview, she had given her interrogators a great deal more information than she had disclosed to Ashton. Not only had her statement been transcribed in both Russian and English, the whole proceedings had been videotaped.

"A word of advice," Zale said quietly. "Stick to the deposition when we see McMurtrie and leave Neville out of it."

"You mind telling me why?"

"It wouldn't go down well with him, he thinks our friend can do no wrong."

"That could make life difficult."

"Something else you should know. McMurtrie is both complacent and aggressive; in fact, he's not the sort of man you would go out of your way to meet. I'm told his family originally came from Ireland in the 1850s and I get the impression that he doesn't like the Brits."

"You got any more good news for me?" Ashton asked drily.

"I think you'll like the Roosevelt."

Ashton thought he would too, even though in the time allowed all he saw was the front desk of the hotel. McMurtrie had agreed to stay on until after normal office hours in order to see them and Zale was keen not to keep him waiting a moment longer than was necessary.

The FBI Chief in Seattle occupied a singularly unimpressive office in the Federal Building, which seemed in harmony with his personality and appearance. McMurtrie in the flesh was everything Ashton had been led to believe; he was middle-aged, fat, bald, aggressive and offhand.

"I hope this isn't going to be a waste of time, Mr Ashton," he growled after a perfunctory handshake.

"Well, I assume Tony will have told you about the joint operation by Trans Globe and Pacific Northwest to circumvent the United Nations embargo?"

"Mr Zale has made a number of allegations without a shred of evidence to support them. I understand you're supplying that?"

"Elena Andrianova has done that." Ashton opened the briefcase, took out a copy of her statement and passed it to McMurtrie. "She used to work for the Third Secretary, Commerce in our Moscow embassy. I can also show a video recording of her interrogation."

"That won't be necessary."

McMurtrie picked up a pair of horn-rimmed spectacles from his desk and began to read the statement. Hostility and scepticism were reflected in his facial contortions, the pursed lips, the occasional raised eyebrow, the down turn at the corner of his mouth. The statement ran to approximately ten thousand words; McMurtrie applied a lawyer's mind to it and went straight to the heart of the matter. Ashton knew what he was going to say the moment he placed the statement on one side and removed his glasses.

"There's nothing in her deposition that will stand up in court. Elena Andrianova claims she was instructed to keep her eyes open for any commercial cables from London concerning the two corporations, but she doesn't say why. Furthermore, it appears she has never heard of Mike Todorvic or this guy Neville who is supposed to be the connecting link."

It was "Mr Zale" and "this guy Neville" but the Executive Vice President of Pacific Northwest Oil and Gas was "Mike Todorvic".

"All we've got here, gentlemen, is innuendo. As such, this statement is worthless."

"I doubt if the people who tried to kill Elena Andrianova would agree with you."

"I'm just playing the devil's advocate, Mr Ashton. I'm a lawyer, not an Intelligence officer. I see things in a different light and I'm telling you we haven't got a case if all you've got is this statement."

"No one in Washington is thinking of a trial," Zale said quietly. "My instructions are to ask Mr Todorvic if he's aware of any transactions between Trans Globe and Pacific Northwest. If something funny is going on, I think he will be just as anxious as we are to get to the bottom of it."

"And I'm sure he will."

"So when do you expect to arrange a meeting with Mr Todorvic?"

"Tomorrow, eleven sharp. We'll leave from here at a quarter to the hour." McMurtrie picked up the statement, waved it at Ashton. "Mind if I hold on to this document overnight? I'd like to read it again at my leisure."

"It's okay with me," Ashton said. "How about you, Tony? It's your copy."

"I've no objections," Zale said.

"Good." McMurtrie favoured them with something akin to a smile. "Well, I guess that's it for now, gentlemen."

And for tomorrow as well, Ashton thought, as they shook

hands again before leaving. Forewarned was forearmed and Todorvic had been given plenty of time in which to prepare his defences. It was all he could do to contain his anger until they were outside on the street.

"We've been screwed," he told Zale. "The way things are, I might as well collect my bag from the Roosevelt and catch the first plane to London."

"I don't think it's that bad."

"You want to tell me how it could be worse? McMurtrie set up this meeting with Pacific Northwest's Executive Vice President before he saw us. How much more could he have done for him?"

"Todorvic isn't just the Executive Vice President of Pacific Northwest, he's also on the board of Consolidated Merrill Industries." Zale stepped out into the road and flagged down a cab. "And you don't get to see him without making an appointment," he added.

"No, I suppose that would be too much to hope for."

"And whatever you may think of McMurtrie, first and foremost he is a law enforcement officer and I doubt very much if he will roll over and die for Mike Todorvic."

The ground was rock hard and although he had dug a hole for his hip, the nagging ache finally got to Neville. Reluctantly, he opened one eye, looked round the bivouac and saw daylight between the tent flaps. He unzipped the sleeping bag, stretched both arms above his head and yawned, then looked at his wristwatch, his eyes still bleary with sleep. Four minutes after six and this was Friday. No good wishing he could snatch another half-hour in the sack when there was a long day in front of him, starting with a twenty-mile hike to collect the Ford Tempo.

It would take him over seven hours to walk that distance, which meant that he would need to be on the way by seven, otherwise he wouldn't get there much before mid-afternoon. He would spend tonight in Beavermouth, which was only a few miles from Rogers Pass, and kill some time there before going on to see Todorvic the following evening. Nothing would come of their meeting; reflecting on their telephone conversation, it now seemed to him that the American had implied that either the FBI or some other agency was on to him and he wanted out. Well, that was okay as far as he was concerned, provided Todorvic grasped what would happen if he tried to gain a few Brownie points for himself by pointing a finger in his direction. That was something he would spell out to him in words of one syllable to avoid any misunderstanding.

It slowly dawned on him that he could hear something moving about outside. Turning round inside the pup tent, he crawled out on hands and knees to investigate. The hairs on the back of his neck stood up and he sensed the intruder was somewhere behind him. Neville got to his feet and turned slowly about to find himself confronted by the biggest Grizzly bear he had ever seen. He screamed just the once, then started running towards the treeline forty yards away.

The Executive Vice President of Pacific Northwest was a good deal older than McMurtrie but looked at least five years younger. Physically, he was in far better shape than the FBI agent and obviously knew how to take care of himself. Todorvic was also a friendly, outgoing man who was particularly good at making a complete stranger feel at home. If anyone possessed charisma, he did. For Ashton, the presence of his attorney was the one sign that he was not quite as confident as he appeared to be on the surface.

McMurtie was in no hurry to exploit the situation. Adopting a very relaxed approach, he introduced Ashton, reminded Todorvic that he had already met Zale and then produced Elena's statement plus a photocopy he'd made that morning before leaving his office. As if to make things easier for them, he then proceeded to give the bare facts and in the process, managed to play down the importance of the information Elena Andrianova had disclosed to her interrogators. Not content with that, he subsequently gave Todorvic and his attorney all the time in the world to read the document. He even suggested they might wish to confer.

"I don't think that's necessary, Mac," Todorvic said easily. "I've got nothing to hide. Hell, you already know this guy Neville used to be on the payroll of Pacific Northwest, but we certainly didn't set him up in business on his own account. And I wasn't aware of Trans Globe's existence until Tony enlightened me the other day. I guess he got that information from you, Peter?"

Ashton nodded. It was all very friendly – Mac, Tony and Peter.

If they carried on this way they would end up slapping each other on the back.

"I don't know what sort of business this guy Neville was doing in Russia but it would seem to me that he was using our name to establish his own credibility."

"Could be," McMurtrie agreed. He had crossed one plump leg over the other and was examining the sole of his right shoe as if he expected to find a hole in it. "I believe he left your employ at the end of 1989."

"Yes. Matter of fact, we were sorry to see him go."

"And I understand you told Mr Zale that you haven't seen or heard from him since then?"

McMurtrie hadn't suddenly come alive, he still gave the impression of being indolent and bored out of his skull, but the smile on Todorvic's mouth had frozen.

"That's what I said."

"This was last Friday?"

"Yes." Todorvic cleared his throat. "However, I should tell you that he phoned me at home on Sunday evening. I was pretty surprised."

"I bet you were," McMurtrie said, his interest now concentrated on the welt of his right shoe. "Did he say where he was calling from?"

"No."

"Did you ask him?"

"No, I was too taken aback."

"Yeah. So what did he want?"

"His old job back. If he had phoned me three days earlier, we would probably have taken him on. But knowing what Tony had told me about Trans Globe and his activities in the former Soviet Union, there was no way I would put him back on the payroll."

"And that's what you told him point-blank?"

Todorvic hesitated. "Well, not in so many words. I stalled, said I was much too busy to see him in the coming week in the hope he would get the message."

"And did he?"

"No. He kept pressing me to say when I would be free and in the end, I suggested he phoned again the following Monday, three days from now."

"Mr Neville is no longer in Seattle." McMurtrie lost interest in his shoe and fixed his gaze on Todorvic instead. "Any idea where he might have gone?"

"Well, as I recall, Neville said he had some business to attend to in Edmonton."

"What made him say that? Was he expecting to meet up with you someplace in Canada?"

Ashton had gone to the Merrill Building convinced they would get nowhere because Todorvic and the FBI agent were too friendly by half. Now, forty minutes into the interview, he was seeing a very different McMurtrie, an ice-cool interrogator who had his man by the throat and was not about to let go. Todorvic knew it too and glanced at his attorney, mutely seeking his advice. He got nothing in return. Left to his own devices, he did the best he could to protect himself.

"Neville may have thought we were going to meet up but that was never my intention. See, he kept pressing me for an appointment, any time, any place, wouldn't take no for an answer. Wanted to know what I was doing over the weekend. Finally I told him Elaine and I were thinking of spending the weekend up in the Selkirks and would probably stay overnight at a motel in Rogers Pass on the Saturday. Like I said, nothing definite was arranged, but Neville could have latched on to it."

"Yeah. Well, I'm sure I don't have to impress upon you how important it is to let me know should you hear from him again."

"You can count on it," Todorvic assured him.

Suddenly it was handshakes all round and McMurtrie was saying how helpful Todorvic had been and how he knew he could rely on him to look into the allegation that had been made about Pacific Northwest's willingness to ignore the UN sanctions imposed on Yugoslavia. There were any number of questions Ashton wanted to raise but they had to wait until they were back in McMurtrie's office.

"So what happens now?" he asked.

"I give Todorvic less than a month," McMurtrie told him. "Consolidated Merrill will launch an internal audit and he will also have the IRS breathing down his neck. His distinguished war record in Korea isn't going to save him, neither is his standing in the community. He's looking at hard time and Pacific Northwest won't be financing any future oil supplies to the Serbs. What more do you want?"

"Neville," Ashton said.

"A small cog."

"He's the only man who can identify the suppliers, the faceless men in the KGB's First Chief Directorate who dipped into the war reserves of oil and gas."

"The KGB," McMurtrie said in a voice heavy with irony. "I might have guessed they would be involved, Mr Ashton."

"The Germans and the Japanese are taking nearly all the oil and gas produced by the Siberian fields, leaving virtually nothing for the domestic market. Still untouched are the war reserve stocks, and who else would have the necessary power and audacity to order their release behind Yeltsin's back but the KGB?"

The First Chief Directorate was responsible for foreign Intelligence and the KGB generals within its ranks had been the real policy makers in the former Soviet Union, not the officials in the 'wedding cake' building on Arbat Street and Smolensky Boulevard. Their power had not diminished with Glasnost, Perestroika or the political demise of Gorbachev.

"Although the men who raided these oil stocks did so for personal gain, there was a secondary motive. Traditionally, the Russians have always backed the Serbs and these people are likely to go on supplying Belgrade no matter what Mr Yeltsin and the United Nations have to say on the subject. You may have destroyed the profit motive but as yet, you haven't cut off the flow."

Ashton fell silent. He had exhausted every argument and felt depressed because it seemed nothing he had said had made an impression on the local Bureau Chief. Then McMurtrie surprisingly asked Zale for his opinion.

"That's easy," Zale told him. "We'll be leaving a job half done if we don't go after Neville."

"He's probably walking around with a different name. Tracing his movements won't be easy even if we make up a Fotofit picture of the guy."

"I can do better than that," Ashton said, and produced a print of every close-up Hicks had taken at the Breakespear Crematorium.

McMurtrie said the pictures would be a help but was still inclined to be pessimistic and warned it could be weeks rather than days before they got a lead.

He could not have been more wrong. That same afternoon, the operations manager of Airspeed at Renton Municipal Airport identified Neville from the photographs. Less than forty-eight hours later, Ashton and Zale flew into Calgary and then made the seventy-five-mile drive to Banff.

The body had been found by two hikers roughly three miles north of the Château Lake Louise Hotel. It had been conveyed to Banff because that happened to be the nearest town with a path. lab and a mortuary. From various items, including a UK passport, which had been found scattered around the bivouac site, the sergeant in charge of the RCMP detachment was satisfied they already knew the identity of the corpse. All he wanted from Ashton was confirmation that their supposition was correct.

"He's not a pretty sight," the RCMP officer said cheerfully, "so I hope you gentlemen have strong stomachs."

Ashton could see he wasn't exaggerating when the mortuary attendant pulled the sliding drawer out from the cabinet. He could hear Zale retching behind him and found it hard to contain the bile in the back of his throat. The left arm had gone, leaving just a four-inch stump below the shoulder and the right ended at the elbow. Both legs from the kneecaps down had been gnawed to the bone and something had taken a great chomp out of the left thigh. The stomach had been ripped open, the chest raked to the breast bone but enough of the face was left for Ashton to know immediately who it was.

"That's Neville," he said in a hoarse voice.

"Figured as much," the sergeant said. "We found the Ford Tempo he'd rented twenty-odd miles from where he had bivouaced. The self-drive agency at Kimberley were a lot more pernickity than Airspeed; he had to produce his passport before they would let him hire the car."

"How was he killed?"

"By a Grizzly. Neville was camping near a river and the bear had either come to do a little fishing or else it had been drawn to the bivouac site by the food he'd left lying around outside the pup tent. Anyway, all the signs point to him suddenly coming face to face with the Grizzly and he panicked. Hard to say who was the more frightened, him or the bear, but he turned tail and ran, which was the worst thing to do in the circumstances because it spooked the animal. I guess he knew a Grizzly can outrun a human so he shinned up the nearest tree. That breed is one powerful animal and the bear simply shook him off the branch, damn nearly uprooted the tree in the process. According to the pathologist who did the post mortem, he must have been dead for some hours before the Grizzly started to eat him."

"I don't think I am going to tell the next of kin that, Sergeant."

"Was he married?"

"Not as far as I know," Ashton said. "He has a sister back in England who lives in Grimsby. I'll have to ask her what arrangements she would like us to make."

"We found his suitcase in the trunk of the Ford Tempo. Maybe she'll want his clothes?"

It was an impossible question to answer. The only thing Ashton could do was collect the effects from the RCMP post before he departed from Banff for Calgary and the UK. After agreeing a time with the sergeant when it would be convenient to do so, he was glad to leave the mortuary and breathe air which didn't smell of Lysol.

"Jesus, that's better," Zale said and filled his lungs.

"It could hardly be worse."

"Hey, do I read you right? Are you thinking you struck out?"

"I would hardly call it a total success."

"You helped to put the moneyman out of the game and the middleman is no longer in place as the go-between. So you didn't get to identify the suppliers, but you've made it difficult for them to continue in business." Zale smiled. "Besides, we ought to leave something for the diplomats. How else are they going to earn their keep?"

"I guess you're right."

"Tell you something, though, I could use a drink."

"So could I," Ashton said. "Let's go find a bar."

Chapter 29

Harriet Egan felt her eyelids droop yet again and reared back in the seat. She had wound the car window down on her side to its fullest extent but the interior of the Vauxhall Cavalier was still like an oven and it was difficult to stay awake, especially when nothing much was happening here on the outskirts of Grimsby at three forty-five on this first hot Saturday afternoon in June. Four of the small shops in the precinct up ahead were vacant, the Army Careers and Information Office was closed, leaving only the butcher's, newsagent's and betting shop open. Judging by the number of customers, there was no last-minute rush to buy a Sunday joint and business next door was only just beginning to pick up again following the delivery of the *Grimsby Evening Telegraph*. The betting shop, however, wasn't doing too badly.

She gazed at the pre-war semi-detached houses on the opposite side of the road and wondered how much longer Ashton was going to be closeted with Neville's older sister, Mary. They had set off from London on the A1 shortly after eight thirty and apart from a brief stop for lunch at Great Ponton, south of Grantham, they'd had a clear run all the way. Door to door, the journey had taken them under seven hours, which meant the heart-to-heart inside number 62 had been going on since one thirty. Still, you couldn't put a time limit on grief and Ashton would have his work cut out keeping the more gruesome details of her brother's death from Mary Neville. Leaning forward, Harriet switched on the car radio and found herself listening to Steve Race.

Ashton would, she thought, find himself on the receiving end of a lot more questions this evening, and she felt sorry for him. They were breaking the journey back to London to spend the night with her parents in Lincoln and she knew her mother would undoubtedly cross-examine him. Harriet supposed it was unavoidable, given her mother's propensity to regard any man she brought home as a potential husband. This fixation had started in her last year at Birmingham University and had become increasingly desperate the longer she had remained unattached. She had promised herself that, to end the speculation, she would tell her mother that Peter was no one special, just a man she was currently sleeping with. That line would have stopped her mother in her tracks, but thanks to Ashton, she could hardly use it now.

Soon after leaving the pub where they had stopped for lunch, Peter had gone all introspective on her and started talking about how well they complemented one another. At first, she had thought he was referring to the office but gradually it became clear that this was entirely personal and she had heard herself asking him if this was a proposal. And typically of Ashton, he had said, "Well, of course it is – why else do you think I am making this speech?" "Then I accept," she had said, and still couldn't quite believe it.

Deep in thought, Harriet did not see Ashton cross the road and was startled when she heard a loud thump above the music on the car radio. She whirled round, thinking some vandal had heaved a brick at the Vauxhall and only started to breathe again when she saw who it was. Heart still pumping faster than normal, she leaned forward and switched off the stereo.

"How did you get on with Mary Neville?" she asked after he'd got in beside her. "Was she very upset?"

"Not really – puzzled would be a more appropriate word. And she certainly didn't want any of the effects, so we'll have to give them to Oxfam." Ashton dropped an envelope into her lap. "Photographs from the family album," he said, "and very interesting they are too."

Harriet opened the flap and extracted a wad of snapshots – a small boy with a cheeky grin in cub scout uniform, a young soldier, his hair cut short back and sides, and other snapshots taken over the years when the boy was growing up in a large family.

"This is George Neville?" Harriet asked in disbelief.

"The real one; the dead man lying in the mortuary at Banff is a substitute. Mary Neville told me that when I showed her the photos Hicks took of her supposed brother."

"But he doesn't even resemble George Neville."

"He didn't have to." Ashton started the car, went on up the road and after reversing into a side street, turned right and headed towards Lincoln. "Everything we learned about Neville showed that he was both a loner and a rootless person. The Russians probably targeted him during those eighteen months he was a prisoner of war in the hands of the Viet Cong. They then kept tabs on Neville after he was repatriated to Australia and took him out sometime after he'd arrived in San Francisco and before he renewed his British passport."

Harriet listened in silence, knowing his reconstruction was broadly correct. The substitute had gone deep and had been given plenty of time to flesh out his newly acquired identity. Any details of Neville's past life which could have endangered him would have been suppressed. No one would ever know precisely what information he had been gathering while he was working as an oil broker in Seattle, but there were any number of attractive targets, beginning with the Boeing Aircraft Company.

Sometime in 1990, his masters in the First Chief Directorate had ordered him to set up shop in England. No real security risk there; you only had to open a telephone directory to realise that Neville was not an uncommon surname and the spymasters would have warned him to give Grimsby a wide berth.

The man who had called himself Neville had ceased to be the dedicated agent after Yugoslavia had fragmented and he had seen how his superior officers in the First Chief Directorate were lining their own pockets by creaming off a lot of the money Todorvic had put up to buy oil for the Serbs. And then, when he was ripe for corruption, Frances Joyner had arrived on the scene and persuaded him to go into business in his own account.

"I thought we had run into a brick wall when he was killed by that Grizzly but now there's a chance we can identify the faceless men he answered to in the First Chief Directorate. It will entail a lot of hard work and it's no use pretending it will be easy . . ."

"Peter?"

"What?"

"We're a team, aren't we?" Harriet said quietly. "I mean, you did say we complemented one another?"

"Yes, and I meant it too."

"So let me ask you a question. Who gave you all the background information on Neville?"

"Clifford Peachey. And yes, you could argue that the subsequent investigation should be turned over to your former colleague in Five but I happen to believe the SIS has more than a passing interest."

"I'm not denying that, but will you do something for me?"

"Name it."

"For once in your life, Peter, do it by the book. Submit a report in writing to the DG through Kelso. You never know, it might do you some good."

"I hear what you say, Harriet." There was a long pause before he added, "And I'll do as you suggest."

It was not quite the whole-hearted response Harriet would have liked and she toyed with the idea of pressing him to give his word, then decided against it. Life had taught her that some things had to be taken on trust and Ashton's commitment to her was one of them.